Readers Love AMY LANE

Sean's Sunshine

"I enjoyed the book so much, I couldn't even be too angry with myself for staying up well past my bedtime to finish it."

—Love Bytes Reviews

The Tech

"This is what Amy Lane is great at! Taking a group of strangers, forming a ensemble, then fighting for a common cause and becoming family."

—Paranormal Romance Guild

The Rising Tide

"If you're looking for a well-written urban fantasy with hot sex, this one will do it. Nicely."

—Sparkling Book Reviews

Fish Out of Water

"Fish Out of Water delivers an intense plot as well as a sizzling relationship between Ellery and Jackson."

—Gay Book Reviews

By Amy Lane

An Amy Lane Christmas
Behind the Curtain
Bewitched by Bella's Brother
Bolt-hole
Christmas Kitsch
Christmas with Danny Fit
Clear Water
Do-over
Food for Thought
Freckles
Gambling Men
Going Up
Hammer & Air
Homebird
If I Must
Immortal
It's Not Shakespeare
Late for Christmas
Left on St. Truth-be-Well
The Locker Room
Mourning Heaven
Phonebook
Puppy, Car, and Snow
Racing for the Sun
Hiding the Moon
Raising the Stakes
Regret Me Not

Shiny!
Shirt
Sidecar
Slow Pitch
String Boys
A Solid Core of Alpha
Three Fates
Truth in the Dark
Turkey in the Snow
Under the Rushes
Weirdos
Wishing on a Blue Star

BENEATH THE STAIN
Beneath the Stain
Paint It Black

BONFIRES
Bonfires
Crocus

CANDY MAN
Candy Man
Bitter Taffy
Lollipop
Tart and Sweet

Published by DREAMSPINNER PRESS
www.dreamspinnerpress.com

Published by DREAMSPINNER PRESS
www.dreamspinnerpress.com

By Amy Lane (cont)

Published by DREAMSPINNER PRESS
www.dreamspinnerpress.com

UNDER COVER

AMY LANE

Published by
DREAMSPINNER PRESS

5032 Capital Circle SW, Suite 2, PMB# 279, Tallahassee, FL 32305-7886 USA
www.dreamspinnerpress.com

Under Cover
© 2023 Amy Lane

Cover Art
© 2023 L.C. Chase
http://www.lcchase.com
Cover content is for illustrative purposes only and any person depicted on the cover is a model.

Trade Paperback ISBN: 978-1-64108-565-6
Digital ISBN: 978-1-64108-564-9
Trade Paperback published May 2023
v. 1.0

Printed in the United States of America
∞
This paper meets the requirements of
ANSI/NISO Z39.48-1992 (Permanence of Paper).

This is dedicated to all the cop-show junkies like myself, who watch them and know they're unrealistic and recognize them for what they are: a desperate hope for heroes and a prayer for a better world. This is also for Mate, who watches them with me, and Mary, Elizabeth, and Karen, who very much understand.

Author's Note

Romantic Suspense gets all the kudos and the cred for being "gritty" and "real," but if you write it, you know it's got as much—if not more—world building and fantasy as hard-core science fiction. For the record, there is no such thing as the SCTF or the Sons of the Blood. If my law enforcement fantasies get anywhere close to reality, I'll be ever so surprised.

Prologue

CROSBY TRIED to slide out of bed stealthily, but he must have failed. When Garcia wrapped an arm around his middle, he mumbled something about going to the bathroom.

Shit.

He used the facilities, but he also put his socks on while he was in there because that got tricky when you put them on after you put on your jeans. He was trying for casual here. No big deal. Two colleagues who'd hooked up after a drink or two when the workday was over.

Happened all the time.

They were professionals, right? And it had been a sucktastic case.

Crosby made the mistake of looking at himself in the mirror when he was washing his face in the bathroom, and unbidden came that moment when the nine-year-old girl had been in his sights as he'd aimed at the murderer behind her.

"Don't take it if it's not good," his AIC had said in his earpiece, but the guy had a knife in his hand. They'd been hunting him, one crime scene after another. So much blood.

And here he was, knife dripping, holding it to her throat, and Crosby wondered which one would make him feel worse—if the killer got her or if Crosby got her, aiming for the killer.

And that hadn't been the worst of it. Garcia… he'd been so close. In Crosby's sights. If Crosby had been just a hair off….

He shuddered then and tried not to retch and splashed more water on his face. Garcia had toothpaste and a fresh toothbrush in the cupboard; Crosby took advantage of it. What was raiding the guy's cupboard when he'd had your cock in his mouth the night before, right?

The memory of the moment overwhelmed him.

Garcia, slighter body moving quickly down the street, Crosby's big blondness lumbering behind him. Crosby had never felt clumsy before in spite of the breadth of his chest, the muscular thickness of his thighs, but Garcia was so tightly wrought.

"Naw, man, I should go home," Crosby had said halfheartedly in response to Garcia's suggestion that Crosby not go back to his uncomfortable living sitch.

"You said she's not your girlfriend!" Garcia laughed. "Besides, you're just crashing at my place!"

From behind Crosby could see the slenderness of his hips, the wiry refinement of his ass and thighs. Garcia wore his black jeans tight—Crosby liked that.

"She's not my girlfriend," he defended. "I knew that from the beginning. We haven't been together since I got hurt."

It would have been awkward to hit her up after nearly six months of not so much as a text. And he didn't want to be needy, although God, tonight he needed somebody.

And Garcia hit him that way. Some girls did, some guys did—just hit.

Even in the spring chill, sweat dotted Crosby's chest under his fleece jacket. He wanted to take off his watch cap, but it was still in the thirties at night, and he knew his ears would be bright purple by the time they got to Calix Garcia's neat little house in Queens.

Sometimes, guy or girl, they hit *hard.*

Garcia had been hitting him pretty hard since he'd shown up in their unit six months ago. Small, quick, compassionate, and with zero ego, the guy was a dream agent. Crosby had looked forward to working with him every day.

And as he followed his fellow agent—and friend—to the door so he didn't have to drive crosstown to the place where he roomed with his old college buddy who was throwing a constant party, he thought hungrily about *working* Garcia, from toes to nipples, from mouth to cock to ass.

Working him. So hard.

Garcia let Crosby in first. Crosby had paused in the doorway, letting his eyes adjust so he could find the light, when Garcia closed the door behind him and came up hard against Crosby's back.

"Tell me to turn on the light," Garcia murmured in his ear, and Crosby's heart pounded. Oh wow. Oh *wow*.

His mouth went so dry he had to clear his throat twice to speak. "No."

Garcia let out a breath, hot and violent, into his ear. They were both still wearing jackets and hats, but Garcia's hands came to rest on his hips, then snuck under the hem of his jacket, and Crosby quaked at the chill of his fingers near his flat, molded abdomen.

"Tell me to back off," Garcia murmured.

Crosby's entire body shuddered violently, and he turned in Garcia's arms and shoved him back against the door. For a moment, they stared into each other's eyes in the darkness, Garcia's gleaming black and excited, before Crosby lowered his head enough to whisper in Garcia's ear for a change.

"No."

"No what?" Garcia baited.

Crosby ground their groins together through their jeans. "Not backing off."

"Good," Garcia breathed and nipped his lower lip.

Crosby nipped his in return, and then Garcia teased the seam of his pursed mouth with his tongue. Crosby shuddered again, and Garcia thrust his package against the placket of Crosby's jeans.

"You gonna tell me it was an accident in the morning?" Garcia taunted him. "You tripped in the dark and fell on my ass with your dick?"

"No," Crosby said, tracing Garcia's jawline with his nose, bumping along his temple, working his hands into Garcia's jacket so he could feel the tight, wiry muscles underneath.

"Gonna tell me you got a girlfriend?"

"I *had* a hookup," Crosby told him, thinking it was honest.

"Now you got two." Garcia grinned and dropped to his knees, dragging Crosby's jeans and briefs down his ass.

Crosby's cock flopped out, mostly hard, and the twinkle in Garcia's eyes as he looked into Crosby's face, mouth open, and engulfed him to the root, almost made Crosby come before the first touch.

It didn't get any worse after that.

Now Crosby looked at himself in the mirror and remembered those sparkling eyes, and his cheeks heated.

He couldn't betray those eyes.

With a sigh he wet-combed his hair and used a cloth on his pits and all points south. He was going to be wearing the same outfit back to work that morning; he didn't want to smell bad.

Then he returned to Garcia's bedroom, taking in the redwood floors, the cream-colored area rug, and the gray-blue and brown bedding, all of it masculine and inviting and clean. He'd been to Garcia's flat before, a couple of times. Spent Christmas in the spare room, which had a bed and everything. Had shared the occasional late-night takeout when Garcia had taken pity on him and rescued him from his living sitch. Garcia had even had the team over a couple of times—once to celebrate his birthday and once to celebrate Crosby's.

This guy had his life together. His room was a little messy but not a pit. He had solid modern furniture in the small living room and even a dinette table in the kitchen/dining room.

Garcia could bring people to his place because his place was *his* place.

Crosby took turns rooming with his old college buddy or with his bestie in the unit, Gail, because he had no place in the city.

He admired someone who could make their mark in a little New York house, and he admired anyone who could work Special Crimes Task Force.

And he really liked Garcia.

With a sigh he went back to the bed and thrust his stockinged feet into one leg of his jeans and then the other. He left the placket open before grabbing his T-shirt and sitting down on the edge of the bed.

Garcia was watching him, head propped on one hand, the covers sliding down his bare chest, revealing a scattering of dark hair between the nipples.

"You going to go back to work and pretend this never happened?" he asked, and his eyes were bright—but not twinkling.

With a sad shock, Crosby realized he could hurt Garcia—hurt his friend, his partner, his colleague—if he played this wrong.

"No," he said, sliding the T-shirt on. It was chilly in the room, although he'd heard the thermostat click on. Probably on a timer.

"Then this was a onetime thing, and we still respect each other in the morning, and I see you with your girl hookup and you see me with other guys and we think, 'Yeah, I'm glad he's happy'?"

There was an edge to Garcia's voice, and Crosby's chest grew tight, his throat swelling as he tried to imagine that exact scenario. He'd never seen Garcia with other guys—had really only intuited that Garcia might be gay... until he'd closed the door last night. But the thought of that, of *his* partner, *his* guy, on the arm of another man was like a big, ugly beast in his stomach.

What came out next was more like a growl.

"No."

"Then wh—"

Crosby turned on the bed and took Garcia's mouth, not wanting any more scenarios, not wanting any "What are we now?" questions. He just wanted the taste of Garcia, and as he swept his tongue inside that warm, willing cavern, he tasted his own come and remembered that last slow, painful orgasm, the final of three, because Garcia had wanted to taste him before they fell back asleep.

Crosby's cock strained against his briefs, the whole works threatening to bubble out of the unbuttoned fly, and he pulled back, breath laboring in his chest.

"I haven't hooked up with Gail's roommate since you started at SCTF," he blurted as he pulled away.

Garcia tilted his head. "Yeah?"

"Yeah." Crosby nodded. He held his hand up because they'd done this quietly, under the table the night before, surrounded by colleagues. It was where they'd started.

Garcia gave him a guarded look and threaded their fingers together. "So what do we do?"

Crosby looked at his sex-swollen mouth, remembered his head tilted back, his eyes closed, as Crosby had pounded into his body and Garcia had begged so sweetly.

"We can't come out to the squad yet," Crosby said, wanting to do that again. Wanting to feel Garcia's come spurting between their bodies. Wanting to hold Garcia's cock, his home, in his mouth again.

Garcia started to withdraw his hand, but Crosby captured it.

"We couldn't even if one of us was a girl," he said, knowing he sounded like a meatloaf and not caring. "'Cause protocol. 'Cause it's dangerous. 'Cause we'd worry every time we had to draw our weapons."

Garcia's eyes, black-brown infinity pools, sharper than daggers. "I already worry about you every time we have to draw our weapons," he said, the brutal honesty stripping Crosby to the skin. He remembered the week before, Garcia catching a shelf to the back of the head, being sent sprawling, and how Crosby had needed to run right past him while Harding checked to make sure Garcia was okay because Crosby had point and there was an asshole with a gun and a death wish who wanted to make everybody else die first.

"But we still do our jobs," Crosby said soberly. The job—it meant everything.

Garcia nodded, and they were on the same page.

"But you don't hook up with Gail's roommate anymore," he reiterated.

Crosby nodded, not bothering to speak the truth one more time. Gail's roommate hadn't been a thing since Calix Garcia had walked in the door at the SCTF six months before. "And you don't hook up with—"

"Nobody," Garcia whispered. "I haven't hooked up with anybody, not for a really long time."

Crosby remembered the sweet yielding of his body, the way he'd devoured Crosby's cock, like he'd been starving for it.

Apparently only Crosby's cock.

"Only me," Crosby said, feeling possessive.

"Yeah."

"You only hook up with me."

"Yeah."

They stared into each other's eyes for a moment, and Crosby took his mouth again, holding Garcia's hands over his head and ravaging, claiming, knowing his short beard would leave marks, stubble burns, proof that he'd been there.

But Garcia submitted, took the kiss, made it more, until the buzzing of both their phones from the charger on Garcia's dresser shocked them apart.

"We have work," Garcia murmured.

"Yeah."

"We can do this. Only hook up with each other."

"Yeah."

"Get dressed, *papi*. We can get coffee and bagels on the way in."

That got Crosby to move. He stood and buttoned his jeans, then gathered his sweater, his fleece, his boots. Garcia ran to the bathroom, probably to give himself the same sort of regimen Crosby had, and Crosby picked up his phone and texted Harding, their Agent In Charge, that Garcia would pick him up on the way.

Nobody would ask, he knew. Buddies coming to work together. Like him sleeping on Gail's couch before the roommate complication. Nothing to see here, folks; no mind-blowing sex, no uncomfortable emotional attachment.

But even as he thought about that, thought about making it clear he wouldn't be sleeping with the roommate again, he fought off the obvious, the thing neither of them had said.

If they only hooked up with each other….

If they worried when weapons were drawn….

If they pretended they weren't doing the thing….

If Crosby marked Garcia like Garcia marked his home, making the man his and fuck anyone else who looked at him….

If these were the truths they were living with now….

It wasn't a hookup anymore. It had never been one in the first place.

Covert—Backing Up to the Beginning

Six Months Earlier

JUDSON CROSBY woke up on his best friend's couch and groaned.

"You awake?" Gail Pearson had long blond pigtail braids and cornflower blue eyes—and some of the keenest knife skills Crosby had ever seen. Unfortunately those knife skills hadn't saved her from a kick from a perp that had caved her knee in exactly the wrong direction knees should go, and she'd been laid up for the last two months, acting as their team's backup hacker because Kylie, their regular hacker, had just gotten married and taken a leave of absence.

Gail was going nuts, and she was driving her roommate nuts, and Crosby had been called in to mediate a week into her "incarceration" at home. Crosby had shown up to be Gail's legs and her ride to work, and had stayed—on and off—for the sex with Iliana, her roommate. Iliana, who was as tall and dusky as Gail was tiny and blond, worked as a commander in Active Crimes in a precinct next door to the precinct that patrolled their street. To say Iliana's sex life was a closely guarded secret was to say Fort Knox was closely guarded. Crosby knew he was a means to an end, a flesh-covered dildo, as it were, because Iliana was straight with him—and that was fine.

But it meant that on the nights they weren't doing the quick and dirty, he was out here on the couch, because Iliana's room was Iliana's room, and he wasn't welcome, and he knew it.

It was a good thing their couch was a sweet, sweet ride to dreamland, or he'd be forced back into his own apartment, where his roommate's other guests had probably had sex on every surface, including the ceilings, with every gender known to or yet to be discovered by humans.

Toby Trotter was a great guy, but he was not—*not*—an ideal roommate.

Crosby's days often turned into weeks in the Special Crimes Task Force. A collaboration that borrowed officers from the police, the FBI, NCIS,

ATF, and probably a few other alphabets as well, the SCTF was funded by the military but under the management of Lieutenant Commander Clint Harding. Clint—formerly covert ops, though some speculated CIA while others speculated black ops, deep—answered to no other master than the Attorney General of the United States, and sometimes they had words. His job—his only job—was to track down felons who had eluded capture in their particular jurisdiction, often felons who were in the middle of a crime spree.

Clint's unit's job was, in his words, to keep the blood from spilling and to bring the bad guy in. He preferred alive, and he made that plain, but he also preferred his guys alive to the bad guy if it came down to that, and his unit was grateful.

Crosby had been tapped for SCTF as a homicide cop in Chicago, but he'd lived in New York for a year to be part of the unit. He'd managed to find a roommate—his old college roommate, actually—who was making a lot of money as a DJ and was happy to let Crosby stay in his spare room. Toby was a great guy, and he'd stayed true to his offer of showing Crosby around the city. The deal had seemed too good to be true when it had first been offered.

After a year and a half of dragging his bloody, bruised, exhausted ass into the apartment to find the party he'd left two days ago still going strong, Crosby had recognized that seeming too good to be true was often *being* too good to be true. He'd jumped at a chance to help Gail out and get some sleep, and then he'd awakened one night to Iliana taking off her robe in the middle of the living room and saying, "I don't want strings, I just want dick. You in?"

Well, if nothing else he'd needed to work off some stress.

With a moan he turned his head now to see Gail holding out a mug of coffee. He whimpered and sat up, taking it from her hands. "We got a call?" he asked.

"Yeah. I told Clint it would take us half an hour. You showered last night, because you're considerate as fuck, and I just need to change." She shook her head. "You know, if you weren't banging my roommate, I'd be afraid you'd perv out on me when you had to help me change, but you seem to be a perfect gentleman."

Crosby sipped his coffee—hot, with cream—and smiled a little. "She make it back last night?"

"Yeah. Late, though. Does she really only let you sleep in the bed when you're having sex?"

He grimaced. "She actually asks me to leave if we don't fall asleep. Don't worry. I have no illusions as to intimacy or monogamy. I know what I'm here for."

Gail sighed, the breath stirring the fine strands of gold hair that curled from her tight braids. "You have to forgive her. I mean, I was super excited when you guys started hooking up—after Danny…." She trailed off. Iliana's boyfriend, Danny Aramis, had been killed in a train derailment up in Pennsylvania on a business trip. Apparently it had been true love for them, and according to Gail, Crosby was Iliana's first step into the land of the living in over two years. Her job at the Forty Third Precinct—she was in charge of the Active Crimes Division—kept her too busy to have much of a social life, and here, neatly delivered, was a person who got law enforcement hours and was pretty decent (if Crosby dared say so) in bed.

It was starting to dawn on them both that Crosby was a means to scratch an itch—he was most assuredly not an emotional act of bravery.

"Yeah, well…." He shrugged. "I was willing. But the good news is I can get up now and get us dressed, and I don't need to kiss anybody goodbye."

Gail didn't answer back. They both knew Iliana didn't care where he went when they weren't fucking, and that was not going to change.

But the thought gnawed at Crosby. He sat through the briefing with Clint and looked over their little unit: Natalia Denison, Clint's second in command, a former ADA with a lawyer's sharp mind and hand-to-hand fighting skills the likes of which Crosby had never seen, who wore a little silver goddess pendant that looked like something from an assassin's catalog; Joey Carlyle, former Marine with the speed and stamina of a gazelle and the patience to stalk a perpetrator through miles of woodland in the snow without a single word of either complaint or victory in case he gave away his position; Gideon Chadwick, Navy covert ops, weapons expert, and psychology major; and Clint Harding, their boss, former top secret badass, who had an uncanny way of looking at evidence and figuring out what their suspect would want, where they would go, and what they would need.

Then there was Gail, who was small, sneaky, and uncanny when it came to judging what a suspect would do in the heat of a confrontation, and Crosby, who, as far as he knew, was only there because he'd run down a serial killer in the middle of a drug war and brought the guy in alive. Doing so had also stopped the war. It had started because two neighborhoods had been losing their young people at a terrible rate, and Crosby had figured out that they hadn't been lost to gang violence, but to Cordell Brandeis, who was currently rotting in a supermax prison with over two hundred kills to his name.

It was either that or the thing that had made his entire department in Chicago want to kill him. Okay—maybe there were two reasons Crosby was in the SCTF.

These were good people, he thought seriously. They had families and kids and spouses or parents who worried about them and a special set of skills he could understand would work in the situations they'd been thrown into.

He'd been with the unit for a year and a half, and he still didn't know—really—what the hell he was doing there.

And that right there was about what he'd been thinking when trouble walked through the door.

CLINT NODDED at the guy who strutted into their small open-air office in the basement of an old police precinct and gestured him to the front of the conference table.

"Folks," he said, his resonant fortysomething voice working with his gentle blue eyes and calm, Nordic demeanor. His hair was dark, but the rest of him was Swedish pale, and Crosby wondered sometimes if he slept in a coffin to avoid being burned to a crisp in the salty East Coast summers. "I want you to meet our new team member. I know we've all missed Kylie, but she wrote me this morning—she apparently got knocked up on her honeymoon and has decided to stay home for the duration. Gail, you're our full-time e-genius, and since you're still here at the admin building running point, this is Calix Garcia. ATF loaned him to us. He's got an impressive resume, and I'd like to keep him around. Be nice."

Crosby eyed the guy—lean build, tight black pants, dark eyes with bright pinpoints of intelligence and interest gleaming in their depths. He had golden skin and dark hair that was buzzed on the sides and only a little longer on top, and he looked about twenty years old but was probably closer to thirty given the lines at the corners of his eyes.

Garcia stood at the front of the room and gave everybody a brief nod and an easy smile. "Happy to be here," he said, his confidence sending something sharp and aching to the pit of Crosby's groin. "Can you tell me what the sitch is?"

And while Clint launched into the details of a gambling operation gone horribly wrong, with the ringleader leaving a trail of bodies in his wake, Crosby tried very hard not to think that the sitch was that he was in so, so much trouble.

New Guy Bennies

"SO, CALIX?"

Garcia had gotten up from the conference table to get coffee and jumpstart his brain. He'd put in for the SCTF six months ago and had just gotten his invite that week. It said something about the unit that once he was pulled, he was pulled. His captain had rung him up the night before and said, "Lucky you, you live in the same city, even if it's a different borough. Otherwise you would have needed to relocate your entire life in, like, a day."

Garcia would have done it too—although he loved his tiny house in Queens. His nana had willed him the place. She and his papa had lived there for forty years, and while Garcia's parents had moved to New Jersey, he'd kept his love for the tiny two-bedroom shotgun-style house—and Queens—through adulthood. When Nana had moved into the old-folks home, where she still resided, thank God, she'd given it to Calix.

Calix had spent the last four years fixing the place up to look like it belonged to someone who knew where Queens was, and not nice little old people who were still trying to decide whether or not they wanted to live in New Jersey.

But he'd wanted to be in this unit so bad, he'd have given all that up to move across the country if they'd asked him. He could put up with a little bit of quizzing from Natalia Denison, a fortyish African American woman with one or two wiry threads of gray hair showing from the tight bun plastered to her scalp.

"Means 'chalice of God,'" he told her. "Go figure."

She laughed. "Natalia," she said, shaking his hand, "means 'Christ's birthday,' which was my favorite swear word all through high school."

Calix grinned, liking her. "Mine was still 'fuck,' but mostly it was 'fuck this stupid name.'"

This got a chuckle from Natalia—and from everybody else. Calix looked around the coffee station and found Gideon Chadwick—thirtyish, hatchet thin, tan, with hair that looked bleached and straw-brittled by the sun; Joey Carlyle—medium height, medium build, with brown hair, brown eyes, the severe cheekbones of Indigenous peoples, and a sweet face a grandmother would give her last dime to keep happy; and Clint Harding himself—early forties, over six foot tall, shoulders like a linebacker, and a Nordic face that was all cheekbones and craggy good looks all gathered to chat.

Only Gail Pearson and Judson Crosby were still at the table, Crosby's dark blond head tilted over Gail's bright blond one as they talked about something, probably case-related.

Garcia felt a little ping and tried to squelch it. This was the SCTF. He had no personal life anybody wanted to know about, and they definitely didn't want his personal life groping them in the ass.

"Well, Gideon means trumpet of God," Chadwick was saying, "but apparently Chadwick means stodgy professor. I do *not* make a good impression in a bar in the Bronx."

Garcia took the opening he was given. "Yeah, and in Queens we'd kill ya," he said, and the group laughed.

And then Garcia's mouth opened before he could stop it. "What about you guys?" he called to the two people still at the table. "Your names got a special meaning?"

Gail grinned up at him, fairy bright. "I'm my father's joy," she said, batting big blue eyes in a way that indicated she probably gave her parents fits.

Garcia laughed like he was supposed to, a stupid part of him soothed because she'd answered so pertly he'd probably been right that they were just concentrating on their work and not snubbing the new guy.

"What about you?" he asked, wanting Crosby to look up.

Oh God. Careful what you wish for!

Those eyes—lined with dark lashes, those eyes were blue-gray, flinty, and fathomless in a square-jawed, almost boyish face.

"My name? Judson?" Crosby gave a short laugh. "Damned if I know."

"Praised," Gail said, her eyes on her keyboard as she looked it up. "And Crosby means 'at the cross.'"

Crosby snorted. "So you're sayin' I gotta die to get some love around here, is that it?" He wasn't from New York, but he did sound urban. Chicago, maybe? God, it didn't matter. His answer was quick and funny, and Garcia's chest and its butterflies were going to get him killed.

"Yeah," Gail said, just as archly. "Much like Daddy's Joy has to die to get some coffee around here. You guys break it up and let him get me some coffee so I can tell you what I found out about our perp."

Crosby stood and shouldered his way to the coffee bar, winking at Garcia as he drew near.

"I never knew that about my name," he said. "Go you for asking the unusual question."

"I live to fuckin' serve," Garcia retorted. He was thinking, *My God, is that guy tall.* Garcia was five nine, maybe, but this guy—he was what? Six three? Oh Jesus. Who went after a guy six inches taller than them, with a chest like a barn and biceps the size of Garcia's head? What kind of crazy was he made of? And Crosby was wearing a black leather coat over a red turtleneck sweater, and Christ's birthday, did he smell *good.*

But Crosby gave an openmouthed grin, like that had been the right answer, and then poured two giant mugs of coffee. One mug—probably Gail's—featured a cartoon cat holding a bloody knife and saying, "What?" and the other featured a photo of a bunch of puppies.

"You like dogs?" Garcia asked, and Crosby grunted.

"I used to love 'em," he said. "Still do, mostly. But my first case here was dog fighters, and I sorta got bit. This was the group's way of saying most dogs are still adorable puppies, but be careful for that one who ain't."

"Bit?" Garcia asked, and Crosby grimaced.

"Don't ask," he muttered, but Natalia apparently had ears like a bat.

"Forty-six stitches," she said. "Two pints of blood. They nicked his femoral artery. He almost bled out."

Crosby grunted again. "Bit," he said. "That's all. Natalia, don't scare the kid. We want him to stay."

Oh Lord have mercy. Strong, silent, brooding—and a little bit funny. Aside from Harding's glass-walled office in the corner, the unit office was one big conference room with six open-ended cubicles surrounding it, and Garcia wished fervently for a broom closet so he could bang his head against a door. This could so end up not well.

"Yeah, but we want him to not be a dumbass like some other dumbasses we know," she said, looking severely at him and then Gail.

Gail rolled her eyes. "That kick came out of nowhere," she said defensively.

"I lost five pounds throwing up to the sound of your knee snapping," Joey said. "I'm with Natalia. Kid—"

"I'm twenty-seven!" Garcia protested.

"And I'm twenty-five," Joey retorted, "and I'm tired of being the youngest, so you get to be the kid for a while. We are after some lethal assholes. Be aware."

"And speaking of lethal assholes," Clint said, bringing everybody back to point, "what do we have on our gambling ring?"

Gail hit a couple of keys on her computer and said, "Clint, hook me up to the screen, would you?"

Clint stood and hit some buttons on a console in the middle of the table, and a screen rolled down at the other end of the room. A few more buttons and a face popped up—a fiftyish white businessman, doughy and self-important, wearing a suit that none of the people in that room could afford, not even Clint, who looked like he made the big bucks.

"This is Newton Sewell," Gail said. "He's the leader of our gambling ring, which is centered primarily around high school sports— football and basketball, mostly boys, and mostly legacy schools. You know, the kind of schools that recruit the best of the best of the best so they don't lose their image of being a good sports school."

"He doesn't look dangerous," Joey said, and everybody at the table groaned.

"Joey, you asshole," Gail said with heat. "Aren't you the one who said, 'Oh, hey, we get to see dogs'?"

"I'm so sorry, man," Joey said, looking Crosby dead in the eyes.

"Don't mention it. Ever. Gail?"

"So the thing is, he's got three runners—see them here?" Three young men appeared. *Not* prep school kids. One was white, and two were mixed race, but all of them had hungry, desperate, and street smart written all over them. There were worse ways to make money than being the kid who ran the money to the bookie, Garcia thought.

"Well, Newton started stacking the odds of the house, and the runners started losing money," Gail went on.

"Tight asshole," Gideon growled. He sounded dangerous. Garcia liked that—but not as much as the Midwest farm boy drinking from the puppy coffee cup.

"Well, he's done all *his* gambling on Wall Street," Gail said. "And he's mostly lost, so he was trying to make up his losses. Anyway, maybe Newton got tired of their bitching, because he offed the kid in the middle. Ryan Peters, aged nineteen." The mouse arrow made a little circle around the youngest-looking, most vulnerable of the runners, who had brown eyes and pale brown skin. Garcia felt a little pang. *He'd* made money as a runner one summer when he was trying to get his degree. The irony was not lost on him that he was paying for a degree in law enforcement by doing something illegal, but it had been honest money in its way.

"Just killed the kid?" Crosby asked.

"Shot him in the head while the others watched," Gail confirmed. "Jesse Campos—the white kid—and Kurt Armbruster were both there. They saw Ryan go down and took off with Newton after them, but there's a reason they're called runners. Anyway, Jesse called the cops and told them where to find Ryan's body, and then the two boys dropped off the grid. And Newton has been trying to collect from his clients since his runners are terrified and AWOL—and he's been doing it with a forty-five."

"Oh no," Natalia murmured.

"Oh yes," Gail said soberly. "This morning he hit the home of Julian Carpenter, his wife, Rita, and his two kids, Jason and Collin. Julian and Rita didn't make it, but the boys hid in a giant toy chest in the youngest kid's room, and they called the cops." A film from a home security system popped up on the screen, and they could all see their doughy insurance agent with thinning hair barge into the front room of a very nice house in what looked like upstate.

"There's no sound, but he's in there for about half an hour," Gail told them, and Garcia put two and two together and realized she and Crosby had been assembling a timeline to present, and they'd done it in the very small amount of time during which he'd been getting coffee and getting to know his people.

Gods, no wonder his former supervisor had told him he had to hit the ground running.

"So we need to do two things," Clint Harding said, deep voice cutting into the uncomfortable silence that had formed as they'd been watching the footage of the house. People were being killed in there, Garcia knew, and the thought slugged him in the stomach.

"The first," Harding continued, "is to figure out where our perp's next target is going to be so we can intercept him and stop him from doing this again. The second is to get our runners and bring them in. They're scared right now, and scared people get desperate."

"Their info might help us anticipate the next target," Crosby said, and Harding nodded.

"But so might the recovery of Newton's laptop or electronics," Harding added. "Natalia and I will go search Sewell's place and the initial crime scene. Carlyle, Chadwick, you're on at the Carpenter house. And talk to the two boys, see if you can get a destination from them. Make sure they land, okay? I know we've got child services there, but make sure they've got some protection in case Sewell goes after them. Garcia, Crosby, you two run down the runners. Gail can provide you with residences and last known locations, as well as known associates. Gail…?"

"I'm here in the office because I can't walk," she said, like they'd gone over this before.

"You're here in the office because you can't walk," Harding confirmed. "But we need you to keep the information flowing because we need to know the first break, okay? Sewell is either completely unpredictable or following a pattern we can't see yet. Let's hope it's the second because the first is a bad, bad thing. Everyone, grab your weapons and don't get dead."

"Right," Gideon Chadwick said, standing up and nodding to Joey Carlyle. "Not getting dead is my favorite part."

With that, they hit their gun lockers and began to suit up. As Garcia was snapping his small Beretta into its shoulder holster, he noted Crosby had a pancake holster with a .45, an ankle holster with a .22, two fixed-blade knives at his belt, and a .38 strapped to his side.

"Expecting an army?" he asked, a little wide-eyed.

Crosby looked apologetic. "I'm not that smart, and I'm not that quick," he said. "And I'm a better shot with a rifle with a sniper's scope. In my case the guns really *are* compensating for something, and I don't want you to end up dead because I wasn't good enough."

Garcia gaped at him, only remembering to follow him out when Crosby finished strapping down and turned toward the exit to the parking garage. As he trailed after his new coworker—and his new partner, apparently—he thought that he'd never had someone work so hard to keep him safe.

Kinds of Meatloaf

"FIRST STOP," Calix Garcia said as Crosby powered the black SUV along the Jersey Turnpike. "James Campos, Jesse Campos's older brother and Jesse's last known address. He lives in Elizabeth, where that smell comes from." All of that information had appeared, via text, on his phone, because apparently Harding hadn't been shitting around when he told Gail she was a vital part of the operation.

Crosby grinned—and shuddered. Elizabeth, New Jersey, had the misfortune of having a giant landfill in the middle. Tourists said it smelled like something was burning year-round. Locals didn't even notice it.

"Great—I-78 it is." Crosby spent a few moments in silence, piloting the car toward the maze of New Jersey freeways, thinking of things he needed to know about Roger Campos, Jesse Campos, and Newton Sewell, when Garcia spoke up, but almost to himself.

"He shouldn't have shot the runner."

"Right?" Crosby asked, completely onboard. "Man, runners don't have control over the operations, and they usually keep the pulse of their network. It was such a dumb, panicky, mean thing to do."

"And they're, like, neutral territory. Like the porters in that Shakespeare play. You don't kill the other guy's runners 'cause they're not in the territory disputes. You certainly don't kill your own. Seems to me that if this guy, Sewell, knew much about running his own gambling ring, he'd get that you don't touch your runners."

"He doesn't," Crosby said, enjoying the give and take. "He's a Wall Street guy. He's making money off the sports bettors in the lowest sectors. Not college. High school and prep schools at most. Not as much competition—he's not stepping on anybody's toes. He's making his bit and sort of sneering at the people who pay him."

He risked a glance at Garcia and spotted the skeptical eyebrow before he turned back to the road. "What?"

"You're making this awfully personal," Garcia said.

"I'm just saying. Taking out the runner in a fit of temper was cold. And then going into that house to take out the father or mother who owed him money was cold, but it was also methodical. We're looking at a true sociopath here. People aren't people to him. They're a means to an end, and his end is paying off his Wall Street debt and playing some more."

Garcia let out a low whistle. "I mean, I'm used to working with scumbags, but this guy—he's elevating the art, you know?"

"I do," Crosby agreed. "But that's why I think finding at least one of the runners is important. I don't even know if Sewell will target them, but *they* know who his biggest clients are and who owes him the big bucks."

"Well, sucks that all his clients are on the other side of the island," Garcia said, staring moodily at the acres of grass-covered landfill they were passing.

"Yeah, but that's where Clint and Natalia are," Crosby said. "We get the runner, he gets us the info, we pass the info to the people close enough to get the bad guy. It's a good system."

"It really doesn't bother you?" Garcia asked. "Who gets the bust?"

"Our team gets the bust," Crosby said, nodding fiercely because he believed it. "Our team gets the big bust, and we get the big cases and the big toys and the autonomy. No bosses telling us which puddle to piss in, you know?"

"God yes." Garcia gave a truly visceral shudder, and Crosby sensed a story.

"Bad?"

"Not this last guy in the ATF, no. Collins was decent. But I worked a small-town police force for a year out of the military. Bad. Man, it was fuckin' bad."

Crosby grunted. He knew from bad. "Bad at the top?" he asked. "Or bad through and through?"

"Dumb," Garcia spat. "Racist. Brown kid always did it. White guy always told the truth."

Crosby swallowed and nodded. "Yeah." He didn't want to talk about this—God, he didn't. But he was a big dumb white guy, and he'd readily admitted to not being the fastest or the smartest. Garcia needed a reason to trust him.

"Chicago cop," he muttered. "Partner shot a kid in the back." For the rest of his life, he would have that horror movie playing in his mind, including the wide, surprised eyes of the unarmed sixteen-year-old who'd been cutting through a neighbor's backyard because he was late getting home. "I testified against my partner in the deposition, because it wasn't a fair shoot. I started getting death threats, and my parents started getting death threats. And then Clint Harding called, and my parents got a nice condo in New Mexico and I got placed with all these frickin' law enforcement geniuses because Harding felt sorry for me, I guess. I'm a meatloaf who can handle a sniper rifle. I'm sorry. You should've gotten someone good."

"Were you able to testify in court?" Garcia asked.

Crosby shook his head. "They didn't even indict the fucker. If you ever see a forty-year-old Irishman asking for 'Mudson,' do me a favor and let me know, because he's got a bullet with my name on it." Collie McEnany—he'd made some of those death threats face-to-face.

"You don't want me to take him out for you?" Garcia asked, eyebrows raised.

"I don't know. Work with me for a week and make your own decisions."

"You've got a criminal justice degree with a double major in history and a minor in comp/sci," Garcia said, squinting at him. "Why the meatloaf routine?"

Oh. Well, Garcia had apparently done his homework on his teammates. Crosby hadn't even known he was coming.

"'Cause that shit didn't come easy," Crosby told him honestly. "I'm so thick sometimes. I… my department, my captain, they kept telling me, 'You're gonna do the right thing, right, Crosby?' and I was like, 'Of course.' Then I talked to the lawyer and my union rep and the internal affairs guy, and before I even had a chance to get crosstown to my apartment after the deposition, my phone was blowing up with death threats and bullshit. And until right that moment, I thought 'Do the right thing' meant, you know, *doing the right thing*. It wasn't until my parents started getting calls that I realized 'Do the right thing' meant, 'Don't make us shoot innocent people because you know the difference between a fair shoot and hitting a sixteen-year-old in the back with a forty-five for running while Black.' I mean, it takes a special kind of stupid to not see that coming."

Garcia grunted, and Crosby thought that was agreement, but then he said, "I don't think it's stupid."

Crosby didn't know what to do with that. "How'd you get recruited?" he asked.

"I'm not sure. I did one tour of Iraq, that shitacular year in Florida—"

"Small-town," Crosby said, making sure.

"Yeah. And when I was in Florida, I blew a drug case wide open, and the ATF took pity on me. And then, to secure my loyalty forever, they stationed me in Manhattan, right when my nana was offering me her house in Queens."

"Oh my God," Crosby said with a laugh. "Someone fuckin' *loves* you!"

"You understand!" Garcia crowed. "And I've spent the last four years getting rid of flowered wallpaper and avocado recliners in between, you know, doing my job."

"Were the recliners comfortable?" Crosby asked, only partially facetious. God, his roommate had horrible taste in furniture. He sometimes thought the only reason he let Iliana treat him like a flesh-covered dildo was because of that couch.

"Naw," Garcia said, snorting in disgust. "I swear, they're the reason Pop-Pop died first. Because that spring in the back was not sending a very positive message!"

Crosby laughed outright. "My roommate's furniture is heinous," he said. "It's all plastic and chrome and plywood, but somehow expensive, right? Like, designer? I mean, I sleep on a mattress on a wooden box when I'm there, and... ouch."

"Where're you at when you're not there?" Garcia asked, and it sounded... well, casual, but studied casual, and Crosby tried not to think about that, because they had to work together. This? In the car like they were doing? This was getting-to-know-you shit, that was all.

"Gail's couch," Crosby answered, blowing out a breath. "Or her roommate's bed, but mostly Gail's couch."

"Wait." Oh God, Crosby could hear it in his voice—he was going to go there. "If you're banging her roommate, why are you sleeping on their couch?"

"Because," Crosby told him, blowing out a breath, "what Iliana and I have isn't really an overnight thing. It's a booty call. But Gail needs transpo and a friend from work to help her out while she's got the cast and all, so I get the couch. Every now and then I get the booty, but mostly, I'm there for the couch."

Garcia let out a disbelieving bark of laughter. "Seriously?"

"It's more comfortable than where I actually live," Crosby said, cheeks burning. "And I have no idea where to live in this city that's affordable."

"Well, it's not like Chicago's cheap!" Garcia said, and Crosby shook his head.

"Yeah, well, all my spare cash is going to New Mexico," he told Garcia. "My folks got the house and the moving expenses, but I'm making the payments and handling the bills. I mean, we get paid decent—more than a detective, for sure—but I've got expenses. We're almost there."

And the atmosphere in the car lit up with electricity.

The neighborhood Crosby had pulled into had seen better days. Once a block of lower-middle-class clapboard homes with stone foundations, all but two of the houses on the block had boarded-up windows and doors. The two that were left were cared for—the lawns were mowed and the hurricane fencing was upright if rusty—but hanging on by a thread. The house they passed had a roof that had three months to see if it would take another winter. The house at the end of the block had needed to rip off the porch overhang, and the debris was stacked neatly on the side. These weren't people who didn't care, Crosby thought. These were people who didn't want to leave their homes but had run out of cash and were running out of options.

Damn. It was possible Jesse Campos was running numbers because he and his brother had nowhere else to run.

"Front or back?" Crosby asked, stopping in front of a vacant place two houses down.

"Back," Garcia said. "Going in hot?"

Crosby shook his head. "Not unless he gives us a reason to. Like Harding said—desperate, but not like the guy who shot his buddy in the face."

"Deal."

Crosby nodded to Garcia, who slid out next to the curb before Crosby opened his door and slammed it shut, drawing attention to himself so Garcia could slip between the two vacant houses next to them. The neighborhood had trees—big ones—that were still thick with leaves in the beginning of September, and they helped shield Garcia as he made his way along the back. These kinds of neighborhoods didn't usually have back fences—all the kids and the dogs and everybody could run around and play in the summer.

Or at least they probably had during happier times.

Crosby reminded himself that these weren't happier times and ventured up the cracked walkway to the porch that might not fall down on his head but might still collapse around his ankles.

Crosby trod lightly up the stairs, and standing to the side, he gave three sharp raps against the brittle door. "Jesse Campos?" he called. "We need to talk to you—"

"He's making a break!" Garcia called from the back. "My left!"

Which meant Crosby's right.

He cleared the porch in one step and leapt over the pile of debris, heading for the backyard. The walkway between the houses was maybe six feet wide, and Jesse, running full bore while looking over his shoulder, didn't even see Crosby as he stepped to the side, stuck out his arm, and caught the poor kid in the chest.

Jesse went down on his back and stayed there, eyes enormous, struggling to breathe.

Crosby dropped to one knee, rolled the kid over and cuffed him before he could recover. Then he sat the kid up with gentle, firm movements and leaned him against the peeling green siding of the house.

"Jesse Campos?" he asked. The kid was stocky but still trim, with wide cheekbones, pale skin, and limpid green eyes.

"Jesse?"

Crosby turned slightly to see a pudgy man in his thirties with a preschooler on his hip come into the side yard.

"Hey, asshole!" he called. "Get off my brother. You didn't identify yourself—"

"SCTF," Crosby said, flipping his leather jacket back with one hand to show his badge. "And we weren't here to arrest him—yet. We need to ask him some questions."

"James, go back inside," Jesse said, voice cracking. "Man, take little Jimmy and go back inside."

"James," Crosby said, "is there anyone inside who can watch the boy? This pertains to both of you."

"Naw," James said. "His mom split last year. Just the three of us since, yanno?"

Crosby thought so. He looked at Garcia, who glanced at the kid. "I'll take him," Garcia said, holstering his weapon. Crosby nodded. Usually he was on for kid duty, but James and Jesse seemed to be responding to Garcia. Crosby checked on Jesse.

"How you doing? Can you breathe yet?"

Jesse struggled for wind before nodding.

"Good. Let's get you up off the ground. Now, I'm keeping you cuffed until I'm sure you won't bolt, because we gotta get through this. You and your family, you might be in danger. You understand?"

Jesse's face, which was flushed and blotchy from the run behind the house and his subsequent capture, turned suddenly gray.

"He'd do that?" Jesse asked, and like that they were in the meat of the case. "I…. He just shot poor Ryan. One minute the guy was raving about how we were costing him money, and the next…." His voice hitched, and he looked beseechingly at his brother. "He accused us of skimming, James. We never skimmed. We wouldn't do that. We didn't wanna work for this guy forever, right? So we didn't skim. We just worked our territory and did our jobs." He gave Crosby a horrified glance, and then, as though it occurred to him what he'd admitted to, turned his face to his shoulder. "Oh shit."

"We're not from Vice," Crosby said. "And we're not here to bust your balls. Did you know Sewell took out Julian and Rita Carpenter after you and Roger took off this morning?"

The horror on Jesse's face told him everything he needed to know. "Julian?" Jesse squeaked. "And Rita? They were on my route! They were nice people! You can't think I had anything to do with—oh God! Their kids! They had these two kids. Sweetest boys. Always wanted to give me a tip. Their dad kept back a few bucks so they could hand it to me. I mean, not what you wanna teach your kids about gambling, but tipping the runner—that's manners. The kids. Sewell didn't get the kids, did he?"

"No," Crosby said, looking from James to Jesse. "No, he didn't. But you said they were on your route? Why would he go after them?"

"They did a lot of business with him," Jesse said. "He's got maybe ten top clients. I had two, Ryan had a couple, Kyle's got some. Sewell's got a real chip on his shoulder about guys with more money. The Carpenters, they were both in TV. Writers. They had some cash, but…." His voice broke. "They were nice. James, they were so nice. They… remember those clothes I brought home for Jimmy? Those were from them. I told 'em how Jimmy was growing like a weed, and they had bags they were giving to thrift stores. It…." His voice broke. "They gave James work. He's a landscaper, and he's not getting work since the crash. And they had him redo their backyard. It's why we can afford to fix the porch. God."

"Jesse, you're rambling," James said, his voice both compassionate and frightened. "You need to let them ask you things." James had the body and face of a high school football hero gone to seed. His cheeks were round, and his neck was steadily disappearing, but Crosby could hear it in his voice—James was good people. "Are we in danger?" he asked.

And he was apparently smart people too.

"You might be," Crosby said, matter-of-fact. "If you want, grab some stuff for the kid, and we'll get you set up in protective custody and a safe house until we apprehend Newton Sewell. In the meantime, me and Jesse need to have a conversation about Sewell's biggest clients and who Jesse thinks he'll go after next."

It took James ten minutes to clear out the house, and in the meantime, Jesse spilled like a waterfall. Fifteen minutes later, Crosby was following Harding's texted instructions to a safe house where he'd have the local police present to take the Campos men into protective custody, and Garcia was sitting next to him, chuckling softly to himself.

"What?" Crosby asked. "What's the laughter for?"

"You. You really had me worried there. 'I'm not that fast and I'm not that smart.' Jesus, buddy, way to bury the lede."

Crosby scowled. "What lede?"

"You read that sitch and those people in a heartbeat, man," Garcia told him. "You don't need the damned guns. You got the instincts of a pro."

Working a Case

GARCIA LIKED the way Crosby's cheeks went a little pink at the compliment—like it meant something to him that Garcia thought he was good at his job. Garcia couldn't help it, though. The way Crosby had dealt with the runner, the big brother, even the little kid, making sure he wouldn't be scared and had his favorite stuffed animal with him as they gathered the family up to take them to safety—all of it. All of it had impressed him.

In the bad place in Florida, he'd watched families get bullied by the cops for having a shitty lawn.

Now it could be true that Crosby was a totally different guy with someone a little darker skinned than the Campos family; Garcia had seen it happen. But so far, he'd been completely aboveboard with Garcia, and Garcia highly doubted that his coworker, Natalia, would have been so worried about Crosby's forty-two stitches if he'd been a dick to her in any way.

And Garcia sort of doubted that anybody who stood up to Chicago PD because of a bad shoot against an obviously innocent kid would *be* a dick to someone because of their skin color. In spite of Crosby's "too dumb to know better" routine, nobody was that dumb. Odds were pretty good he'd known it was going to be a rough ride when he saw his partner shoot an unarmed Black kid in the back.

Yeah, Garcia had read up on it. The official report on the incident had been sketchy at best, but Garcia could read between the lines. Crosby's bitter recitation had only confirmed what Garcia had guessed: Crosby had been screwed, but not nearly as bad as the dead kid and his family, so Crosby wasn't going to bitch.

Oh, this could be bad. So bad. So deliciously, decadently bad.

But it was too soon to so much as scent the wind to see how he'd taste. Garcia hadn't survived that hellish year in Florida—or the last four in the ATF—without once outing himself to screw up his dream job posting now.

Still, he couldn't help listen in as Crosby bid goodbye to the Campos family in the midlevel safe house one suburb over from their own neighborhood.

"Okay, now, you've got Officer Gibbs and Officer Swan here to keep you company," Crosby said, smiling at the two officers wearing plain clothes. Swan was young, African American, and male, with one of those round faces that seemed sweet and trustworthy. Garcia knew this could be a lie, but the rapport between Swan and his partner—older, female, with no-nonsense brown eyes and a tight braid of graying brown hair—was sound and efficient. "This shouldn't last more than a night or two. We want to make sure it's all clear before we send you back to your home."

"Won't be much of a home left without that check from the Carpenters," James said, his voice bone weary. "God rest their souls." He grimaced, probably aware of the crassness of mentioning his own problems when the couple had been murdered that morning but also afraid of losing his house.

Crosby nodded. "Look, I don't know what to say. But we've got some money people who might be able to help you guys get some loans or grants or something. I'll ask my boss. There's almost always money lurking in corners, but nobody knows how to find it. How about you, Jesse? How you doing?"

The boy hadn't stopped crying since he'd first talked, and Garcia wondered if he was grieving for his friend. He gave a quiet sob now and shook his head, and Crosby frowned.

"Kid, you want to talk to me privately?"

And with that he pulled Jesse Campos into the living room while Garcia, the two protective officers, and James and the boy all stared at each other.

Officer Swan glanced around and said, "So, uhm, anybody want pizza?"

Garcia would have *killed* for some pizza then, but he figured it wasn't his call. James and little Jimmy said that was fine, and they sat at the table, the boy on his father's lap, and drank sodas while nice Officer Swan used his expense account to order a family style with the works.

And Garcia glanced into the prefurnished living room to see how Crosby was doing with the kid. He didn't want to look pointedly at his watch, but they *did* have the other runner to track down. Crosby must have sensed the urgency, because Garcia watched his brows knit in that apologetic grimace people get when they have to bail.

Finally Crosby put his hands on the kid's shoulders and said, loud enough to carry, "Kid, that sucks. I can't even imagine how much that sucks. But you gotta tell your brother, or he'll never know how much it sucks for you, okay? It's good info for *me* to have, because I know how to talk to your friend, but it's gonna take some time before *you* feel better, and only your family can help with that."

The kid said something inaudible, and Crosby's expression softened. "Kid, trust him. He seems to like you fine. Besides, you're here with nice police officers. He can't kill you here." And with that, Crosby gave the kid a brief, hard hug and then pulled out his wallet and gave the kid his card. "Look, I've got to go, but I don't want to leave you hanging. You give me some time to get the bad guy so your family is safe, and then if you feel like you need a friend, give me a call, okay?"

Jesse nodded, obviously dumb with misery, and Crosby squeezed his shoulder before striding through the kitchen, nodding to Garcia without breaking stride.

"Guys, it's been real. Gibbs, Swan, can I speak to you for a moment?"

She followed them outside, and Crosby handed her a piece of note paper with an address. "I need a unit sent out to this place to patrol. The people inside aren't great, but they don't deserve to be shot in the face, you read me?"

She nodded and pulled the radio at her belt, and he stopped her. "Look, the kid's fragile. You two take care of our friends here for us, okay?"

She nodded, and then Crosby and Garcia were out of there, trotting toward the agency-issued SUV with all of the urgency Crosby had been trying not to show the kid in the living room.

Garcia waited until they got back into the SUV to ask, "What was that?"

Crosby grunted and held up a finger, pulling his radio out to contact Gail. "Elsa, you there?"

"Yeah, Olaf, speak to me."

Garcia held back a snicker—if he ever wanted to know about their relationship, the Disney references clued him in.

"Look, I've got three names for you to run down on potential victims for Sewell, but I got more."

"Gimme the names first," she said, and he rattled off the top three names from memory, which impressed Garcia, because that's why he used a notebook.

When he was done he said, "We got three more that might be a possibility, and Garcia's going to get those from my phone and send them to you," he said, pulling the device from his pocket and handing it to Garcia after unlocking it with his face. "It's in Notes, and she's in frequent contacts," he murmured as Garcia got moving, listening as he followed directions. "But I got more than that. I also got a line on Kurt Armbruster, and it's in the city. I need to know if the chief wants us to track this guy to Queens, or if he wants another team to do it."

She grunted. "You sure this tip is live? We've got him living in Elizabeth, same as your last boy."

"Yeah, well, my last boy met his two friends while bussing a gay club in Queens. Nobody's parents knew, but the guys were pretty tight. Kurt and Ryan had shitty home lives, and they used a little flop above the club to hook up with each other and dodge fists and lamps and baseball bats and shit. Jesse thinks Sewell found out—he'd had a crush on Ryan since the beginning—and that's what sort of tipped him over the edge, if you know what I mean."

"Oh dear God," she muttered. "Does Sewell know about the flop?"

"The answer there is maybe. I guess Sewell had been dogging the kid pretty hard before he shot poor Ryan in the face. So we know Kurt's probably there, and we know where Kurt's family lives. I sent a unit there to keep an eye on the family, but someone needs to check out the flop."

She grunted. "Give me five. Find a drive thru or something, get some coffee, and let me run names and locations and work."

Crosby signed out and scowled, brows knit like he was thinking of a place to go while they waited for directions.

"Burger? Taco?" Garcia asked, taking advantage of the situation. "Sorry. I usually carry granola bars with me—I've got the metabolism of a rat on meth."

Crosby grunted. "Can do. But we gotta work on your taste in takeout. There are food carts all the fuck over the city. You don't got one you can wait for?"

Garcia bit his lip and held up his shaking hand. "Sorry again. Skipped breakfast," he admitted, feeling dumb. He knew better. The blood sugar thing wasn't bad enough to be diabetes, not yet, and he usually ate right to make sure it didn't head that way. But he'd been nervous, riding the high of the quick turnover, spending his night reading up on his team. He'd burned off more than he'd bargained for, and he hadn't come prepared.

Crosby said nothing, but as they neared a fast-food-studded strip mall before the turnpike entrance, he turned into the parking lot.

"Take your pick," he said. "I'll find something."

Garcia picked the least offensive place that looked like it sold coffee too and ordered a chicken sandwich. Crosby ordered coffee and then, grimacing, a hamburger.

As they pulled into the queue, he patted his stomach. "More crunches for me."

"Metabolism is nobody's friend," Garcia consoled. Privately, he was thinking that he liked a little bit of a tummy on a guy. It usually meant he was a more generous lover, but in spite of Crosby's sympathy with the Campos kid, he wasn't going to push his luck. You didn't break an eight-year streak of nobody at your work knowing about your social life on the first day of your dream job.

Besides, something like that would probably be interpreted as the come-on it was.

Crosby shrugged, his handsome face set on "buffering," but Garcia wasn't fooled. He was probably thinking about the case.

"So where in Queens are we heading?" Garcia asked.

"Jackson Heights, if the chief gives us the go-ahead," Crosby responded, eyes still far away. "The club sounds like one of those places you can get to from an alleyway easier than a street, and the flop is on the third floor, under the staircase. It used to be storage, but the club owner turned it into a sort of hideaway for peeps who needed it, I think. I guess the three of them have been renting it for… uhm…." His eyes sharpened, and unexpectedly his ears turned pink.

"A place to hook up?" Garcia asked, trying not to laugh at him.

But Crosby shook his head. "More than that," he said. "A safe place. I mean, sure, I guess Ryan and Kurt would hook up there, but I got the feeling it was more a place they could, you know, go and *be* gay. Jesse loves his brother, I think, but he doesn't have rainbows coming out his ass. Both Ryan and Kurt tended to have strained muscles and bruises that don't come from a bicycle, if you know what I mean. I hate the idea of invading this kid's safe space, but worse than that, if our scumbag knows about this place…." He bit his lip.

"It's a trap," Garcia said, horrified.

"Yeah. It's a trap. Now so far our scumbag looks more venal than vengeful, so I think Natalia and Harding are on the right path, but just in case…."

Garcia got it then. His thousand-yard stare was impatience more than anything else—although he didn't seem to hold it against Garcia.

"Sorry about the food thing," Garcia said weakly anyway.

Crosby shot him an amused glance. "Not your fault. Gail put us on ice, so it's a good time to stop. But tell me what kind of protein bars you like—if we all keep some in our pockets, we can back you up."

Oh, that was embarrassing.

"It's not a medical thing or like that," he said, although his teeth were beginning to chatter.

Crosby shot him a hard look. "Because you're careful," he deduced. "Gotcha. We'll help you be careful. Nobody wants to end up with something like that in their file. How much notice did you get you'd be coming in today?"

"Last night at six."

Crosby grunted, but then they were up to the window. Crosby asked for a side of fries to be added to the order and paid, handing the bag over to Garcia before taking the two coffees and putting them in the holders. He'd just pulled away from the building when Gail came on the radio.

"SCTF Four, you there?"

"Yeah, One, what's the news?"

"Chadwick and Carlyle are closer to the addies you gave me. He says Queens is yours if you want it."

"Well, who wants Queens, but I'll run down the address."

"Ten-four. Let us know when you get there and if you need backup."

"Fuck backup. I need fucking *parking* is what I need in Queens!"

Gail snickered. "Hey, I'm a goddess, but I'm not a miracle worker, yeah?"

"I hear ya. If you can scare me up some place this thing won't get towed or creamed, you'll really be earning your salary, right?"

"Right, Olaf, I'll see if I can't get some uniforms to set you up."

"Thanks, Elsa. Signing off."

He set the radio in its receiver, and Garcia chuckled through a mouthful of chicken sandwich.

"What?" he asked, the Irish cop twang in his voice more noticeable than ever.

"What do you have against New York parking?" he asked, swallowing gratefully.

Crosby sheepishly rolled his eyes. "You ever been to Chicago?" he asked.

"No."

"Well, you know how New York streets are so narrow you can't see the tops of buildings and shit?"

"Yeah."

"Chicago's streets are wider, and I'd say it's because we're not barbarians, but fact is, the one street they made to New York spec turned into a fuckin' wind tunnel. It faces the lake, and people get blown backward if they try to walk on the ice in the winter. But that doesn't change the fact that the streets are wider and the sidewalks are wider and there's fucking parking where you don't think parking's gonna be. But it is. So yeah. I got a healthy distrust of being able to park the great Cop Whale here anywhere that's not the structure at our office, you hearing me?"

Garcia nodded and took another bite of his sandwich. From anyone else, he'd say Crosby was griping to hear himself gripe, but he heard a healthy dose of longing for his hometown in Crosby's voice, and Garcia got it.

Crosby could never go home.

He wasn't going to bitch about that, so he'd bitch about the parking instead.

But apparently one rant was all he ever spent on something because as the car hummed along, Crosby let out a breath and looked unhappily at the fast-food bag on the center console.

"You feelin' better?" he asked, and Garcia managed an "*Mmf!*" through another mouthful of food.

"Great," Crosby said. "You can have my burger. Lookit this traffic—we got forty-five minutes minimum before we're anywhere near Queens." Fucking New Jersey. Freeways there like vermicelli. Forty-five minutes was generous.

"What about your lunch?" Garcia asked, but Crosby shook his head. "Man, those poor kids. I ain't hungry after that, you know?"

Outside, Garcia nodded, but inside, he was thinking how funny it was that he could happily hook up his way through his twenties and think that was the way things were going to go until he was ready to retire, only to be brought low by this broad-chested Adonis who was entirely clueless as to what he was doing to Garcia's constitution.

Garcia refrained from the burger, thinking maybe they could split it after they checked out the locale.

THE LOCAL po-po had done what they'd been asked and staked out a parking spot across from the club itself without going in. Crosby and Garcia were out of the vehicle and crossing the street after a cursory wave to the boys in blue. Garcia had done his best to make sure he didn't have mayo on his shirt or his mouth before the car stopped, but he resisted the urge to double-check that now. He'd have to get used to having the sort of clout that meant he barely had to talk to other cops if he didn't need to.

Not that Crosby was rude, but it was clear he was on a mission.

They passed the front of the building, which hosted a tiny newsstand, and moved to the alleyway between that high-rise and the next. There were businesses on the bottom and apartments on the top, like a lot of NYC, but Garcia was getting the feeling of classic funkiness here—the precursor to gentrification. Jackson Heights wasn't the *worst* area of Queens, and it was the sort of place where people knew each other, even just to recognize them and curse them out for walking too slow.

As they trotted down the alleyway, which was wide enough for dumpsters and probably lines of people in the night but too narrow for a car to drive without losing paint, Garcia heard sounds—thumps, yells, some serious destruction.

Then he heard a shout, anguished and desperate, "*Run, Kurt, run!*" before a muffled shot.

"Shit!" Crosby cried out. He paused to pull his radio from his belt. "Elsa, shots fired, our location, get an ambulance here and some uniforms stat. Garcia and I are on scene, going in."

"Crosby, *stay*—"

Before the rest of the order could come through, Crosby hooked the radio to his belt and pulled his largest gun from his hip before he looked at Garcia grimly. "I'll stay put if you want," he said. Garcia got it then, that he would. This was dangerous, and he wasn't going in alone, but he needed Garcia's okay for them both to check out the situation without someone on their six.

"I heard nothing," Garcia said. He pulled his own weapon and sank to a crouch, moving to the other side of the door.

"Law enforcement," Crosby called when they were both in position. "SCTF, on-site and coming in!" They heard nothing, so Crosby kicked in the door and Garcia went in low while Crosby went in behind him, aiming over his head.

When the Case Works You

GARCIA WAS used to his days moving fast—from researching to confabbing to making a bust—but not this fast. Later he'd reflect that it's what happened when your perp was committing homicides and needed to be stopped *now* as opposed to building a case against a criminal enterprise, but right at this moment, he was letting Crosby take point while he followed, weapon out, checking their left, right, and six while Crosby kept his eyes front.

Which meant that when Crosby muttered, "Well shit," and crouched to the floor, Garcia had to take in the victim on the floor amid a destroyed table and a couple of chairs reduced to kindling with little flashes of sight while he kept his partner safe.

The victim on the floor was a tall, broad-shouldered African American male wearing a powder-blue sequined jumpsuit with false breasts in the bra and bright blue shimmer eye shadow with false eyelashes that were still fluttering as they struggled for breath through a lushly painted mouth. Crosby took a pulse and nodded, sucking in his breath.

"Gunshot," he said to Garcia. "Through the abdomen, to the side. Lots of blood. Need an ambulance stat. You stay with the vic. I'll go look for Sewell."

Garcia opened his mouth to protest. They should stay there for backup, he knew that, but Crosby was obviously thinking about the runner. Garcia pulled out his radio and sent terse instructions on the law-enforcement frequency, detailing location and need. The whole time his mouth was running, he was scanning their surroundings and listening to Crosby.

"Ma'am," he said, "ma'am, help is coming. Hang in there. I need to know where Kurt's gonna go, though. He's got a flop here. How do we get to it?"

"Up the stairs," the victim wheezed. "Fourth-floor landing, down half a flight behind utility closet. Can't get to it from the elevator. Tucked behind."

"What'd that asshole take?" Crosby asked, and Garcia looked just long enough to catch the grim smile on their victim's face.

"Elevator. Fucker's slow."

Crosby squeezed her shoulder. "I'm not," he said. "This is Garcia. He's gonna look after you. Hang tough."

With a curt nod, Crosby stood and caught Garcia's eyes for a moment before hauling ass across the club floor for the stairs with the speed of a gazelle and the bulk of a bear.

"Fuck," Garcia muttered, kneeling on the black rubber floor. Their victim's breaths were getting labored and panicked, and Garcia needed her to calm down. "Ma'am," he muttered. "Please, take it easy. Ambulance is already coming."

"Got blood... on my floor... dammit."

Garcia had to smile. By day, dance clubs lose a lot of their luster. The mysterious cavernous interior with graceful glimmers of color becomes a black rubber floor with walls painted black and poly-tinsel streamers, and the much-coveted stools and tables become the shoddiest of woodwork, held together with shellac and spilled beer.

But the place was clean, and the disco ball in the center of the floor had most of its mirrors. There was hand sanitizer in every corner, and the bar at the far end of the building was sparkling clean, without a whiff of spilled alcohol or spoiled bar fruit.

"This your place?" he asked, to keep her focused. He was focused on the elevator dial in the corner. It said six floors, and, as promised, it was inching slowly toward the fourth. He couldn't hear Crosby's footsteps pounding in the stairwell anymore, but he was trying to imagine how quickly he was running, if he could sustain that pace for four floors.

"Yeah. Should see it at night. It's swingin'."

Garcia spared the proprietress a wink. "I'm surprised I haven't been by. But don't tell anyone, okay? I'm po-po."

She let out what was supposed to be a cackle, but it came out a wheeze, and Garcia could have wept with the need for the ambulance to get there. Their vic needed help, and Crosby had run up the stairs alone, and—

The EMTs hit the doors hard, the stretcher between them.

"Gunshot victim," Garcia said tersely. "Assigned male at birth. Responds to ma'am."

"Roger that." The EMTs, both painfully young and female, elbowed Garcia aside and knelt by the victim, speaking firmly. "Ma'am? Ma'am? Can you hear us?"

"Send back the cute boys," she rasped.

"Check on you later," he told her. "Hang in there."

With that, he took off after Crosby, cursing his partner for running into the fray.

He was two flights of stairs up when he heard the first gunshot, and his heart roared so hard in his ears he almost didn't hear the second. By the time he got to the fourth floor and followed the directions to the utility closet, he was seeing stars from holding his breath. He took two steps down the tiny stairwell and almost tripped on the sprawling body.

He bent down to check the pulse and found it fluttering under his fingers as he heard Crosby on his radio, asking in a choked voice for another ambulance, giving directions to the utility closet on the fourth floor.

Garcia almost wept. God. He was alive. Sewell might not make it, but Crosby could radio for help. Gingerly he picked his way around Sewell, making sure to kick the gun he found far down the stairs as he continued.

"Crosby?"

Crosby was sitting upright on a bed that took up maybe half the room, talking into his radio while fighting for breath. The bed—a four poster—looked directly out the half window that made up half a wall in the tiny little room, and Garcia had a fleeting, aching impression of two lovers in this room looking out into the city and pretending the new day was starting for them alone.

"Yeah," Crosby gasped, clutching his side. "Runner's safe. Sewell's down. Ambulance is on its way." He glanced up at Garcia and gave a ragged smile. "New guy isn't dead." Crosby winced as a very irate voice came in through his earbud, and then grimaced at Garcia just as Garcia's came online.

"How is he?" Clint Harding said, sounding very, very worried.

"I think he took a round in the vest," Garcia said, glaring at Crosby. Crosby nodded and struggled for breath again, his arm wrapped around his middle.

"Any broken ribs?" Clint asked.

Garcia watched Crosby labor for breath and hazarded a guess. "Cracked at the very least," he said. "He's definitely getting sent in for X-rays."

Crosby glared. "Traitor!" he mouthed.

Garcia rolled his eyes. "Where's the kid?" he mouthed back.

"What about the victim in the club?" Clint asked.

"Medics had just arrived when I came to back up Crosby, sir."

There was an arctic silence over the comms. "He left you to come after the perpetrator?"

"We had reason to believe our boy was at risk, sir," Garcia said, looking Crosby dead in the eye. "Detective Crosby probably saved the kid's life."

"I'm sure he did," Clint snapped. "Make sure he gets his ass to the hospital. Tell him I want X-rays before he's cleared for active. We'll be on scene in ten. Goddammit, that kid needs to take a breath before he rushes into things."

The comm clicked and went dead, and Garcia let loose his own sigh of relief before sinking to his haunches and looking under the bed.

Kurt Armbruster was a good-looking kid—he had been on his ID shot during the presentation that morning anyway. But his pale brown skin was smudged with dust and grease and tears, and what had probably been a nice pressed button-down was torn and none too clean.

"Hey," Garcia murmured. "It's all right. You're safe. Come on out."

Kurt nodded, but he didn't move.

"'M I crushing him?" Crosby gasped, and Garcia glared at him, then decided to use it as an advantage.

"Look, buddy, my partner probably has a couple of cracked ribs, so if he has to get up, it's gonna hurt. Let's save him the pain of standing up to pull you out, okay? He took a bullet for you."

Armbruster nodded reluctantly, and Garcia bent to help him crawl out from under the bed before sitting him on top of it and covering both their shoulders with the comforter. The kid was shaking from head to toe, probably shock, and Crosby looked like he was fighting the same condition all the way.

"Ooh, Crosby," Garcia murmured when Armbruster was settled, leaning his head against Crosby's shoulder, "Daddy's mad at you."

Crosby nodded. "Figured."

"I'm not too happy myself," he muttered, "but I'm glad the kid's all right."

Crosby took another gulp of air. "You ready for that transfer yet?"

Garcia met his eyes directly and took a mighty risk by smoothing that dark blond hair from the pale brow. "Not on your life," he said, meaning every syllable.

Crosby's lips twitched back in a smile, but he was still trying to catch his breath, so it didn't last long.

Hospitals Suck But Nobody Else Does

CROSBY HAD gotten a scholarship to Illinois State University playing defensive back. He'd been injured in his senior year—two cracked ribs and a dislocated shoulder—and had barely escaped going pro.

He remembered what broken ribs felt like, but the bullet impact, even through the vest, was a special sort of panic. He didn't even want to think about the ways Garcia made it better.

But he did, starting with that touch on his forehead, pushing his hair back. Maybe Garcia was just a handsy guy. Some people's families were like that, and Garcia seemed like the type. But that didn't mean it hadn't been a comfort. In a way, so had the ration of shit Garcia gave him for running up to the room behind the stairs without backup.

"I was right, wasn't I?" he asked, carefully spacing out his breaths.

"I'm glad the kid's okay," Garcia admitted, but maybe that's because the kid was sitting on the bed next to him, leaning his head on Crosby's arm.

The kid started to talk, his voice dreamy, his teeth chattering from the shock.

"Is… is… is Jesse okay?"

"Yes," Garcia said immediately. "He and his brother and the boy are in protective custody."

"Good." Then Kurt whimpered and said one more word. "Ryan." He started to cry silently, and he didn't move until the EMTs got there and started to shout directions to each other on the landing. The general consensus was they had to move the body on the staircase before they could treat anybody in the little closet/room, so Crosby and Kurt had to wait to be seen.

As much as Crosby wanted an apartment of his own, he figured he wasn't going to move into the closet anytime soon. The room may have *sounded r*omantic as a little hideaway, but the truth was, only the window saved it from being a deathtrap. Listening to the EMTs swearing as they tried to fit the dead perpetrator onto the stretcher was dark comedy.

By the time they'd figured out how it was going to work, Crosby decided he wasn't going to sit there and wait for them.

"Help me up," he said to Garcia.

"No."

"Help me up!" he insisted. "Do you want to make them come down here to get me? Here, you help me, the kid helps me, we can be up the stairs before the next unit gets off the elevator."

Garcia grunted. "This is stupid, and your commander is going to kill me."

"He doesn't have to know," Crosby breathed. "He's your commander too." Adrenaline and injury were giving him the shakes—he could feel it coming on. But he needed to stand up, and he needed Garcia to stop hovering over him because it gave him ideas he shouldn't have. "Kurt, I'm going to lean on you. Are you game?"

"Sure," Kurt said, his voice low and sad. "Here, hold on to my hand."

Crosby trusted him and pushed up, while Garcia offered him a hand from the front. Lev-er-*age*! He stood, eyes watering from the pain in his side, and remembered all the squat thrusts he'd been doing, not to mention the hours running to amp his cardio. He locked his core and used his thigh muscles, one hand on the railing and the other wrapped around Garcia's wiry, hard bicep.

Ooh. Nice.

It was a good thing he was in too much pain to get handsy, or he'd be down for a good grope, and he had no cultural excuses for it. His parents were repressed Irish, down to his mother's sensible shoes. Gah! He'd known it when the guy had bopped through the door, all tight and hard like that. Crosby didn't really think of himself as gay, but he'd had a few exceptions that probably made him bi. Guys who hit him just right, guys he liked to look at, and a few who'd hit on him that he'd gotten to touch. In the end he'd accepted it, that he could like it with a guy same as with a girl, but he hadn't had a relationship of more than a week or two. Cop work was too demanding—and too homophobic.

But Lord, this guy was hitting his spots.

His foot slipped a little, and white lightning zapped him in the side, stopping his breath, forcing his thoughts to the here and now of what his body was doing. He must have made a sound because Garcia was suddenly closer, one arm wrapped around his waist while he gripped Crosby's bicep with his far hand and took some of his weight. One step at a time, one breath at a time, he made it to the top of the stairs, arriving as the next crew burst out of the elevator.

"You tried to do our job for us?"

Crosby recognized the girl—sweet, early twenties, blond and blue-eyed. She'd been there when he'd gotten mauled by the dog.

"Didn't want… you to…."

"He didn't want you to get stuck on the stairs," Garcia muttered. "Jesus, Crosby, you say bupkis all day, and now you want to talk?"

"This is Garcia," Crosby said, smiling in spite of the clammy pain-sweat enveloping his body. "He's… impatient."

Wendy Parsons and her partner, a fit Asian man in his early forties named Brian Kim, both snorted and hustled the stretcher to where he stood.

"He's the impatient one?" Kim asked acerbically.

"They had a hell of a time getting the body out of the stairwell," Garcia told him. "I think he didn't want to have to hear all the bitching if you had to go down into that tiny room."

"That's the Crosby we know and love," Wendy said, coming to his other side and helping him sit. She glanced up, and her blue eyes took in Kurt, who was huddling back in the stairwell. "Who's your friend?"

"Kurt Armbruster," Garcia said. "He's probably in shock. He's had a super shitty day."

"Aw." Wendy moved to let Brian help Crosby while she went to coax Kurt out of the darkened hallway. "Come on, baby. You're gonna be okay." She stretched out her hand, and Kurt reached to take it. Crosby couldn't turn to watch them anymore, but he did hear her say, "Oh honey. Your hands are ice cold. Let's get you downstairs with your friend here. We'll check you out and make sure you're okay."

"You… you… can't tell my family I'm here," he managed.

Crosby was going to open his mouth to say something, but Garcia touched his shoulder. "Lift your shirt, Cowboy, and let your guy tape your ribs. I'll see if we can get him someplace safe."

Oh wow. That was nice. Crosby nodded and let him do that while he moved his hands to the Velcro of his Kevlar, wincing when he disturbed his side.

Brian took over for him, taking out the vest before unzipping his hooded sweatshirt and lifting the shirt underneath. The sound he made sucking air through his teeth was not promising.

"Oh man. There's some swelling here. It's looking bad. Wendy, get your ass over here. We need to get him to X-ray, stat!"

"Oh Lord. Crosby," Wendy said, because she definitely *did* remember him, "could you not make things shittier on yourself? That would be great, yeah?"

Crosby was suddenly grateful he couldn't look past his bunched sweatshirt to see the bruising on his ribs. Somehow that always made it worse. At that moment the elevator doors swung open and Clint Harding strode through the doors, looking pissed off and frustrated. He took in Crosby with a sweep of his eyes and said, "Crosby, lie down."

"Yes, sir," Crosby rasped, but Brian shook his head no, pulling out an ace bandage.

"Not tape?" Harding asked.

Brian pushed gently at the swollen flesh, and Crosby let out a little moan, hating himself for the noise.

"Possible internal bleeding. X-rays first, tape after we know if we're going in for surgery."

Clint glared at him. "You could not fucking wait?"

"He saved my life," Kurt said, and Crosby had to give it to the kid. He approached slowly, almost like a feral animal, but still, Clint was on a tear, and that was something to behold.

"We're so very glad he did." Harding said it through his teeth, but he didn't bark.

"Chief," Garcia said quietly, "this is Kurt Armbruster, one of our runners. He's a little shocky. We were going to take him to the hospital with Crosby to check his vitals."

Clint Harding gave Garcia the kind of look he'd been giving Crosby for a year and a half, which made Crosby think maybe the new guy was going to make it for a while. That was good, because at that moment, breathing got a lot harder, and he found himself being helped onto the stretcher while he became the unwilling center of attention once again.

EIGHT WEEKS. That's how long it took to recover from the broken ribs, with an extra week thrown in for the punctured lung. On the one hand, it was two weeks spent in the hospital, which was the suck because everybody came in to tell him that the new guy was really earning his oats.

On the other hand, it was six weeks spent in Toby's apartment, in a bed he'd ordered from the hospital and made Toby promise on his life not to let anybody have sex on. Which was also the suck because he sort of missed rooming with Gail. Not Iliana, though. He didn't even miss the sex, which had been impersonal. He really liked the emotional connection he usually made during sex; he hadn't had a girlfriend since Chicago, and he missed that.

Gail's cast had come off a week after Crosby went into surgery. She wasn't back to full duty yet, but she did get to go out on calls on occasion. She came by and updated Crosby on Garcia and the others too.

When he was out of the hospital and stuck at Toby's, trying not to bitch like an old man about the five thousand people doing the ten thousand illicit substances in the other parts of the apartment, Garcia himself came to visit.

Crosby was lying on his side, trying to rest and wishing he didn't feel like such an asshole for begging Toby's guests to open the window in the living room while they were smoking, when Toby let him into Crosby's room.

"You doing okay?" Toby asked, and Crosby smiled weakly.

Toby was little—five three, five four—with bandy legs and contorted joints. Crosby remembered Toby saying he hadn't been able to absorb nutrition as a child. He had a puckish little face and an ugly-beautiful smile, and his sense of humor was spot on. As a DJ—a DJ with a communications degree and an IQ of 145—Toby was widely popular, and Crosby got it. Toby had been on the outside looking in for his entire childhood. Now, in the most happening city in the world, Toby was cutting edge, cool, and interesting. He knew Crosby's job was exhausting, and when Crosby got home after a week of chasing bad guys, Toby had the fridge stocked with his favorite foods and beer, and when he ambled into his room to crash, Toby asked his guests to tone it down.

Crosby didn't like to impose, and Toby did his best to accommodate a big oafish cop with zero cool in his fascinating milieu of artists, actors, and writers who wandered in and out of the flat. It seems they'd formed a legitimate and real bond while Toby was helping Crosby through his classes at Illinois State and Crosby was introducing Toby to the football team—and the cheerleaders—and watching his snarky, magnetic personality blossom into who he was now.

But that didn't mean living in his flat was optimal, and Crosby suppressed a wave of embarrassment as Garcia made his way into Crosby's sparsely furnished room.

"Wow," Garcia muttered, grabbing the desk chair and moving it to the side of the bed without asking. "It's like going from Studio 54 to my old army barracks through one open door."

Crosby grinned tiredly. "Yeah, but the moldings." The apartment was old-school, circa early 1900s, retrofitted for electricity, HVAC, and modern plumbing. The bones were good—hardwood floors, solid doors, more space than New York probably allowed by law in this day and age.

Garcia laughed a little. "The apartment is nice," he admitted, "but is that"—he gestured with his hand toward the sophisticated goose-babbling chaos that filled the front rooms—"always a thing?"

"Unless Toby's out at a gig," Crosby confirmed. "Then the whole menagerie just sort of follows him out on the town. That's three, four times a week."

Toby may have had a perpetual party in his apartment, but he rarely, if ever, partook of it. He actually slept regular hours, in his own room, usually alone, and he worked hard drumming up gigs and negotiating top price for them. When the money had started flowing in, Crosby had been first on his invitation list to come out and party in the city, and Crosby had taken him up on it, back when he worked in Chi-town. When the SCTF offer had come up, he'd called Toby asking for apartment advice, and Toby had extended a hand. The situation *wasn't* ideal—and Crosby was sure Toby could use his bedroom to set up his equipment and work, practice, whatever, but neither of them complained, Crosby figured, because the basics hadn't changed. Crosby was still a stand-up friend who had protected Toby and his friends on more than one occasion, and Toby was still a really decent guy who hadn't let fame and experience change him.

"Toby's cool," Garcia said, sounding sincere. "But I swear there was a guy out there smoking something the ATF doesn't even have a name for yet."

"Was the window open?" Crosby asked, a smile twisting his mouth.

"Yeah."

"Sometimes that's all I can ask." He appreciated the smile. "How's work?" The truth was he resented the hell out of being laid up.

"We miss you," Garcia said, so much feeling in his voice that Crosby felt warmed.

"They been treating you okay?" Crosby knew his team wouldn't leave the new guy out to flounder—they hadn't let *his* sorry ass sink, right? But he also knew that his streak of protectiveness toward Garcia hadn't faded during the two weeks in the hospital, or this last week on bed rest either. The new guy had been snarky, funny, and well, fun to look at, although Crosby would keep *that* thought to himself.

What he *could* admit, though, was that after three weeks off duty, he really missed the damned job.

The hunt and chase was fun in a way he hadn't known could happen in law enforcement. A lot of a patrolman's life was walking or driving beats or handling petty crimes or domestic disturbances. This job was higher stakes, usually, and once they had a perpetrator in their sights, they were all bullets from the same gun. There was no rousting people, no giving poor people crap because rich people said so, no worrying that standing up to do the right thing would get him on somebody else's bad side. The right thing was the right thing with the SCTF. If he'd even known the job had existed when he'd been in Chicago, he'd have hunted for it himself.

"Yeah," Garcia said, smiling slightly. "Thanks for telling Gail about the food thing, though. The eating thing. We were out on the job three days ago, and I guess my face got a little pale, and suddenly three people were shoving protein bars into my hand. As soon as the case was over, Chadwick stopped at a burger joint for 'no reason at all.'" He held up his fingers in air quotes. "It was like everybody knew, nobody was going to say something, and damned if I wasn't going to get fed." He gave Crosby a wink. "Best group of people I've ever worked with if the last few weeks are to judge by."

Crosby nodded, pleased. "Yeah. I'll second that. I'm glad they're treating you right."

"Well, they want to treat you right, and Gail said you were having a hard time getting to PT. I get it. The elevator here would make my lungs burst too if I had to ride that thing down to street level and call a cab. Anyway, we have a solution for you."

"Yeah?" He was suddenly feeling a little more awake and, at the same time, more relaxed than he'd been since he'd gotten back from the hospital.

"Yeah. Gail's back. *She* needs PT too, but she's good for on-site stuff and showing me the ropes—who to talk to, what to look for. We figure that if we give Chadwick and Carlyle a feeb buddy—"

Crosby suppressed a snort at the disrespectful appellation of the FBI, and Garcia twinkled those dark eyes at him and kept going.

"Anyway, they get a feeb buddy to train other divisions of SCTF folks and maybe do some SCTF magic themselves, and I get Gail to maybe slow my roll into the division until she can run without throwing up. And you get to run point on our ops, like Gail did, since Harding informs me that your 'I'm not that fast and not that smart' routine is pure bullshit and you have a minor in computer sciences to back up your double major."

"I'm a meatloaf," Crosby joked. "Everybody knows it. My first gig I got taken out by puppies, remember?"

Garcia snorted and leaned forward on his elbows so their faces were very, very close. "You'd get to come in, run point, and use your off time in the gym with the spotter who works with the feebs. Your brain works fine, and Gail needs to not be running balls-out, so she can back you up when you need to rest. What do you think?"

Crosby's eyes burned as he contemplated another four to six weeks lying there like a lump while Toby tried to channel Andy Warhol through a new music mix.

"Sounds like a plan," he rasped. "Did you and Harding cook that up?"

"Whole team," Garcia said softly. "Gail came back and said you were miserable. We didn't want to let you suffer. Yeah?"

"Like I said—best team on the planet." He smiled and closed his eyes, suddenly exhausted. "What happens if there's no need for a point man? I do paperwork?"

Garcia laughed. "You sleep, big guy." He stood and did that hair pushing thing, and Crosby wished he had the balls to capture his hand and keep it on his face. It felt so good. Warm and reassuring. God, it was nice to be cared about. "Just like now," Garcia finished, his thumb giving a careful brush against Crosby's cheekbone.

Crosby wanted to say something—acknowledge the tenderness, thank his new partner and friend for the solution to what was going to be a four-to-five-week problem, *something*—when Garcia withdrew his hand and said briskly, "Enjoy your nap, right? We'll all be seeing you in a week, 'cause that's the earliest Harding could get you approved back for duty. Take it easy, right? Don't breathe too deep, and I promise if the

DEA raids this place, I'll back up your complete ignorance of all that stuff in the front room, sweartagod."

Crosby might have laughed—he wasn't sure—but he did know he was asleep before Garcia closed the door behind him.

GARCIA DIDN'T seem to think the time away or the temporary change in assignments was any sort of divider between them. As far as he was concerned, they were still partners after that one eventful day. The morning Crosby returned, taking Gail's spot as point man when everybody was out, Garcia greeted him with a new coffee cup that said, "Let's keep the dumbfuckery to a minimum today" and was filled with something fresh-ground and cinnamon-y with what tasted like real cream.

He closed his eyes and inhaled first, then gave Garcia a look that probably carried far too much gratitude.

"You let Joey make the coffee, didn't you?" he breathed.

"Well, yeah!" Garcia grinned. "We let Joey make the coffee, let Gideon find the places to eat, Natalia orders the pastries, and Gail has healthy snacks—protein bars, cheese sticks, beef jerky. She'll hook you up."

Crosby nodded, remembering those conversations. Feeling vulnerable in the field was no good. Garcia had to know they were looking out for him.

"And don't ask Harding for shit," Garcia continued. "In fact, maybe have some peanuts or something to give *him*, 'cause he's as intense about a case as you are. Dude. You gotta give props to Natalia—she keeps up with that!"

"Yeah, he's scary," Crosby muttered, his ears on sonar, like a bat's, to make sure Harding didn't overhear them talking about him.

Garcia nodded and took a sip from his own coffee cup, which featured a lounging cat and the text No Fucks Given.

Crosby nodded to the cup. "There a story behind that?"

Garcia shrugged and then grinned shyly. "Man, my first week, after you went into surgery, I stayed late every night to work out, do paperwork, listen for news on you. They found me asleep in the weight room one morning and told me to chill out."

Crosby couldn't laugh his way past that. "You were worried about me?" he asked, something in his chest pinging.

Another one of those shrugs—all his movements were so quick Crosby enjoyed watching him. "I know it was only a day," he said, "but it was a really good day. You were probably the best partner I've had. I'm sort of pissed you got shot so we don't get to go out together for another few weeks."

It was Crosby's turn to give a shy smile. "Me too," he said. He sobered. "But you're being good to Gail, right?"

"Yeah. We mostly get interviewing witnesses. She's pushing herself, but her leg's still weak."

"I'm surprised Harding hasn't gotten more people on the roster besides the feebs," Crosby pondered, and at that moment, Harding walked in and heard him.

"Garcia, get me coffee," he said pleasantly, coming to sit down in Garcia's spot.

"Hey, sir."

"So we let you come back early," Harding murmured. "But you can't overdo it."

Crosby grunted and tried not to let his eyes go to Garcia, who was filling Harding's mug like he knew everybody's coffee orders by rote. "Wanted to make sure you didn't abuse little brother," he said, trying to keep his voice light.

Harding wasn't buying it. "Look. You were right a minute ago—we need people. I'll be honest, I need a special sort of skill here. Not just people who run down the perp, but people who are careful about not leaving collateral damage and who are good at dealing with the other victims who are left behind. Don't get me wrong. I don't approve of you going after the perp without backup, but I do approve of your priority not to have another innocent person die that day." He sighed and rubbed his eyes. "Chadwick and Carlyle are telling me they practically have to retrain their shadows from the very beginning because those priorities aren't necessarily the Bureau's. You tell me where we can find someone with that same agenda built into his bones and I'll train them myself."

Crosby's mind went back four weeks ago. "Sir, Officer Swan from the detail in New Jersey who was keeping Jesse and his family safe?"

"Yes?"

"He got the older brother some financial help so he didn't lose his business because Sewell killed the people who were going to get him through the winter. And he apparently talked him into letting Kurt

Armbruster stay with them because Kurt's father was beating the shit out of him. And he even mediated when Jesse came out. I'm just saying—I don't know his gun skills or his dossier, but if that's who you're looking for…."

Harding smiled, nodding. "That's the kid I need. You sure you're good for a couple weeks as point man from the information center until you're back in the fray?"

"I am, sir." He was. He and Gail had worked together often enough that he felt like he had a good handle on things.

"Then I'll look into young Officer Swan and see if he'd like to take some tests. How's that?"

"As long as I get to keep Garcia, sir, that's fantastic."

"Not Gail?"

Crosby grinned. "She'd kill me, sir. I'd call her Elsa one too many times, and that would be it. You'd have a homicide on your hands."

Harding laughed like he was supposed to, and Crosby didn't have to explain. He'd loved partnering with Gail before she got hurt, but Gail could take care of herself. Garcia, though, there was something vulnerable about him. Crosby didn't want to leave him out there again without Crosby to watch his back.

Whites of Their Eyes

"YOU ONLY got me for one more day," Gail said brightly. "You good with that?"

Garcia grinned at her as he piloted the SUV through Pennsylvania Amish country. They'd been doing background questioning about a perpetrator who had originated there and then disappeared during his *Rumspringa* nearly ten years ago. He'd come up on the bad side of a drug deal gone wrong, and they'd been hoping to find somebody who could help them find the guy before he hurt somebody else. All their intel said he had an addiction and a helpless yearning to go home. He hadn't killed anybody yet; if they brought him down carefully, he might not spend the rest of his life in prison.

"Gonna miss you, Elsa," he said, meaning it mostly. Next to Crosby, she was the best partner he'd ever had. Conscientious, tough, willing to play helpless female if it would help them get their way, but anything but helpless when shit got busy. As her leg had gotten stronger, they'd been given more active duty, and the week before she'd had his six as they were running down a perp. When they came to a six-foot fence, she actually vocalized, "Going around!" to let him know to watch his back because she couldn't have made the climb—not yet.

Garcia eventually chased the perp into a two-by-four she wielded like a pro ball player, because she'd made good on her threat and then grabbed whatever was nearby to make the collar. He'd been impressed as fuck.

Everything his old job at the ATF hadn't had—honesty, quick thinking, the sense that someone having his back really meant having his back—had been present in that six-minute chase behind a Quick-E-Mart in Paramus. It almost made him think that the thing he'd felt with Crosby had been just him overreacting to a bunch of professionals honest-to-God acting like professionals, and that Crosby hadn't felt the chemistry too.

Then they'd released their perpetrator into custody at the jail, and the two of them had gotten back to base, telling the story on top of each other, their words tumbling like child's blocks, they'd been so excited.

And Crosby had listened to every word avidly, gray-blue eyes big and bright, mouth slightly open in excitement. When they were done, he'd laughed and said, "So I guess you don't need me after all, right?"

And Gail had stuck out her tongue. "No, he needs you because I get to boss around the new guy for a while and I'm looking forward to that."

"You sure?" Crosby had met Garcia's eyes. "I mean, I got put out of commission for a while, and you got to trade up."

Garcia felt it again. The connection. An emotion he couldn't define flickered over Crosby's face—it might have been hope.

Garcia was willing to trade Gail's chirpy, sarcastic company in on the hope that this Jethro with the big heart was a completely different kind of partner than Garcia had first signed on for. Silly, maybe, but Garcia figured that even if the interest was purely platonic, he was still better off than he ever had been in the partner department.

So now, driving back to base in Manhattan because their information had helped Carlyle and Chadwick get their perp to a rehab detention in Philly, they could joke a little about their nine-week stint as partners.

"You say that," Gail told him now, laughing about his crack about missing her. "But you and Crosby make bro-eyes at each other like you're the thing missing from each other's chest."

Garcia snorted and tried not to panic. "Bro-eyes. How do you know we're not soulmates, and the whole medical leave thing interrupted the true romance of the century?"

"Oh, it totally did," Gail said, her voice so light he assumed she was still kidding. "I haven't seen Crosby that interested in someone since he got here."

Garcia snorted. "Wasn't he banging your roommate?" He pretended like he wasn't hanging on her answer.

"Iliana… well, she was using him for sex," Gail said, letting out a disappointed breath. "At first I hoped it would be more. Crosby's a great guy. She had her own damage, and I wanted to see her get past it. But nope. I think it hurt him more than gave him a release, you know? I mean, he left everything—family, friends, the job he thought he'd have his entire life—to work here. I wanted to see him have something, you think?"

"Not you?" Garcia asked, taking advantage of her willingness to talk on the subject.

Her laughter reassured him. "He's the big brother I've never had," she said. Then she sobered. "Seriously, there's a… a thing in him. He wants to care for someone. I'm sort of care resistant. Or, I should say, I'm the caretaker in all my relationships. I think we'd mother each other to death."

"Don't you mean smother?" Garcia quipped, but inside he was trying desperately not to melt. A caretaker? His entire life, he'd wanted to be cared for. God. This sucked. This sucked this sucked this sucked.

Except it might not suck, and it was that hope that sucked more than anything else in the world.

He'd managed to calm down his expectations as he walked into the office, which was good because Crosby was no longer running point now that the team had reported in. Instead, he was in the weight room, working out and talking to their newest, Almanzo Swan—Manny for short.

Garcia had been pleased to see the young officer from that fateful day running down the runners. He'd liked the guy but, being the new man on the team himself, had been in no position to recommend him for shit. Knowing Crosby had landed him on their team had given Garcia warm feelings everywhere he shouldn't have had warm feelings, but it had also given him some jealousy where nothing green had the right to sprout.

"Garcia!" Crosby called as Garcia stuck his head in the work-out space. "You've met Swan before. He's just passed at FLETC with flying colors and is starting with us now. Come say hi!"

Manny Swan nodded his head and extended his hand for a quick shake, and Garcia accepted. If Swan had done well at the Federal Law Enforcement Agency Training Center, where they had all experienced the rigorous program at some point or another, he would be a solid addition to the team.

"Did everybody report in?" he asked, mostly to make conversation. Crosby wouldn't have been there if anybody had been out in the field. Gail had confided that she took her laptop to the ladies' room when everybody was in action because being the hub of their operation could be so critical.

"Yup. Joey and Gid are stopping for food, Natalia's springing for pastries, and we're having ourselves a paperwork party in ten minutes. Since Manny's starting full-time tomorrow, I thought I'd show him around."

"Do you know who I'm getting partnered with?" Manny asked. "I thought it would be you at first, but I guess you two…?"

"If he wants me," Crosby said with a shrug. "We're throwing you on Gail's tender mercies. Where is she, by the way?"

"Changing," Garcia told him. "We had to run down the perp's little brother so he could answer some questions." He shuddered. "There were... cows."

Crosby grimaced. "How fragrant's our state-issued vehicle?"

"She promised to talk to the guys in the vehicle department," he said, remembering his desperation. "I, uh, didn't want to give you an excuse not to come back."

Crosby's chuckle was music to his ears. "Man, I'm stoked. Someone's got to run point—I know that. But after nine weeks, I want a chance to be out in the field. Let Harding do his bit now!"

"Who's Natalia going to run with?" Garcia could do math. There wasn't anybody left. They'd released the feebs the week before, and Chadwick and Carlyle were back in each other's pockets again, where apparently they belonged.

"She's going to survey some new recruits so we have a permanent point person and another team," Crosby said. "I, uhm, freed up some money while I was stuck behind a desk—"

"What he means," Harding said, coming into the weight room and looking around at the men, "is that he applied for some grants and wrote emails and did some serious good work and got extra money in our budget so we're not operating on a shoestring anymore. There's food in the meeting room. Swan, go get some and meet Gail Pearson, your new partner."

Crosby and Garcia were left looking at Harding expectantly.

"Sir?" Crosby asked.

"You two...." Harding shook his head. "You two need to keep each other out of trouble," he said after a moment. "I mean, I've approved our personnel placement, and I know it's coming, but you two...." He let out a breath. "You two could either get each other killed or save the city. Maybe find a compromise between the two extremes, you think?"

"I have no idea what you're talking about," Crosby replied cheerfully. "I'm just looking forward to working with Garcia some more."

Harding's eyes—flat cop's eyes—went round. "Sure," he said. "Garcia, I'll expect you to report to me if he starts taking unnecessary risks. Do you understand?"

"My pleasure," Garcia said, giving his best ass-kissing smile. He'd had inscrutable bosses before. This was no exception.

"And you know that expression 'Don't fire until you see the whites of their eyes'?"

"Yessir!" they both said.

"Fire way, way before then. You hear me?"

"Yessir," they repeated.

"Good. Go eat. Natalia got the really good pastries to make the paperwork go down."

"Sir."

And on cue, like in the military, they saluted. Harding stalked out of the room in disgust, and they waited until he cleared the door to crack up. Crosby bumped Garcia's arm as they turned toward the conference room.

"We're gonna have so much fun," he promised.

Garcia shook his head and tried not to think about his ulterior motives. "My God, I hope so."

COMBAT TRAINING was the best and worst, Garcia thought the next day.

They had no cases, so Harding sent them to the gym for a refresher course on nonviolent takedowns given by the local branch of the FBI. It was also, Harding had confided to Garcia before they left, a way for the team to check on Crosby, make sure he was 100 percent since he wasn't doing light duty as Gail had.

But that didn't mean the combat training was awesome. The feds had said very seriously in their brief of the class that it was hard to get information from a dead suspect, so it was important not to kill unless necessary. Garcia had heard Harding tell Natalia that dead *anybody* was a bad thing, but he'd take dead suspects over dead task-force members any day.

But the upshot was running through takedown methods that didn't block airways or threaten breathing in any way and hopefully kept the suspect comfortable in case they were innocent but jumpy. Because that happened *way* more often than law enforcement ever wanted to admit.

Their instructor was even taller than Crosby, and Garcia was probably typecasting, but he sort of disliked the guy on sight. Maybe he just didn't like buzzcuts, or maybe it was the beady little eyes. Or the extreme muscles or lack of neck. The guy screamed attitude, and Garcia tried to overcome his aversion to blond, blue-eyed boys in law enforcement before he dug his own grave here. He liked Crosby, right? And Gail was his friend. Clint Harding, Gideon Chadwick, Joey Carlyle?

They were all okay. But as the instructor—Morrison—had them line up military style while he paced in front of them and shouted instructions, Garcia caught Crosby's eyes.

Crosby crossed his eyes behind the instructor's back and pulled his chin in to mimic having none.

Garcia didn't even let his lips twitch, but Manny Swan wasn't so lucky.

"Do you have a problem with that?" Morrison yelled in his face, and Manny, being the new guy, recoiled.

"No, sir," he responded calmly. Not afraid—Garcia liked that— and not subservient or sarcastic. Just quiet. Mild.

"Then what was that smirk about?"

Manny opened his mouth to respond, and Morrison yelled in his face again.

"You don't got an answer to that, do you, smart guy?"

"I do," Crosby said behind him, and Garcia grimaced. Oh no, white boy, do *not* get into this.

"You sticking up for your buddies?" Morrison sneered.

"My team knows I've got their backs," Crosby said composedly. "But if you'd let Swan talk, he had an answer for you. You wanted to wave your dick around, and you didn't give him a chance."

Morrison's arm shot out in what Garcia would later recognize as an attempt to take Crosby down the way the class advocated—without excessive force.

But Crosby dodged the hand coming in, grabbed the arm attached, and pulled Morrison's shoulder forward while sticking out his own leg. The result was he took Morrison down from behind. Morrison ended up on his ass, looking *very* surprised, and before he could launch himself at Crosby—and Garcia read the intent in his eyes—Crosby held his hand out. "Nice charge," he said smoothly. "Want a hand up?"

Morrison took three deep breaths and glared, and Crosby kept his hand out, saying, "Swan, do you want to tell us what was on your mind?"

"Thank you, sir," Manny Swan said, and Garcia could tell it took all his courage to do it too. He was the new guy, and this situation had gotten ugly fast. "I was laughing because Morrison was telling us that the easiest way to take a guy down was from behind, at the knees, and we'd just finished a psychology seminar on de-escalation. I was going to say the easiest way to take a guy down was to talk to him and get him to see reason if you can, and if you can't, to make sure your partners are behind him to initiate the takedown. You can have force without excess, sir."

Crosby grinned. "God, the kid's smart. Anybody see a hole in that plan?"

"Well, it helps if you wait for your backup," Natalia drawled, and Crosby grimaced good-naturedly.

Morrison made his move then, grabbing Crosby's hand and trying to yank him down to the mats in what Garcia thought was an instigation to an out-and-out brawl.

Crosby leaned back, though, falling back onto the mat and pulling Morrison forward so he sprawled on his stomach in front of Crosby's outstretched legs. While he was there, Gail took one arm and Natalia took the other, while Joey Carlyle sat on his ass and hollered, "Ride 'em, cowboy!"

Gail hauled Morrison's arm behind his back, and Natalia took hold of both wrists and pushed Morrison's face against the mat.

"Now I'm sure," she said, barely breathing hard, "that what you just did was part of a teachable moment, Agent Morrison, but you need to be very, *very* careful how you present your lessons to this team. We aren't held back by protocol, and very often we are pursuing perpetrators who have killed, and we expect them to kill again. So we aren't all starry-eyed about our jobs, and we *will* respond with force, do you understand me?"

"Yes, Special Agent Denison," Morrison said meekly.

"If I let you up, are you going to try that shit again against my team?"

"No, ma'am," Morrison said, his words muffled by the mat.

"Then we're going to let you up. But I warn you, one more attempt to take one of us out *not* in the parameters of the course will lead you to a world of hurt."

"Understood, ma'am."

Gail got up first and Carlyle next, but they stayed close enough to help Natalia up while the rest of the team closed ranks against Morrison.

"Do you have any exercises you'd like us to try?" Natalia asked sweetly.

"Sure," Morrison said through gritted teeth as he pushed up to his feet. "The takedown I was attempting against your man puts your opponent flat on his back." He glared at the unfriendly faces around him. "I'm sure you'd love to tell me why that's a bad idea."

"Agent Swan?" Natalia prompted.

Manny answered, "If your opponent has a weapon anywhere on their person, you're toast." Morrison grunted in response.

"Garcia?" Denison said, nodding at Calix.

"Even if they don't have a weapon, pulling them to their feet requires an officer to let their guard down. It should only be done if you have backup. Otherwise you're putting yourself at risk from an accessory, if there is one around, or the opponent, if they're in the mood for an out-and-out brawl."

Morrison grunted again. "You've been trained," he said. He gave Natalia a sour look. "What in the hell am *I* doing here?"

"We believe that all the agencies have something to teach us," Natalia said pleasantly. And then without changing her expression by so much as a whisker, she lowered the air temperature in the gym by at least ten degrees. "We usually hope it's not by negative example."

Morrison inclined his head. "Of course." And with that, he turned toward the rest of them and had them practice the takedown—and effective countermeasures—in pairs, which was fine with Garcia.

He'd been wanting to wrestle with Crosby since he'd shown up that first day. Seeing him take on an opponent twice his size hadn't eased that itch one bit.

They circled each other Greco-Roman style for a few, sizing each other up, looking for an in. Garcia was watching carefully to see if Crosby's ribs still hurt, but if they did, he was masking it well.

Then Garcia saw it—an in. Crosby put his foot out wide and a little pigeon-toed, opening up his legs for a takedown, and Garcia went all in.

Only to find himself on his back while Crosby straddled his torso and held his hands over his head, an apologetic smile on his face.

"Nice try," he said encouragingly. "You gotta watch out for the thunder thighs, though." He flexed his muscular thighs and glutes. "It makes a takedown through the legs a little harder. Center of gravity is wonky. My turn?"

Garcia nodded mutely and hoped Crosby didn't think he was sweating too much. Because he was. Sweating. Because being that close, that intimately, with Judson Crosby and his muscular tree-trunk thighs was *not* good for his equilibrium, although it seemed to be *great* for his libido.

They circled some more, and then Crosby straightened, smiling thoughtfully. "Hey, did you want to go for takeout after work? My roommate's having another party, and Gail and her roommate are having a girl's night. I'd love to not go back to my apartment yet."

Garcia straightened, trying not to show his delight. "Sure, man. I don't got—"

And he found himself tied into a delicate knot, his face against the mat as Crosby pretended to restrain him.

And he was even more delighted. "Man, that's *dirty*!" he complained. But smart. And funny. And it was the kind of thing that implied they were friends and more, partners.

"Yeah, but it worked," Crosby said, straddling his back. "So, what kind of takeout did you want?"

"Thai," Garcia said promptly. "We got some of the best places in Queens. Let me show you around, Chicago. We'll treat you right."

"Great!" Crosby released him and then set up for the next takedown. "I promise not to do that to you again," he said, and for a moment, their good-natured sparring was completely sober. "I, uh, only do that shit with friends."

"Count me in," Garcia said. His heart was still hammering from Crosby's strong "thunder thighs" straddling his hips, and he had memorized the little gold fleck in Crosby's right eye after their first encounter.

It was a good thing they were both wearing cups, because otherwise, this whole exercise would be a lot less goddamned fun.

THE NEXT day Garcia was awakened at five in the morning by his phone buzzing insistently with Foreigner's "Urgent," which was his ringtone for work. He yawned and stretched reluctantly—gah! He'd heard about calls at fuck-you a.m., but this was his first.

"Garcia," he mumbled. Did his bed—new in the old Queens house—smell like sex? He'd been *dreaming* of sex. He'd been *dreaming* of Judson Crosby's big thunder thighs straddling his head while Garcia took his entire cock down his open throat, and it was by far the most graphic, sweaty, *detailed* sex dream he could ever remember having.

And now he had to go in to work?

"Hey, Garcia?"

Like he was summoned by Garcia's dreams alone, Crosby's Chicago tenor came across loud and clear.

"The hell're you doin' there?" Garcia asked because he was calling from the work number.

"I was sleeping on the couch," Crosby said through a yawn. "I was here when the alerts started pinging like crazy. We've got a guy who walked into an ob/gyn clinic where the doctor and staff were setting up for the day and shot his wife's doctor in the head. He's got his two daughters in the car with him, and we think they're headed to Westbury. Harding gave me permission as I called you to come pick you up and try to cut them off. Harding lives in Great Neck. He's working to set up roadblocks, and Gail and Swan will meet us there."

"Who's running point?"

"Chadwick. He's coming from Jersey, so he'll be in office soon. Carlyle's riding with you and me." Which made sense because Carlyle had an apartment on the Upper West Side—he'd reach the office before Crosby could get to the garage to check out a vehicle.

"Shotgun," Garcia said grimly, throwing off the covers. "I'll be ready when you get here."

"Deal," Crosby said. "Make sure you eat."

"Deal. Out." Garcia figured he had about half an hour before he needed to be outside on the steps. Was that time enough to take a shower? It had to be if he didn't want to smell like the come that caked his lower abdomen now when he hopped in the car with Crosby.

Island of Hope

GARCIA WAS sitting out on the step in the early November chill, a travel mug of coffee in one hand and an english muffin in the other as Crosby pulled up.

Crosby glared at Joey Carlyle in the passenger seat, who gave him a disbelieving stare back. "But I brought coffee!" Carlyle complained, gesturing to the three giant spill-proof paper cups in the holder. "And sausage biscuits for all of us!" Joey's thin, appealing face and boyish features probably got him laid a lot and most definitely had gotten him out of scrapes when he'd been a kid, but Crosby knew where his duty lay.

"You were a totally stand-up guy," Crosby said, meaning it, "and I hope to return the favor many, many times. But you do not understand how completely possessive Garcia can be about—"

"Move," Garcia said, opening the passenger door. "You're a good guy, we owe you, but I'm the partner. Git."

"Gitting," Carlyle said, conceding defeat and sliding out of the passenger seat so he could get in the back. As they were getting situated with seatbelts, he added, "I probably just added years to my life anyway. He's driving like we can pass through solid objects while vibrating like the speed of sound."

"Sweet," Garcia told him. "Get us there fast, partner."

Crosby did his best to oblige.

He may have done his job too well, he thought fretfully as they exited the interstate and hit the Old Country Road. Garcia had finished his muffin—and started on his sausage biscuit—in grim silence, using one hand and practically strangling the chicken stick, and Carlyle had been uncomfortably silent as Crosby had driven.

"I didn't mean you were supposed to *try* to pass through solid objects," Carlyle rasped as Crosby slowed down for Holy Rood Cemetery.

"Crosby, you there?" Gideon Chadwick crackled over his radio, and he pulled up the receiver.

"Roger that. We're here by Holy Rood. Do you know where the suspect is?"

"Natalia and Harding almost caught up with him in Westbury, but he lost them. We caught up with him here using GPS, but we don't know what he's doing. He's armed, and he's got the two little kids. We've got his Dodge Charger in the parking lot, but we don't know where *he* is."

"Does he have family in Holy Rood?" Crosby asked, frowning.

"No, but...." Chadwick paused for a moment, probably scanning all of the information as it arrived. "Okay, bear with me here. *Cops just* found the guy's wife, whom he killed *yesterday*, after her ob/gyn appointment. Then he grabbed the two little girls, spent the night in the car, and then left the girls in the car while he ran into the clinic to kill the doctor. Then he took off for Holy Rood. You follow?"

"People suck," Crosby said flatly. "Yes, I follow."

"Holy Rood is an old Catholic cemetery. One of the things it's known for is the Island of Hope," Chadwick told them, and Crosby frowned, because now he was lost.

"That's sick," Garcia said, getting it before Crosby, because apparently Crosby lost points for not growing up in New York.

"I don't get it," Crosby said. "Explain it to me."

Carlyle spoke from the back. "The Island of Hope is where they bury victims of neonaticide—babies killed right after birth. Think about it. What if his wife had a miscarriage or, God forbid, an abortion. This guy's finances are in the tubes"—he raised his voice—"right, Gid?"

"Nailed it," came the voice from their console. "Yes, his financial penis has been cut off."

Carlyle picked up the thread again. "So his wife does something at the ob/gyn that he disapproves of or, hell, doesn't understand. For all we know he thinks getting a pap smear is the mark of the devil—these fucking tools and women's bodies. Whatever. That's his tipping point. Somebody is lord and master over his woman's body, and he's not going to take it. Kills the wife. Kills the doctor 'cause he's a fucking tool. He's a... whatyacallit?"

"Family annihilator," Garcia said, his voice flat, and Crosby was with him because damn, those were some of the worst.

"Yeah, that brand of asshole. And 'cause that's his brand, he wants to kill the kids, but he's a good Catholic, so he's got to do it someplace where they'll be close to God."

Crosby's stomach roiled. "That's... ugh. It's fucked up and twisted, but it's good Catholic logic."

"You in recovery?" Carlyle asked.

"From being a Catholic? Isn't every cop in Chicago?"

Carlyle snorted. "Protestant. My great-grandparents lived in Ireland as British citizens before coming over here and exploiting the natives. Apparently this sucked ass and made that whole branch of the family bitter, which is funny because all the men are still misogynistic fuckheads. But what I'm saying is we've got to put on our body armor and give our boy here a sniper rifle or this could get...." His voice dropped, and Crosby could hear his audible swallow from the front of the car. "Ugly. This could get ugly."

"Fuck." Crosby's stomach was *not* getting any better. Kids. Being taken to a place where babies were buried. And fuck him, they were not prepared.

"'Sup?" Garcia was looking at him, those fathomless brown eyes not missing a thing, and Crosby felt sweat popping out on his forehead.

"This shop," he said, gesturing with his chin to the standard agency-issued SUV. "It's got limited tactical in the back. Harding drove his agency issue home last night, so they've got the sniper rifles and the semiautos."

"So what do we have?" Garcia asked, alarmed.

"Beanbag guns and tasers. And our personal weapons, of course." He was keeping both hands on the wheel, but he felt the reassuring weight of his holstered Glocks at his sides and the extra at his ankle.

"That's unfortunate," Carlyle muttered. "I mean, you gotta admit, that's unfortunate. I mean, what are the fuckin' *odds*?"

"About the same that our boy here would be awake to catch the case early as it came down the wire," Garcia said perceptively. "What were you *doing* in the office at fuck-you in the morning, Crosby, that would make you catch this case?"

Crosby grunted. "I don't want to talk about it." Toby and his fucking parties. This one had sort of "sprung up." Toby had worked a club late, and Crosby's sleep had been invaded by ten to twenty of Toby's new best friends, who all wanted to "detox and chill" while Toby was riffing hot. Crosby hadn't wanted to encroach on Gail's goodwill—not since Gail's cast had come off. Iliana hadn't sent him so much as a text when he'd been laid up, and while on the one hand he'd figured that was self-protective because she couldn't deal with someone she cared about being hurt, on the other hand, in addition to his visit, Garcia had called or texted him at least three times a week.

Although why he should draw a parallel between Iliana and Garcia was beyond him.

Sure. Sure it was.

But as much as he wanted to hang with Garcia, it was still too much to ask to just show up at his door in the fuck-you a.m. to crash in his guest room. And he didn't want to seem like a charity case. He'd started to develop a certain… pride around Garcia. The guy had been his probie, his trainee, and Crosby had caught glints of admiration in the guy's eyes. Crosby didn't want any of that to go away.

"His roommate was throwing another rager," Carlyle said knowingly, and Crosby cringed.

"Crosby, why didn't you crash on my couch?" Chadwick asked over comms, and while the offer was kind, Crosby took a millisecond to think bitterly that his old partner in Chicago hadn't given a good goddamn if Crosby had slept on the street, and he sort of missed those days.

"Couch at work's fine," he said briefly. "They even have showers. Now when we get there, I say we suit up, helmets too. He's armed with a Beretta with a silencer. Reports at the clinic say he seems competent at firearms—there was no hesitation when he shot the doctor—and he was in a hurry. He had kids in the car, right? Walked in, shot the doctor in the head, walked out, ignored the two nurses working the early shift. He coldcocked the security guard even—could have taken the guy out. If he's going to sacrifice his kids at the Island of Hope, I'm thinking he's just going to have them look away and do it cleanly. If we threaten him, we will pull his attention away from his kids, but he might also put them in the crosshairs. We need to take him out clean when his back is turned. One of us in front, two others on the side he can't see."

"I'm sneaky," Joey said. "I'll take the back. Crosby, you're a good Catholic boy—"

"Chadwick," Crosby said before they locked this into stone. "Ethnicity of our dirtbag."

"White boy," he returned. "Carlyle's right—you're our negotiator." Fair.

"Just as well," Garcia said with a snort. "My people are Jehovah's Witness. I didn't get a birthday party until I turned eighteen at college."

"Bummer," Crosby said. "Was it a good one?"

"Got laid," Garcia said, and then he blushed.

Crosby thought of asking what her name was, but something—a stupid hope, maybe, or a fantasy even more likely—kept him from doing it.

Boy or girl, they were lucky ducks.

"Good for you," Crosby said and then narrowed his eyes. They were passing through the cemetery, which was old, dignified, well-kept, a carpet of greenery padding row upon row of marble headstones. The roadway through the cemetery looped several times, with a parking lot near St. Brigid's church and enough space on the loops for mourners to park on the wide lanes.

"Our suspect was last seen driving a hunter-green Dodge Charger, entering the cemetery from the east," Crosby said, pulling himself to the here and now. "Pearson, give me the quickest directions—"

"Turn left now," Gail said, a hint of panic coming over the radio.

Crosby did, ignoring the protest from his passengers, who seemed to think that was something of a surprise.

Gail had them park a quarter of a mile from where the suspect's GPS was pinging, and the three of them unloaded and suited up quietly, pulling their Kevlar and helmets from the back, as well as the limited armaments.

Carlyle, surprisingly enough, went for a small but powerful crossbow with steel bolts, and when Crosby raised his eyebrows, he replied tersely, "Smaller boom, smaller mess, more accuracy. If you're not taking this shot, I want the thing that's going to traumatize the kids the least."

"Fair," Crosby said. "Just, you know, don't miss."

Carlyle gave him a grim smile. "Don't get in the way," he said before turning and running silently through the graveyard, his path wrapping around a stand of trees that, according to the map Gail had sent them, served as partial boundary for the Island of Hope.

Crosby slammed the hatch shut and turned toward Garcia, expecting him to be on his way through the light snow toward the small, tragic cemetery plot, swinging wide to come in the opposite side as Carlyle.

"What?" Crosby asked. "Also, watch out for the others. Gail and Manny are about ten minutes out, but Harding and Denison are here already and searching."

Garcia nodded, his gaze boring into Crosby's until Crosby could feel the heat rising up his cheeks.

"What?" he asked again, defensively.

"Don't get shot," he said, obviously troubled.

"Well, that's the idea—"

"No, don't put me off here. Don't get shot. I'm not screwing around. You scared the shit out of me a few months ago."

Crosby grimaced. "Yeah, but that was an anomaly—"

Without warning, Garcia pulled him into a hard, masculine hug, thumping him twice on the back before letting him go and disappearing into the closest stand of trees.

Crosby watched him go, surprised, before turning toward the small path that led to the Island. He'd just started jogging along the path when he heard a high-pitched child's scream.

His jog turned into a sprint.

The path led him to a small enclosed triangle plot of earth with privacy walls on two sides. In the center of the triangle was the nightmare scenario he and the others had anticipated.

A portly middle-aged white man stood with his daughters at his feet, shaking hands aiming the Berretta at them.

"I said," he screamed, "you two need to get on your knees like good girls and pray!"

"But Daddy," wailed the oldest one, a green-eyed princess with tangled hair past her hips. "Why do you have a gun? I want Mommy. Why can't we see Mommy?"

"In a few minutes, baby," her father promised, tears washing his face. "I promise—"

"But can you really promise that?" Crosby asked, walking through the stone entrance passage with his hands relaxed at his sides. "I mean, I get as a Catholic you'd like to *think* they can see Mommy, but will they really be able to? Is that how the whole thing works?"

Their suspect—Tyler James "T.J." Kennedy—stared at Crosby blankly, his gun wobbling in front of him.

"What? You ask me that *here*?"

Crosby casually reached for the holster on his right hip, keeping eye contact with Kennedy and trying to be as nonthreatening as possible.

"Well, I'm asking you because your daughters are kneeling in the snow over infant graves, and it looks really uncomfortable and sort of scary. I wanted to make sure you were absolutely certain you were doing what God intended."

Kennedy gaped at him, and in the stillness all Crosby could hear was the muffled suppressed sobs of Kennedy's daughters.

"Of course I am," he said, his voice broken. He held the Beretta up, not tensely, but still he could fire at Crosby in a heartbeat. "I… I believe in the sanctity of life. Their mother—their mother didn't. She… she was going to commit murder!" His voice broke. "Our son. She was going to kill our son."

Crosby breathed out carefully through his nose. "But your son wasn't even born yet. Were there complications?"

"They said he had no brain," the man gasped wretchedly. "And she was going to kill him when that's God's job. How could they kill him when that's God's job?"

"Well, those babies go through a lot of pain when they're born, and they die within a week," Crosby said, remembering everything he could about the last reproductive health pamphlet he'd read while bored at his GP's office. "Do you really think God wants them to be in pain if he's given us the power to spare them? Your daughters—they're freezing in the snow, Mr. Kennedy. Can't you see that?"

"But they're supposed to join their mother," he said, staring at Crosby in confusion. One of the girls whimpered, and his confusion seemed to end. "And you can't stop me from sending them there!" he snarled. But as the gun rose to Crosby's chest, suddenly Kennedy's entire body stiffened, and he gaped in surprise.

Blood trickled from his mouth as his knees buckled, and Crosby turned toward the little girls and said, "Come on, guys, come over here. Your daddy needs to lie down for a little. Come on. Come toward me. Don't turn around, okay? Look at me. Just, you know, you don't want to make him mad."

He hunkered down to a squat, and Gail, Manny, Harding, and Natalia appeared from nowhere, forming a wall between the girls and their dead father as the girls rushed into Crosby's arms.

CROSBY SNUCK in a quick look before the ME arrived and after he'd handed the girls off to the social worker, after making promises to visit. Joey Carlyle had shot one crossbow bolt, silent as a shadow, a little to the left of Kennedy's spine.

Straight through his heart from behind.

Like he'd said—no big boom, no blood, less trauma.

"Chilling as fuck," Garcia said, coming alongside him as he checked out the body.

"Yeah, but I'm glad he's got my back and not the bad guy's," Crosby conceded. They both looked up to where Carlyle was getting congratulations and "I'm sorry, you have to do desk duty next, you know that, right?" from Harding and Denison.

"I had your back," Garcia said, sounding wounded.

Crosby threw a companionable arm around his shoulders, feeling like a fraud. It looked very good-ole-boy being a buddy, but that's not why he did it.

"I know you did. But it's good to know our unit has ours."

Garcia nodded and cast him a grin. "Do they have our back enough to let us stop for food? I'm starving."

Crosby laughed a little because Garcia had embraced being the guy everybody either fed or ate with to keep company, and he kept his arm over those shoulders, staying close to that tight, muscular, compact body.

Garcia didn't move away. Crosby's insides were shaky from the terrible, terrible confrontation, from the fear of facing an opponent unarmed, and from the sheer awfulness of the morning.

Garcia's warmth gave him hope.

Gail and Manny wandered over, and he dropped the arm, keeping it casual, just as Gail said, "For God's sake, Crosby. I'll give you a fucking key. If you'd been sleeping on *my* couch, we could have let NYPD take care of this."

"NYPD might have fucked it up," Manny Swan said. "I mean—" He swallowed, trying, Crosby suspected, to be loyal to both units, and then flashed a quick grin at him. "—I trust Crosby to get those girls out more than my old unit mates, you know?"

"Carlyle made the shot," Crosby reminded them as they turned away from the grim reminder of the worst part of their job.

"Yeah, but you kept his attention," Carlyle said, joining him. Harding and Natalia were still working cleanup, and as a unit, they moved through the cemetery to their vehicles, waiting where they'd been parked.

"But," Garcia added, lest they all forget, "can we get back to feeding me?"

"Sure," Carlyle said. "But if we don't bring Chadwick back some breakfast, that asshole's so thin he may fly away." There was a brief moment of quiet laughter. No, what had just happened was never going to be okay—and it was never going to be better. But if the team could huddle together for animal warmth, keeping their psyches grounded and as steady as they could get in their companionship, then that was going to have to hold them.

It was going to give them hope.

Miracles and Missed Moments

CHRISTMAS SEEMED to hit them all differently.

Gid and Joey both had family—one in Philadelphia, the other in Boston. They both took three days off in the hope that nobody did anything bad and they wouldn't have to be called back. Gail's folks lived down in Norfolk, and she got a week.

Natalia had kids, and she lived in upstate, so she was off from three days before Christmas until the day after when she came in to relieve Harding. Same with Manny, except he took the train from Brooklyn.

Harding apparently sprang from a mushroom and answered to nobody because he volunteered to man the helm, do paperwork, and get quietly snockered after his official time on the clock was called—or at least that's what Garcia supposed.

Garcia's folks had moved to Florida with most of his family, but he didn't visit often. He'd grown up in New Jersey and had loved visiting his Nana and Pop-Pop in Queens. Florida didn't have the same vibe.

Besides, he wasn't out to his parents and had no intention of ever being out to his parents and would as soon not sit through any more of his mother's dinners while she told him he should find a nice girl and settle down.

And Crosby's folks were in New Mexico, which left the three of them—Crosby, Harding, and Garcia—to settle in for a long, quiet day at the office, drinking eggnog, playing poker, and eating... well, eating a shitload of sugar. So much so that Garcia was wondering who did takeout on Christmas, because he was going to need some protein, dammit!

Crosby and Harding seemed to have a curious big brother/little brother relationship, and Garcia was pleased to see that warmth extended to himself. They took turns telling stories—Harding talking about his deployments overseas and some missions he'd run with some absolutely crazy assholes, in Garcia's opinion. There was a guy named Lee Burton who figured big in a lot of his stories, as well as a Colonel Constance— Garcia heard enough absolutely batshit things about the two of them to wonder if they were real.

"So, that's true?" Crosby asked, incredulous at the last story, which had the two men working a secret military op to recover homemade serial killers from the wilds into which they'd been released.

Harding lifted his shoulder. "Far as I know. That's where Constance ended up, last I heard. Burton followed him. I guess Burton figured the whole thing out in the first place. Something to do with a target who became his boyfriend." Harding smiled softly. "Sounds like a fairy tale, I know, but those are good to believe in sometimes."

Garcia nodded, but inside he was thinking, *He knows guys in the military—badasses—who have boyfriends. Maybe I can come out. Maybe it's okay.*

And the thought was terrifying and exhilarating at the same time. He glanced at Crosby, who was frowning at his phone.

Crosby looked up and said, "Boss—so many questions. But my folks are calling. Gotta go be the good son, right?"

Harding nodded, giving a lopsided grin, and Garcia shook his head. He'd called his folks that morning, said a cursory hello to his sisters and their kids, and had then rung off, desperate to escape to this quiet man cave where they could play poker and tell stories and watch the snow fall from the big office window.

Something about Crosby's pained grimace when he answered his phone told Garcia Crosby had it worse.

He hadn't realized he'd followed Crosby across the office with his eyes until Harding said softly, "They keep begging him to come back to live near them. It's hard on him, but I think he really likes it here."

"He does," Garcia said without a doubt. "I... I think he misses Chicago."

Harding grunted. "I got word that his old partner got a promotion to a federal job. He's some sort of internal affairs officer for joint special projects. I have no idea how that happened, and I'm not sure who he reports to."

Garcia sucked air in through his teeth. "Man, that's the worst. I hate it when good things happen to super shitty people."

Harding snorted softly. "That's one way to put it." He frowned. "But it did give me the excuse to recruit Crosby. That work he did on the Brandeis case was top-notch."

Garcia looked over to where Crosby was sitting on a table in the conference room, swinging his legs as though bored. "I couldn't find much on it," he admitted, because he'd done his best to research the incident. Crosby wouldn't talk about it. "The only files I saw talked about kids getting abducted from bad neighborhoods and the local gangs blaming it on each other."

Harding shook his head. "Fuckers. The cops were pissed, you see. He was still a rookie. From what I can gather, there'd been a local gang throwdown, a drive-by. The kid at the trigger was a mess. Too fucked up to hit anything and so, so angry. Our boy there—he was the one who did the takedown, and the kid yelled something about how he was trying to kill the fuckers who killed his sister. Now anybody else would have assumed it was another drive-by—makes sense, right? At least to a white cop in a nonwhite neighborhood. But Crosby, he'd paid attention. The kid was well cared for, and he had no gang activity whatsoever in his jacket. In fact he and his sister had been school superstars—they'd been going places—before his sister had been found dead in a playground the month before. So Crosby tells the kid that if he calms down enough for Crosby to get him representation, he'll look into the girl's murder."

"Sounds like him," Garcia said, and from across the room he noted the quiet unhappiness that seemed to emanate from Judson Crosby as he tried to wish his parents a Merry Christmas. Ouch.

"Yeah, to us it does. But apparently he had to go off book in Chicago. Nobody would talk to him. So he puts on his jeans and his T-shirt and goes door to door, talking to the kid's neighbors about the girl and about the circumstances of her death. No gun. No uniform. No backup. Just that sweet little puss asking earnest questions, right?"

Garcia's gut clenched. "He could have been killed."

Harding shook his head. "Yeah, but I personally think he was safer in his civvies. Look at him—he screams sincerity, right? Anyway, he finds out a lot of stuff. First, the girl was on her way home for her *birthday*, and she was apparently abducted after school. So the cops blew that off. They were like, 'Kid probably just went somewhere besides home and ended up in the wrong place, wrong time.' Crosby was like, no way. The other thing he found out was that she wasn't the only one this had happened to. She was one of a *dozen* Black kids—boys and girls, ages twelve to fourteen—who had disappeared after school and had been found in another neighborhood, in a public place, with some big fucking knife wounds in their stomachs."

"*Bwah!*" Oh God. Everything Garcia knew about law enforcement, about investigative technique, about profiling and running down suspects and perpetrators told Garcia that one lone rookie cop should not have been the only one to see that pattern.

But apparently Crosby had been the only one to care.

"So did they listen?" Garcia asked, although he already knew the answer.

"Fuck no," Harding muttered. "No, but by this time, he'd started to contact people outside his department, ask some questions, poke some badgers, and he got the attention of one of the top profilers in the FBI, a friend of mine, Dr. Harman Blodgett—also works as an MD 'cause he's Superman. So Harman calls me for a consult, and together we come up with an MO and a profile, and Harman starts feeding Crosby information. And Crosby keeps doing what he was doing, but now he's asking specific questions, and he's figuring out that the knife wounds are personal and they're dominant, and that this is probably someone in authority who wants these kids to know he's the boss. And then he starts trying to figure out the common denominator, because this perp is killing kids in different gang territories and then dumping them in enemy territory. It's somebody who knows the gangs and who is trying to show he's more powerful than them too. And then he figures out that this is someone the kids trusted, someone they felt comfortable around, because all of the abductions were from school, and these kids were told to be careful of strangers."

Garcia's blood was icy in his veins. School counselor? Doctor? Cop? He said that last one aloud.

"SRO," Harding said, shaking his head. "Student Outreach Officer. Knew how to do all the things that would make a racist white cop think this was gang violence except use a gun. Crosby ran him down on foot, alone, after he stalked the guy at one of the three schools he worked and saw Cordell Brandeis try to abduct his next victim. Called the takedown in on Brandeis's own radio and had him confessing to every crime, all recorded on Crosby's cell phone."

"Jesus," Garcia breathed. Then it hit him. "So... when McEnany shot that kid...."

"Oh yeah. Killed a kid in cold blood to bait Crosby into calling him out. Nothing can convince me otherwise. It was calculated departmental revenge."

"And his department didn't give him *anything* for the Brandeis collar?"

"A write-up for working the case alone," Crosby said, coming in from the other room apparently in time to hear them gossiping about him.

"I'll cut them," Garcia promised, looking his boy in the eyes so Crosby would know Calix Garcia had his back.

Crosby gave a gentle, pained smile. "I'd rather arrest them," he said gruffly. "McEnany, the union lawyer, the lieutenant—none of them should be on the streets or breathing free air. But given that McEnany is now IA for the feds and the others are retired and shit, I'll have to settle for working here."

"Ouch," Harding said, giving Garcia a wink. "Talk about a scant second place."

"Hey, if I'd known this unit existed, I would have applied here instead of Chicago and gone through FLETC right out of school," Crosby said—not the for the first time. Then he sighed. "And that way I could have left my folks there and they wouldn't be so confused as to why I can't just apologize to that nice police officer I offended so they can move back home."

"Gah!" Garcia and Harding both reacted pretty much the same way, but Garcia was the one who kept going. "Dude, why aren't you spiking your eggnog!"

Crosby chuckled, but it sounded strained. "Because while you guys were gossiping about my painful past, I heard chatter from the radio in the conference room. I give it five—" He held his fingers out, counting down. Four, three, two, one, and at one, Harding's cell phone squawked.

"Well done," Harding said with a grim nod as he picked up the phone.

He did *not* say, "Merry fucking Christmas," but Garcia could read between the lines.

"SCTF, Harding," he said crisply. His craggy face had automatically assumed the hard planes of his "game face," but as the dispatcher spoke, he grew a little softer and frowned. "Yes, you were right to call. Put her through." He glanced from Garcia to Crosby and mouthed, "Chartreuse Victor?"

Garcia met Crosby's eyes, both of them cocking their heads in concern. The club owner from the first case they'd worked—the one who'd been bleeding from a gunshot wound as Crosby ran to save the runner hiding under the bed—had recovered from surgery with flying colors. Garcia had gone to visit her, and so had Crosby. They had been in the hospital together after all. Chartreuse, who identified herself as "Classic queen, my darlings—everything your mother warned you about," had been funny, even when in pain, and very, very grateful. Garcia had never made it to the club to dance—for a lot of reasons he didn't want to put voice to—but he and Crosby had sent her a Christmas card from the both of them, knowing she'd gone back to work.

A moment later, Harding's voice went to that tone they associated with him talking to a victim or someone under fire. "Ma'am, I'm putting you on speaker with Crosby and Garcia." His grim mouth twitched. "The cute boys."

"Oh, thank heavens," she murmured. "I'm so glad. Where's my hunky blond boy?"

"I'm here, honey," Crosby answered. "You sound upset. What's doin', you calling on Christmas?"

"We've got a gunman here," she said, and Crosby straightened immediately while Garcia hopped up as though zapped. "He thinks we can't see it, but he keeps fondling his piece. I've got my bouncers passing the word to clear people out, but I don't want the po-po here, darlings. That's a good way for a lot of rainbow blood to hit the streets, if you know what I mean."

"We do," Crosby said, jerking his chin toward the gun lockers. Harding followed them, phone out so they could converse while Garcia and Crosby armed themselves. "But baby, you know we're in Manhattan. It's a good twenty minutes if we drive like the wind."

"Yeah, I hear you," she murmured. "But I'm saying, this guy's jumpy, but he's looking for someone. Please don't come in here guns blazing and shoot up my club. The po-po hates us bad here, boys. You're the only ones I trust."

"On our way, sweetheart," Crosby said. "Hold tight. And I'm gonna have my boss call the po-po and have them on standby, no lights. You stay on the line with our boss here, and if things start to go bad, have him talk to the po-po. Everybody's afraid of him. He'll keep them in line."

"Thanks, boys," she murmured. "I'm not going to tell you to hurry because I want you to get here alive. It's snowing out there."

"Sit tight, Chartreuse. We're on our way." He made eye contact with Harding with those flinty blue-gray eyes, and Harding nodded, picking up his cues. Without breaking stride, Harding wheeled and went back to his computer, probably accessing cameras around the club so they could get a feel for their possible gunman, as well as calling the local police and filling them in on the sitch.

They were in the department-issue SUV and heading down the I-278 Expressway when Harding came on comms.

"I talked to the local police, and Chartreuse isn't wrong. They were willing to go in with guns blazing, but sitting and letting someone calm the situation down isn't their thing. So you guys hit the place with lights, no sirens, take charge, and go in as patrons. Your girl says she's getting people to trickle out the back exits, a few at a time so as not to arouse suspicion. She's found the man's kid—trans female—and the girl thinks her father is there to... I don't know. Get her to change her mind? It's going to be tricky there. I'm going to say Garcia should take point on this one."

"Roger that," Crosby said, and Garcia was warmed by the idea that he didn't even hesitate. They worked hard to tailor the best person on the team to the situation—the club wasn't a place where good Irish Catholic ex-football players went to hang out, no matter how much Garcia had been dreaming of that guy walking through the doors on any given night.

THEY ARRIVED at the club and took a moment to suit up, pulling their coats and sweaters off to put Kevlar on underneath, and then putting sweaters on over the vests. After that they pushed past the puzzled, worried club goers wandering out of the building in ones and twos. A bouncer—a woman Crosby's height with the muscles of a body builder and a granite jaw—stood monitoring the door. She wore a T-shirt stretched tightly across her chest, but a T-shirt as opposed to a bikini top was her only acknowledgment of the snow that fell softly from an ash-gray sky. She scowled at the two of them until Garcia said, "Chartreuse called us. She wants us to handle the sitch so the police don't escalate."

The woman nodded and stepped back, but her expression didn't soften one bit. "He's in the far corner, hugging the bar. She's kept the music on so he hasn't noticed the crowd thinning."

Her voice was a low bass rumble, and Garcia sort of wished she was Kevlared up and ready to party with them.

They were about to enter the club when Garcia, acting on impulse, grabbed Crosby's hand. Instead of jerking away or asking why, Crosby moved in closer, like they were a couple out on Christmas, going into a club to celebrate.

When Crosby tightened his grasp and his breath brushed Garcia's cheek, Garcia had to fight not to lean into him, to turn toward his warmth, to run his lips along that strong jaw. Crosby gave him a guileless smile and spoke directly into his ear.

"He's by the bar," he murmured.

Garcia's eyes flickered around the place, and he gave a nod and a smile. "Spiked eggnog?"

"Beer."

That brought a sudden grin Garcia couldn't contain. "That's my boy," he murmured. With a little chin nod, he sidled up to the bar and found a seat two seats down from a middle-aged white guy hunched over in a trench coat, a caricature of a bad guy, a dark figure emanating anxiety and clutching something to his chest under the coat. He was one of three white males in the room, including Crosby and the bare-chested bartender in black pants, a bondage harness, and a red bow tie.

He wasn't hard to spot.

Chartreuse was at the corner of the bar, letting the very butch, very blond bartender serve their nervous gunman, and Garcia nodded to her. She plastered on a smile and sauntered over, looking festive in a red Santa Clause skinsuit with flesh-colored tights and a Santa hat. Her lashes were flecked with glitter, and glitter makeup adorned her cheeks. Garcia caught Crosby's unfettered grin and felt his chest—cold from the proximity to the gunman—warm a fraction.

God, the guy was perfect.

"How're my cute boys?" Chartreuse purred. "We having a Merry Christmas?"

"We are now," Crosby said, his innate courtliness making the statement charming instead of smarmy.

"What can I do for you boys?" She gave a furtive glance to her right, where the bartender was blocking their suspect's view of her.

"Soda water with lime," Crosby said. "And a twist. You know what the twist is, don't you?"

"Whisper it to me," she murmured, and both of them leaned over the bar while she put her face near theirs.

"Who's he eyeballing?" Garcia whispered.

"His daughter. She went to the ladies' when I called you. See, he keeps staring at the door." The ladies' room was on one back recess of the bar and the gentlemen's on the other—that made sense. Their guy was closest to the ladies'.

"Any exits from there?" Crosby asked, and she shook her head and gave a subtle, flirtatious laugh. Their perp flashed her a look of both agony and hatred, and Garcia's heart thumped double time.

"We need him to switch his focus somewhere else," Garcia murmured. "Do you have any performers tonight?"

He watched a look of determination cross her face. "I sent most of my girls home," Chartreuse said. "But I've got one trick left."

"Honey, don't put yourself in danger—" Crosby began, but she arched an eyebrow at him.

"Baby, I absolutely refuse to be shot out of my place one more time. Another asshole with a gun is not gonna keep this whore down."

And with that she swung beyond the bar and sauntered up to the little stage across from it, whistling to get her DJ to switch the track.

"How you all doing here tonight?" she asked, and the remaining patrons clapped happily—it sounded as though Chartreuse was a favorite. She rolled her eyes at the applause. "Yeah, you say that. But we all know why you're here. It's 'cause ain't none of you want to be someplace else for Christmas, amirite?"

Some more applause and some sheepish laughter greeted the statement, and the DJ pulled up the building chords to a time-honored Christmas standard.

"Yeah, yeah, I hear you. When it's Christmas, you want to be with someone you love—even if it's just for a night." The mood shifted, a sort of desperate sentimentality filled the room, and Garcia swallowed. Without meaning to, he met Crosby's eyes, and Crosby shrugged. They'd both volunteered for this duty tonight because damned if they had anything else to do. They could sympathize with the people here at the club, looking for a good time with a family of strangers because the family they'd grown up with might not be as kind. But Chartreuse wasn't done speaking yet.

"'Cause if you're with someone you love," she said, giving a sultry look and a wink, "even for a night, then at least for a night, you're home."

With that, she launched into a surprisingly poignant version of "I'll be Home for Christmas" that had everybody, even their gunman, turning toward her.

Crosby and Garcia met eyes, and both of them started to edge nearer to the gunman.

He seemed unlikely as a mass murderer, Garcia had to admit. His hair—blond, probably, in his youth—was still thick, curly, and graying. It was a little mussed, as though he'd been running his fingers through it, but still fashionably cut. His trench coat was newish, a practical beige, but it showed few scuffs and no rips at all. Lightly used, but not worn on the streets, made dirty by sleeping or too much distraction with thoughts of, say, murdering a bunch of people in a nightclub.

And underneath the trench coat were a pair of khaki slacks, shiny loafers, and a bizarrely bright and ugly Christmas sweater.

This man, hugging a semiautomatic weapon under his lapels, was very much somebody's father, somebody's husband. What in the hell was he doing at a drag club on Christmas?

Garcia was just about to cross his line of vision so he and Crosby could grab his arms when a miracle occurred.

Garcia hadn't seen the woman come in; she suddenly appeared near the entrance, as spectacularly suburban and average as the man they were about to take down. She had frosted hair pulled back in barrettes and a skirt that came down to her knees over a pair of sturdy black tights.

She was wearing a garishly colored Christmas sweater that looked like a dead match to the one their guy was wearing, and next to all of the girls wearing glitter and sequins and not much else—or the guys in their leather pants and shiny satin shirts—she was so badly misplaced it was almost physically jarring to look at her.

And then she called out over the sound of the club, her voice shaking and frightened enough to make even Chartreuse quit singing.

"Glenn!" she called out, her voice ringing through the club. "Glenn, you've got to stop! What in the hell are you doing here?"

Glenn turned toward the woman, his hand under the coat falling to his side, the gun in plain sight now but held by the stock, his fingers nowhere near the trigger. "Patsy? Patsy, you don't understand!"

"Explain it to me, Glenn—like I was five!"

Their boy's face crumpled in anger and confusion. "Don't use that tone of voice with me, Patsy. That's what our son says when he's… when he's…."

"When he's putting on his high heels," Patsy snapped. "And his club dress. And getting ready to run away from our Christmas table because you won't see *her* for who she is."

Glenn's face crumpled. "I just came to get him back. This place, this place stole our boy from us. You don't understand—"

"I understand plenty." Patsy started to walk across the club toward him, and Crosby met Garcia's eyes before he looked up at the lights.

Garcia met Chartreuse's eyes, and she nodded to the bartender, mouthing, "Lights," softly, but neither of the two people who didn't belong there noticed.

"He was our boy—you remember that? I took him to games, I taught him to play catch, how to work on the car." Glenn's voice trembled slightly, and his wife drew nearer, her face a mask of grief and of pity.

"I get it, Glenn," she said, her own voice soft. "None of that is gone now—"

"It is!" he half sobbed. "Gone! It's all gone!"

"No!" she sobbed back. "It's still there, Glenn. It's like... like you don't know everything about your kid when they're born. We don't know if the kid is gonna be tall or short, or have my dad's eyes or your mom's. Neither of the kids—we guessed wrong for years until they grew up, remember that?"

"But we at least knew if they were a he or a she!" he yelled. "That—*that* we knew!"

"But we didn't," his wife wept. "And that's not our fault. Don't you understand? Our child—*your child*—loved going to games, loved playing catch, loved working on cars with you. That kid is still there." She tried a watery smile. "She just wears a sequined dress to parties now."

Glenn shook his head at his wife sorrowfully. "It's not the dress, Patsy. You heard him—"

"Her," his wife said firmly. "It's got to be 'her.' I heard our child tell us that they needed to fix who they are on the outside to match who they are on the inside."

"So you're saying all these years we been wrong?" he yelled.

"No!" she yelled back. "Glenn, we raised our kid the best we could. We didn't do anything wrong. But if we... we reject our kid *now*, because we didn't know everything about them and they're trying to tell us and we don't listen, *then* we've done something wrong."

"I just want to get my son back," he wept, the gun falling unnoticed to his feet. "That's all. I want my little boy back."

His wife finally reached him and took his hands in hers, and Garcia bent smoothly and grabbed the gun before anybody could notice it and shoved it securely in his waistband under his Kevlar.

"Glenn, we're never going to get our little boy back, but we can have our *child* in our lives, if only we work at it."

"I miss our kid," he sobbed, and she wrapped her arms around her husband's waist as he fell apart on her shoulder.

The lights came on as a pretty trans woman, wearing the hated white-sequined party dress and kitten heels, emerged from the bathroom. Her jaw was soft from hormone treatments, and her emerging breasts fit the dress nicely, but Garcia could still see the man's little boy in her changing features.

He wondered if that made it harder on the parents struggling to see the child they thought they knew.

But then the girl said, "Daddy?" her voice alto but still the voice of a woman, not a young man, and Glenn and his wife turned toward their baby.

"Danny?" her father whispered, still hugging his wife like she was the only thing solid in the world.

"Sure, Daddy. Just… you know. Spell it with an *i* now."

And he broke all the way, still sobbing in his wife's arms, while his daughter, their child, came and was welcomed, engulfed in the hug.

Crosby glanced at Chartreuse, who made the signal to the bartender to turn lights off again, and then Chartreuse murmured into the microphone, "I think we can get this party started again."

Several people brought out their phones, and Garcia had no doubts the place would be rocking by the time he and Crosby left.

But that didn't mean they were going to leave the happy little family there in the middle.

Garcia guided the two women while Crosby used his bulk and height to quietly intimidate Glenn to the exit door. Together, they emerged into the alleyway, the cold almost a slap in the face of reality after the dark heat of the club.

"What—" Glenn the distraught father began, but Crosby took him by the upper arm and shook him gently.

"Mr.…?"

"Dickson," he rasped. "Glenn Dickson."

"Okay, sir. You know how people talk about a Christmas miracle?"

Glenn Dickson swallowed. "Yes."

"You just lived one. You had a semiautomatic weapon in a crowded place. It could have been very easy for you to become a mass murderer if your wife hadn't stepped in and brought you to your senses."

"A mass murderer...."

The horror on Glenn Dickson's face told Garcia everything he wanted to know about why gun control was so damned important.

He held up the gun Glenn had dropped by his side. "Sir, when and where did you buy this?"

The alleyway was wet and smelled strongly of wet garbage and piss, but it wasn't snowing hard enough to stack up on the sides of the building. Which was how this nice suburban dad came to be on his knees in a filthy mud puddle, vomiting up his Christmas meal in the snow.

THEY PISSED off the local po-po, declared the situation handled, and told them to resume their usual duties. The officer in charge—a middle-aged, sagging Viking named Brigham—was none too happy about it.

"You called us out here on the word of a hysterical drag queen—"

"She had a very legitimate call," Crosby said, while Garcia quietly explained to Glenn that he would be charged with a misdemeanor for bringing a concealed weapon to a crowded place without a permit, and then helped to install the family in the back of their unit, after making sure none of them were armed with anything more than a nail file.

"Legitimate my ass—"

Garcia turned from shutting the door to the SUV and pulled out the semiauto, glaring at the guy. "This is legit. More importantly, it's *legitimately* a weapon sold to a distraught man the same day he walked into the gun store. No waiting, unlike the state law, and no check for a jacket or a history of depression. So yeah, this could have been a legitimate nightmare if your guys had rushed in, and it wasn't, but we appreciate the backup."

"You slimy little beaner," Brigham snarled, and before Garcia could even register the slur, Crosby popped the guy in the nose. The other cops—there must have been six or so—stared blankly in response, although none of them went for their weapons or even shouted, "Hey!" Apparently the respect for a federal officer was burrowed deep.

Brigham wobbled and fell backward onto the pavement while Crosby and Garcia hopped into the department-issue SUV. Crosby rolled down the window and called, "We're not writing you up for this 'cause it's Christmas. You pull that shit on anyone in my department again and we'll paperwork you into retirement, you understand me?"

From what Garcia could see, Brigham was still too dazed to do more than nod, but then he might have nodded if they'd asked him if he liked cheese, so there was no guarantee this was going away. As they pulled away, his men gathered around him and helped him to his feet.

"You didn't have to—" Garcia muttered as Crosby plugged the address Patsy Dickson had given them into the GPS so they could take the family home. Apparently they'd all come to Queens from Secaucus by train. Because New Jersey turnpikes were just the fucking worst, and it was going to take Crosby and Garcia forty-five minutes to get to Secaucus, even in the thin late-Christmas traffic.

"I did," Crosby said, shaking out his hand. His knuckles looked bruised but not torn, and Garcia fought the urge to grab the hand and kiss the knuckles, because who did that? Who fought for a guy's honor like that?

"It's not like the whole world's been all sweetness and light since I was born, you know," Garcia chided.

"Yeah, well, fuck them. Fuck the guys in Florida who called you 'boy' all the time, and fuck that guy for being an asshole when you were being a professional." Crosby put his hand back on the wheel to negotiate traffic. "Nobody does that to my partner, you understand?"

Garcia was going to have him. Oh dear God, it was going to have to happen. With a sigh he peered behind them to the Dickson family, who were talking softly, Glenn in the middle, his wife and daughter on either side, hashing out the rest of their lives.

Yeah. Garcia and Crosby were inevitable—but it wasn't going to happen in the next forty-five minutes.

Instead, Garcia got on the horn to the ATF, and with Harding's backing, they had people in place for a sting the morning of the twenty sixth.

Without the gun, that would have been a little family drama. With the gun, it had the potential to be a fucking tragedy.

After unloading the tearful, shaking family—and reminding Glenn Dickson he was getting a misdemeanor firearms charge added to his record and would have to appear in court, all the better to make it harder for him to make another purchase—they turned around to come back.

"You need food?" Crosby asked, and Garcia groaned, the sugar crash from all those cookies hitting him hard.

"Fuck. Yes. Stop somewhere—"

"There's a steakhouse on the next exit. Text Harding. Ask if he wants takeout if we stop."

"Sure."

Harding did, indeed, want steak, and they pulled off the turnpike and went in.

It was a classic steakhouse—pretty girls in white shirts and black miniskirts served whiskey, beer, and big slabs of beef. The décor was dark wood and dark leather with white tablecloths, and the two of them sank gratefully into a booth, shedding their outerwear to leave on the seats beside them in the blessed warmth of the restaurant.

After placing their orders—they both went with the biggest cut of prime rib, the better to leave half in the work fridge for the next day—Crosby seemed to sink into the restaurant babble with a sense of peace.

"That was… that really was a miracle," he said, his eyes closed. He opened them, and Garcia was arrested for the thousandth time, surprised and attracted by their infinite gray-blue depths. There was a deep sense of relief in those depths tonight, and Garcia felt an answering echo in his own soul.

"You mean that Brigham didn't press charges?" he asked facetiously, and Crosby rolled his eyes.

"That's coming back to bite me in the ass, don't think it's not," he said soberly. "But I'm talking about the family. I saw it going so bad back there. I was thinking, 'God, let's not have to shoot this freaked-out family man on Christmas Eve.'"

"I was so relieved," Garcia admitted. "God. I mean, in my head I know Christmas is no different than any other night. In fact with families? It gets worse. That girl—I think she sat down at the dinner table, trying to be Danny with a *y*, and her dad said one too many things about—I don't know. Gay people. Trans people. *Her* people. And she snapped. Went and put on her slinky dress, her kitten heels, the red lipstick, the pushup bra. Said, 'Dad, this is who I am.' And boom. Dad's got to believe it or fight it, and, you know. Hard to swallow the real."

Crosby nodded before tilting his head back again and taking a deep breath, blinking those marvelous eyes out of existence.

"Families are so hard," he said on a sigh. With a little shake, like he was trying to get rid of the sad, he straightened and gave Garcia a look. "I mean, I'm pretty sure Harding doesn't have any family, which is a real shame. But I *know* I was avoiding going home this holiday. I was so grateful Natalia had Thanksgiving at her house I almost offered myself for babysitting for a year. I get the feeling you were doing the same."

It wasn't an invitation to talk so much as it was an *opening*, should Garcia choose to walk through.

Tonight, feeling vulnerable and a little alone on one of the happiest nights of the year, Garcia chose. "My folks... let's just say they don't approve."

"Of what? Being in law enforcement? The military? What?"

Oh, so so many things—even the one big thing he'd never told them about but was pretty sure they suspected.

"All of it," he said, gesturing with his coffee. "They didn't want me to join the military—wanted me to join Dad's business. Didn't want me to join law enforcement, because same. When I was in Florida, they were mad because their neighbors knew I was a cop. When I left, they were mad 'cause I was gone. When I was in ATF, they were mad because, well, most of the people they know are on the watchlist. When I started this, they were mad 'cause Nana gave me the house, even though they *still* don't fucking visit. My dad's mad 'cause of the LEO. My mom's mad 'cause I haven't married yet. Take your pick." He shrugged, realizing he hadn't even acknowledged the resentment that had come coursing out of his mouth. "Not a picnic."

"No," Crosby murmured, taking a sip of his coffee.

"What about you?"

Crosby grimaced. "I *was* the perfect son. Football scholarship, and then when that went south, I got to be a neighborhood cop. My dad was a cop, my grandpa was a cop—they *loved* me."

Garcia sucked in a breath. "But then...."

"I fucked up. They had to move out of the neighborhood. I moved here, which, you know, feels like the moon to them. Last year I couldn't wait to see them for Christmas, but I swear, it almost ended as bad as that family's we just met. I moved hell and high water and got a plane back to Virginia and then rented a car and drove twelve hours north. I'm the reason Denison got to see her kids last year, 'cause I left New Mexico on the twentieth and was showered and napped by Christmas Eve morning. Spent the day with Joey Carlyle, a lot like I spent it today with you and Harding. Didn't regret a thing."

Oh. "Do you miss them?" Garcia asked, wanting to touch him *so bad*. Wanting to stroke his thigh, cup his cheek, nuzzle his temple, soothe the bruises on his knuckles. Comfort. Couldn't anybody see his boy needed comfort? Garcia had never felt so loved, so *right*, as he did with the SCTF, but Crosby had lost *so* much to get there.

To his surprise, Crosby shook his head. "I miss who they *want* me to be," he said after a moment. "I miss being that kid who could do no wrong in their eyes. I mean, I know that kid was a myth. I know nobody's that perfect, and I also know it's not a prize to grow up just like your old man. My old man would have backed his partner, dead kid at their feet. He told me so himself. Me? I'm not that guy. I don't ever want to *be* that guy. So if that's who I had to be to stay where I was, I guess it's okay I left."

"Would you go back if you had a chance?" Garcia almost took it back. God, he was surprised he'd asked it. What was in him that had to know that bad?

But Crosby shrugged. "I'd like to visit," he said after a moment. "I'd like to let my folks go back, 'cause that was no goddamned good." He looked up and flashed a grin so unfettered by sadness, so untouched by bitter regret, that Garcia had to *fight* not to clutch his chest. "I'd love to show you around," he said. "You and me? We could go to the dance clubs there. I'd show you the sights. The tacky stuff like Navy Pier and the shopping district—you'd go nuts over the shopping district. Leather jackets for *miles*. The architecture. God, even that giant fucking dinosaur head—"

"Chicago Sue?" Garcia asked, delighted. He'd been in Chicago as a stop, never as a destination.

"That's the one. *Loved* that museum. Not that the Met isn't great. But, you know."

"Familiar," Garcia said.

Crosby's smile lost none of its luster. "Yeah. It's like I want to go back to remember there was good shit. I want to *show* you the good shit. You'd appreciate it, I'm sure." His face eased into thoughtfulness now, the bitterness gone. "But I don't want to go back. Not for good. I-I mean for one thing, I'm *smarter* now. Harding trains us up right and keeps us smart. Sociology, criminal justice—our down time isn't a joke, you know that."

"Always an online class," Garcia said, winking.

"Fuckin' always. I love it. It's like all the bad stuff that festers with the old street cops, it gets flushed away with new knowledge. The whole *world* should be doing this shit." He nodded. "But more'n that. If I could only get a fuckin' apartment someplace in the city, this would be perfect." And again that smile. Garcia would have wept, but Crosby would have stopped smiling then. "I love what I'm doing right now. I love my team. I feel like we do some goddamned good." He made a frustrated gesture with his bruised hand. "That thing we just did? It could've gone wrong. I know a thousand different ways people in that club could have gotten hurt. And all of those people—did you see them? They looked like us. They were there 'cause they wanted to be home, and that was the closest thing they had. They could've gotten hurt, and all that safety, all that hope, it would've gone away. That family—dad, well, you know. Picking up a gun isn't the best idea, *ever*, but his wife, his daughter, they could've been hurt just loving someone with issues like his. It could've ended so wrong. But 'cause we didn't rush in being all high-and-mighty cops and shit, everybody there's got a second chance. You and me, partner—we *did* that. I'm not giving that up."

Garcia grinned, and there must've been something in his grin like there had been in Crosby's, because they ended up staring at each other, smiling, quiet, until Garcia's heart started thumping. He thought, *This really* is *it. This will be the night. I'll make my move. Something quiet. Christmas movies on television, us on the couch. I'll sit close.... God, he can't smile at me without it meaning something, can he?*

Their food came, and the moment ended. They talked about other things—football and the best stuff to look at when they were at the Met—and eventually they left and took Harding his meal.

Harding was napping on the lounge couch when they got back to the office, covered with his own coat. He struggled awake when they walked in and thanked them for the food. He was about to tell them to leave—Garcia could tell—when Crosby met Garcia's eyes and Garcia nodded.

"You know, Chief, we got a pie in there. Like, an *entire pie*. You, uh, wouldn't want to share that pie over a game of poker, right?"

Harding gave a quiet, melancholy smile of his own.

While he never told them *his* lonely Christmas story, it didn't matter. They stayed the rest of the night, leaving when Denison checked in, and in the meantime, they spent Christmas playing poker.

Didn't make sense for Crosby to go back to Garcia's place then. Just as well to go home, right?

Garcia wouldn't have traded the night for anything. Being there for Harding was important. He risked his ass to back them, time and time again.

But Garcia spent the next few months wondering, the idea niggling at him. Building. Growing from a hope to a want to an unbearable need.

God. One day he was going to reach for Crosby, because even if he was denied, he'd at least know he'd tried.

Under Protest

CROSBY ALMOST hated himself for this skill sometimes. It felt cold and bloodless, when the results could be bloody as hell, and right now he couldn't afford for that blood to be spilled.

He did *not* like this op.

"Garcia, to your left," he murmured into his comm.

Through his scope, he watched the back of his subject's head and *willed* his partner to shift to Crosby's right. Crosby couldn't see the subject's face, but that wasn't the problem.

The problem was that he was firing a 700-gram projectile 2000 miles an hour into a combined half inch of bone, front and back.

Best case scenario, the bullet stopped inside the subject's head.

Worst case, it blew the subject's head off and then blew right into the nine-year-old girl that he was holding hostage—or into Garcia, who was standing close enough to catch the bullet too if Crosby missed.

He was *not* taking the shot unless the victim was in the clear—and Garcia too. But Garcia was there to try to keep him from having to take the shot anyway.

With a deep breath, he turned his attention to what was going on in the comms.

"So, you got that big-ass knife to her throat and you got all the power, right?" Garcia said. From around the subject's back, Crosby could see his expressive hands, one on either side of their subject—but he couldn't see the nine-year-old girl in their subject's arms. A minute ago, she'd been all he could see, and then Garcia had stepped in to distract their perp. Dammit. *Dammit.*

"Don't give me that," snarled their perpetrator. "I'm a *cop*, remember? You assholes probably have snipers all over me."

Local deputy Pete Thomas had been in service of the small Maryland sheriff's office for over ten years, and he had a jacket of complaints for unnecessary force to prove it. He might have gone on beating up people of color for traffic infractions if he hadn't hit a pregnant teenager in the stomach with a baton in full view of a gas-station camera.

The guy behind the counter had seen Thomas in action one too many times. He made the moment viral, and the DA had been forced to arrest and prosecute.

And Thomas had run like the coward he was.

He'd ended up in this stop-and-rob near a New Jersey turnpike, and his first action when he'd sensed the team gathering around him had been to take a hostage.

Gail and Manny had been first on the scene, and as they'd attempted to make contact with the guy, he'd used both a racial slur and the word "cunt," so they'd backed off. As Gail said, "Our very existence is pissing this guy off, and he's got a kid with him. He's got crazy eyes, people. We need Crosby to do his thing."

Well, since Carlyle and Chadwick were still stuck in traffic from DC and Harding and Denison were hauling ass from Manhattan, it was the best call they could make.

But it made Garcia, with his definitely Latin features, their only other bet for negotiator. Crosby had been able to set up from a nearby rooftop as Garcia had tried to de-escalate the situation, but in spite of Crosby's many injunctions to stay out of the line of fire—even if the subject was on the side of the bullet—Garcia hadn't been able to edge his way sideways.

"Maybe we do have snipers everywhere," Garcia said, and Crosby hoped his heart didn't explode. "But, you know, you still got the kid. What is it you want? What can we give you?"

Crosby's eyes—squinting through the rifle scope—shot wide open. Bad question. *Bad* question! Thomas knew all the angles. All of them. He'd killed three people on his way to this impasse, all of them Black. The only thing that had saved the little girl's life, Crosby was convinced, was her pale skin, and that might not do it in the end.

"Give me?" the man sneered. "*Give* me? Who are *you* to give me *jack*? All day long, swimming in the fucking sewers with the animals—I *take* what I want!"

Crosby heard Garcia swallow, but his voice when he spoke was just as even as it had been. Except he'd started inching around to his left, bit by bit.

"Okay, so you take what you want," Garcia murmured. "I get that. Do you really want to take that little girl's life? I mean, there's other cops here—you were right about that. Do you really want to go out slitting her throat?"

There was a moment's pause, and Harding must have shown up somewhere, but Crosby couldn't afford to look away.

"Don't take it if it's not good," Harding said soothingly into his ear, now in comm's reach.

"Garcia's not clear," Crosby said, agitated. "The *girl* isn't clear."

"You can't see his face," Harding said. "I can." Which meant Harding must be inside the service station. "He's got nothing to lose. You're their best bet if we can get Garcia out of there."

And Crosby saw the infinitesimal shake of the head through the scope. Oh God. Garcia was going to keep holding out for the girl.

"Oh come on, kid," Harding muttered. "C'mon, guys. The girl's as safe as she's going to be."

"Keep moving him, Calix," Crosby begged. "A little more to the right—"

"*Who are you listening to*!" Thomas roared, and Garcia gave a smile, smooth as silk, no worries here, and to Crosby's relief didn't let his eyes dart either in Harding's direction or Crosby's.

"Bosses, man," Garcia said easily. "Can't live with 'em...."

"So don't," Thomas said and spat at Garcia's feet. The little girl he held under one arm gave a whimper, and Thomas shook her like a rag doll. "*Shut up, bitch*!"

"Do it!" Harding commanded. "He's gonna pop!"

"Please, Calix," Crosby prayed. "Just a little more...."

"*Now*!" Harding roared, right as Garcia shifted the last little bit and the subject followed him, raising his weapon toward the girl's throat.

Crosby saw Thomas's body fall before he heard the report of his own rifle.

Garcia stepped in and grabbed the girl, running away from the body as it fell, half its head missing, leaking blood and brains onto the pavement. Her screams could be heard from the top of the building as Crosby sucked in a hard breath of relief.

"Good shot," Harding praised.

"Thanks, partner."

Garcia's voice, not quite as smooth as it had been when he was trying to talk their subject down, was the thing that made Crosby break into a cold sweat. With a gasp, he unclenched his hands from his rifle and buried his face in his bicep, keeping it together. God, it had been close.

"Let's not do that again," he said gruffly.

"I'll make it a priority."

Below him, he could sense the chaos that came with a dead body after a standoff—including getting the little girl checked out and probably treated for shock, and letting Harding and Denison talk to the authorities. He would imagine Harding and Denison would spend some time putting Thomas's cronies in their place and telling them that if they let their personnel issues slide under the carpet, situations like this were the best outcome they could expect.

Crosby stayed on the rooftop, pulling together his collective cool, until he heard Harding murmur, "Garcia is swinging around the street. He's going to pick you up. I want to keep your name and face out of this. So far they haven't figured out where the shot came from. You guys go home. Don't come by the office in case the cops stake it out. Consider this your desk leave after the shooting, are we clear?"

"Yes, boss," Crosby muttered, his heart still hammering in his chest. Over and over again, like a bad movie, he saw the man he'd shot go down. Taking a life like this was different from taking one in the heat of battle. *His* life hadn't been threatened, but the stakes had been just as high.

He swallowed down queasiness and started packing up his gear. When he got downstairs, after having used the roof access of the insurance building to get to the stairwell, he found Garcia on the west side of the building, idling in an empty parking space. As efficiently as possible he stowed the sniper-rifle case in the trunk of the SUV before swinging into the passenger seat and securing his belt.

"Go," he ordered, leaning back and closing his eyes. He wanted to check out Garcia—personally. Wanted to hold Calix's face in his own big hands and carefully examine him, make sure nothing in that dangerous situation had hurt him.

Wanted to make sure his heart was okay, as Crosby's didn't seem to be.

God. His insides were going to be shaky until next week.

"Where to?" Garcia asked. "And don't say home."

Crosby grunted. It was no secret, apparently. Whatever privacy he'd tried to maintain about his shitty living sitch was out.

"I'll be on desk duty again," he mumbled. "Maybe this time I can find an apartment or something."

"Knowing you, you'll get more funding for the squad and end up living in a dumpster," Garcia scoffed. "And don't worry about a destination. I've got one. It's walking distance from my house. You can crash in the spare room, like before."

Crosby should have protested. He really *did* have an apartment, although God knew who was sleeping on his bed *today.* But he didn't want to go there. Even if his roommate *wasn't* having a party, the space left when everybody was sleeping it off—or not there—was just… empty and sad. Like a hangover. Because the place wasn't really home to begin with.

"Okay," he said, letting go for once. Garcia was okay. *Garcia* was okay. It was enough to make the sweat saturate his underarms to his leather jacket, and he tried to turn off the emotion.

But the thought scared him. If he turned off *relief,* what was he left with? Fear? Longing? Maybe relief was the one he should be sticking with, yeah?

His breath started coming in fast and hard, and it took him a moment to calm himself down as Garcia deftly managed the Queensboro Bridge.

"You okay?" Garcia murmured. "You're sounding sorta rough."

Crosby breathed out slowly. "This," he said, "is the reason they put us on leave after a shooting."

"Yeah, buddy. How about you and me, tonight we go out, drink too much beer, pass out in my house, and pretend today didn't happen."

Crosby gave a harsh laugh. "Sure," he murmured. "Sounds like a plan to me."

THE BAR wasn't a dive.

Crosby noticed after Calix had parked, using the government sticker to make sure the SUV was secured, in a local pay lot. They were in one of the fun, trendy parts of Queens, sort of kitschy, sort of eclectic, very ethnic. Crosby was probably one of the few Irish white boys in the area, but that never bothered him. The Park was full of brass and dark wood and a surprisingly well-stocked kitchen. Bottles of every stamp lined the walls, including some of the top-shelf brands that would need a step stool and possibly an acrobat to access. A mixture of accents babbled around them as they plowed through, but mostly it was men and women there for no-nonsense drinking.

Garcia led the way to a table big enough for eight, and Crosby frowned.

"Everyone else coming?"

"Yeah, I texted. Harding and Denison might not be able to get away until later, but you and me—we're the advance guard."

Crosby gave a weak chuckle. "Let's get a pitcher and some food and get started."

He really didn't feel like a beer and chatter, but he also didn't feel like being alone. His insides were jumpy, edgy, and he felt like he needed something, someone, to hold on to him and keep holding on, to ground him or he'd jump away forever.

Don't take the shot if it's not good.

Or maybe he could just grab hold of Calix and crush him to his chest and make sure he didn't let go.

"Hey," Garcia asked, coming back to the table with a pitcher of beer and some glasses. God, Crosby hadn't even realized he'd gone. "You okay? The food's coming."

Crosby nodded. "Yeah. Sorry. Not sure what I'm doing when I tune out like that. Just…." He looked anywhere but into Garcia's brown eyes. "Today sucked," he finished weakly.

"Yeah." Underneath the table, Garcia patted his knee in what was probably supposed to be a gesture of comfort and camaraderie, but Crosby shuddered and held his hand there, not sure if it was sexual or animal or what but just… needing to be touched.

When Garcia gave his knee a squeeze and then turned his hand up to lace their fingers, his heart stopped. He turned his head, not sure what to say, and saw instead Garcia's expression, infinitely sad, expecting rejection. His brown eyes were overbright, and his lower lip trembled faintly, and for the first time since the trigger had given under his finger, Crosby knew exactly what he wanted. His lips parted, his breath froze, and he wasn't sure what they looked like, sitting so close, hands laced under the table, eyes locked, but the bell over the door sounded unnaturally loud, and both of them jumped as though shocked.

They turned toward the entrance, and Garcia waved and flagged down Gail and Manny with his outside hand, but he squeezed Crosby's hand under the table before disentangling their fingers.

Crosby managed a smile and a wave of his own, but neither of them moved away from the other, so their upper arms were touching and their thighs were touching for pretty much the next two hours.

Crosby thought that contact was the only thing that kept him from spacing off, from bursting into tears, or from rage-trashing the very nice bar during the course of the night. It kept him human, kept him *grounded*, and he was so grateful he couldn't stand it.

Gail and Manny Swan were good companions, though. Swan was young—fresh out of the academy young—and not sure what he was doing in the company of people who had cut their teeth in the military, like Gail, Garcia, Chadwick, Carlyle, or Harding, or alphabet ops like Denison, who had been to Quantico. Crosby was the first one to tell him that he'd been a flatfoot too, on track to being a detective, but he hadn't made it yet.

"Really?" Swan said. "How'd you get to be the designated sniper?"

Crosby had shrugged. "Harding believes in training. All the training. You've seen that. My dad and I used to hunt when I was a teenager, and one of the first training sessions Harding had after I got posted here was long-distance shooting." He shrugged. "I've got a knack, I guess." He didn't sound proud—not even to his own ears.

"I get the feeling it's not a, uhm, comfortable skill," Manny said softly.

Crosby looked away. Under the table, Garcia bumped his knee against Crosby's, and Crosby remembered to breathe.

"It saved my partner today," he said, realizing it was true. "I'm grateful."

Manny nodded and rubbed his close-cropped hair. "Yeah, I'd be glad for piano training if it kept this one safe and sound."

Gail sent him a look of mock outrage. "Piano? You think that's going to save me?" She turned to them, obviously sensing they needed a mood shift. "He sings. He sings to the radio. Hip-hop, blues, even rock. And the thing is, he's got a *dynamite* voice, but it's incessant! I can't listen to Green Day anymore without hearing the Manny Swan rendition!"

They laughed, and Garcia patted Crosby's knee. "Stay right there. I'm gonna go test this out."

Crosby watched bemusedly as Garcia made his way to the jukebox in the corner and put in a pocketful of ones. By the time he came back, the first few chords of Eminem's "Lose Yourself" were starting to echo through the bar, and Swan gave Garcia a droll look.

"You can keep up?" he asked.

"Game on," Garcia said. The two of them locked eyes, and as a table all of them began to rock in time to the music.

Manny Swan knew every *word*, and in a rhythm notoriously hard to capture, he hit every beat.

Garcia kept up for the chorus—and Crosby was impressed as hell—but Garcia wasn't the only one. As Chadwick and Carlyle walked in, Gail and Crosby were shouting the chorus too, and the table burst into cheers as the song rollicked to a close.

The next song up was Tupac's "Gangsta's Paradise," followed by Linkin Park's "Bleed it Out." By the time Sam Cooke showed up on the rotation, Denison and Harding had shown up, and Crosby had relaxed fully into the beer and the pizza that Calix had ordered, and the day, the terrifying, horrible, *shitty* day, had been pushed into the background.

THEY ALL had to work the next morning. They didn't close the place down by any means, but by ten o'clock the others had left, and Garcia had quietly promised Harding he'd see Crosby home.

"Is he okay?" Harding asked as Garcia put more money into the jukebox as a farewell gift for the bar, and Garcia felt honored by the trust—and protective too.

"I think it was rough," he evaded. "The little girl, me... he knows what a bullet can do."

Harding looked surprised. "Of course he does. That's one of the reasons I put him on my team."

Garcia nodded, aware that Harding's craggy features were looking more tired than usual.

"It's been a tough year for our boy," he said at last, and Harding nodded.

"I don't think he's healed yet from what happened in Chicago. You know what I mean?" Harding asked.

Garcia nodded again, casting a surreptitious glance to where Crosby sat. He'd been quiet all night—unless they were singing. There was a passion, a *fury* in the way Crosby had been belting the lyrics out from his diaphragm that told Garcia he wasn't okay.

Crosby met his eyes then, and he gave a faint head tilt, probably indicating it was time to go. Garcia gave Harding a sideways look, and Crosby nodded understanding and turned back to Gideon Chadwick, who wanted his attention. The lean academic-looking man had been dry and funny all night, and Joey Carlyle had been devilish per usual. Garcia appreciated them both.

"I do," Garcia said, in answer to Harding's question. "I think it hurt him—bad."

"And today he killed a bad cop," Harding told him. "It's going to eat at him. I'm glad you can read his mind, because I think someone needs to."

Garcia tried for swagger. "It's what partners do."

Harding's expression softened, and his eyes—a soulful brown—went incredibly gentle. "The good ones," he said, and Garcia felt as though he had missed something.

It didn't matter. Harding turned away and went to catch a car, and Garcia came back to the table and made a big deal out of needing to pour a drunken Crosby into bed.

Crosby protested—fairly, since Garcia had kept track. He'd had a couple of beers, not enough to impair his judgment, and that... that was important to Garcia.

That Crosby be in full possession of his faculties.

Garcia couldn't admit to himself why, not even after they'd put their coats and hats back on, gloves too, and made their way out into the chilly night.

"Lead the way!" Crosby said, keeping his strides purposeful and slow. Garcia stayed half a step ahead after that, although they bumped shoulders a lot. Every time they did, the power of Crosby's muscles shuddered underneath Garcia's skin.

Oh God. Could he really do this? He... he wanted to do this. Could he really do this?

But he had to. His partner's heart... it was growing thin, thinner every day. Garcia wasn't sure if it was his time in the hospital or TJ whatsisface threatening to kill his little girls in the cemetery or that awful choice about whether blowing a guy's head off was going to kill the man's victim *and* Garcia, or maybe it was all of it, plus Chicago, plus a sort of infinite loneliness that Garcia longed to soothe.

They did a hard, dangerous job, one that broke people's hearts routinely. Garcia used to get by on one-night stands, on dancing in mosh pits, on screaming songs like "Sabotage" to the sky.

But he couldn't do the one-night stands anymore, not after having a partner like Judson Crosby for the last six months. And he couldn't stand to watch such a good man, such a good *partner*, float in the New York tides without an anchor. Crosby *needed* someone tonight, and Garcia… well, Garcia was getting desperate to see if the hugs, the arms over his shoulder, the unabashed touching… was that what he thought it could be?

Crosby was such a Boy Scout! Garcia couldn't read him for desire, for sex, for need. But he hoped. He hoped because *he* needed. *He* wanted.

And he trusted, more than anything, that if he made his needs and wants known, Crosby wouldn't hate him, wouldn't reject him cruelly, but would simply say, "Sorry, man. I wish I swung that way."

He was going to count on that trust to maybe get Crosby to give him a chance to serve both their needs.

He'd been thinking maybe a slow seduction, sitting on the couch and then moving closer and then a kiss… he'd been *thinking* that.

But then he'd ushered Crosby into his house, and when Crosby had looked around the place and then back at him, Garcia had seen *yearning*.

Garcia was up behind him before he could think about what he was doing, before he could dwell on the many ways this could go wrong. He pressed his body along Crosby's back, grabbing his narrow hips to hold him in place.

"Tell me to turn on the lights," he growled, and time seemed to collapse in on him while he waited for an answer.

"No," Crosby whispered, and Garcia shuddered against his heat.

Good.

The words they muttered in the dark were hot after that, charged, and their first kiss was searing, a gnashing of tongues and teeth. Both fed a hunger in Garcia that peaked the moment he fell to his knees and pulled Crosby's pants down, palming his thighs before making eye contact and taking Crosby's cock—as massively sized as the rest of him—into his mouth.

He shuddered as it shoved up against the back of his throat, needing to feel it, needing to *gag* on it, needing to make it the focal point of both their lives—anything, anything to take that hopeless, lost look from Judson Crosby's face.

He became lost in the blowjob, dedicated to slurping, to teasing, to stroking, all in the name of making Crosby come.

He'd been needing this for so long.

Crosby spurted a little precome, and Garcia groaned, wanting more. Crosby's fingers threaded through his hair, and he tugged Garcia's head back, meeting his eyes.

"A bed," he said gruffly.

Garcia whimpered, opening his mouth again to suck Crosby's cock, but Crosby did him dirty then, smiling the tiniest bit. "Please."

Garcia stood and traced Crosby's lower lip with his thumb. "Please what?"

"More kissing," Crosby whispered. This time when their lips met, it was slower. Tender. Garcia was suddenly hesitant, shy, and almost afraid.

Not of what would happen between them that night, but of who they would be in the morning.

He couldn't stop it, though. The moment he'd pressed his body against Crosby's, felt him tremble, felt him *need*, he knew that this moment *right now* was the most important he'd ever live.

His entire life of quick hookups and putting his career first—and of never knowing if the guy he needed to watch his back really *had his back*—and this guy here, the one with the powerful hands, the muscular body, had watched his six from day one.

Garcia couldn't stop them. They were like a freight train, had been from the very beginning, the first moment they'd met and Crosby had given him that inscrutable, sober look from those blue-gray eyes and had made keeping Garcia alive his priority.

This moment here was going to keep *Crosby* alive, keep his heart from shriveling in his chest, keep his soul from exhausting itself, always wondering if he'd have a place to rest.

The need in Crosby's touches told Garcia he wasn't alone. *They* weren't alone.

Garcia broke away, panting, and led Crosby to his bedroom, and clothing flew everywhere. Garcia was still wrestling with a sock when Crosby almost tackled him, pushing him flat on his back on the bed and looming over Garcia, a shyly playful smile on his face.

"You feel that?" he chided, grinding up against Garcia's thigh. "You got me revving this bad, partner, and you're gonna hang out and worry about your *socks*?"

Garcia laughed harshly. "You think I'm not primed?" He arched his naked body up against Crosby's. "You been looking at me with them Irish-boy eyes for six months, and I've been losing my mind!"

Crosby sobered. "You liked personal combat class, didn't you." It wasn't a question.

Garcia stared up at him with smoldering eyes. "I wanted to eat you alive."

Crosby's kiss was starving, nearly savage, but Garcia answered it just as harshly, his blood thundering in his ears. Oh God. He'd been wanted before, had been the cute guy at the club, had been the onetime hookup that some hungry top had absolutely *needed* to have that night.

He'd never been wanted like this. He'd *never* been someone's long-term, smoldering crush, had never had a yearning for one man and one man only. These last six months with Crosby had been the best and worst of his life. The best because he'd finally found someone he could partner with and the worst because he'd wanted to partner all the way.

Garcia kissed Crosby with his passion on his sleeve, stroked his shoulders, his waist, cupped his neck, urged him closer. Augh! He needed to be taken *now*!

But Crosby had other ideas. One kiss, one love bite at a time, he made his way down Garcia's chest, pausing to nibble on first one nipple, then the other. After flicking with his tongue while pinching the other nipple, he gave a hard lick and glanced up.

"You have until I get to your cock to find the lube," he growled, licking the nipple again.

"What happens then?" Garcia panted.

"I suck you down my throat and stick a finger up your ass and you come."

Garcia groaned, already scrabbling for the lubricant in his side drawer. "What happens... ah!" Crosby had moved to his other nipple. "What happens if... oh fuck—*there it is*—I get you the lubricant?" Crosby was kissing down his stomach and Garcia was wild with need, but at his words, Crosby paused to look up and meet his eyes.

"I lick you," he promised. "I stretch you. I fuck you." He said it with absolute commitment, and Garcia gasped and shot a little precome and tried really hard not to lose his nut.

"Here," he gasped, handing over the lube, unable to play this game. "Suck me and stretch me. Make me come. Fuck me until I pass out."

Crosby kept moving down his body, where he took Garcia's cock into his mouth and fumbled with the lube. In a moment Garcia felt the invasion of Crosby's thick fingers up his ass, and his thighs trembled as he held them open.

With a moan around Garcia's cock and a hard, long suck up the shaft with a frantic lick of the head, Crosby kept the two fingers scissoring, loosening, while his mouth worked. Garcia let go of his noises, gave up on control, until Crosby pulled his fingers out and he keened.

"You still want the whole package?" Crosby taunted. "I sucked your cock and stretched your ass. You want me to—"

"*Fuck me!*" Garcia commanded. "God, fuck me. I will fucking *end you* if you don't—*gah!*"

Crosby was true to his word. With a swift predatory motion, he lunged up the bed and positioned himself at Garcia's entrance, thrusting slowly in.

Garcia lost himself for whole moments, a circle of fire forming behind his eyes as he allowed Crosby to invade his body, to possess him wholly, to fuck him raw and without inhibition. They were both on PrEP protocol—Harding asked all his people to be on it, because the job could get bloody. In this case it meant he didn't have to worry about Crosby taking care of him, but he wouldn't anyway.

Crosby wouldn't let anything happen to Garcia—not on the job and not here. Garcia knew that in his bones, which meant every thrust of Crosby's cock was more than just a sublime explosion of nerve endings, it was a merging of two people who had been dancing toward this for a long time.

It was coming home.

And then it was carnal, sweaty, absolutely committed sex. Crosby fucked him blindly, and Garcia urged him on in guttural shouts. Home wasn't always comfortable. Sometimes it was sweaty, angry, needy oblivion, and Garcia was starving for that too.

"*Harder!*" He demanded. "*Harder!*"

The slap of their flesh was almost brutal, and Garcia knew he'd have bruises on his ass in the morning, but he didn't care. Something desperate in both of them demanded this, and Garcia craved Crosby's release, wanted to beg for his come like a wanton, greedy slut, but he didn't have the breath.

Crosby arched his back, flexed his stomach, and the ridges of his abdomen caught the end of Garcia's cock. With a snarling moan Garcia cried out, his entire body convulsing in orgasm, and Crosby gave a shout, hips stuttering as he hammered his climax into Garcia's ass, thrusting deeper, deeper, until his come became part of Garcia's DNA.

Garcia felt the heat of it, filling him, seeping out of his destroyed entrance, and almost wept with the relief of it. Crosby collapsed on top of him, and for a moment the two of them panted in the shattered peace of afterglow.

With a grunt, Crosby rolled off him and was about to get off the bed.

"Where you going?" Garcia mumbled, trying to take stock.

Crosby kissed his temple. "Washcloth. I'll be back."

"You're staying here," Garcia ordered, frowning. "I don't need a washcloth. Come back to bed."

Crosby paused, frowning. "I won't leave you," he said softly. "I wouldn't do you like that. I just want to take care of you. Nobody likes to sleep in the wet spot."

He got up then and disappeared, and Garcia heard him moving around in the bathroom. In another moment he was back. He had Garcia roll over and gently sponged him off, fingering his abused asshole gingerly.

"I didn't hurt you, did I?"

Garcia chuckled, facedown on his own bed. "God no. I needed that like you wouldn't believe."

Crosby's kiss on his tender buttock was a sweet surprise. "Good. I don't want to ever hurt you."

Garcia moaned, and without his permission, his legs spread as his greedy asshole tried to offer itself up to Crosby in supplication.

Crosby chuckled gently and lifted him bodily so he could pull his knees up to his chest, presenting his ass to anyone who wanted it.

Crosby apparently wanted to lick it, from taint to dripping hole and back again, leaving Garcia to moan into the pillow, drifting in and out from want to need to absolutely would die if he didn't, without a single word to beg for it.

Finally Crosby paused in his absolute heaven of a rim job and squirted a healthy dollop of cool lubricant on Garcia's body.

"Can I?" he whispered, rubbing his backside, and Garcia had enough words after all.

"Please. Oh God, please."

He stayed facedown while Crosby used him, but this time was slower, with tenderness and care. Crosby's hands drifting over his bottom, spanning his waist, caressing him from his flanks to his shoulders—they drove Garcia up more than anything else.

Finally they drove him into a second orgasm, and Crosby collapsed on his back, rutting gently.

This time when Crosby rolled off him, they were facing each other, and Crosby looked like that was it, he was crashing, no more for tonight.

"Thank you," Garcia slurred, "for that."

Crosby chuckled, and Garcia snuggled up against his chest. Crosby pulled him in before covering them both with the comforter, and for a moment in the spring chill, Garcia was in a warm fortress, cared for and sated, and all was right with the world.

Mornings After, Promises Before

CROSBY COULDN'T help it. They'd managed to get dressed and had run down to the bar to pick up the SUV, also getting bagels and coffee on their way. Now he was on the bridge to Manhattan, trying desperately to get his head in the work zone.

He couldn't do it.

"What?" Garcia demanded through a mouthful of bagels, lox, and capers. Crosby gave him crap about *all* the salty food, but Garcia never seemed to care.

"Nothing," Crosby mumbled, keeping his eye on traffic. The bridge could get squirrely at morning rush hour, and New York traffic was not quite as friendly as Chicago's had been.

"Come on, brother, you need to spit it out now, while we're alone, or you're going to dwell on it when we're trying to have a day. Say it!"

"Why?" Crosby muttered.

"I just told you why!"

"No, not why should I say it—why did you go down on me at three a.m.?"

Garcia sputtered coffee all over himself and spent a minute wiping it up. "Now I'm *really* glad you asked me that while we were alone," he said, and Crosby reached into the door compartment where they kept the extra napkins. He handed a couple to Garcia, because his piddly single one wasn't doing it, and waited for an answer.

After a few minutes of fussing—and a few more of stalling—Garcia finally pitched the napkins in his empty paper bag and said, "Because I didn't know if we were going to get another chance. Six months I wanted you and told myself I couldn't have you because what a way to fuck up the best partner I ever had, right?"

Crosby grunted in assent. Yeah, he'd pretty much been exactly there for the last six months himself.

"So," Garcia kept going, and as traffic came to a stop, Crosby caught his wistful little smile, "I thought if this was what I was getting, I'd get it all. I wanted your come in my mouth, man. Grabbed a washcloth, went for it."

Crosby's entire body flushed. He could feel his *toes* tingle. "Next time," he said, "maybe make sure I'm all awake for it. I, uhm, would like to remember the whole blowjob. I'm pretty sure it was prime, but, you know… now I'm going to be wondering until the next time we hook up."

"Tonight," Garcia said promptly, without shame.

"I mean, next time—"

"Tonight. You said just us. You said we're a thing. You're coming home with me tonight."

Crosby wasn't exactly sure how to respond to this. "I need clothes, Garcia. People are going to get weird if I show up to work wearing the same clothes three days running."

"We'll get them on the way back. I can check out the SUV tonight. Nobody cares. Do it all the time. You'll stop by your horrible apartment, get all your stuff, and move it into my place."

Crosby took a hurried sip of coffee to see if he could find an argument for this. "I said exclusive, Calix. I didn't say *married*—"

"I don't care if we never do the thing again and you end up spending five years in my spare room," Garcia snapped. "You look like hell because you don't get any fucking sleep there. We're doing the thing, so you might as well sleep at my place. When we're done doing the thing, you can sleep in my spare room and I'll help you get a decent place of my own." He paused, and his words echoed in the SUV. "I mean *your* own."

Somehow, Crosby had lost complete control of the conversation. "I, uhm, was just wondering why the three a.m. bj—"

"Now you know. I wanted to taste your come, and I was afraid that was my last chance. I'm super thrilled it probably won't be, but now we're on to another subject."

Yup. He had zero control over the narrative. "You can't just adopt me because we had a good night—"

"Good?"

Oh hell. Now Garcia sounded hurt.

"*Great*," Crosby corrected.

"Cowboy, you are such a shitty liar. You were honest this morning. Be honest with me now."

A cab driver narrowly avoided death under Crosby's grill, and he had a sudden wish they weren't doing this in morning rush-hour traffic, but he couldn't seem to escape this conversational quagmire. He couldn't deny the things he'd said that morning, the absolute possessiveness that had come over him or the need to keep Garcia's eyes from showing that fathomless hurt they seemed capable of. It had been a time for honesty, a time for rawness, to be real and to confess that he wanted this, this *thing* between himself and his partner, more than common sense should have allowed. But he was trying to do damage control, trying not to obligate Garcia any more than necessary, trying to slow his fall into a relationship that experience told him would only leave him flat on the concrete and bleeding.

"It was really fucking awesome, okay?" Crosby retorted, his heart still beating fast with the near miss. "It was fucking amazing. But… you don't get it. Every time I tried a relationship with a guy, it just… just disintegrated. A week of a guy putting up with my schedule, putting up with my job, with not knowing if I could text to break a date, with not being fucking out—and pfft! All that excitement went up in jizz. They didn't even fucking *speak* to me or look at me or whatever. One of those guys was a *cop*, man. He should have at least gotten a clue, right? I mean, it was worse than the girls. The girls could at least tell their girlfriends I was a cop. The guys, they couldn't tell anybody shit about anything. So you and me had this fucking amazing moment, and I'm not lying—I want *more.* But I don't know what'll happen when we move all my shit into your house and in a week you don't want a fucking thing to do with me. It'll be hard enough working with you when you think I'm a piece of shit."

Garcia was quiet for a moment, and Crosby glanced over at him to make sure he was still good. He'd turned his eyes back to the road—and a good thing too—when Garcia said, "But man, we've already done that week. We did that six *months.* You haven't left my six once. Not even when you were back doing overwatch and I was out in the field. Do you really think I'm going to desert you now because we had a fucking amazing night?"

Crosby let out a sigh. "But if you do, I won't have any place to live."

Garcia's hand over the console to pat his knee was one of the warmest, sweetest things he'd ever felt.

"*Papi*, you don't have any place to live now. At least if we move your shit into my place, you can sleep on a really comfortable guest bed, okay?"

"I'll think about it," Crosby muttered, coming up to the garage where the SCTF parked.

"Well, if you don't give me an answer by tonight, Crosby, I will *meet you* at your shitty apartment with the SUV and get your deadbeat roommate to help me move your shit."

"I just got a new bed!" Crosby remembered.

"Which your deadbeat roommate needs to give him credibility," Garcia countered as Crosby found the bank of spaces to check the SUV back in.

"And Toby isn't a deadbeat—"

"If I was in ATF, I could have his place raided and get a commendation," Garcia told him seriously. "I mean, I like the guy, but anybody at his flat has so much shit in their blood on any given day, you could give somebody a transfusion with it to treat them for chronic pain."

Crosby had to laugh at that. None of his roommate's friends had ever done drugs *in front* of Crosby. Probably because Crosby had begged Toby not to let them so he didn't have to pretend not to see anything. But Crosby was under no illusions about how much "chemical enhancement" went into his roommate's constant parties either.

"I'm not sure this is a good idea," he muttered as he killed the motor. He looked at Garcia unhappily, perfectly aware this would be the last moment they had to talk about this in private before they became all about whatever was going down at op center right now.

"I am," Garcia said, nodding vigorously. His expression softened, and for a heartbeat, it was just them and the memory of what had transpired the night before. The first moment Crosby had merged with Garcia's tight, responsive body filled his senses like wine or chocolate, and Crosby's heart was singing a steady song of how everything was possible.

"Have some faith, Judson." Garcia tilted his head beseechingly, his dark eyes tender. "I can't promise much, but I can promise that by the end of the day, I'll still feel exactly the same about you as I did last night. That's all two people got, really. That promise that tomorrow nothing's going to change."

Crosby bit his lip, remembering that one day when he'd testified against his partner and everything had changed.

Apparently Garcia remembered too. He gave a quick look around before leaning forward and taking Crosby's mouth in a short, hard kiss. "Won't be us," he said. "I swear. You and me, we've got honor in our veins."

Crosby nodded and backed away. "I'll *think* about it," he said, "and let you know at the end of the day."

Garcia cackled as he let himself out of the vehicle. "Famous last words. Seriously. I don't even know why you bother."

Because he'd been burned before, and often, he wanted to retort. But looking at the joy—and the devilment—in Garcia's black eyes, he didn't think he could actually say that.

How often could you give anyone—friend, lover, partner—so much joy?

Walking through the garage and into the elevator became like the old *Batman* show, Crosby thought. Once they hit the elevator, their "new lovers" faces disappeared and their "federal agents" costumes plastered on. They walked into their office on the eighth floor shoulder to shoulder, ready to be briefed.

What Crosby saw, sitting at their happily battered conference table, made his breakfast threaten to rise up in his gorge.

"Mudson, my friend," McEnany said. "I'm so glad you are not dead."

Crosby took a breath and looked to Harding, whose expression was stony with displeasure.

"Crosby, Garcia, my office, now. McEnany—"

"Agent McEnany to you," said Crosby's former partner. Fortyish, balding, ginger, McEnany was wiry and living proof that redheads needed sunblock and a lot of time indoors. His skin was leathery and freckled, even the skin under the remaining hair on his head, and the sneer he delivered to Crosby was one of his best weapons.

Or it had been. It used to give Crosby an upset stomach just looking at the guy, but not now. Now Harding was regarding the man with absolute distaste.

"And that's *Special* Agent Judson Crosby to you," Harding replied icily. "If you get unprofessional on him one more time, I'm giving my entire unit permission to call you McAsshole. Try me." And with that he spun on his heel and into the office, not even looking back to see if Garcia and Crosby were following.

Of course they were.

Harding's office door slammed behind them, and Harding made a show of closing the blinds as McEnany looked on with that patented sneer contorting his features.

When the last blind clicked into place, Crosby sank into one of the chairs across from Harding's battered wooden desk and scrubbed at his face with his hands.

"IA?" he asked gruffly. Harding had mentioned that McEnany had gotten a federal job after the DA in Chicago had failed to prosecute him for the bad shoot. He'd just never, ever thought the two of them would have to cross paths again.

"IA," Harding confirmed, sitting on the desk in front of his chair. "But here's the thing. He has no authorization to grill you here. There's been no internal affairs case opened on yesterday's incident—and there wouldn't be. Not on you. I authorized the shoot. The entire team heard me screaming at you to take the shot. He shouldn't be here, and as far as I know, the only reason he *is* here is that our perp's CO took it upon himself to call in a favor with McEnany's superior."

Crosby took a breath and met Harding's eyes. "So I don't have to deal with this guy?" he asked, to be sure.

"Absolutely not." Harding ran his hands through his dark hair, rucking it up in all directions and making the occasional strand of salt stick out wildly. "That said, I'd *really* like to know what he's doing here. But we can't. Not right now. I suspended your desk duty and called everybody in because we've caught a live one. We need to shut McEnany down and work around him. Do you think you can ignore him?"

Crosby nodded, feeling his face harden. "It'd be my pleasure," he snarled, thinking about how happy he'd be to be able to plow the guy over while he and his team did their jobs.

"Excellent." Harding nodded and then paused. "But I've got to ask. Are you still rooming with your DJ friend in midtown?"

Crosby winced, but Garcia spoke up. "I was going to move him into my spare room today, sir. Those digs are no good."

Harding lifted an eyebrow and blinked so slowly Crosby *knew* he was thinking three things at once.

"Well, I think that's a good solution for the moment." He gave Crosby a compassionate look. "You're too old to be couch surfing, kid, and your friend may be a stand-up guy, but for people like McEnany, he's one more reason to hassle you, you got me?"

"Yessir," Crosby said, trying hard not glare at Garcia. "We can move me out after we clear the case."

Harding nodded. "Okay, so let's go out there and show this McAsshole fucker what a real group of professionals looks like when they work. Don't respond to him, don't look at him, and don't tell him anything about the op that he wouldn't hear as a fly on the wall. You feel me?"

Crosby and Garcia both nodded and then turned to leave.

"And guys?" Harding said, causing them to turn.

"Yeah?"

"Same thing I told you months ago. Fire long before you see the whites of their eyes. I do *not* like this guy in my situation room. He is not our friend."

"Understood, sir," Garcia told him, and together they walked back toward the conference room. In the short time they'd been in there, the others had emerged from their open cubicles and were ready to lay out the sitch and talk strategy. McEnany had apparently spent *his* time staring at the door to Harding's office, and as Crosby and Garcia stalked back toward the conference room, he didn't appear to notice that they weren't alone.

"So, did you have a nice little confab?" McEnany sneered as they emerged. "Were you told to cooperate with—"

"Gail, do you have the sitch board ready?" Crosby said like the guy wasn't even there. Finest bit of acting he'd ever done. If he hadn't felt the clamminess under his arms and down his back, he would have sworn he wasn't on the verge of puking.

"Yeah, me and Swan are ready to throw down. Who's your friend?"

"Not authorized to be here," Crosby replied. "Treat him like a fly on the wall, per Harding, but he's not to interfere with our op."

"The fuck?" McEnany spluttered. "Crosby, are you fucking kidding me? I'm here to investigate your shoot yesterday—"

"No you're not," Natalia Denison said, emerging from the coffee corner to hand Crosby and Garcia their own mugs before turning to get her own. "We're not stupid. We know why you're here and why you're zeroing in on Crosby. Go to your corner and let us work." She made a little shooing motion with her hand, and McEnany's eyes narrowed. He advanced on her, shoulders swinging.

"Look, you fuckin' bi—"

Gail stuck her foot out and tripped him.

McEnany went sprawling, and the mood in the situation room was grim enough that not one person laughed.

Instead, they turned toward Gail and Manny. "What do you got for us?" Garcia said.

"It's a hot one," she told them, like that foot thing hadn't happened. "See this guy?" On the screen at the far end of the table a picture appeared of a fleshy businessman in a very pricey suit. His thinning hair was coarse and black, like his eyebrows, and his scalp showed pink underneath.

"Mobster," Natalia said, taking a sip of her coffee and stepping delicately around McEnany as he was trying to pull himself up.

"Winner, winner, chicken dinner," Gail told her. "This is Maurice St. James, but that's an assumed name. His real name is Mauritz Stoya. Businessman, illegally in this country from Russia, master of imports and exports, owner of one of the biggest strips of warehouses off the Hudson in New Jersey."

"I take it he's been under observation?" Harding said, strolling in from his office. McEnany was reaching for a chair to help pull himself up, and Harding pulled the chair away from him and sat on it.

"For a number of years. FBI and NYPD Vice both have dossiers on this guy, boss," Gail said. "He's slippery, but my contact at the FBI says they were closing in on him—the sting was supposed to go down this weekend."

"Ah," Harding said. "That explains a lot."

"It does," Swan replied. He hit a key on the board in front of them and another face appeared on the monitor at the end of the room. "This is his six-year-old son, Kosta, by his mistress, Tatya Zarim." The boy appeared, smiling shyly, in the lap of a thin, tired-looking blond woman who had obviously lived happier days. She was doing her best, though, kissing the boy's ear, holding up a favorite toy. The boy was reaching for the toy as the photo was taken, and Crosby got the impression of a dragonfly captured in amber at a perfect moment.

"The boy's okay?" Crosby asked, suddenly not aware of McEnany in the least.

"As far as we know," Gail said. "He disappeared from his bedroom last night, and while his mother is doing all the batshit crazy things you'd expect from somebody worried to death, his father is not."

"So, uh, what is Stoya doing?" Gideon Chadwick asked. He and Joey Carlyle were seated on the far side of the table, shoulder to shoulder, as focused on the case as Garcia and Crosby. McEnany had managed to get himself upright by now and was glaring at Denison. He'd taken two steps toward her, mouth opened in a snarl, when Harding stood fluidly and blocked his path.

"Stoya," Gail murmured, checking her notes, only a little oblivious to the byplay, "is gathering his goons. I've got possibles—a private jet booked to Moscow and another to Prague. Moscow is closer to home, but given the current political climate there, I think Prague is safer."

"And he's going to want a safe place, isn't he?" Harding murmured, frowning.

Garcia asked, "Do we have a family history for him?"

"Hm…." Gail went to work. "Gimme a second here…."

"Got it!" Swan said. "Yes, yes we do. His father bailed before he was born. Raised by his mother, but she bailed too when he was a kid, and his maternal grandmother took over. She was… oh."

Gail looked over his shoulder to see the intel on his laptop. "Ugh."

"You guys are freaking me out here," Garcia said, and Crosby felt the tension that had wrapped his face in eel wire since he'd come in and seen McEnany relax with Garcia's easy presence. "It's gotta be bad." Garcia was working; Crosby could work. Right, relax—just enough to get into the swing of things, to do what his team always did.

"She ran the family business," Gail said, glancing up.

"Same business Stoya inherited," Swan added. "She was apparently very good at it." He met everybody's eyes. "According to the data available to the FBI, Stoya probably saw his first murder at age ten."

The room recoiled. "That's fucked up," Carlyle said, and there was an exhalation of agreement.

"So what's that got to do with anything?" McEnany asked, apparently drawn into the puzzle more than he was upset at the players.

"It means we know where he's going," Harding said crisply. "I know the political sitch is bad in Moscow, but our Stoya's going to want to bring his son into the fold. He's taking the plane that will take him home. Where's that one departing from?"

"La Guardia's private jet field," Gail said, tapping. Manny pulled something up on his computer and showed her. She nodded and *hmm*ed. "Chief, it looks like Grandma Gargoyle had two properties. Prague is still in the running."

"Good work, Swan," Harding said, correctly interpreting the source. He paused. "Why didn't you bring that to me yourself?"

Manny gave McEnany a side-eyed glance. The IA officer had moved into Swan and Gail's space as they worked, uncomfortably so, and Crosby fought the sudden urge to grab him by the scruff of the neck and throw him from the room.

"I can smell his breath, sir," Swan said darkly. "Two words. Tic Tacs."

Crosby hid his snicker behind his hand, and to everybody's relief, Harding grinned.

"McAsshole? Get out of their laps. They're fucking working."

McEnany backed up hurriedly, ruddy face flushing more. "I was just checking their work," he blustered, and Harding rolled his eyes.

"As if you could," he said, raking McEnany with a razored gaze. "So we've got two potentials. Where's the one to Prague departing from?"

"Teterboro," Swan said.

Harding groaned.

"What?" McEnany said, sounding legitimately invested. "They're, like, twenty minutes apart!"

"On a *map*," Chadwick muttered, voice dripping disdain. "You're not from here, are you?"

"How long does it really take?" McEnany asked, glancing around humbly.

"This time of day?" Carlyle estimated. "Forty-five minutes if we all go lights and sirens."

"We'll have to split up," Harding muttered, and before he could slice and dice the group, Crosby had an idea.

"Wait a minute," he said. "I know we're in a rush, but has anybody talked to the mistress? She wants her boy back, right?"

Harding nodded. "Yeah—yeah, she does."

"Where's she live?" Crosby pursued.

"Right outside Teterboro," Swan said. "What're you thinking?"

"That we secure a helicopter," Crosby said. "One unit drives to visit Tatya and pick her brain, and everyone else goes to La Guarda, with a helo on standby there. If it's in Teterboro, we've got a unit close by and everyone else hops the helo. If it's in LaGuardia, most of the force is there and it's worth losing an extra car 'cause we can have backup from the copter. What do you think?"

"I think you're a genius," Harding muttered. "Suit up! Denison and I will take Tatya. Everyone else to La Guardia, stat. Helo's on its way."

"Wait!" McEnany protested. "What about my interview with Crosby?"

"Get in the back," Garcia said, and Crosby noted he had an evil, evil smile on his face. "Crosby ain't killed us yet."

Son of the Blood

"YOU DID that on purpose," Garcia muttered as they practically flew out of the SUV after Crosby screeched to a halt on the tarmac reserved for private jets in La Guardia. They left McEnany behind, still retching into the plastic bag Garcia had given him after Crosby had tried his patented "Let's vibrate through the traffic in front of us" driving method.

It had apparently worked—they'd beaten Gail and Manny *and* Carlyle and Chadwick and were currently making their way toward the clearly marked helo while waiting for Denison to conduct her quiet, painful interview with the boy's mother.

Denison had kept comms on as she'd talked, and Garcia and Crosby could still hear the woman's hesitant voice under the screaming wind of the airstrip.

"I'm sorry, no. I do not know. I thought he hate Prague, because his grandmama—she was not kind. But you say he wants to go there. But Russia, it holds no healing for him. Not yet. Not yet."

"Well," Natalia asked patiently, "what sort of healing does he need?"

"Don't you see?" Tatya asked plaintively. "He needs a happy childhood, and he needs it to see the man he's become." She sniffled. "He's... for all the things he does are illegal, he is very kind."

"He stole your child!" Natalia snapped, and at first Garcia had grimaced, thinking that she made so few missteps, it surprised him this was one.

But then Tatya had answered, and Garcia's respect for Natalia went up a notch, and he hadn't thought that was possible.

"He did! But he give me option! He tells me he can take our baby to Moscow and I never see him again, or I can step aside, give boy his blanket, his stuffed animal, and they will go to Prague, and I can visit."

Carlyle, Chadwick, Gail, and Swan all screeched to a halt near the helicopter and stared at Crosby.

"Folks," he said, looking stunned that his gambit had paid off. "We're in the wrong goddamned airport."

They'd loaded onto the helo and taken off before Garcia remembered they'd left McEnany puking in the back of the department-issue SUV.

"Goddammit," Garcia muttered directly into Crosby's ear. "We were gonna get your stuff!"

"What?" Gail yelled from Garcia's other side. "You finally moving him into your spare room?"

Crosby groaned comically above the propeller noise. "I don't believe this!"

"We can't!" Garcia yelled back. "The IA asshole is throwing up in the SUV!"

"No worries," Carlyle yelled from across the bench. "Chadwick drove in today. We'll help you move."

Garcia grinned, and Chadwick nodded enthusiastically. Apparently operation Move Crosby was a go whether or not their department issue was going to be ready to drive.

THE OP TO get the boy away from Stoya went cleaner than any of them expected. It made Garcia a little sad, in fact, because the big man, the mobster, responsible for people bankrupted, lives ruined, people killed, had taken one look at the agents, armed and ready to take out his entire entourage, and had held up his hands.

"Guns down," he said with authority, and then he'd dropped his voice and met Harding's eyes. "May I hug my son before you take me away?"

He'd sounded so damned sad, as though every life choice he'd made to lead to this moment had betrayed him in the worst way.

He'd held his son then, for a long time, murmuring in his ear, and the boy backed away with a watery smile, kissing Stoya on the cheek. "Yes, Papa. We will visit another time."

And then he'd walked down the ramp from the plane to his mother, whom Denison and Harding had brought after that seat-of-the-pants interview.

In the aftermath, Harding ordered Crosby and Garcia into the back of his and Denison's department issue while the FBI took away the suspects, and had the helicopter drop everyone else off on the top of their building in Manhattan.

"Hey, Chief," Garcia began as they clambered in, and Harding snorted.

"I've already got the route planned, Garcia. There's a Shake Shack on the way back."

"Yes!" Garcia pumped his fist, but that was mostly for effect. Crosby's expression—which had become animated and kind when dealing with Stoya's young son—had slammed down as closed as a steel door once the op had cleared. Garcia knew that their treatment of McEnany that morning would not go unanswered, although leaving him barfing in the back of the government-issue shop would do a lot to keep him from opening his mouth, because that rumor would not help him in *any* department, but he was starting to get worried.

Garcia had gotten so close to getting Crosby to hope, maybe even to plan for the two of them, but McEnany.... God, that was a bad break.

"You both belted?" Harding asked, and they hummed assent from the back.

Crosby broke the silence by saying, "Good job, Tal, getting the mistress to talk. That was pretty prime."

Natalia shrugged, and Garcia—who was behind Harding—could see her modest smile in profile, her pretty silver goddess pendant glinting in the sun through the window. "Good plan," she said. "Don't let anybody tell you you're not good at strategy. That was good thinking."

"Thanks," he responded, and Garcia glanced at him.

He couldn't even look pleased, he was so worried.

"Crosby," Harding said softly, "we're not going to let him take you."

Crosby's body gave a giant involuntary shudder, and Garcia—who had never wanted a long-term relationship, never wanted visibility, had not given a *damn* about LGBTQ rights at the workplace—suddenly wanted the right to hold him. God, look at him, the big dumb Irishman. Just holding all that fear inside.

"It's good of you to say so, Chief," Crosby said, sounding shell-shocked. "But you may not have a choice. I mean—" He swallowed, and his gaze flickered to Garcia with the tiniest of smiles. "—as *rewarding* as it was to make the guy throw up in the back of our government issue—"

Harding and Denison guffawed.

"Seriously?" Denison asked, holding her hand delicately in front of her mouth like a debutante at tea.

"It was epic," Garcia said, nodding like a bobblehead. "Crosby was at his best today. I mean, I don't think McEnany has ever seen traffic like we got in Queens, but our shop swapped numbers with a couple of cars and maybe got a delivery truck pregnant."

Denison dropped the hand into her lap and threw her head back and laughed, as did Harding.

"Oh, Crosby," she said when she could talk again. "Do you really think we'd let you go?"

"Garcia's the one with the good lines," Crosby told her, and the look he sent Garcia was so full of gratitude Garcia thought he might actually melt into a puddle. Right there. In front of the two best AICs he'd ever had.

"But you're the one with doubts," Harding said astutely. "What's troubling you, son?"

Crosby's cheek ticked, and he let out a breath. "The fact that he's here. We never got a chance to ask him why he'd come when you were right. You were the one who ordered the shoot, and the shoot was good. Everything I know about chain of command says they should have sent *your* festering asshole and not mine. McEnany was *waiting* for a chance to crawl up my ass, and I'm not going to rest easy until I know what he's got planned."

Harding let out a long noisy breath. "That's fair," he said, and Denison sobered instantly. "That's fair," he repeated, "and you're right. Look, you two were supposed to spend the day doing paperwork. I say we get back to the office, you check out *a new* shop, and then you move into Garcia's house while I make sure that's the address on all your paperwork. That way if anybody shows up to interview your roommate...."

"He shows up at my place," Garcia said. "Not the Magic Mystery Tour—we hear you."

"Fair enough," Harding said. "In fact, I may have to make you two have your little moving party without me and Tal. The others can help you, but we'll do your paperwork, and after that we all may be doing some investigating of our own."

Denison nodded. "McEnany's bad shoot should *not* have gotten him promoted this far up the food chain. He had to have help, and that help might have it in for you. We need to look."

Harding made an affirming sound. "Chadwick worked in the FBI as an analyst for a while before I tapped him as a field agent. He might know the ways and means that asshole became everybody's asshole."

"What if we can't make him go away, sir?" Crosby asked, and Garcia could tell the question came from the depth of his fear.

Aw, Crosby. C'mon. Trust us, buddy. Trust us.

"We find out what's driving him," Harding said without compromise in his voice. "And we make *that* go away. But first, he's got to interview you in front of me, and he can't do that until tomorrow. If our luck holds and we can go without calls for two more fucking days, we might be able to get a jump on him or whoever he's working for. So I repeat, Crosby—"

"Don't lose hope," Denison said softly. "I know you're thinking this is the best team you've ever worked with and you don't want to lose that. Well, you need to know, this is the best team *any* of us has worked with, and *nobody* wants to lose that."

Crosby swallowed. "Thanks, ma'am," he said, the humility in his voice hitting Garcia right in the feels. "It would be a shame if I ended up someplace they didn't give me coffee mugs to remind me of my fuckups."

Everybody in the car laughed softly, and Denison and Harding went on to list avenues of investigation they could take. They ended up picking Crosby's brains for names and connections *he* might know about, and Garcia listened to this part avidly. Crosby had given him that bare bones explanation on the first day they'd met, and after that most of Garcia's knowledge had been in breadcrumbs, most of those Crosby's skittish behavior regarding friends, colleagues, or anything, really, reminiscent of the day he'd lost everything by standing up to do the right thing.

And now, listening to him talk, Garcia was struck by something that surprised him.

"You're hiding something," he said, and the look of anguish Crosby shot him was enough to make him almost regret that he'd said anything.

Almost.

"I noticed that too," Denison said. "Something about the way everybody in your precinct reacted—it was almost choreographed. You were told to do the right thing, and you did, and your story has always been you thought that's what they meant. To tell the truth. But the minute you told the truth, the death threats started flooding in. I mean, Harding was called *the day* you were deposed. What gives?"

Crosby grunted and threw a glance at Harding through the rearview. Harding was busy negotiating traffic around the Shake Shack, but he nodded.

"Say it now, Crosby, before we're out in the open and anybody can hear you."

Crosby grunted. "I hope your department issue's clean," he said apologetically, meaning bugs, Garcia presumed, and then he spoke. "You all ever hear of the Sons of the Blood?"

Garcia's veins iced over. "That racist cop group that everybody's saying doesn't exist but you always have the feeling it does?"

Crosby grunted. "It does. It's… it's almost like the Elks, right? But guys tell their wives it's poker night, and the wives all get together and decide that any cop who's not invited to 'poker night,' well, that cop's wife doesn't get invited to dinners and lunches and stuff. It's… it's generally a bunch of old farts sitting around a table and telling each other stories of the good old days, when they could just round people up and hold them indefinitely and nobody could say boo to a mouse."

Garcia tried not to shake all over. "That… that was how they—"

Crosby looked him in the eyes. "That was how they kept people of color in line," Crosby said grimly. "I know that. And the reason I know that is because my father was one of the Sons of the Blood, and McEnany was his trainee." He grunted. "A thing I did not know until McEnany invited me to 'poker night' three days before he shot a kid in the back."

Garcia sucked in a breath, trying not to gag. "Did you know?" he asked, trying to trammel up the betrayal until he knew if it was a thing.

"*No!*" Crosby barked, his voice ringing with authority and hurt and *conviction*, some goddamned *conviction* for the first time that day. "I went to that poker game, and finally, *finally* what those assholes were saying about 'the right people' and 'guys like us'—it *finally* fucking sank in. I finally got it. Every time I'd said, 'I didn't *see* that guy do something, but if you *say* so,' I hadn't been a clueless rookie. I'd been a fucking racist enabler. And I was sick realizing that. I wanted to rip off my own skin. And just about the time I wanted to run and hide and quit the force and never see any of those laughing bozos again, it really hit me."

Garcia was so relieved—so goddamned relieved—that he almost hadn't seen this coming.

"What?"

Crosby shook his head, devastated. "Ohmygod. My *father* was part of these guys. My dad. The guy I joined the force to be like. He was a fucking racist asshole. He was all that was wrong with the force, and with my city, and with my fucking country." His voice was shaking. "I…. God. I remember that night. We'd been drinking scotch, and everybody was smoking cigars, which were fucking foul, and suddenly… like the light of goddamned God from above. I ran outside and puked, like McEnany did in our SUV. They gave me shit about it all the next day and told me I'd learn—I'd *learn*, you hear—how to drink like a fish, how to pull over random Black people to make my conviction rate better. And… and that thing I did, with Brandeis, that thing that took me months to do because nobody was listening and kids were fucking *dying*—that thing, that was a *mistake* I'd made. I'd *fucked up*, because who cared about those kids anyway, and I should've known better not to show up the guys who'd been there longer."

His voice was fracturing, getting close to breaking, and Garcia snuck his hand behind him, palming the small of his back behind the seat, not sure if Denison and Harding could see him but almost not caring.

"That really sucks," Garcia whispered. "What did you do?"

Crosby laughed, and it was an ugly sound. "I told McEnany the next day that I'd really rather not play poker anymore. He said, yeah, sure, as long as I remembered to do the right thing. And two days later, we were pursuing a suspect—a sixteen-year-old kid who had been trying to get into his buddy's house to get his backpack, as it turned out—and McEnany pulled out his gun and looked me in the face as we were running."

"Did he say anything?" Garcia asked, horrified.

"Yeah," Crosby said bitterly. "He said, 'You damned well better show up at poker.' And then he fired."

Harding pulled up alongside the Shake Shack and killed the engine, and Garcia tried to control his breathing.

"Oh God," he said, the words coming out through a dry throat. "This is bad."

Crosby pulled in a shuddering breath. "And then they all told me to 'do the right thing'—and I had to. I had to do the *real* right thing, 'cause I couldn't be a part of that. I… I didn't think I'd make it home."

It took Garcia a heartbeat to realize what he meant by that. That he'd fully expected McEnany or his stupid secret man group to *kill him* on the trip between his precinct and his house.

In the sudden silence of the vehicle, they could all hear Harding swallow. "The FBI had—*had* mind you—a mole in with your precinct," he said softly. "That's how I knew to tap you that day, and to get your parents the hell out of there. I… I thought I'd give you a shot at the SCTF and maybe place you with NYPD later. I just thought that that kind of courage—it shouldn't be repaid with a bullet in the back. But you were so good, kid. I mean… *everything* about you was so good. The way you got on with the team. The way you treated the wits *and* the perps. Every day of the last two years, I thought, 'Wow, that was some lucky break that landed that kid in my lap.'"

Crosby took in a ragged breath, and Garcia heard the tears he wouldn't shed. "Thank you, sir," he choked.

"No." Harding turned around in his seat. "Thank *you*. For not once making me question that decision. And I don't question it now. You were right to tell the whole story. And I know it had to be hard—"

"My father, sir," Crosby whispered. "*My father.*"

Harding closed his eyes and nodded. "Which is why New Mexico is making so much sense right now," he said, a dry smile twitching at his lean lips. "I was thinking you'd send them to Florida, but you really didn't want them close enough to visit, did you?"

"Christ no," Crosby said with feeling. "I can't even explain to them what they did wrong."

"But *you* know," Harding murmured. "And you've worked your damnedest to make it right. I think everybody in this car respects that."

Denison nodded soberly, and Garcia did too. What he wanted to do was hold Crosby in his arms until all that shame shuddered itself out into the wide open and only that goodness Harding had seen remained, but he couldn't.

"I think everybody on the team will too," Harding said softly, and Garcia wanted to cry at the betrayal on Crosby's face.

"Sir?" he asked, agonized.

"We have to tell them," Harding told him. "Because it's part of the reason McEnany is here. It's part of the reason he's going after you now and trying to break up our team. I know…." His voice dropped. "I *know* why you'd want to hold this close to the vest, Crosby. But I hope you'll trust me that this is the right call."

"Sir?" Crosby asked again, and this time, it was Denison's hand on his knee.

"Trust us," she said softly. "All those things you're afraid of being? We know you're not. You have proven to us, every day, that you are not McEnany, and you're not your father. I've trusted you to have my back for two years, Crosby. I've never regretted that."

"It's been a privilege," Crosby whispered, and he dashed his eyes with the back of his hand.

"Let us take care of you," Harding said softly.

His only answer was the shudder of Crosby's breath, and Garcia spoke up. "Could you guys maybe go get me some food? All the meat and a giant shake for me. This guy wants a chicken sandwich 'cause he's nuts."

Crosby gave him a weak smile. "And a diet soda."

Denison barked out a laugh. "I'm gonna go in and fuck up that order," she pronounced. "Do you want me to fuck it up chocolate, or fuck it up strawberry?"

"Both," Garcia said, because he'd been there on the few days Crosby had broken. "And a truly disgusting amount of pickles on that burger."

Denison grinned at him. "That's a good partner right there. Don't lose him, Crosby, you hear?"

And with that, she and Harding shut their doors, leaving Crosby and Garcia in the sudden silence.

Garcia moved his hand from the small of Crosby's back to take Crosby's hand as it sat on his thigh. He half expected Crosby to draw away, because their bosses were *right there*, beyond the tinted glass, but Crosby laced their fingers together and squeezed.

"I'm sorry," Crosby whispered.

"Baby, as far as I'm concerned, you ain't told no lies. You didn't talk about the Sons of the Blood or whatever 'cause that involved your dad, am I right?"

"I'm so ashamed," he confessed, leaning his head forward against the seat. "I felt so stupid. I mean… who doesn't know that the people around them are racist shitbags?"

Garcia leaned his head against Crosby's broad shoulder. "A person who doesn't think that way and doesn't understand that others do," he said softly. "You got a helluva education, and you got it quick, papi. But as far as I can tell, you learned all the good stuff, am I right?"

Crosby turned red-rimmed, shiny eyes toward him, and his mouth twisted crookedly. "You're good," he rasped. "You're one of the good things."

Garcia felt a flutter in his chest, just as real as the first one he'd felt six months ago, walking into the conference room and seeing Crosby's gray-blue eyes. But this flutter was bigger. Stronger. This flutter would knock him on his ass if he wasn't careful.

And he hadn't been careful.

"That's what I needed to hear," he said, squeezing Crosby's hand. With a quick look in either direction, he brought that wide-palmed, big-knuckled hand to his lips and kissed it softly. "You and me, we've got some being together to do. Tell me you still want that."

Crosby's sigh practically floated out of him. "So bad. You got no idea."

"Then let's get you moved into my place. And *not* in the guest room, although we can put your clothes there so everybody can play stupid, okay?"

Crosby let out a crumbly sort of laugh. "What makes you think they'll have to play?"

"Aw, baby. 'Cause anybody can see I'm gone over you. But we'll pretend as long as you need to, okay?"

Crosby's full mouth parted in protest, but Garcia shook his head. "Don't argue. Don't say anything. You, son, have had something of a *day*, as they say. Let's go get your stuff and pretend that's all we have to worry about. Tomorrow will come, and it'll be hard, but tonight we get to play house. You good with that?"

Crosby nodded and sat up a little straighter. "Man, you haven't even heard me snore yet. I say this lasts about a minute and a half."

Garcia snorted. "Oh, you wish. I've already got plans for earplugs. Your snoring is as epic as your driving."

Crosby looked around them furtively, and Garcia hated that he had to do that, but a moment later, Garcia felt Crosby's breath against his temple and the whisper of a kiss.

"I thought," Crosby murmured, "that if we hooked up, it would all go away. We'd go back to being partners. We'd be fine."

"No?" Garcia felt naked when he turned his head to meet Crosby's eyes.

"I thought I was scared yesterday, when I had to take that shot and you were right there. Man, I'm sweating so hard right now. I had to tell you that fucking story, and… and what if you didn't look at me the same?"

Garcia squeezed his eyes shut. "Nope," he whispered. "All that wanting—it's still there."

"Thank God," Crosby murmured. They heard voices outside the SUV, and they both straightened up, Garcia shifting so he wasn't practically in Crosby's lap, seat belt or no.

HARDING AND Denison very quietly put the rest of the squad in charge of moving Crosby out of Toby's loft while they did paperwork and tried to get to the root of the IA problem. Before everybody disbursed, Harding got in one quick admonition.

"Look, everybody," he said softly, all of them eyeballing the elevator like they expected McEnany to materialize. "This guy has it in for Crosby, and he'll tell you a little more about that tonight. Before he does, though, here." He nodded to Denison, who came by with some tiny devices the size of a key fob that she distributed. "This is a portable scrambler. If any place you go is bugged, this will scramble the signal ninety-five percent of the time. I do not like this guy moving in on my people. I have *tapped* the IA division of the FBI and NSA, both of whom hold jurisdiction for special procedures over us, and *nobody* knows where his authorization came from. As far as I'm concerned, he heard about the shoot and weaseled his way into my office, and he wants Crosby's ass for a reason all his own. I know we were supposed to run one team in the office tomorrow unless a call came, but I'd like Swan and Pearson to work with Denison and me to research while Chadwick and Carlyle answer any calls."

"What're we doing?" Garcia asked, feeling generous. He and Crosby were supposed to be off the next day, barring any big cases.

"You're off," Harding said with a snort. "I assume that's why you picked tonight to move? Tomorrow you guys can fight over where to put the furniture, right?"

Garcia simply nodded, but inside he was doing backflips.

A day. Maybe they'd spend it in bed; maybe they'd spend it picking out curtains. He didn't really care. He wanted to spend it with Crosby and maybe make the man feel at home.

Fly by Night

TOBY TRIED not to look hurt when most of Crosby's department showed up to move him crosstown.

"Man, I know it wasn't a picnic for you," Toby confessed while helping Crosby throw all his clothes into trash bags, the better to stow over the gun safe in the back of the department issue. "But I really enjoyed having you here."

Crosby grinned at his roommate, remembering the times Toby had gone to hide in Crosby's room when his own party had gotten too big for the once shy honors student.

"You're gonna have to learn to kick people out now," he said. "I mean, I'll come over to do it for ya, but I'm sayin', you can't use me as a shield anymore."

Toby hid his face in his shoulder. "Man, you could see right through me!" He gave a furtive look behind him, into the main part of the apartment, where even now there were three or four people crashing on his couch or curled up on the floor watching his big screen. "Could you maybe kick everybody out *now*? I mean, you'll be gone, I'll be here alone. The thought's giving me a boner!"

Crosby laughed softly and dodged out of the way as Garcia swooped in. "Oh good," Garcia told him, looking at the garbage bags. "More jeans and shit to go under the leather jacket. I'm all aflutter with your wardrobe choices."

"The leather jacket makes it all look good," Crosby said with dignity, and Toby laughed softly and tugged Crosby even further out of the activity.

"Leave the bed!" Garcia told Gideon Chadwick and Joey Carlyle. "I know it's new, but I've got a decent one in my spare room!"

Yeah, Crosby wasn't touching that with a barge pole. Instead he let Toby bring him into his own room, which was surprisingly neat, a wooden queen-sized pedestal in one corner, a small conversation pit by the window, and an en suite bathroom.

"Hey," Toby said softly. "Judson?"

"Yeah?"

"Look, I know this isn't something you want people to know about, but I was there, in college, remember?"

Crosby's face flamed. Yeah. Toby had been away with his parents when Crosby had his first one-nighter with a guy—a cheerleader, actually, athletic as hell and out and proud, and willing to walk Crosby through his embarrassment and keep Crosby's little bisexual secret. Stevie had been leaving their dorm room, obviously debauched and proud of it, when Toby had gotten back and seen him.

He'd taken one look at Crosby, still climbing out of bed and looking *very* satisfied but also terrified, and said, "What happens in the dorm room *stays* in the dorm room," and that's the way things had stayed.

"Yeah," Crosby muttered, knowing where this was going and not sure how to stop it.

"Just…." Toby looked around, his ugly/cute countenance contorted with worry. "Be careful, man. This guy—I remember him visiting when you were laid up. He seems like a good guy. I'll have faith that he's a good guy. But I know what you're up against. Be careful." He gave a flutter of a smile. "The last two years, like I said, I know it was rough on you, and my place was a complete and utter circus, but you've always been there for me, man. I hope I was able to be there for you, just a little."

Like that, two years of Toby sneaking into his room to talk, of Toby confiding his dreams and his hopes for his career, for someday finding a girlfriend who was all about being real and not about Toby's success, for someday moving out of the city to a suburb, coming in on the weekends to perform—all of that, as well as watching movies and eating takeout, often in Crosby's room while the party raged outside.

"You were the best," Crosby said, meaning it. "Man, I showed up here, and I had no place to land. None. You were here, and I had a friend and a place to keep the rain off. It meant the world." He grimaced. "Like you said, not optimal for my profession but, you know. You really are the greatest guy in the world."

Toby grinned at him, his eyes a little shiny, and Crosby engulfed him in a tight hug, remembering how strange this city had been after leaving his little cop-centric suburb in Chicago, where he'd lived with his parents. Toby had taken him on "field trips," introducing him to the subway system, to the good places to eat, to the good bars for drinks, the ones for music, the ones for hookups. Crosby could admit it now that he was leaving: One of the things that had taken him so long to go was that Toby, for all the hectic noise of his apartment, had himself been a bastion of kindness against a scary new sitch.

The hug ended before it could get awkward, and Crosby went back into his bedroom, grimacing at the new bed and remembering that Garcia wasn't kidding. He really did have a good one in the guest room.

"Hey, Garcia," he protested, going to the closet. "I've got some nice sheets and a comforter and shit!"

"Fine," Garcia muttered. "Would it kill you to buy a color? I mean, navy blue alone doesn't count."

"What about navy blue and brown striped," Crosby retorted sourly, holding up the sheets.

"That sort of attitude will get you a floral print," Garcia replied smartly, and Manny Swan, who was helping Carlyle carry out Crosby's supremely comfortable and built for someone "big and tall" stuffed chair, grunted in affirmation.

"Concede now," he said. "People who like color always win."

Crosby laughed softly and booty-bumped Gideon out of the way so he could take the other side of the chair.

"He was the one having trouble!" Gideon complained, his long, thin frame unfolding as Crosby took the weight.

"He was having trouble because he was carrying all of it," Garcia said dryly. "Look at those shoulders. Think he doesn't know how to carry a chair?"

"What about my shoulders?" Manny asked, but they were disappearing out the front door and toward the freight elevator, so Crosby didn't hear Garcia's reply.

He did hear Manny's chuckle, though, as they waited for the freight elevator.

"What?" Crosby asked.

"You're going to find yourself wearing orange shirts and turquoise slacks," he said. "And I'm here for that shit. Gail and I will bring popcorn. We'll all watch you guys come in arguing and sing the theme from *The Odd Couple.* It'll be great."

Crosby had no comeback to that. He chuckled, and the elevator got there, and they had other things to do, but inside he was starting to adjust to the idea, the hope, of him and Garcia in the same house. In the same bed. Nobody would have to know. The things that happened to couples—

quibbling, spending time together, knowing the same jokes—that had happened already. They were partners. They were already a couple.

And he wasn't moving to prison. Garcia wouldn't mind if he made the guest room his—stacked some of his books, used his bedding, used the weight equipment when he was restless. And if this—this thing between them—faded, the other stuff—the banter, the chatter, the trusting the other to have his back—that would stay, wouldn't it?

Toby was a good friend, would always be a good friend, but suddenly the idea of having somebody there who got him, got the job, got the pressure, and could hold him through the shakes after a day like the one before seemed like something so good, so perfect, he should have been dreaming about it all along.

But first, he thought, as he and Garcia piled behind Manny and Gail, letting the other car hold the big stuff, he had to tell his team what had really gone down before he'd been forced to leave Chicago.

They moved shit in, and Calix was on the horn to get pizza and beer delivered before every item was pulled out of the vehicles. By the time they'd set everything down, more or less in an appropriate place, the food had arrived, and they made a rough circle around Calix's coffee table, some people on the floor, some of them on the furniture, and Crosby settling in happily to his big-and-tall chair.

And it was sort of amazing how everything fit.

After two of the pies disappeared and everybody was down to the last two, the serious eating tapered off and glances more and more drifted to Crosby.

Garcia was sitting on the floor at his feet, and he bumped Crosby's knee with his shoulder and gave him a neutral glance.

Crosby nodded.

It was time.

"So," he said on a big exhalation, setting his paper plate down on the nice pine coffee table. "I know that when you all started, you read everybody's jacket, and when you read mine, you saw a couple of things. One was the Brandeis case, and the other was the shooting in Chicago."

All his friends—his entire team, save Harding and Denison—all stared back at him, except Calix Garcia, who knew this story and was still there.

In the end, that was what gave him the courage to go on.

"The jacket told the truth," he said and then sighed. "But not the whole truth. And now that McEnany is here and you guys are all signed on to help me stay out of IA clutches, you need to know the whole truth. If I take a round to the back of the head in the next week, I want you all to know why—ouch!"

Calix glared at him from where he'd elbowed Crosby in the thigh. "Jesus, think of another way to put it," he muttered, and Crosby resisted the urge to rub his knuckles along Garcia's cheek to calm him down. Instead, he ruffled his hair, buddy style, and told his story.

It had helped, that terrible moment in the car with Harding and Denison and then the quiet moment of absolution with Calix. He was still girded for the worst, but hopeful... so hopeful... that these people here, whom he'd trusted with his life and who had trusted him in turn, wouldn't turn their backs.

When he was done, Manny was the one who let out a low whistle. "Man, that's fucked up."

"Fucking twisted," Joey said, the low light from Garcia's lamps throwing his cheekbones in stark relief, reminding all of them that he'd grown up on a Native reservation in upstate and had seen his own share of racism firsthand.

Gideon blew out a breath. "Yeah, fucking white people, man. I mean, I've got the rich white people in my family, and they're not as blatant as the blue-collar racists, but boy, do they know how to exclude someone who 'doesn't quite fit in.' This is like a nasty mix of both brands of awful, you know?"

Crosby nodded. "It was bad enough," he said softly, "but the thing to remember is that the guy who dared me not to report a murder is the guy who's trying to put me away for the shoot yesterday. He showed up here with the assumption that Harding would simply hand me over, but even though that's not happening, we think he wants me for a reason."

There was a general nod. "And we should be figuring out what that reason is," Gail said. She gave Crosby an astute glance. "We love you, Judson, but this is even bigger than our love for you."

Crosby laughed, as she'd no doubt intended him to. "I know it," he agreed. "This Sons of the Blood thing—it goes bigger than just my precinct or the department. If it's up here in the alphabets, or even in New York, we need to find it, and we need to kill it dead. Look at the firepower, the technology, the toys we've got. Nobody should have all that at their disposal if they're hunting people down out of sheer prejudice. I mean, the prejudice is awful...." He shuddered, remembering making the shot the day before, and for a moment… for a moment he had a strobing impression of the perpetrator's head shattering before the body hit the ground. "So awful," he whispered. "But higher up—that's gotta be the first place we kill it."

There was a general assent, and then Joey spoke up.

"I get why you didn't tell us," he said. "There's a stink on that shit. My buddies at school didn't know my mother was Delaware. You just sit there through the dumb jokes and the Pocahontas bullshit and the 'I'm gonna make that girl my squaw' bullshit because your dad's Irish Protestant, and that protects you. Keeps you safe. Lets you not fight so damned hard every day. And whether they're degrading you or people you think are okay, sometimes it goes right over your head because you're not ready for it. We're not raised to listen for hatred. We don't always recognize it because, you know. When you're a kid, you think your dad is the best person in the world. You have to see him from other people's eyes to know he's not."

Crosby nodded. "But then you see it," he said. "And you can't unsee it. And you hate yourself for being so blind."

"That's dumb," Manny said. "That's like actually *being* blind and hating yourself for not knowing what the color blue looks like. Even if *boom*, you can magically see, you still have to learn the difference between red and blue and yellow, and then you have to decide which one you want to paint your walls with, and then you have to accept that someone you love might want to paint your walls a totally different color."

There was a silence—almost puzzled but mostly thoughtful—and then Garcia, oh God bless him with the quip or the retort or the one-liner, said, "Is this a nice way of telling me I should let him keep the chair in the living room?"

There was general laughter, and Crosby followed it up with, "I'm not giving up this chair. Your scrawny ass fits in anything. I got this chair and the department issue, and that's about it."

More laughter, and Garcia stood to collect trash. The rest of the team rose to help him clean up, and it was time to break up the party.

Gail was the last to leave, and she stood on tiptoe and kissed Crosby on the cheek before she followed Swan out the door. "Judson?" she said softly.

"Yeah?"

"I'm… I'm glad you found a place. You know. Where you can sleep." Her eyes kept darting to the guest room, and he had a cold feeling at the base of his spine.

"Uh, Elsa?"

She blew out a breath through her nose. "Olaf, if you want people to think you're staying in the guest room, you need to keep Garcia from bitching about your choice in sheets, okay? I'm not sure if anyone else caught it, but me and Swan—"

"Oh God," he said, his stomach a ball of icy hell.

"Yeah, well, Chadwick and Carlyle don't care either. I'm just saying, McEnany might." She gave him a sudden, fierce hug. "But anyone who's been working with you—and isn't phobic and blind—has seen it brewing for months. Swan made you the day he got recruited and realized you were hurt. I was like, 'He's in the hospital,' and Swan said, 'His boyfriend is probably losing his shit.' I was like, 'Hey, they just met,' and he was like, 'My bad.' But he saw it. I saw it. I'm glad you're in this place now, but... but don't lie and say it's to protect Toby, okay? Garcia deserves better."

Crosby wanted to argue. Hell, he wanted to tell her the whole story and explain they really *were* new, but now was not the time.

"He does" is what he said instead, because it was true. "I won't do him dirty."

She smiled a little and nodded. "Take care. See you day after tomorrow, 'kay?"

"Yeah, Elsa. Thanks for having my six."

"Always." And with that, Gail waved gaily at Garcia, calling loudly, "Gotta go. Swan's gonna leave without me, and I don't want to take the train from Queens!"

"Later!" Garcia called, in the middle of shoving the trash down so he could take the bag out to the can on the side of the building. "Hold the door for me," he told Crosby, easy as breathing, as he left. The rapid patter of his feet could be heard down the walkway, and Crosby leaned against the door idly, watching as Gail hopped into the SUV Manny had pulled around the curb. He wondered if all of them would be couples, Chadwick and Carlyle, Swan and Pearson. The thought broke off with Harding and Denison because Natalia had a wife, and as far as he knew, Harding had no life.

No. Maybe just him and Garcia. Or maybe that's all he needed to know about for now.

Garcia walked up the steps, and Crosby backed up to let him go by and lock up. As Garcia walked through the house, he turned off the lights—the living room, the kitchen, the hall—and Crosby followed him through the house, getting a feel for the place, listening for the noises, wondering what it was like to live in a tiny house in the middle of the city. Then Garcia passed the guest room and turned to him as he switched on the light in his own room.

His dark eyes glinted slightly, and Crosby was remembering that hit, that kick to his stomach he'd felt the first time Garcia had walked into the conference room. He was remembering the way he'd longed to crush Garcia's mouth to his for months and the raw noises he made when Crosby had been deep inside his body and how there'd been nothing in those moments of their jobs or law enforcement or pretend.

"Whatya thinking, Cowboy?" Garcia murmured as Crosby drew near.

That was easy. "Thinking I want you," he said softly, bending his head to breathe in Garcia's ear. With one hand he tilted Garcia's head so he could kiss along his neck, while with the other, he switched off the light Garcia had just switched on.

"Yeah?"

Crosby ran his lips down from earlobe to shoulder, flickering his tongue along Garcia's skin as he went. "Yeah."

Garcia shuddered against him. "Anything else?"

"Thinking we're not fooling anybody with this guest room bullshit," he said, thrusting his hands up under Garcia's T-shirt and hoodie. Garcia lifted his arms above his head and let Crosby pull the shirts off, and Crosby grew a little giddy with the thought of his naked body, the smoothness of his shoulders, the little bit of hair on his chest, the puckers of his nipples, all there for the taking.

Feeling decadent, he lowered his mouth to a brown nipple and welcomed Garcia's fingers tightening in his hair. But not to stop him.

To urge him on.

"Only person you were fooling," Garcia gasped, "was yourself."

Crosby pulled hard at his nipple, and when those fingers tightened in his hair, he moved to the other one. He only teased this one, tickling with his tongue, until Garcia whimpered and bucked against him.

"I don't know," Crosby whispered, still teasing. "You seem to want me. Guess I fooled you too."

"Augh!" With a groan of frustration, Garcia yanked Crosby up by the hair and lunged into a hungry, almost violent kiss.

Crosby returned it, shoving at Garcia's jeans, his stomach shaking in relief as the button gave and they slid down Garcia's thighs.

Garcia pulled away long enough to hiss, "Whatcha doin'?" before Crosby put his foot in the crotch of the pants and briefs, wrapped his arms around Garcia's waist, and lifted him out of his clothes, leaving him naked and clinging to Crosby's shoulders as Crosby practically threw him on the bed.

Oh wow. He was naked. He was naked, and Crosby wanted to take his time.

Garcia must have seen something in his face, something a little frightening or a little awe-inspiring. "Cowboy?" he asked tentatively.

Crosby fell to his knees in front of the bed and pulled Garcia's legs toward him. He raised up a little between them, and there was Garcia's cock, hard and dripping, waiting for his attention.

"Do you think I didn't want to taste your come too?" he rasped, remembering their conversation that morning—was it just that morning?

Garcia let out a low moan and propped his heels on the bed, opening himself up for Crosby's use.

Crosby planned to use.

But first, he had to taste. He'd been going to tease, but his own clothes were binding him, chafing him, torturing him with reminders of how badly he needed to be touched. He struck, pulling Garcia's cock into his mouth and down his throat in one quick thrust, leaving Garcia to cry out, to prop his feet on Crosby's shoulders and beg, partly in Spanish, partly in English, for Crosby to suck him harder, faster, oh God, more!

Crosby obliged, swallowing to make his throat accommodate Garcia's length, letting his spit drip freely down Garcia's shaft, between his balls. He heard Garcia suck in a breath when it trickled between his cheeks.

Crosby slid his fingers along the same path as he sucked, using his lips, his tongue, even flirting with the edges of his teeth, every movement designed to drive Garcia higher, to make him quake, keep him begging.

He skated his forefinger down Garcia's taint, into his cleft, into—

"Gah!" Garcia finally stopped talking and simply cried out. "Papi— God, please—"

Crosby thrust his finger in, finding him a little loose from the night before, but so, so sensitive. He pulled off enough to gasp, "Lube!" and spent a delirious few moments continuing to suck, continuing to thrust, while Garcia gibbered, stretching his hands to reach under the pillow.

When he finally found the lubricant, he swore and handed it off to Crosby desperately, still pleading.

Crosby removed his one finger so he could snick the cap. With a dump, he coated three of his fingers and thrust them back inside.

Garcia cried out, back arching, heels digging into Crosby's shoulders as he came, and Crosby drank him down. Again and again he spurted into Crosby's mouth, until he subsided against the bed, limp and sated, legs dangling over the side.

Crosby rocked back on his heels, taking in the sight of the body, so tight, so muscled, so *alive* in the ambient light from the window, and wiped the come off his mouth with the back of his hand.

And smiled.

Garcia shuddered one more time before trying to talk.

"Cowboy, you'd better have your clothes off by the count of five or I'm making you sleep on the floor."

Crosby rested his forehead against Garcia's inner thigh for a moment before standing and stripping. While he did, Garcia stood and peeled back the covers, sliding between the sheets and shivering in the spring chill. When Crosby slid in next to him, Garcia wrapped his limbs around Crosby's body, offering his body heat, and Crosby sighed into the space between them, overcome with the amazing feeling of their bodies, skin to skin, nothing between them but need.

Garcia's mouth on his was lush, decadent, and Crosby returned the kiss full throttle, flexing his hips and arching his cock against Garcia's thigh. In response, Garcia moved to his back and spread his thighs again, welcoming Crosby inside, and Crosby positioned himself, needing to go.

With a grunt and a smooth thrust, he was there, held in the haven of Garcia's chamber, warm, safe, sensitized, *aroused.*

Garcia let out a sigh of completion and wrapped his legs around Crosby's hips. "Yippee kai-yay," he moaned, and Crosby gave in to the compulsion that had nearly consumed him, rocking back and forth, fucking his lover—yes, his lover, not his partner or his colleague—with all the heart he had.

His climax rushed him, starting at the pit of his balls, roaring outward, an explosion of synapses, a climax of desire, a megaton force of *come*. It left him, cold and shaking, rutting inside Garcia's ass, face buried in the hollow of his neck and shoulder, trying to go deeper, to crawl inside Garcia's warmth, to be sheltered from pain, from loneliness, from isolation, forever.

Garcia gave one of those soft moans—a sweet sound Crosby never would have suspected from such a tight, hard man—and came a second, easy aftershock sort of climax that allowed Crosby to let go of the shaking fear of getting lost and finish his own.

He fell into Garcia's arms, gulping in air, dazed and still a little frightened of everything that happened between them when the lights went down.

"Hey, papi," Garcia whispered. "Easy. Easy. You're shaking."

Crosby nodded, unable to stop. "Was good," he said, not knowing what else to say. "Intense."

"Yeah. Me too." Garcia raised an unsteady hand to push Crosby's hair from his eyes. "I've had lots of sex, Crosby. This here, you and me—this is new."

Crosby nodded and gave a shy smile before turning his head. "Haven't had *lots*," he muttered, "but it's still new."

"Mm...."

Crosby rolled to his side and studied Garcia's expression in the gray light coming through the top of the window, the part not covered by curtains.

"You had lots of sex?" he asked, fishing without shame. They hadn't talked about their sex lives—apparently Garcia because he exclusively preferred men, and Crosby because, with the exception of Iliana, he hadn't had much of one since moving to New York.

Garcia gave a sly smile. "Not to speak of...."

Crosby laughed. "C'mon. I'm living in your spare room now. Isn't this where we offer full disclosure?" He sobered. "You already know I like both, but my relationships with men—those haven't worked out so well."

"What about women?" Garcia rolled to his side too and, with a little bit of fussing, situated the covers over their shoulders, creating enough space between them to whisper in.

Crosby's mouth turned up a little. "Had a few good ones. Had a college girlfriend I thought might go the distance."

"What happened?" Garcia asked, lacing their fingers together between them.

Crosby liked that. It was intimate and playful, possessive and kind, all at the same time.

"She was kind of shitty to Toby," Crosby said thoughtfully. "It... it sort of turned me off. Later on, after... after Damir Calvin—"

"The kid McEnany shot?" Garcia rasped.

"Yeah. I… it's hard to say his name," Crosby confessed. "But I make myself. I need to remember that kid was human. He had a family that mourned him. He wasn't *my* cross to bear. He was a whole person, with hopes and dreams and a girlfriend—all the good things. If I forget to say his name, McEnany gets closer to erasing him, you know?"

"Yeah," Garcia nodded, agreeing with him.

"So anyway, after Damir, it occurred to me that Brittney would have been one of those wives, you know? Perfectly happy to let me turn a blind eye to the bad shit if meant her life wasn't disrupted."

Garcia nodded again, his eyes troubled.

"What's wrong?"

"I'd never expect you to turn a blind eye," he said softly. "And I'll hold your hand and jump off the cliff with you. All you gotta do is ask. But Crosby—Judson—you… you attract these sorts of moral dilemmas. You know that, right?"

Crosby tried to pull away, hurt. "Not on purpose!"

"No! Of course not!" Garcia paused. "But you are always ready, aren't you? To see the line in the sand and walk away from it. You were with me. I could have waited our entire lives for you to make a move—"

Crosby snorted. "Oh no, I could not have," he rumbled. "Do you think you were the only one planning what would happen when we got to your place last night?"

Garcia chuckled, but it sounded strained. "But what if I'd said no?" he asked.

Crosby swallowed, suddenly cold. "I would have asked if you wanted a new partner," he said, the words costing him. He'd thought of it. Every day for the last six months he'd thought of it. Of the moment his restraint broke and he'd needed to touch Garcia like a lover more than he needed him as a partner.

Of the consequences of that move.

Garcia nodded sadly. "But if I said we should stay partners, would you have ever tried again?"

Crosby frowned. "Not if you weren't consenting, no."

"What if I just needed reassurance?" Garcia asked, voice soft. "That I wasn't about to fuck up one of the best relationships of my life."

It hit him then that Garcia was scared. They'd made a helluva leap in the last two days. He wasn't talking about Crosby, he was talking about his own fears, the things that had held *him* back.

"We would have fumbled our way into it," he grumbled, dropping their laced hands and pulling Garcia to his chest. "I would have tried again. I couldn't have just walked away from you. You're not a line in the sand to me, Calix. You're a living breathing human, and I want to be part of your hopes and dreams, you hear?"

"Yeah," Garcia said, snuggling against his chest. "Don't mind me, Crosby. You are seriously the best thing I've ever had in my bed—or in my life. I didn't expect to have a relationship. Not before I retired. I thought my life would be made of one-night stands until I didn't have anything to lose with whatever agency I was working for. But God, I hadn't even shaken your hand and I knew that had changed."

"Now you're scared," Crosby said. "Like I am. 'Cause it doesn't seem right that this is gonna work, does it?"

"Not this easy," Garcia said. "But I'll be damned if I give you up now."

That's all they said for a while, and their breathing slowed down, and Crosby was almost asleep.

"You awake, Cowboy?" Garcia's voice was so low he didn't even know he was supposed to respond.

"Good," Garcia said, apparently assuming Crosby was out. "'Cause I need to say this to you sleeping before I try it awake. I love you, Judson Crosby. I knew it that first day. It's worse now. You need to stay alive, stay hopeful, hold on. I'm not gonna let you go now. You understand?"

Yeah. The gods'll have to pry you out of my arms.

It was the last thing he thought before he fell asleep.

THE NEXT day was like a photo blueprint for what life could be if he let down his guard and enjoyed Garcia's company, their living situation, and even their little spot in Queens.

They woke up, legs tangled, and threw on sweats while Garcia hit the thermostat and Crosby made coffee. After spending twenty minutes drinking coffee while scrolling on their phones, they were both awake enough to want to get out of the house and enjoy their day.

Calix grabbed Crosby's hand, taking him to the bagel place he loved most for breakfast and then to every shop in the neighborhood. Sweets, sheets (of which Garcia bought a set), and a cat café, all of it called them in. They bantered, looked at prices, discussed whether a thing should go in Garcia's house or not (mostly not), and let little bits of their personal history slip by too.

"So did you really get laid on your eighteenth birthday?" Crosby asked while they were looking at a lawn ornament for the six-by-six stretch of what Garcia called his front-yard mange.

"Yeah—lots," Garcia admitted. "I was on PrEP, everybody had condoms—I didn't just punch the V-card, I ripped it into little pieces and burned it."

Crosby chuckled like he was meant to, but he regarded his friend—lover—closely. "Why? What made you so... I don't know... violent about it?"

Garcia sucked wind through his teeth. "'Cause my pops had just finished an epic rant about gay people, I guess. I don't know—some election, some politician or TV show got stuck in his craw, and the next thing I knew that rant was on at the table, twenty-four seven. Anyway I turned eighteen the next week, and I'd planned to tell my folks as soon as I moved out, but I suddenly knew I couldn't. I mean, I'm not close with them, but I don't hate them either. I'd like to see them occasionally. And I knew suddenly that coming out would never happen, and it pissed me off. So I spent a weekend in Miami—they'd moved by then, and I was still going to college up here and living in this house with Nana and Pop-Pop—and I hit South Beach like hurricane Calix. By the time I caught my flight for Queens, every daddy for a mile radius knew I liked dick, and I was proud of it."

Crosby nodded, something hitting him then that he'd never thought of but maybe should have.

"Yeah," he said softly. "I... I can't come out to my folks if I ever want them to talk to me again." He paused, remembering how things had been over the last two years, with him patiently explaining that racism was bad, and his father's bluster about "the way things always had been."

"Maybe that's not a bad thing," he said after a moment. He gave Garcia a melancholic smile. "They wouldn't understand being both, and they wouldn't care, really. It's all gay to them. And I wouldn't have to have any of those awful conversations with them when they're just begging me to say I'm sorry so we could move back to Chicago."

Garcia swallowed and set down a ceramic zombie gnome so he could reach over and grab Crosby's hand. "It's a hard way to set yourself free," he said, voice gruff.

Crosby nodded. "Yeah, but I'm not the first person to do it." He gave a little shrug. "I'm even sort of a late bloomer. And pick that up again. If I'm sleeping in the guest room, I want a zombie gnome on the porch."

Garcia blinked at him. "A zombie gnome?"

"Yeah. I'm such an average sort of vanilla guy. I think a zombie gnome makes me look more interesting, don't you?"

"Cowboy," Garcia said, something funny happening to his voice. "You can have anything you want. Anything. If you're average and vanilla, I'll eat this fucking gnome."

Crosby blinked at him and then grinned. "Always about food with you."

Garcia's eyes heated. "Not always," he said huskily.

Oh. "So, uh, you want to get the gnome and, uh, go back to my spare room?"

"Yeah."

Slow this time. Playful. They had all the time in the world. Nobody cared about who they were or what they were doing. They had their phones on chargers on the end table, but nobody was texting. Nothing urgent was happening that demanded their attention. They were free, in Garcia's bed. Free to touch and to tease, to taste and to sigh.

Does this feel good?

Yeah.

This?

Tickles!

More of this, papi—I need to hear you laugh.

And he did, so much. He laughed more with Calix Garcia than he had with any friend, any lover, he'd ever known.

And when their climax came, Calix's back arching as Crosby moved above him, the look of freedom, of trust on his face, was everything Judson Crosby had ever needed in his life and had never dared to hope for.

Sometime in the night, after a dinner of toast and eggs and a dozy evening of watching TV in bed, they fell asleep. Calix backed into Crosby's big spoon like he'd been everything missing from Crosby's arms, and Crosby tried to pull him closer, to bond souls like they'd bonded bodies.

At 2:00 a.m. his phone rang. It was Toby, his voice pitched to panic.

"I'm sorry, man. They put me in the jail. I… they say they'll put me back. There were no drugs, I swear, but this McEnany guy, he pulled a baggie out of his *ass*—"

His phone buzzed, so he put it on speaker so Calix could hear and he could look at the picture texted to him from a number he didn't recognize.

It was Toby, distorted features made even more distorted by bruises on his face, cuts on his lips, and an obviously broken nose.

Crosby sat up, blood cold in his veins. "Is he there, Toby?"

"Yeah."

"You put him on."

McEnany's voice had a smug quality—just like it had every day they'd worked together for a year and a half.

"So, Crosby," he said, like they were sitting at the conference table. "Ready to play poker now?"

Empty Nest

"YOU ABSOLUTELY cannot," Garcia said, his panic beyond being a bird in his chest. It was a fucking pterodactyl, a T-Rex, and it was going to crush him and leave his body twitching on the ground.

"I don't have a choice," Crosby said, sliding into his jeans and finding his gun belt. Garcia had a safe for firearms—he'd shown Crosby where it was when they'd been moving him in. Crosby was on the fingerprint lock and the whole nine yards, but Garcia wished right now that he hadn't been. That he'd have to ask Garcia for his service piece like he was a guest and not… oh God. A resident. He fucking *lived* here in Garcia's house. Yeah, it was for two and a half nights and two days, but that was enough—his DNA was imprinted there, on Garcia's sheets, in his skin.

"But Crosby, he wants to kill you!" Garcia burst out, beyond being tactful. "That man wants you to report for a bullshit cover operation so he can use your dead body to cover his ass!"

Crosby paused in the act of shoving his shirt in his pants. He stared at Garcia, agony in his eyes, and nodded. "Yeah. Yeah, you're right. I can't argue that. But before I get dead, he wants to use me. And while he's using me, we'll be using him right back."

Garcia dragged a hit of oxygen into his lungs. "We?" God, such a hopeful word.

"Yeah. Yeah, we. Look, you think I want you to go fetch Toby from the precinct and then let me waltz into the night? Are you fuckin' kidding? You're going to call Harding and—"

"What am I going to tell him?" Garcia asked bitterly, the panic still raw in his chest. "That your old boss wants you to go undercover with the Sons of the Blood so you can get him back in with them?"

Crosby nodded, resuming his dress routine, and Garcia contemplated smashing him over the head with the zombie garden gnome they'd left on the kitchen table. At least that way he'd be safe—unconscious, but safe.

"That's about it," Crosby said. "But first, get Toby the fuck out of there. Call Harding on the way if you have to, but use your scrambler, and I'm serious, man. Either they're going to turn Toby loose the minute I show up at McEnany's meet or they're not. If they don't, they're throwing him back in the pond, where he'll die, and if they do, they're going to let him loose into the streets and put him through a meat grinder. Either way he's fucked. If there's not people there for Toby, I don't see him walking away alive from this. I told McEnany I'd have a friend run him down at the precinct and make sure he was okay, so I think the action is gonna be on the streets, but man, if McEnany's serious about trying to propagate the Sons of the Blood from the inside, I don't trust him not to take our boy out in the jailhouse either." Crosby gulped in a breath, and Garcia had to close his eyes against his worry. Toby Trotter, the sweet, almost shy little man who'd been Crosby's one friend for over a year. As Crosby had said—repeatedly—it wasn't Trotter's fault his place wasn't a good match for Crosby's hours. In the last few days, Garcia had really begun to see why Crosby had hung in there so long with the guy.

A friend that tight? That wasn't anything to sneeze at.

"God, Judson—"

"You heard his voice on the phone," Crosby said, all his frantic activity halting for the moment. "He was so scared."

Garcia nodded, not able to turn his back on this. "I know, man."

"He's so fuckin' gentle, Calix. He… didn't even turn on me, did you hear that? McEnany said he knew I was staying with my girl. Toby covered for us, man. They sent him to get the shit beat out of him, and he kept your name out of it. Said I still lived with him—I was just going to stay with a girl in Flushing. He's… he's five three, do you know that? He's got six kinds of things in his body that try to kill him on the regular, and those assholes gotta put him in with gen pop? Calix, we… we *gotta* get him out of there. We gotta. There's no fuckin' reason for the police to *exist* if we can't get Toby the fuck outta there, you hear me?"

Garcia took a stuttering breath and swallowed. "I know, Judson, I *know*. But why can't you go get him now, and we tell Harding everything and—"

"And someday one of us gets that bullet to the back of the head?" Crosby said, the quiver to his lower lip firming up. "And I'd *hope* it was me, you know? But there's a reason my folks are in New Mexico bitching about the heat. They'd start with Toby, maybe move to Gail, and maybe they'd find out I was banging Iliana back in the day. And then they'd find

out you and me spent two days together with nobody watching, and...."
His voice clogged. "And God. You're everything they hate. You're brown,
you're gay, and you're mine. I got to go, and you got to get Toby and tell
Harding. I'll get a burner on the way, put your numbers—"

Garcia could do one thing here to help.

"Don't worry about the burner. I got something better." He reached
into the gun safe and pulled out his old ATF phone, which still held a
partial charge. He had a battery on his desk, and he was hooking it up as
he pulled Crosby to look over his shoulder. "It's got two SIM cards," he
said softly, wanting Crosby's heat at his back always. "See? Hit this—"
He hit a spare, almost invisible button on the side. "—and you're texting
one group of people. Hit it again, you're texting the other. When I worked
undercover, I always made Group One my cover group and Group Two
my backup. See this light, here?" He showed a tiny green light in the
lower corner of the phone. "Green is one, red is two. This way you don't
have to worry about texting the wrong guy with the wrong number. See
this app?" He showed Crosby the icon. "This app lets you spoof numbers.
So if you want to text someone but make it look like you're texting
someone else? And you can do spoofing presets. So you text me, and
it looks like you're texting Gail. You text Harding, it looks like you're
texting me. That way you can...." He turned to Crosby in agony. "You
can keep us posted. We can know where you are." He swallowed and
hit a couple of buttons, sending a text to his own phone. "And I've got a
tracker on you, because I've got the number in my phone. Use Harding's
scrambler when you need to, okay?"

Crosby nodded. "Good. Hold that for a sec. Let me put on my boots."

He wore lace-up cross-training urban boots—the kind you could
run in, but that could take some punishment. Garcia had another thought
and ran to the gun safe again, coming back with a tracker and a couple
of new batteries.

"Here," he whispered, bending down to find a place in Crosby's boot
lining. "Another tracker." He stood so Crosby could put his stockinged
foot in the boot and slid the batteries in his back pocket. "I've got this
one loaded into my phone."

He went about getting his own boots and his own piece, and silently
the two of them finished getting dressed—Kevlar under their sweaters,
because they were all business.

Right up until Crosby stood at the door of the darkened house.

"I'll text you on the way," Crosby said gruffly. "And you and Harding at least once a day. I…." He squeezed his eyes shut, and Garcia couldn't help it. He cupped Crosby's face and pulled his head down, taking Crosby's hard mouth in a kiss made of desperation and iron.

"Stay safe," he ordered, trying not to be broken.

"You too," Crosby rasped.

"And do what you have to," Garcia said, hating this might have to come up. "I don't care if you're faithful, Crosby—I just care if you're alive."

Crosby sucked in a tortured breath. "I care if you're fucking faithful," he rasped. "I do. So help me, I do. I don't want you with anyone else, and I don't want to *be* with anybody else. If we gotta to stay safe, we gotta, but I don't wanna, you hear me?"

Garcia nodded. "I hear."

For a moment, a heartbeat, Crosby's face lost its hardness, and his body lost its urgency. He pulled Garcia close in an embrace made of tenderness, like they had all the time in the world.

"This was the best two days of my life," he said, and Garcia fought the urge to cry. "I want them back. I want them back with you. I'm gonna work real hard to get them back, you hear me?"

"I hear," Garcia repeated.

In reply, Crosby kissed him on the forehead and ghosted out the door.

Garcia waited ten minutes, so anybody watching Crosby would see him heading for the nearest platform and could follow him there, before going to the side door and sliding out, cutting through the neighbor's backyard to catch a Lyft halfway down the block.

It would take Crosby about half an hour to get to Bed-Stuy and Garcia a little less time to get to Manhattan. He was taking the Lyft to get there sooner, and he was grateful when the driver stared moodily ahead, speaking tersely in sentences heavy with a Slavic accent when he did talk.

First things first. Harding picked up on the first ring, and Garcia wondered how hyped he had to be to still be awake and ready for bear at this hour.

Or how scared.

Garcia outlined the sitch, using "our boy" and "the good ole boy" for Crosby and McEnany, and "liability package" for Toby.

For a moment, Harding was nonplussed. "Liability package? Who's our boy's liability?"

"Same guy we thought two days ago," Garcia said, thinking about how close they'd come to having Crosby forced into this because he'd been the one arrested.

"Oh dear God." Harding's voice pitched. "Seriously? You're going to collect him now?"

"Yeah. But we're not sure if there's a welcome party when he's released or not."

"Fuck me. Wait. Go inside, get the package, but wait for a text from me before you walk outside and into the party, you understand?"

Garcia sighed. "Sir, if he goes back to the... to the nonparty room...." He sent Harding the picture of Toby that McEnany had sent Crosby.

"I'll kill him," Harding muttered. "There was no goddamned reason for that."

And Garcia hated saying this—he did, because he wanted to believe Crosby had just left him, carted off in his own goddamned heroism and bailed on a relationship. It was so much fucking easier to deal with him being gone if Garcia could be mad at Crosby for leaving.

But Crosby had been right. Damn him, he'd been right about the whole sitch.

"No," Garcia said, keeping his voice steady. "That's why our boy had to go."

Harding's short, hard burst of air into the phone told Garcia he'd made a point.

"Hang in there," Harding said in a moment. "Wait for our signal before you leave one party room and dive into another, you hear me?"

"Roger that."

"We'll have some medical professionals ready to take care of our package. Goddammit. Goddamn all these fuckers to hell."

"Roger that too, sir. Out."

Garcia hit End Call and glanced up at the Lyft driver. The guy hadn't even checked his rearview mirror as Garcia had cleared with Harding.

CROSBY TEXTED him as he was getting out of the Lyft at the precinct.
Here. He should be released inside.
Roger that.
Be safe.
You too.

And that was that. Garcia hated that he'd had to wait for Crosby to text "Be safe" before Garcia could respond, but he also appreciated the warning. Crosby had a shiver up his spine, and so did Garcia.

He went in and flashed his ID, asking where he'd go to pick up a released prisoner, only to be told they didn't have anybody by the name Toby Trotter there.

Garcia was about to go nuclear, pull his rank, call every lawyer he'd known through ATF when he heard an agonized scream coming through the double doors leading to the jail.

Oh fuck *that*.

He shoved his way through the smirking cops and through the doors that separated the front offices from the detainees' spaces in the back. The precinct was old, with stucco walls and cracked beige tile, but sound carried like an arrow, and he followed the direction of that scream. He arrived at a crowded hallway in time to see a cop retracting his nightstick while Toby writhed on the ground at his feet.

The rest of the squad was about to close in when Garcia pulled out his phone, hit Record, and held it over his head.

"Smile for the fucking camera, guys," he yelled. "I got you going straight to the press!"

It might not have won him any popularity contests, but it had the desired effect.

The beginning melee of police officers stopped what they were doing, standing up straight while Toby huddled on the ground cradling an arm that looked broken. His clothes were bloody and ripped, and Garcia thought sickly that if Crosby hadn't had his boy's back, he would have died here tonight, a victim of a beating from the police or from the inmates of the crowded jail. Nobody would ever know the difference.

Garcia was streaming the video to Harding. Harding would know the difference.

"He resisted arrest," snarled the officer with the telescoping nightstick, but Garcia shook his head.

"In fact, he did not," he said. "Believe me, I know exactly how he ended up here. Toby, can you get up on your own?"

Toby's voice was as broken as his body looked. "I... I think my ankle's broken."

Garcia nodded, scowling at the officer who had spoken. "You. You get the fuck away from him." He eyeballed a kid, a rookie, who was looking green, as though he might actually wet himself with fear and revulsion. "You, boot, you help him up. Gently. Unbroken arm over your shoulder, that's it." He glanced around and saw another cop—this one Latino—whose face was molded in granite lines of disapproval of the entire scene. "You, next to him. Doba. You help Trotter too. One on either side. Yes, the video is still streaming. Is it the press? Is it the DOJ? Is it the FBI field office? Who wants to find out?"

There was some grumbling, but the sea of blue parted to let the rookie, Henderson, and the older guy, Doba, help Toby to his feet and toward the double doors Garcia had just crashed through.

One step back and another. And another. And another. In spite of the cool March night, sweat ran down Garcia's back, under his arms, and while he kept his expression locked, he was just waiting for it to run into his eyes.

There was a minor scuffle at the door, and then Chadwick's voice. "Special Agent Gideon Chadwick. Open up and let them through. Garcia, I have my piece drawn, and I am facing the room."

"Roger that," Garcia said, still backing up, phone raised. "Doba, Henderson, keep him coming. We've got a bus outside to take him to the hospital. If this guy dies in your custody, it's not going to be an accident, and now *so* many people know that."

He continued to back up, aware that the eyes of the now-crowded precinct were staring at him, at Chadwick, even at Henderson and Doba, with absolute hatred. When he got to the door leading outside, he made sure his head was *not* aligned with the little lined window and the steel door was between himself and anything somebody outside cared to throw at him.

"We clear outside?" he asked, and Chadwick shook his head slightly.

"We're going to stand, backs to the door, while your two friends there haul Trotter out," Chadwick told him. Then Chadwick blinked, and Garcia knew he had his commlink in his ear. "Not good," he responded to the voice in his ear. "It's a good thing we've got the ambulance."

Garcia didn't have to see Chadwick's flinch to know Harding had just let loose with a string of curses.

But it was Chadwick's grim look that had Garcia's back up.

Chadwick shook his head again and called to their friend with the nightstick who had followed hard on the heels of Doba and Henderson. "You? Asshole with the nightstick—yeah, we all saw you, you bullying motherfucker. We need you to walk out first."

They both watched the guy with the nightstick blanch, and knew they were on to something. Well, shit. They couldn't stay here, in this tiny old cracked-paneled room with all the hostile armed policemen advancing on them either.

But Chadwick wasn't done.

"And you, Desk Sergeant Montillo. Yeah, you. You think I haven't seen you pushing the button, asking for help? We're federal fucking agents, and we are saving an innocent man from getting beaten to death by the police. If you're looking for help, you're looking for thugs in blue, and that makes you a bad person. You get out here with Nightstick. You two go out first."

"But...." And Nightstick guy—his badge said Nichols—was shaking. "They'll *kill* us if we go out first."

It was funny... Garcia liked Gideon Chadwick. Liked his fancy coffees. Liked the tender way he seemed to keep the volatile Joey Carlyle in line. Liked his spectacularly dry conversation and how he seemed to know all sorts of useless shit that turned out to help them at the oddest times.

But until the moment he looked Garcia in the eyes and nodded, ever so slightly, and said, "Better you than us," Garcia had not known what it was to love a guy in a way that had nothing to do with sex and everything to do with their cold-fucking-blooded ability to make a decision.

Garcia nodded back at him and took point. Taking a breath, grateful for the Kevlar Crosby had insisted he put on, he got in front of the Toby Trotter protection sandwich while Chadwick got behind, back-to-back with Doba, his weapon out, as Nichols and Montillo preceded them, their hands raised in the air.

Nichols dropped first, the headshot so clean he didn't have time to cry out, and before the report reached Garcia's ears, Montillo dropped next. Garcia's weapon was out, his cell phone still recording in front of him, and for a breathless moment, they stood there, Toby in the middle, the two cops on either side, Garcia riding point and Chadwick bringing up the rear.

From out in the darkness beyond the blazing lights and foggy halo that encircled the precinct, came two voices—Carlyle first. "Clear!"

Then Pearson. "Clear!"

"Bullshit," Henderson practically whimpered. "I didn't hear any guns go off. How can we be clear?"

Then Denison. "Clear!"

Then a muffled shot. "Clear!" shouted Swan.

Then Harding strode past the ambulance, his department-issue windbreaker ripped, a bleeding wound on his shoulder, and a honking bruise on his face. He pounded on the side of the ambulance and snarled, "Trust me, fellas, we're clear. We're gonna need a couple of coroner's vans, though. If you could call for those while you're working on Mr. Trotter…?"

Toby gave a moan, and that seemed to galvanize the three people who'd been hiding inside the bus. In a moment, they'd emerged and were swarming around Toby while Henderson and Doba helped him onto the stretcher.

Garcia slowly lowered his phone, his hand shaking. He didn't realize how much until Harding walked up to him, two hands out, and coming from the side, he helped Garcia holster his weapon.

His hands were shaking too. For a moment they stood there, glancing around like feral animals, until the others emerged from the fog surrounding the precinct.

Gail was first, her hands covered in blood and a knife literally dripping from a holster at her waist. Denison came next, winding a string of bloody piano wire into the silver goddess necklace he'd seen her wear on the regular. Swan was next, his weapon held at rest position, and then Carlyle, who held the crossbow he'd apparently purloined from the last time he'd needed something silent and deadly.

Harding glanced around. "Garcia, I know you probably want to accompany Trotter, but you're needed at the debriefing. Chadwick?"

Chadwick, who had coldly consigned two men to their deaths, nodded his hatchet-thin face and then turned those absurdly gentle eyes to Toby.

"Mr. Trotter?" he said as the medics moved the stretcher to the ambulance, "Allow me to introduce myself."

Harding gave a decisive nod, then took in Doba and Henderson, both of whom had the half-angry, half-terrified glare of guys who knew they'd just walked away from the life they'd known—possibly forever. "You two, any family in the city?"

They both shook negative, and Harding nodded as though that made it easier.

"You're going to report to my office for the duration, and I think we can secure you an apartment for the next month."

"No offense," Doba said, voice suspicious, eyes hard, "but what's going to change in the next month?"

Harding's lips pulled back from his teeth. "We're going to find the sources of this," he said, gesturing around them with his chin, "and we're going to uproot it, and we're going to kill it, and we're going to salt the earth around it. And if you still want to grow there, we'll buy you a fucking pot. That good with you?"

The two men met eyes and nodded slowly. "I have a cat," young Henderson said faintly.

Doba shrugged. "I'm only allergic to lead," he muttered.

"Settled," Harding replied, his anger still a palpable thing—but not aimed at them.

The team gave a collective sigh then, and Harding nodded, almost to himself, before unhooking a radio from his belt and issuing orders, asking each member of the team to tell him where their kill was.

Garcia looked toward each coordinate and shuddered, his heart suddenly thundering in his ears. Five dead bodies. Five men, lying in wait for a member of the SCTF to emerge with the innocent man they'd been trying to kill.

The police precinct had been surrounded, although Garcia didn't know what the enemy looked like yet. McEnany had anticipated somebody coming for Toby, and whoever showed up had been slated for death.

They had wanted Crosby—and wanted him badly. And they'd wanted to take out anybody who might come to get revenge or protect him, with a vengeance.

"God," Garcia breathed. "What's our boy into?"

Harding shook his head. "Not here," he said, voice gritty. "Team, get your vehicles. We're not talking again until we're in the office and the place has been swept. This shitshow was just the first fucking act, people. Crosby needs us all to live to the finale."

Various forms of "Roger that," and "Understood, Chief," were murmured around the steps, and as the first whispers of dawn could be heard over the city's rooftops, they all moved to start their day.

The real work had just begun.

Snake Pit

"SON OF a *bitch*!" McEnany yelled, making all the men in the shitty room in one of Brownsville's most infamous tenements jump. Except Crosby.

He'd put his game face on as he'd ridden the train from Garcia's awesome little house in Queens to this project dump in Brooklyn's Brownsville. He'd already decided he was going to be the baddest ass in the room, no prisoners, no mercy, no surprises, and that was how he had to play this thing if he wanted to survive to get back to Queens.

Garcia had texted him as he'd been walking to the tenement. *All safe. Lots of casualties on their side. Someone's gonna be pissed.*

Understood, he'd texted back, because he did get it. Toby had been a trap for Harding's team, but Harding wasn't stupid. SCTF was safe. The same couldn't be said for the guys who'd been trying to kill them.

And McEnany couldn't even blame Crosby. He'd been following orders, right? If he showed up here in Brooklyn, Toby would be released back in Manhattan. Here Crosby was in Brooklyn, no blood on *his* hands. Apparently sitting in their conference room listening to the team work hadn't been enough of an object lesson for McEnany. He hadn't seen the intelligence, the intuitiveness of the team—he'd just seen that Crosby was a valued member and needed to be removed.

And apparently McEnany had been an awful enough person to try to take out the whole team in a fit of prissiness.

"What's up, Cap?" said Donny Mazursky, one of the ten or so guys in the room, sounding worried, like a real cop, and Crosby tried not to seethe with hate.

What was up was that McEnany had coopted his own little fucking army—that's what was up.

Being born into the Sons of the Blood did *not* guarantee a person entry into the local PD. All the things that held true for the general populace still held true for the wannabes. They had to be sponsored through the academy, pass all their criminal justice classes, get a trainer to sponsor them through their rookie years.

But these guys—they'd been born into families as the sons and grandsons and great grandsons of cops. And they'd been told they'd fallen short.

That entitlement—and that denial—it rankled. It festered. It left a big chafing, rotting sore on their fragile souls and poisoned their blood.

McEnany had met Crosby at the stairwell and given him his cover. He was Rick Young, a six-year veteran of NYPD, Twenty Fourth precinct, tired of the liberal bullshit and wanting to integrate the local police force with his Sons of the Blood brethren. It was a good cover. The Twenty Fourth was one of the older precincts, diverse, beat the hell up, and Crosby knew some of the guys there because the SCTF was stationed in midtown, and they got to know (and piss off) most of the locals. Crosby would remember the assholes and could now deduce which ones were friendly to McEnany's cause.

McEnany had been thorough. In addition to the job at the Forty Third, "Young" had a furnished flop in the same building as the leader of the local chapter of the Sons of the Blood, a guy named Creedy. The keys to the flop came with the badge, the hiring papers, and the fake IDs.

"What's my goal?" Crosby'd asked sourly as he'd studied the papers—expertly made, he realized. They might even be the real thing. The badge, the driver's license, the backstory, even the job that was legit—McEnany had been planning this awhile.

"Your goal is to get in good with the deputy chief of the Active Crimes Division of the Forty Third," McEnany said, his face set into ugly lines. "Davies. That bitch has turned down more of our guys than I can count. We need *somebody* high up in every division, or someone, sometime, is going to get all fucking liberal and fuck up the department."

Crosby kept his face impassive, but part of him was jumping for joy, and part of him was icy cold. Iliana Davies. Gail's roommate. Explaining that he was undercover with the Sons would be helpful—and hopefully keep him alive—but he didn't like that they'd had a connection, or that she was so close to Gail and the other members of the SCTF. If McEnany had done just one more layer of research on Crosby, he'd know that Crosby and Iliana had done the wild thing, and instead of sending Crosby undercover with her, he might have sent Crosby to take her out.

Fuck. *Fuck.*

With that cold realization in his gut, Crosby didn't care what the bullshit excuse was—fucking bad guys fucking monologuing. It was fucking twisted how the guys who wanted to blow up the world thought their feelings were so much more important than their victims'. If Crosby hadn't been aware that roomfuls of enemies were right inside the high-rise he and McEnany huddled next to, he might have reached out and snapped Collie McEnany's neck with sheer rage. But he kept that part of him controlled. What Crosby *needed* to know was why him? And why now?

"What do you get out of this?" Crosby asked bluntly. "You pulled me from my team, and you did it by blackmail, in a way that's going to arouse suspicion. That's a helluva lot of risk."

McEnany glared at him sourly. "God, look who grew a fucking brain and a fucking spine alluvasudden. When you were my fuckin' boot, I couldn't get you to commit to full sentences, and now you're asking *strategy*? Which idiot made you think you had it in you?"

Crosby thought miserably of Harding but kept his expression neutral. "What. Do. You. Get?" he asked with no inflection whatsoever.

"I get back in," McEnany hissed. "You defected. I got nailed with that kid's shooting and my partner didn't back me. Suddenly Chicago PD can't get the stink off fast enough. A friend pulled some strings, and I got this bullshit job as an IA rat—"

"On the federal level—not enough power for you?" Crosby asked. God, he'd *loved* working for the SCTF. It was a tiny, almost invisible federal agency, but it had well-trained, well-briefed people, and he'd *loved* it. He'd embraced every class Harding had thrown at them. He hadn't wanted the promotions, dammit; he'd wanted to be better at his job. It seemed like McEnany could have taken his own lemon and made some rocking lemonade too, but instead he seemed to want to blow up the agency that gave him the better paycheck, the better status, the better everything. Fucking *why*?

"*I'm a fucking Captain,*" McEnany snarled. "In the Sons of the Blood, I'm a *Captain*. And with the feds I'm a *rat*? Bullshit. But if I want my connections with the Sons to pull me up, to give me some power, I gotta prove I'm not a liability. What better way to do that than to get the guy who jammed me up in the first place to find someone in a new division to pull over to our side? The Forty Third Precinct is clean, my friend. Not a single Son in the ranks, and a lot of that is the new Deputy Chief of Active Crimes. So guess what? I've got just enough juice to get someone with a clean record into the ranks. But you're going to report to me now."

Crosby tilted his head and decided he was going to make McEnany say it.

"So I want you to spell it out for me," he growled. "Like I was five. Why am I leaving my team to report to you?"

McEnany's smile was all yellowing, crooked teeth. "Because if you don't, I'm gonna have my guys stalk your team, one at a time, until you are just as alone as I was two years ago. You don't get the good team and the hero's welcome—not after leaving me out in the cold."

Crosby let a razor-thin smile escape. "Damir Calvin," he said deliberately.

McEnany's eyes narrowed. "What?"

"That's the name of the first corpse you walked over. I thought you'd want to keep a list."

Those rheumy blue eyes darted a little to the right, and Crosby knew he'd hit a nerve. "There'll be others," McEnany said snidely. "Now follow me up. You gotta meet Creedy and the boys. Then you can go to your flat and press your dress blues, flatfoot. You start your new job day after tomorrow."

The introduction with the guys at Creedy's flat had been both everything Crosby expected and less.

It was a basic apartment with old, battered plaid furniture, a small kitchenette covered with takeout boxes, a fridge full of beer, and guys on the couch doing lines and playing video games. The guys were all white, some of them thin and raggedy, a few of them buzz cut and stacked— but all of them had either the snarling, hyperaggressive posture or the cringing, obsequious fear of dogs who'd been whipped too much as puppies and now had the devil in them as adults.

Creedy himself was a ruddy-skinned, oddly magnetic man with a square build, dark hair graying at the temples, and an almost perfect rectangle of a face. Like McEnany, his teeth were crooked, and some of the back ones were missing, but his swollen hands and battered knuckles testified to a life working in warehouses, and his sneer told a story about how he thought he was better than that.

The men took McEnany's intro at face value—which told Crosby he was going to have to watch his back at all times, because these guys were squids and slippery as fuck—and there was lots of bro-hugging and locked hands at the heart level, which Crosby tried not to compare to the easy and authentic camaraderie of the SCTF. He'd hugged every member at one time or another, but not as a ritual, and definitely not when they'd first met.

It made him squidgy.

But that was all on the inside. He kept the itchy, almost automatic dislike for everybody locked away behind his badass face and listened as McEnany helped Jimmy Creedy spin bitterness into spiderwebs, talking about how their friend, Rick Young, was their ticket to getting that bitch cop to let their group into the Brooklyn PD, and their guys could stop, as they put it, "suffering under diversity oppression."

Which meant that Active Crimes was an equal opportunity shop—everybody could be arrested, and everybody got the same choice of overworked lawyers looking to plead out.

Crosby hid his disgust at the same time he hid a little glow of pride for Iliana. They were never going to be a real forever thing—but God, she had these guys on the run. Good for *her*. He hoped he'd live long enough to give her the compliment.

The intro session had devolved into the usual—how somebody's brother's cousin's buddy had gotten wronged by the cops—when McEnany's pocket buzzed.

"Sonovabitch!"

Crosby kept his game face on as his former boss, the guy with Crosby's balls in a vise, stormed around the little room, raging about five dead operatives—and two other stalwart Sons who'd gotten caught in the crossfire.

As McEnany was kicking over the coffee table, Crosby had glanced at the kid next to him, one of the scrawny, underfed young men—twenty-two, twenty-three—who looked like he was still getting beat up on the daily.

"Kid," he said on a yawn, and the guy skittered his been-whipped-too-many-times eyes to Crosby.

"Junior," the kid said.

"Like Jimmy Junior?" Oh God—nothing like being a legacy member of a hate division.

Junior nodded, glancing at his father. "Yeah," he whispered. "I… uh…."

"You want to show me where my flop is?" Crosby asked, not having to fake exhaustion. The guys in the flop looked like they were wired for sound—and he'd heard noises about them usually working nightshift at the warehouse. Not Crosby—thank fuck.

"Yeah, you want I should get you settled?" Junior replied, looking almost eager.

"McEnany said he got me all set up, but I need to count my underwear and shit, you know?"

Junior watched McEnany lose complete control again, his father yelling rather desperately, "Collie! Collie! Calm down. We'll get the bastards!"

"My sister's kid was in that clusterfuck!" McEnany shouted. "How'm I gonna tell her you sent him to fuckin' die!"

Junior gave Crosby a desperate look, and Crosby nodded. While Jimmy and McEnany were on the far side of the room, Crosby started for the door like he had every reason to want to get the hell out of there.

"Where the fuck're you goin'?" McEnany snapped, and Crosby pulled his bullshit suit on.

"Look, man—I'm real sorry for your loss. It just seemed like you all needed the space to mourn your brothers, yeah? I thought it would be more respectful if I left you all to do that."

Jimmy nodded, his eyes red-rimmed and shiny. *He lost people too. God, whoever's behind this needs to fuckin' pay. These guys are deluded, but they coulda been led somewhere else.*

"Good man," Jimmy said, sounding choked. "Junior, you show him where his apartment is. Your shift is day after tomorrow. Collie tells me he got you all moved in?"

The thought of "Collie" with his fingers all over Crosby's underwear made him want to vomit. "Yeah. I may need to check my shaving kit, though. You know, every guy's got his toothpaste and his aftershave, right?"

"CVS on the corner," Jimmy said. "Junior'll show you that too after you get some winks. Night, Rick. Thanks for the time, man. We lost some good people."

Crosby put his hands together and gave a short bow. "We'll do 'em proud," he said, because he figured that would be of comfort to a man like Jimmy.

Apparently not. Jimmy's eyes spilled over, and Crosby used that moment to slide out the door, Junior on his heels.

His flop was three floors up, and it was easier to take the stairs because the two elevators were both gross *and* rickety. McEnany had made a point of telling him that the one on the south end of the building perpetually smelled like shit. The stairway smelled like wet metal and mold, but it had to be better than shit.

Crosby let himself into the room and grimaced. It was smaller than the one the rest of the Sons met in, with a closet, a bed, a few chairs around a tiny table, and a kitchenette. Microwave, hot plate, coffee maker—everything a growing boy needed, right?

With a grunt, Crosby realized he hadn't even brought his laptop with him, which was just as well, because Jimmy Junior was making himself comfortable in one of Crosby's chairs, a rickety affair next to the pasteboard table. He yawned and laid his head down on the table, and Crosby realized the kid was as tired as he was.

Jesus.

"Kid," Crosby said, eyeballing the bed, "you want I should give you a blanket and a pillow? You can take the little couch?"

Junior looked up at him, gratitude profound on his thin face. Another kid with no dental work, crooked teeth, a crooked nose, a crooked chin to go with it.

Maybe he'd been hit often enough that braces weren't the only problem.

"Yeah, Rick. That'd be great. Thank you."

He appeared to have no artifice in him, and Crosby had to wonder what the downside was to this kid. He was, technically, the enemy, but Crosby wondered how he'd respond if Natalia tried to mother him. Would he be disdainful because she was Black or just so fucking grateful that a kind adult paid attention to him?

So many ways that could go.

You can't fix the whole world, Crosby.

He wasn't sure whose voice it was—coulda been Harding's, coulda been Natalia's, coulda been Garcia. But whoever was talking in his head, it set up a howl of homesickness he wasn't sure he could drown out.

He pulled the quilt and one of two pillows from the bed and threw them at Junior before kicking off his boots and hunting around the place until he found the tiny chest of drawers next to the closet.

Sweatpants and T-shirts, clean but used, with the Goodwill tags still on 'em.

Fuckin' subtle, McEnany. Subtle.

Didn't matter. Crosby would get new clothes tomorrow when he bought socks and underwear, so he didn't have to worry about McEnany feeling like he owned Crosby with his gesture of "goodwill," and in the meantime he'd share the bed with his gun belt and cover up with his Kevlar on top of the blankets. He was aware any one of the heavily armed guys three apartments beneath him could crawl up the stairs and take him out when he was sleeping.

He locked the door—and the two chains and three bolts—to make himself feel better about not dying in his sleep, fully aware that Junior on the couch might be the one to do the honors.

But Junior was curling up very much like the whipped puppy he seemed to be, and Crosby was *beat* to his toes. He slid out of his jeans and into one of the pairs of sweats and took off his Kevlar before putting his sweatshirt back on.

As he crawled into bed, his phone banged against his hip from his hoodie pocket, and he pulled it out, figuring he had the excuse of texting his girl.

But Junior didn't even shudder as Crosby pulled up the one blanket and the sheet, trying not to shiver in the spring cold, and Crosby figured that his fleece jacket, the vest, and the sweats should actually give him a little bit of warmth—enough to sleep, maybe—and he hid under his Kevlar tent and pulled out his phone.

Following Garcia's directions, he found Garcia—whom he'd listed as Callie, spoofing Gail's number. Get it? Callie, Calix? God, he was pissed off. His humor was fucking savage right now.

Garcia had sent a text about half an hour after his last text, saying he'd gotten to the building safely, and about half an hour before the text that had made McEnany go insane.

Toby's in the hospital but safe.

Took out five Sons assassins—well financed, well trained, waiting for me and Toby to emerge. They didn't expect SCTF to hit them like Navy SEALS.

Two other cops loyal to the Sons taken out.

Harding's PISSED.

Gonna be open season on SCTF. Watch your back, Cowboy, I'll watch mine.

Ca.

Crosby read the text string six to eight times over, making sure again and again and again that Garcia was okay.

God. He didn't want to be here in this shitty apartment with this puppy who needed training up and a Kevlar blanket. He wanted to be *home*, wherever Garcia was, secure in the knowledge that the warm body next to him would keep him safe.

It took him a whole thirty seconds to remember he had info to deliver.

They want me to infiltrate the Forty-Third's Active Crimes division. Gail's roommate won't hire any Sons. Tell Gail to give Iliana fair warning I'm there.

Then, because he had to: *God, I'm glad you're all safe.*

And then because he had to say something—something—although he couldn't say *I love you,* could he? Garcia had said it when he'd been asleep. They weren't there yet, were they? God, he wanted to be there. But he had to say something. Something to say he missed the haven he'd had in Garcia's arms, in his house. He wanted more.

Take care of the zombie gnome, he wrote at last. *I'm gonna want more of them.*

He yawned then and reset his phone to the bad guy's presets before shoving it in his pocket, still on the battery. He had a power cord—he'd plug the whole works in the next day—but right now it was the closest thing he had to home.

"I got work at seven," Junior said softly into the air. "I'll be up in a few hours. You can have the other blanket back then."

Shit. "Thanks, Junior," Crosby murmured.

He was wondering how long he could go without sleep and if it would be possible to really keep one eye open.

He dozed lightly, his body welcoming even that. At seven, the buzz of the kid's phone woke him up, and after Junior had stood and yawned, he gave Crosby his blanket before he left.

Once the door closed, Crosby stood and triple-bolted it, then used the kitchen chair under the doorknob to shore it up before going back to bed.

At nine his stomach woke him up, and he figured that was as good as it got. He was ready to start his day as Rick Young. Bad guy.

CROSBY SPENT part of the next day getting shit for the flop—an extra blanket, his own fucking socks, underwear, sweats, and T-shirts, as well as toiletries and, please God, a couple of books to kill the time when he wasn't trying to die—and familiarizing himself with his surroundings. He knew where the bodega was, knew where the food trucks camped out, knew where the dealers lurked and where the school was and on which corners the cops hung out. By the end of the day, he retired to his flop, legs aching pleasantly from walking all day, secure in the knowledge that he knew which hiding places to run to and which ones were flat-out traps, and that he could find a bus stop and a train stop on a dime.

And that he knew how to avoid the cops, because God knew which side they'd be on.

Garcia had been texting him throughout the day, keeping him updated on the investigation. And on his day.

God, Chadwick's coffee. Lifegiving. After stepping up like a badass at the precinct, it's almost criminal that we depend on him for coffee too.

He'd sent the video of the precinct, and Crosby had watched it in the bathroom at McDonald's while he was getting breakfast, his blood running cold. Oh God, it had been such a trap. How could he not have known he was sending Garcia into a meat grinder?

I'm so sorry. I shouldn't have had you do that. He shuddered, thinking of what could have happened. *I'm such a fucking meatloaf.*

Bullshit. You had me call Harding. I wouldn't have otherwise— saved me and Toby like a boss.

Crosby swallowed and tried to pull his shit together. He knew better than to let this anxious, awful feeling overwhelm him. What—he finally had something good in his life, something his, and he had to lose his mind about keeping it?

He'd fucking keep it all right.

With a deep breath, he remembered all the good things that came from working with Garcia.

Tell me about the dead assholes. One of them was McEnany's nephew—that might be a good angle.

Ooh—see, we didn't know that. All we got was five guys, ages 21- 35. Hard living—bad livers, bad skin, bad teeth—one guy had nth stage syphilis.

Nice.

Elsa got that one in hand-to-hand—I think she's still in the shower.

Poor kid. Crosby smiled. He could hear Gail bitching now. *How's Toby?*

Shook. Not gonna lie. You saw the video—he got beat pretty bad, but he's mostly worried about you. How're you?

And he wanted to spill everything. He'd never asked for undercover gigs, had known he'd suck at most of 'em. Couldn't hide a damned thing with his face. This was a tightrope, and he was wearing his God-given cement shoes.

Shook. Not gonna lie. But I need to tell you—Jimmy Creedy is the guy who runs this division of the Sons and has headquarters in a flop three floors down from mine. McEnany claimed Creedy sent those guys to die. Don't think I was supposed to hear that—I bailed on the convo. I'll try to get bugs. He missed the toys from the SCTF; not that they'd ever relied on more than tactical gear, but still. A bug would have come in handy as he'd been watching McEnany roll the place.

What do we know about Creedy?

Works warehouse jobs—seems to lead a crew—pissed 'cause he tried to be a cop. Has been wiping his feet on his son Junior a couple of times a week. Junior stayed in my flop last night on the couch. Kid is freaked the fuck out.

Aw, Crosby—you got a puppy!

Crosby let out a sad chuckle for the slang. It's what cops called someone who became emotionally dependent on an authority figure, particularly one who seemed sympathetic. The thing, they all reminded each other, was that puppies were needy, and if they didn't understand that their "owner" had other priorities, they could get aggressive and dangerous—just like a real puppy. Crosby's puppy had a lot of different ways he could go wrong.

Yeah—looks like a Chihuahua, could be a cross between a rattlesnake and a pit bull. Sleeping with one eye open.

Good boy. Any other nuggets of info we can run down over here? You've got Elsa and Swan pounding away like Mozart here.

Yeah. Meth. It's what's for dinner. McEnany knocked over a coffee table full of lines, and not one person whined about their hit. Someone is flooding the place with drugs—I need to find out if our guys are slinging or just using or some combo of the two. Where is that shit coming from?

Ugh. Drugs are the fuckin' devil, man. Watch your coffee, watch your water bottle, watch your food.

Because it would be *so* easy to get dosed when not looking. One of the primary rules of undercover was flat out don't do it. Ninety-nine times out of a hundred, users would accept "I only deal, I don't use," as truth. A lot of criminals didn't. And if you got that one guy who didn't buy it, you turned around and walked away, even if it meant bailing from the operation. Using on the job could lose you the bust—and the job. And your life. But Crosby had no way of getting out here. Even if he went hauling back to the SCTF, there were enough Sons of the Blood out there to throw his entire team into WITSEC just to keep them safe.

No, he had to bring down McEnany, bring down the big guys he was trying to impress, and bring down as many little soldier-criminal-cops as he could point a finger at, or his team might as well be shot out of a cannon and used for confetti.

I wouldn't mind some Narcan for my flop—or my pocket. Or some testing kits. I'm about to become nth level paranoid, if you know what I mean.

I'll see what I can scare up. We need a meet place and some protocols.

Let me see how tight my follow is—gotta go.

He'd been so comfortable texting Garcia that the knock on the door startled him into a cold sweat. He quickly switched his phone to the first setting—McEnany and Jimmy Creedy, at this point—and then to his Kindle app, where he was reading a Tom Clancy novel, before striding to the door to open it.

McEnany barged in. "You jerkin' off in here or what?"

Crosby held up his phone, where the first page of chapter five was displayed. "Finishing my chapter. Is the world coming to a fuckin' end?"

McEnany squinted at him. "You read?"

"Four years at Northwestern, McEnany. I've got a BA, double major in criminal justice and history. Yes, I fuckin' read. What do you want?"

McEnany snatched his phone and squinted at the screen. "Jesus, you really are reading this. What is he talking about?"

"Military strategy during naval battles. You want me to pull up some Craig Johnson and you can read about cowboys, or you want to tell me what you're doing here?" Crosby snatched his phone back and made sure McEnany hadn't flipped the pages.

McEnany held up his hands. "Take it easy! Man, you need to go downstairs and hang. They're just playing video games, eating some pie. Creedy said you were being a grouchy asshole, and he's going to suspect something's up if you don't go mooch with the losers."

Crosby eyed him with distaste. "You know, I'm not a fan of cop-killing criminals, but those puppies don't deserve to be thrown to the wolves when you finally get your promotion."

McEnany shrugged. "I can't help how many bodies I have to walk over in order to get the fuck out of this job. Now get your ass downstairs. Ask if anybody's got some food. Jimmy's kid ordered extra for you."

Yeah, Crosby could do that.

"Fine. Make sure nobody doses me with any fuckin' drugs. That's on you, McEnany. You know that'll get me pitched from the department, and then I'm no goddamned good to anybody."

McEnany had the good sense to look worried and nod. "I hear ya. Yeah, these bozos have no clue what it's like to have to piss in a fucking cup once a week. Now are you gonna follow me down?"

"I'll be down in a sec," he said. "I left some burritos in the microwave—let me wrap them and put them in the fridge."

He headed that way, relieved when McEnany walked out. Crosby waited to hear his feet clatter on the stairs before he shoved almost an entire burrito in his mouth so he didn't get too hungry for pizza. God, he did not want to be in that pit with all the fucking vipers, but he *really* didn't want to be in there hungry or thirsty.

He grabbed the six-pack he'd brought for just such an eventuality and followed McEnany down the stairs.

THE BEER turned out to be the smartest fuckin' thing he'd ever done. Once he shared the beer, ate the pizza, and wiped the floor with Junior and his friends Kinsey and Pidgeon on *Overwatch*, everybody in the apartment was either high or asleep. He told everyone he had to be up early so he could get to his job and do the Sons proud and then made his way up the stairs.

When he reached the second-floor landing, he realized Junior was in the stairwell too.

"What're you doing here?" he asked, thinking about how bad he wanted to be alone in that apartment.

Junior's eyes flitted left, then right. "Uh, my dad... he, uh, doesn't want you alone. He, uh, seems to think you might not be straight with us."

Crosby sighed and leaned his head back, pinching the bridge of his nose. "What the fuck ever. Good thing I bought my own fucking blankets. You can have the couch again."

The relief—and the gratitude—on the kid's face told Crosby everything he needed to know about how much of what he'd just said had been a lie. Garcia hadn't been wrong; he had a puppy.

Well, fine.

Crosby had bought a lock for his food cabinets and his refrigerator, and he was starting to trust the kid wouldn't slit his throat when he slept. He might get twenty winks tonight.

He watched the way Jimmy slunk up the stairs.

Maybe only ten.

WHATEVER IT was, it was not enough, because when Iliana called Rick Young into her office to interview her department's newest recruit, she barely waited for the door to close behind him to say, "Jesus, Crosby, you look like shit!"

After the last few days of living on stress, beer, and pizza, his stomach rumbled unhappily, and he fought off a yawn.

"One word, Iliana. Fiber. You have no idea how lucky you are to be able to eat a bran muffin and an apple without defending your life to every scumbag in Brooklyn."

Her eyes widened, and she went to her drawer, coming out with a packet of laxatives and some Tums. He took one of each gratefully and washed them down with coffee he'd bought from a local place, and then handed her the giant kiddie-pool-sized cup of the same brew that he'd gotten as well.

She took the cup and swigged before sighing. "Crosby, this is bad. This is so bad." She wasn't talking about the coffee.

He nodded. "Yeah, in one way it really is. These fuckers are organized, and they're everywhere. I spent my time exploring Brooklyn yesterday, and I had two tails. The good news was they were easy to shake, the bad news is they know where I live 'cause they're paying my rent."

She pulled back her glossy black ponytail, the movement accentuating her trim figure, and he had a moment of regret for the fact that it was never going to have worked out for them. She really was cute.

"So what's our play?" she asked, looking at him worriedly. "I mean, I've worked really hard to build a clean house here—and if you think that's easy, being Latina and being in charge of Active Crimes, you haven't been paying attention."

Crosby nodded. "See, I'm just here to harvest information. The good news is I was a good fuckin' flatfoot. Hire me. Use me. Let me do a flatfoot's job, and when I see what McEnany has planned, I feed that to you and feed him a false report in return. You get all the bennies and none of the noise, you understand?"

She nodded, looking resolute. "Yeah—it *is* good for me. But not so good for *you*, Crosby. Like I said, you already look like shit."

He grunted. "Man, I got no fuckin' place to sleep. They got the Sons of the Blood division chief's son coming up to my room to make sure I don't call the wrong people."

At least that was Junior's excuse for showing up—Crosby was starting to believe Junior just liked the fact that Crosby had no inclination to casually lash out and backhand him like his father or his friends.

Iliana nodded, crossing her arms in front of her uniformed chest. "Most undercover operations give us a little time to organize, get our operator some place for decompression, make sure there's some safe spaces. We don't got that for you, and that means we've got to move quick. Anything you need me to do?"

"See, McEnany has me here to front for the Sons, but he's trying to impress someone. Somebody in the upper echelon—PD or Alphabet, I'm not sure—is gonna be watching me, seeing if I get in tight with you. So if people start checking on my progress, getting nosy. If someone you never heard from before wants to know if that Rick Young is a fast-track guy? You need to tell Harding's people."

She nodded. "I've got a couple of names already. Courtland Cavendish, police commissioner's lawyer. I've never heard from him before, but suddenly I've got a memo on my desk from him. About you. Marshawn Devereaux, NYPD brass, who was apparently asked to push your transfer through but hadn't met you himself, and Marcy Beauchamp, also from the police commissioner's office, who was told you were an up-and-comer and needed to pull somebody since she'd just lost a couple of people she really valued."

Crosby grunted, nodding. "Okay, I don't recognize those people...." He frowned. "Except Devereaux. I'm not sure why the name rings a bell. But good. That's who we're talking about. Rick Young shouldn't have a fan club yet. And that's the sort of stuff I can't get while I'm off being Rick Young. Now I've got to tell you something so you can push it to Vice. There is a *lot* of product flooding the streets from our particular area." He pulled out a dime bag he'd let Creedy push on him the night before, just in case he changed his mind and needed a little taste. "It's tagged—" He indicated a stamp, a revolver, because you might as well shoot yourself as take this shit, right? "—and from what I can see, it's pretty potent." He'd needed to caution two of Creedy's thugs the night before because he'd been afraid they'd OD out of sheer carelessness. "I'm guessing it might be cut with more than a smidge of fentanyl, you know, 'cause first responders don't have enough to do."

She took the packet and put it into an evidence bag that she had him sign before signing herself. Smuggling drugs into the precinct hadn't been easy; he'd needed to cut the seam in the waistband of his trousers to fit the thing in under his belt.

"Wow," she said, letting out a breath. "Anything else you can tell us about the drugs?"

He shook his head. "Only that I get the feeling some cops are turning a blind eye. One of the guys asked me if I wanted some baggies to flash in case—and I quote—'my blue brothers start giving me shit.' So if you've got any cops who are using…."

"This might be the stuff," she said on a sigh. "This is fabulous. Don't take this the wrong way, Crosby, because I realize you're not the elephant who shit on my stoop, but…."

"It's still a lot of shit," he said, agreeing. "Look, if it's any consolation? I'm here, in your department because you are so fucking squeaky clean, they can't get a cop in edgewise. I wasn't sent to Vice or Robbery/Homicide. I was sent to Active Crimes, where all the shit is going down *right now*. So they want somebody who can maybe not suck their guys into the system." He shrugged. "Turns out that's what my old job trained us to do—not look at the system, just look at getting the victims out of a bad sitch so we can get the perps. So I can do the job you need me to do, keep the victims from getting sucked into the system, and maybe figure out who the real bad guys are, all while letting the Sons think they got a guy in play."

She shuddered. "Yeah. Sounds like an easy win. Except somebody's gotta be you."

He let out a humorless laugh. "God, it'll be worth it if I can cop a nap in a crib or something. I just…." He shuddered, and she nodded.

"Can't do it every day, but if you're really hurting, you can use my couch." She indicated the couch in the back of her office. "And there's a crib in the squad room if you need it. Active Crimes tends to run hot, so there's not a lot of use for it. If nobody's there and you're off shift, go for it. Fuck McEnany—tell him you're doing paperwork, right?"

Crosby cracked a quiet grin. "Right. Now, where do you want me?"

She sighed, then turned to pull out a file she'd obviously had ready. "Here's your beat," she said, "as well as a patrol breakdown of the precinct and hot spots. You're with a veteran training officer and his rookie for the first week, then you're on your own, but you need to know you're their backup. I…." She didn't turn the file over. "Look, Crosby, this is hard. I know you're a nice guy, because let's face it, you didn't give Gail all that help for the living conditions." Her apologetic smirk was the closest thing he'd gotten to an acknowledgment that they'd been lovers once.

He reached out a gentle hand to take the folder. "Your couch was better for my back," he said softly. "And you both needed a certain thing at that time. I'm glad I could help."

For a moment her lower lip crumpled. "You're nicer about it than I was," she said, her eyes on the floor as she gave up the folder. Then she raised her chin and met his eyes. "And I… I'm still broken. But I'm asking you to be the kind of cop you just bragged about. To take care of my guys, my veteran and my rookie, and make sure they're okay as best you can. I…." She shook her head. "I know that your unit is hot shit, and I'd have Gail in my division any time. I just need to know I'm being responsible here."

He nodded and swallowed. He knew the horror stories of UC cops who'd left a trail of human wreckage in their wake. Cast-off families, burned sources, as many people in the morgue as in jail. "You know what I like about SCTF?" he asked, and she shook her head.

"We have the resources to help people. Cops don't. Cops stop crime, and the good divisions have contacts—social services, rehab, that sort of thing. But our division is about minimizing the damage path. Why else do we have guns and badges, right?"

She nodded, a faint smile at the corner of her mouth.

"I know…." He shuddered. Was it less than a week ago, he'd taken that shot? "I know you look at my record and think 'this guy hates cops.' That's not true. I love cops. I wanted to be one since I was a kid. I hate *criminals*, and they don't got no business with a badge."

"Truth," she said softly before sticking out her hand. "Fair enough. Go back to your flat, catch some Zs, start tomorrow."

Oh *sweet*. McEnany thought he was wrapped up all day! It was only 10:00 a.m.…

"Can do," he said, before looking down at the dress blues he'd been given for his induction day. "But first can I get a locker? I'm going to leave these here and catch a train."

Going Gnome

QUIET DAY, thank fuck. Garcia was still filling out paperwork on Crosby's shoot, the Stoya case, and, God help them all, getting Toby out of the Twenty Fourth.

His phone buzzed, and he was almost ashamed at how quickly he jumped on it.

Bring electronics and Narcan. Meet by the gnome.

Oh wow. It had been three nights since Crosby had been called out of bed, and Garcia was so ready to see him. After six months of rarely going more than a day without being in company—whether at work, in training, or hanging out in general—those two days of furtive texting were a terrible taste of the time ahead.

And Garcia needed to know he was okay.

In one moment, Judson Crosby, the most dependable man Garcia had ever known, had been sucked into a terrible underworld where every breathing moment was filled with ways this one could be his last, and all Garcia had to do was… wait. Wait for people to run down leads, wait until the paperwork was done, wait for some direction that would help them get Crosby the fuck out of Brooklyn.

He hadn't expected Crosby to find a way himself, although the "bring electronics" was a pointed reminder that this wasn't a social visit.

Garcia picked up his phone and was about to head toward Harding's office when *his* new shadow spoke up.

"What's up?"

He grimaced, not wanting to share anything with Lou Doba but not wanting to brush the guy off either. The officer—sergeant, actually—who had ended up helping Toby Trotter out of the Twenty Fourth wasn't a bad guy. Single, in his thirties, he'd seen very clearly what was going on, and having watched his precinct, which was in the neighborhood in which he'd grown up, get worse and worse and more corrupt by the day hadn't been easy on him. He and young Henderson had been offered places in the local field office. They'd both easily passed government clearance, and Henderson had been sent to electronic filing, something he apparently had an aptitude for.

Doba had asked, respectfully but with confidence, if he could work with the—in his words—badasses who had taken on the Twenty Fourth in a war and won.

Well, they were down a Crosby, and while Doba would need a *lot* of training, not to mention FLETC, before he was field ready, having someone to help with the paperwork, organize the training schedule, and feed them intel on Crosby's general area and the criminals he'd need to watch out for while he was undercover was gold. While Doba hadn't worked the place, he had friends and family at the Forty Third, where Crosby was, and a solid knowledge of what drugs, gangs, and criminal rackets were flooding the streets of Manhattan and where they were coming from.

Helpful, smart, and—a blessing—humble, Doba knew the difference between federal level training and state, and while he was older than most recruits, he wanted in.

And, well. Crosby wasn't there.

But since Garcia was the one without his partner, Garcia was left to train him, and Garcia wasn't ready to trust another partner just yet.

But he really didn't want to blow the guy off either. *He'd* been the new guy, and the team had taken him in. He felt like he owed this guy a little of what he'd been given.

"Got a meet with a source," he said. "Ongoing case."

Doba cocked his head. "You mean your guy who's under, right?"

And he was smart. "Look, we're not going to talk about that. Other cases, sure. But—"

"The missing crewman that everybody's terrified for? I'm not supposed to notice that?" Doba scoffed. "Sure. I'll try to forget his name."

Oh God. Garcia rubbed the back of his neck. "We do not know who to trust right now," he said after a minute. "And we want to trust you—you've been great! But it's been two days. Everybody in this room wants our boy back in a week, but we're smart enough to know it's going to be longer than that. So give it some time. Man, you still got tags on your civvies, right?"

Doba gave half a laugh. They'd been trying to explain their dress code—classy but functional, works well with Kevlar, helpful for running, holds the badge case firmly but makes it easily accessible—and in the end Harding had ended up taking him shopping on his lunch hour.

He'd come back looking slick and able to work—and run down a perp—and highly uncomfortable about not wearing a uniform.

Garcia, Chadwick, and Carlyle had been giving him tips for the last two days, and he'd been embarrassed but grateful with every pointer.

"I just...." He looked around. "You may not know this, but you probably saved my life... and Henderson's, because I do not think the Twenty Fourth would have let that kid walk away. I'd like to help."

Garcia gave a quick smile. "You *are* helping. And tomorrow we'll be running active shooter drills and the like, you and me, and you'll be learning a buttload. I came up from a small-town deputy through the ATF to this—you'll be super excited to know how much fun we'll be having and how you'll be fucking exhausted in the morning—and the dress code is real simple. Combat boots, tactical clothing, black T-shirts. Boom. You're in." He allowed his expression to gentle. "But this? This goes high up. I think I can tell you that. This goes high up, and we do not want to leave our boy with his ass swinging in the breeze."

Doba nodded. "Tactical gear, you say?"

Garcia tilted his head back. "Doh! Go see Pearson. She's got the number of the uniform department. Sorry about that, brother, I've been—"

"Thinking about other things," Doba said. "Understood. Hope your boy stays safe."

"We all do," Garcia told him. *Me most of all.*

Harding looked at the text as Garcia held out his phone, then held up his hand. Without a word, he headed toward a filing cabinet in the back of his office. He came back with two small boxes, one with five tiny plastic listening devices in it and another with fifteen tinier batteries.

After another trip to his magic filing cabinet, he had a small recorder that could be programmed for every listening device.

"Range is twenty, twenty-five feet at most," he said quietly. "Go see Denison. She's got trackers and Narcan."

"Thanks," Garcia told him. "I'll be back—"

"Tomorrow's soon enough," Harding said and then grimaced. "I just got a call from Gail's old roommate—said the guy's looking for a place to flop between gigs—a night at the most. You might hear from him."

"I'll be ready," Garcia said, his heart thundering. A night. Or at least the rest of the day. It was a gift he hadn't dreamed of. "In the meantime, I'll go meet my CI."

"Fair. Let us know how it falls out. I've got some names to run down too."

Meaning Crosby and Iliana had been exchanging information. Good. Good.

"Mañana!"

Garcia practically ran out of the room.

THE FIRST thing he noticed when he got to his little house was that the gnome, which he had parked outside on his porch, looking creepy and kitschy and weird, was gone. It didn't stop him from keeping his hand on his piece as he let himself in, but when he saw the thing on his coffee table, a thick file folder underneath, it did let him relax just a tad.

Venturing farther into the house, he saw the boots he'd put the tracker inside were sitting in the hall outside the spare room, and the door was open a few inches. Crosby lay, shirtless, in a pair of sweats, facedown on the bed, his bare shoulders hunching slightly in the spring chill.

Garcia had been undercover a few times in his career. He murmured, "Crosby, it's me, Calix. I'm coming in."

He was prepared for the sudden stiffening, the instant alertness, and relieved when Crosby reached under the mattress for his weapon and not under his pillow, which could be so much more dangerous.

"Calix?" Crosby muttered, his words obviously catching up to his reflexes. "Izzat you?"

"Yeah, papi." Garcia ventured into the room and placed a soothing hand on Crosby's back. "Why you in here and not where you belong?"

"Didn't want to be there without you," Crosby muttered, sitting up and looking so utterly exhausted Garcia gave up any dreams of having a quickie before they talked. "Didja see the folder?"

"Here, let's move to the other bedroom, I'll lock up our weapons, and you can sleep while I look through it and share some info, okay?"

"Yeah, sure."

Crosby allowed himself to be led, meek as a child, to the room they'd shared so passionately three nights before. This time, he took off his sweats and slid between the sheets in his boxers, pulling the covers tight around his shoulders.

Garcia bent and kissed his temple. "Get some sleep, okay? I'll wake you for lunch in a few."

"Anything but pizza," Crosby mumbled. "Maybe a nice salad." And then he was asleep.

THREE HOURS later, Garcia's stomach grumbled, and he yawned and stretched from his place on the bed next to Crosby. He'd spent time with the file and his laptop—a clean one, with no connection to the SCTF or the federal offices they were stationed in—looking up the names and the connections Crosby had brought back. He had some info to share, mostly with Harding, but he didn't want to talk about that now.

Instead, he ran his hand along Crosby's shoulders, smoothing away the tension that had haunted Crosby even in sleep.

Crosby moaned faintly, his shoulders relaxing, and then rolled over, smiling sleepily up at him.

"You okay?" Garcia asked.

"Needed that," Crosby mumbled.

Garcia smoothed his hair back from his head. "Never done undercover before?" He knew Crosby hadn't. The story of how he'd tracked down a serial killer by putting on his civvies and going door-to-door ran through his mind. This guy wasn't a UC kind of guy—Garcia's boy was all out there, without reservation or artifice. Those words from his first day kept repeating. *I'm not that smart and I'm not that quick… I really don't want you to end up dead because I wasn't good enough.*

That was his boy, and that boy had no business swimming in the shark tank that was his current sitch.

"Their apartment is all drugs and old food. I think the meth is driving away the cockroaches, and… I can't even. How bad's the meth gotta be?"

Garcia managed a broken laugh, but he couldn't seem to stop touching Crosby's hair, his face, his neck.

Crosby seized his hand and kissed it, those flinty blue-gray eyes going sly. "You, uh... you know, wouldn't need to take a break or anything, would you?"

Garcia needed him inside so bad. "I thought you'd never ask." He set his laptop aside before sliding down the bed, capturing Crosby's mouth, and pushing at the covers to touch more skin.

Crosby grunted. "You're wearing clothes."

"Too many?"

"Obviously."

Garcia grinned and hopped out of bed to strip. This time he slid under the covers to tangle legs with Crosby, to kiss, to feel their bare skin together.

They had so little time—he would take all the Crosby he could get.

Crosby's kisses turned hungry, *starving*, and his hands demanded things Garcia was more than willing to give. His hand on Garcia's cock was no bullshit, and he wasn't gentle stroking Garcia to an erection.

Garcia recognized the hunger, the need, for what it was—the shaking comedown of being someone else, of knowing the world was just waiting to kill you, the need to be with someone on a human, animal level that had very little to do with romance. He fumbled for the lubricant and handed it off but refused Crosby's pressure on his shoulder to turn him to his stomach.

"You look me in the eyes," he rasped. "There's nothing there I can't handle."

Crosby swallowed, his eyes growing bright, and for a moment Garcia thought he'd lost him. He lunged upward, taking Crosby's mouth again and spreading his legs. Crosby's slick fingers weren't gentle as they stretched him, but Garcia didn't care. The rough burn in his asshole was secondary to taking Crosby inside, to being with him as he rode out the shakes, the anxiety, the comedown.

Goddammit, Garcia needed this so badly.

"You sure?" Crosby asked, poised at his entrance with little preparation.

"Go, dammit, now!"

Crosby's jaw flexed, and he breached. For a moment Garcia could do nothing but tilt his head back and force himself to relax, *let* his rim be stretched wide and hard, *allow* his body to widen, to accommodate, to surrender.

A moment of pain, that was all, and Crosby was sheathed inside him, his arms shaking as he held himself up, one palm on either side of Garcia's head.

"Good?" Crosby asked, and Garcia knew it took all his patience, all his control, to ask that before thrusting.

"*Fuck me!*" he ordered, and Crosby threw his head back and complied.

It wasn't lovemaking—it was barely sex. It was an animal coupling, Crosby's body rocketing into Garcia's, his eyes closed, his entire being focused on chasing his own climax, answering to his own pleasure, soothing his own need.

Garcia spread his legs wantonly and took it, letting the pounding wash through him, his arousal building to an unbearable peak.

"Oh God," he moaned, entire body in a sweat of desire. "God, I need to—" He didn't wait for Crosby's permission. He slid his hand between their bodies and squeezed his own cock, stroked it hard, dug his thumbnail into his slit, needing his orgasm so bad the bite of pain was necessary.

The first ripples up his spine bowed his back, and he grunted, feral, needing... oh fuck, Crosby, hit him, there... there... *there, goddammit, there!*

With a cry, he let his climax take him, his ass clenching hard enough to make Crosby cry out too, the sound ripped from him like his come, filling Garcia's body with fierce, hot spurts.

For a moment Garcia went limp, his body shivering with aftermath. When Crosby pulled out, and he wasn't proud of the sound of want he made.

And then Crosby slid down his body, heedless of the spatter of semen across his abdomen, hitting his chest. It smeared between the two of them before Garcia felt Crosby's mouth on his still-dripping cock, and it occurred to him in a very dim way, past the shuddering of the orgasm that was fading and over the whispers of the new one that was building, that this interlude was *far* from over.

"DAMN," CROSBY breathed, falling onto the pillow next to where Garcia fought for breath. "You good?"

Garcia's asshole ached, and he was covered in a wash of come—on, in, or gushing from all orifices. Round two had been a fumbling sixty-nine, and Garcia had barely time to wipe Crosby's cock down before it was in his throat.

Round three had been facedown, because his arms and legs couldn't hold him anymore. He was pretty sure he had bite marks down his back, across his chest, on his thighs, on his neck… and his ass.

"Great," he mumbled. "Destroyed. Wrecked. All same. Jesus, Cowboy."

Crosby gave a rough chuckle and kissed Garcia's bare shoulder tenderly. "Sorry. I was…."

Garcia turned his head in time to see Crosby bite his lower lip. "Driven," he whispered, rubbing his thumb along it.

"Yeah. I… I needed as much as I could get." He kissed Garcia's shoulder again. "I hope it was okay."

Garcia nodded. "Yeah. Hearts and flowers are nice, but sometimes…." He waggled his eyebrows, but Crosby didn't laugh.

"I am afraid," he said softly, "that I'll get the hearts and flowers sanded out of me. These people. God, Calix. This world—I…." He shook his head and held out his hand, scooting backward like he was going to roll out of bed.

Garcia wouldn't let him, grabbing his hand, pulling himself toward Crosby's heavily muscled chest and making sure they were eye-to-eye.

"I've seen this world," he said worriedly. "I *did* go undercover in ATF. And it's… it's bad. And the worst thing about it is that people assume that one hit makes someone the devil. But it's not like that. It's that the person they're supposed to be is always so clear. And sometimes that person's an asshole and the drugs sand away the clown mask, but most of the time, they're just…."

"People," Crosby said, proving he got it. "Just people. They… they didn't see their lives turning out like this, that's all."

Garcia was going to say something light, something to make Crosby feel better, but it stuck in his throat.

Crosby—for all his talk about being a "meatloaf"—wasn't near stupid.

"You didn't see your life here either," Crosby whispered. With a shaky breath, he rolled out of bed and started fishing for his boxers under the covers. "I'm sorry. I… we can meet somewhere else next time. I can move my stuff out—"

"*No!*" Garcia bit out, not even conscious of moving but suddenly right there next to Crosby, standing naked in the unheated house. "Stop! Cowboy, fuckin' *stop!*"

Crosby stopped moving, but he kept his face averted, probably so Garcia couldn't see the hurt there.

"Look, I'm sorry," he said gruffly, eyes at the wrecked bed. "You didn't sign on for this, for me in undercover. You probably want another partner so you can start living your life—*ouch*!"

Garcia wasn't aware he was going to slap Crosby's face until his hand made contact.

"The *hell*, Garcia!" Crosby was staring at him in pain and confusion, rubbing his cheek.

"Don't you fucking *dare*!" Garcia snarled. "You think you haven't made promises to me, Judson Crosby, you think again!"

"But that was when I was going to be here!" Crosby retorted. "Not when I was gonna be out in the wind, with McEnany just itching for a reason to off me or feed me to the sharks. You know that's where it's going, right? As soon as I'm not useful, he tells his higher-ups, they come gunning for me to shut me up?"

"Then we go into WITSEC together," Garcia snapped, replacing Crosby's hand with his own. "But you don't back out. Not now. Not when.... *God*, Crosby. I never had anything good before like you. I never ever thought someone would have my back like you. I've waited my entire *life* to have you in it. Don't threaten to take that away *now*!"

Crosby started to nod, and then he stopped and leaned into Garcia's palm. "I," he said succinctly, "am going to be a needy fucking disaster every time we meet here." His voice was thick with frustration and longing. "You think I've ever had someone like you in my life? I don't want you to see me this... this fucking needy. This fucking sad. And...." He pulled in a shaky breath. "It's like I can be a badass, and my game face is locked down, but the minute I was in your bed, I was... I was safe. And I don't want to be your puppy, Calix. I want to be your man!"

Garcia swallowed. "You are," he said softly, leaning into Crosby's body so Crosby *had* to hold him. "We're still partners, Crosby. We're more partners than before, okay?"

They both stood, breathing hard, trying to get a handle on the hard emotions coursing through them both like an electric current, binding them tighter in a rictus of fear.

Crosby shuddered, and Garcia stepped away reluctantly, finding Crosby's boxers with one fish under the covers.

"Thanks," Crosby muttered, sliding them on.

"You will come here whenever you can," Garcia said gruffly. "No hanging out in your shitty flat because you think it's what you do. You will not last out there in the wind, Judson. You need shelter—it's why there's so many songs about it."

Crosby nodded and gave a slight smile before making his mouth into a tiny O and singing the first notes of the Rolling Stones classic.

By the time they were both completely dressed, Garcia had called it up on his phone, and much like that night—God, less than a week ago—they were screaming the lyrics at the top of their lungs.

Shelter was, after all, just a kiss away.

GARCIA MADE them late lunch/early dinner. He sauteed chicken and steamed some veggies and some rice. It was very basic, but he used a nice marinade and made a lot. He wasn't letting his boy back into the lion's den with no fuel to sustain him.

Crosby watched him from the counter that divided the kitchen from the living room, his eyes hot, but they were both all business as they talked about the case.

Garcia asked him where he planned to leave the bugs, and Crosby had three places picked already—Creedy's flat, his desk at the station, and the locker room. He figured he'd leave the other two to place later, when he got a feel for where things would be happening. The hard thing with bugs was the need to replace the batteries. It couldn't be a place that would seem too suspicious to hang out nearby.

When they sat down for dinner, Garcia gave a very brief, very silent prayer to whatever god his grandmother had prayed to, mostly for safety, a remnant of his childhood, and then turned to what he'd learned while Crosby had slept.

"Okay, so Marshawn Devereaux, Chief of Police for the Brooklyn precincts, is probably not your guy," he said, shoveling chicken into his mouth.

"What makes you think that?" Crosby asked, leaning just close enough for their shoulders to touch.

"Well, for one thing, he's Denison's father-in-law."

Crosby blinked. "Isn't Denison's family…?"

"Black?" Garcia nodded. "Uh-huh. Yeah. So that's a whole lot of nope."

Crosby gave a chuckle. "Be sure to tell her he was on our list." Then he sobered. "But maybe ask him why he was interested in Rick Young, or, you know, have Natalia ask him. Because it would be good to see what kind of motives the average higher-up has when asking about a new hire."

"Good point." Garcia bumped his shoulder in emphasis and realized they'd been communicating like this—grunts, half-finished sentences, reading each other's minds—for the better part of six months.

How had they not known from the beginning that it would lead to this?

Maybe he would ask Crosby that someday when the undercover work was over.

"What about Marcy Beauchamp?" Crosby asked, pushing his plate away.

"Finish that," Garcia ordered, noting that Crosby had left about half his chicken and vegetables.

"I thought I was hungry," Crosby said apologetically. He rubbed his stomach. "Turns out it was just stress."

"Eat it anyway," Garcia said, trying not to let worry gnaw at him. "Food is fuel, and admit it." He grinned and made the "all that" gesture at himself. "I can cook."

That earned him a shy smile and the plate getting pulled back into position.

"Happy?" Crosby asked through a full mouth. He swallowed. "Now what about her?"

"She's a gray area," Garcia told him, frowning with what he'd learned. "She works for the commissioner's office overseeing imports and exports, grew up in California, of all places, and her father was a cop. She served ten years in law enforcement—but not in New York—before climbing the promotion ladder like a squirrel to end up here, but I get the feeling the whole Sons of the Blood thing wasn't ever supposed to be a Daughters of the Blood thing, so that's where it could fall apart."

Crosby grunted. "Yeah, that's a tough one. The culture in that flat is so toxically male, I...." he trailed away and bit his lip.

"What?" Ooh, this was worrisome.

"I... man, I'm wondering if those guys don't... you know, fuck with Junior because they don't want to get all contaminated by girl cooties, if that makes any sense. It's just... listening to them, listening to the way they talk about women, it's never by name. It's always by... you know. Body part. I just don't see a woman getting to the top of that food chain and then giving it all up for an organization that would sooner gangfuck her bloody than talk to her like a person."

Garcia let out a low growl. "Yeah, I don't see it either. But we've both seen it happen. We've *both* seen people so poisoned, so resentful and wanting to prove something that they fight against their own best interests, you know?"

Crosby thought about McEnany, who was betraying an office that offered more power and more money in order to further a cause of hatred, and nodded. "Fair. Give her information to Iliana. Maybe she can get a read on Beauchamp for us. Rick Young has no reason to talk to her. It would be weird coming from me. What about Cavendish?"

Garcia frowned. "City police commissioner's lawyer. I can't get a bead on his upbringing, though. Attended Harvard Law, so that's something, but I have no idea if he's a lawyer legacy or a cop success story. There's nothing here. I've been tracking down his write-ups in law review journals and stuff, but I don't even know if he's got a wife. I mean, lots of briefs, lots of bailing the NYPD out of the fire for everything from police brutality to closing down precincts, but I have no idea which side he's on. A lot of this shit's settled out of court."

Crosby grunted. "Look, you know when I was being debriefed for the Brandeis trial?"

"By the ADA?" Garcia asked, because he'd studied this in the last few days.

"Yeah. I had to give my depositions about six thousand times before Brandeis took a plea for a supermax instead of the death penalty. At one point the defense attorney was practically ripping my nails out to get me to change my story, and my ADA snapped, 'Marty, if you don't back off and put on your human skin, I'll tell your wife how you're treating this kid and we'll see if you ever get laid again.'"

Garcia snickered into his hand. "What did the defense attorney say?"

"Well, first he said, 'Fuck you, Alan, and see if I invite *you* to poker night,' and *then* he turned off his tape recorder and looked at me and said, 'Kid, you're holding pretty tough, but you gotta be a steel wall, coated in Kevlar, coated in goose shit. If the jury sees you crack, it is my *job* to drive a truck through that crack and get my client off. It's your job to make sure they know why that shouldn't happen.' Then he turns back to the ADA and goes, 'Fair?'"

Garcia gave a slow nod. "It *was*," he said, surprised. "I mean, the guys defending the scumbags really are doing their jobs. And you and I *both* know if more of the little bad guys had a lawyer, the cops would spend more of their time with the real criminals."

"Yeah," Crosby agreed. "But also, you know, who knows you best?"

And *now* Garcia got it. "The guy whose job is to stick it to you."

"Yeah. Someone smart must have said that if you really want to know someone, know their enemies."

Garcia had brought a legal pad out to write down ideas and take notes as they ate. He wrote that down and double underlined it. Then he wrote down a list of places to look to find the people who had gone up against Cavendish in the past.

A silence fell, and Crosby yawned, then peered outside. "Getting late," he said on a sigh. He stood and took his plate to the counter.

"Leave the dishes," Garcia told him, waving his hand. Then he went to the top of the fridge and grabbed a bakery box of bran muffins, the kind he'd seen Crosby eat every morning for the last six months. "Here, put this in your gym duffel. You'll have something to eat tomorrow."

Crosby did, giving him another one of those shy smiles. "You thought of that for me?"

Garcia nodded. "You know, someone always brings them for you. I just... you know me. Always thinking about the next meal."

Crosby's grin almost undid him. He sobered quickly, stepping into Garcia's space and bending to kiss him, warm, strong, kind—all the things Garcia treasured about Crosby were in that kiss.

"I'll be in touch," he promised.

"Be safe," Garcia begged.

"You too. We both work the same job, you know."

Yeah, but you're working it through the looking glass. You're going to get some stuff backward, Judson. There's no way to avoid it.

"Yeah, but you know. First day we worked together you ran into a sitch without me and got shot. Bad things happen when I'm not there to have your back."

Crosby's response to that was another kiss. "I'll text you the uplink for the bugs," he said soberly. "You'll have my back."

And then he was gone.

Garcia closed the door behind him and fell against it, closing his eyes against the gnawing worry and the empty echo of the house.

He swallowed, working for resolve, and went back to the kitchen to load the dishwasher, which was when he realized Crosby never really *had* eaten his dinner.

Fuck.

He finished the kitchen and then wandered into the bedroom, saw the sheets rumpled and marked with their lovemaking, and lost to temptation. He picked up the pillow where Crosby—*his* Crosby—had slept like the dead, secure for the only time in three days that his partner had his back, and held it in his arms, smelling his body wash, his shampoo... and his fear. Oh, it was in there, the faint scent marker of fear.

And that's when he gave in, hugged the pillow to his chest, and cried.

Flatfoot

"HEY, BEER!" everybody in Creedy's little apartment cried, and "Rick Young" put on his best face.

"Beer's always welcome," he said, because it was true, but also because it was part of his schtick. Yeah, sure, he spent five days a week, sometimes twelve to sixteen hours a day, working as a patrol officer in the neighborhood, but when he was off, he was expected to "socialize." He was well aware it was the only way he was getting out of this sitch alive. A lot of the guys worked night security at the warehouse with some sort of loading device called a "big bitch"—those were the nights they stayed out late. The next day, they were sleepy and hungry and high.

Always a good day for beer.

He looked around the room today to see who was there and let out a sigh of relief. He'd been taking covert photos of everybody who'd appeared in Creedy's flat while he'd been there over the last six weeks, and thank God, he knew everybody's names and jackets today, because he was not in the mood to pull his phone out and play with it and get tricky right now.

His pretend job was hard enough, thank you—having to do his real job was not on his agenda.

"How you doin', Ricky?" Junior asked, and Crosby wanted to groan. Junior was sitting next to Kinsey Sizemore, a fucking behemoth who liked to turn around randomly and whale on Junior for fun. It was like little kids wrestled sometimes, but Crosby *had* been a flatfoot for two years, and he recognized the actual pain on Junior's face when it happened, and he also recognized the short, feral bursts of fear that seemed to wrack Junior on the regular.

Kinsey Sizemore was probably doing more to Junior than socking his arm, and Junior was not exactly thrilled about it, either. Crosby didn't think Kinsey was gay so much as he was *violent* and a bully, and he'd bend Junior over and fuck him bloody just to hear him whimper.

Because the look on Junior's face told Crosby he'd stopped screaming a long time ago.

"Not so bad," Crosby answered. "Just, you know—working backup for a veteran and a rookie. The rookie's a good kid, but wet behind the ears." Crosby had lost track of the number of times he'd run drills with the kid for following your partner through a house, one hand on the shoulder, looking behind you so nobody got caught by surprise, but Crosby had gotten there just in time that day, right before Sweeney had almost gotten jumped by a guy spiraling on meth. The meth seemed to be everywhere, and Crosby had needed to use his baton on the back of the guy's head to get him to drop off Sweeney's back.

Thank God there'd been no knives or guns involved or Sweeney and his partner, Barnes, might have been dead, and Crosby would be eyeball deep in paperwork too.

Junior gave him a slight smile, the kind that made Crosby's stomach bunch up like it had been for the last six weeks. He'd been running hard, taking pictures, planting bugs, getting called in for extra shifts. There'd been no time to visit Queens in the last six weeks, and Crosby could feel Garcia's absence like he'd been torn from Crosby's skin.

No time to talk about his misgivings regarding Junior, how he thought maybe the kid *was* gay and needed to be extracted from this situation *now*, before it was too late. Crosby had caught him the other day about to do a line of the meth that sat fucking *perpetually* on the table at Creedy's.

"That shit'll rot your brain," he'd said harshly, and Junior had dropped his hand.

"I just…." He'd shifted where he stood, obviously in a little pain. "Everything hurts," he'd whispered, giving Kinsey and his smaller, meaner buddy Pidgeon Smalls a surreptitious look.

"Take Advil," Crosby had advised, also quietly. "Learn to run faster. Maybe don't hang out in your father's apartment so much, Junior. But don't start with that—man, I don't know how these guys hold down jobs at the warehouse with all they do!" It was true. Kinsey and Pidgeon and their buddies always seemed to be in Creedy's apartment whenever Rick Young visited, and they always seemed to be high.

At that moment, Kinsey had looked up from his huddle around the table with Pidgeon and the others. "C'mere, Junior," he'd said, laughing meanly. "We want you to help us settle a bet. Maybe your buddy Rick can hang out too! C'mon, Ricky, have a snort and come play poker!"

That had been Crosby's intention that day—minus the "snort"—but looking at Junior's anguished, terrified face, he realized he was going to have to improvise.

"Me and Junior gotta go down to the bodega and get some water and shit for my mini fridge. Sorry, guys—I got a double shift tomorrow, and I need some stores."

There'd been protests as he pulled Junior out into the corridor and down the stairs. He'd discovered the tiny elevator on the south side of the building, but it stank like shit, just like McEnany had told him. The stairs kept him fit, he told himself virtuously.

They also kept him off McEnany and Creedy's radar, because they were lazy bastards, just like the thugs who hung out in Creedy's flop.

That day, Junior had told him that his father, while not the union president, had pull with the union. Kinsey, Pidgeon, and their friends were night security at the warehouse, but they seemed to be able to miss a lot of days without anybody caring.

The thought teased at his brain today as he watched Junior try helplessly to distance himself from Kinsey and Pidgeon again.

Shit. Well, it wasn't like he was going to be able to see Garcia tonight, or tomorrow either. He knew the teams were working on the info he'd been feeding them. He'd gotten jackets on all the criminals, with everything from sexual assault to manslaughter behind their names, but so far they couldn't figure out the connection between Creedy, his goons, and the higher-ups that McEnany was trying to cozen up to.

And it wasn't going to happen today, he decided.

"Junior, got another shopping run to make," he said, which flat out wasn't true. He had noodles, waters, even apples, bran muffins, and yogurt, which he tried to eat every day no matter *how* bad his stomach felt, but God. He couldn't see Garcia. He couldn't fix the whole situation in just this minute.

The least he could do—the very least—was get Junior out of this apartment, where Kinsey or Pidgeon or Rod or Clyde or any of the other assholes might pull him into his own bedroom and work out their meth boner on his poor, abused, scrawny body.

"Yeah?" Junior popped up from the couch, moving nimbly from Kinsey's clumsy grasp. "Sorry guys. Gotta go!"

And with that, Crosby led him to the stairwell, but as soon as the door had closed, he started to go up instead of down.

"No groceries?" Junior said, sounding depressed.

"Cup-o-noodles and a salad in my flop?" Crosby asked. "I got some mac and cheese."

"Hot dogs?" Junior asked.

Crosby grimaced. "No room for hot dogs in the mini fridge," he said.

"I'll run and get hot dogs," Junior told him, sounding excited. "Don't worry—those guys were really fucking stoned. They won't be looking for me for a good two hours."

Oh God. "Well, in two hours, I'm gonna be asleep. I hope you brought a book or something."

Junior gave him a hopeful smile. "I've been, uhm, reading the paperbacks in your room. I like the fantasy ones."

Crosby frowned and realized that he'd let Junior sleep on his couch enough times that Junior might have had plenty of time to do that.

"Fair," he said. Then, because he didn't want Junior to think this was a date. "I've got to text my girl for a bit. It's been a while—she's getting needy." The truth was just the opposite. Garcia sounded like he was doing okay. He kept Crosby briefed on all the team was doing every day, and they would talk personally if there was time. Courtship language; Crosby could recognize it.

He treasured it.

"Yeah," Junior said. "I figured. Just...." He didn't need to finish that sentence.

Anything to get him away from his father's thugs.

"No worries, kid." He turned around and pulled out a ten. "Bring some hot dogs—and maybe some cookies or something." Crosby's stomach was all acid, but God, Junior may have been twenty-one or so, but he was a kid who needed some fucking cookies.

And then he smiled, and Crosby's stomach gave a volcanic churn.

"Sure, Ricky. Anything you want!"

As the kid turned down the stairs and Crosby hauled his exhausted, depressed ass up the three flights to his flop, he knew, deep in his bones, that Junior really meant that. And while Crosby had no intention of taking the kid up on it, he couldn't help but wonder exactly how much trouble having a puppy was going to be.

"BARNES," CROSBY said into his comms three days later, "if you do not get your boot out of my line of fire, he's going to get shot, and I'm going to feel really bad about that."

"*Sweeney!*" Rufus Barnes was a solid training officer, but a rookie was a rookie, and in this case, Corrigan Sweeney was fresher than lettuce.

"Sorry, Barnes," Sweeney said apologetically and then took a step to the left, which was more in Crosby's line of fire than he had been.

"Sweeney," Crosby said through his teeth, aiming his service revolver at the front door of an old walk-up building which emerged next to a hardware store. Their suspect was on the first floor of the walk-up and had shot twice through the door—the plan was for Crosby to aim for the long shot, while Sweeney and Barnes stood on either side of the door, their backs to the thin brick façade that went halfway up the wall, to take out the perp while Crosby distracted him.

Except Sweeney kept moving directly over the doorknob, which put him in the line of fire.

"*Rookie!*" Crosby snapped. "If the suspect doesn't shoot you, I will. He has been shooting through that door all day. The fuck you think you're doing?"

"It's just," the rookie said hesitantly, "I can *hear* him behind me—"

Oh shit. "*Get down!*" Crosby screamed, and just as the kid started to drop to his knees, the shot came from the plain stucco behind him and shoved him on his face.

And Crosby aimed at the shattered wall and emptied his clip.

In the ensuing silence, the rookie whimpered, but his back showed, thank God, no blood. The Kevlar had held, although at that range, he might have some bruising on his spine and ribs to contend with.

Crosby called in shots fired and asked for a bus, and then he took point while he and Barnes burst through the house.

Sure enough, their dead suspect was lying on his back behind the wall the rookie had been propped up against, looking surprised as a gutted fish.

Crosby bent and took his pulse, because that was procedure, and when he felt the guy's flesh already cooling, he motioned that he was heading up the stairs, and then for Barnes to follow him, facing the other way.

Barnes nodded—he assumed the guy would have his back.

He'd gotten to the third floor when he heard the slamming of the door behind him, and he turned just in time to deflect a kitchen knife wielded by a whippet-thin woman covered in blood.

"Ma'am!" he shouted, wrestling her for the knife. "Ma'am! We're the police! You're safe now! He's dead!"

Dispatch had reported a hysterical female calling about her husband, who'd done all her stash and was trying to slit her throat. Crosby hated domestic disputes—all cops did—but the drugs, the violence, and the location near a business put it directly in Active Crimes patrol.

"You killed him!" she screamed. "You killed him! He was all I fucking had!"

She swung the knife outward, and he blocked with both hands, waiting for her swing inward so he could take her wrist and bring her close. Apply pressure… apply pressure… and the knife clattered from her hand as she screamed. With quick, efficient movements he swung her around and to her knees, then prone on the ground, where he held her in place with his knee and one hand and then cuffed her, still screaming.

While he was doing that, Barnes lumbered heavily up the stairs, puffing with exertion.

Crosby stared at him, both concerned and furious. Barnes wasn't in great shape—Crosby was used to his team being in top form, and he really hoped the guy didn't fall over. But he'd also expected the man to have his back!

"Sorry, kid," Barnes puffed, leaning forward to rest his hands on his thighs. "I'm really sorry. I was trying to run and tell you to slow down, and God, I'm just not where I used to be."

Crosby nodded, some of his fury subsiding. "I'll pay better attention," he promised, grunting when the woman under his knee gave a jerk in an attempt to escape. "Ma'am, where do you think you are going?" he asked, out of patience. "You are under arrest for assaulting an officer with a deadly weapon. You have the right to remain silent...." He finished reading her rights now, while he had a witness and before he forgot. He usually was part of running a suspect down. If they brought the guy in alive, they handed him off to officers who read them their rights.

He finished the recitation and stood, assisting the woman to her feet again, and she jerked against his hands, then whimpered, "You're hurting me!"

Like her words were magic, he felt the blinding burn of a slash across his forearm and realized he was bleeding all over his new perpetrator.

"You fuckin' think?" he muttered, not even wanting to look at the slash. "C'mon, lady, I think we need to find a new police officer to take you in. Officer Barnes and I have shit to do at the hospital."

"Oh God," Barnes muttered. "You think the kid's okay?"

Crosby nodded. "He was getting his breath as we went in. But he's going to have to be checked out. I got shot close range through a vest earlier this year—six weeks desk duty on account of cracked ribs and a punctured lung. Fucking sucked."

Barnes turned his head as they were escorting their prisoner down the first flight of stairs. "Seriously, kid?"

"Yeah." He finally got a look at the slash through his uniform and the blood trickling down his hand and dripping onto their suspect and then the floor. "This is nothing. Let's check on your rook."

By the time they got downstairs, Sweeney had been loaded on the stretcher already. Barnes made Crosby go talk to the medics for some on-site medical assistance and so he could check on the rookie.

The rookie was pissed.

"That was dumb," he muttered, still trying to get his breath.

"You heard him," Crosby said, trying to gentle his voice because his adrenaline was still high. "You had the instincts, rook. Why didn't you speak up?"

The kid—gah, he was twenty-three!—gave Crosby a look of mute appeal. "Got a badass...." Breathe. "Backing me up? Can't whine!"

Crosby crossed his eyes and held up his bleeding arm. "Not so badass. Go, get checked out, take your medical leave and study up on procedure. Memorize it. Use it to your advantage. God, rook, I'm so glad you're not dead."

Against everything, a slow smile crept into Sweeney's wan face. "Me... too...."

The medics loaded the kid onto the bus, and the driver paused to talk to him. "Kid's losing feeling in his toes," he warned. "I'm betting a bruised spine, possible cracked ribs, maybe some internal bruising. Six weeks minimum."

Crosby nodded. "I'll tell the cap."

The captain of their unit was Cosmo Gambini, one of the most Italian people Crosby had ever met. Crosby liked him—he was midsized, with a sharp goatee, surprising blue eyes, and a habit of singing Frank Sinatra when he was preoccupied. Once again proving that Iliana only hired good peeps, Gambini was on the scene, had probably started out the minute Crosby made the shots-fired call.

"Young!" Cosmo called, and Crosby barely remembered that was his name now.

"Yo! Cap!"

"You getting checked out?" Gambini was jogging toward him, looking pointedly at his bleeding arm, and the medic grimaced.

"You couldn't have led with that?" he asked Crosby with irritation.

"Wanted to check on the rookie," Crosby mumbled.

The medic grunted. "You talk to your cap about the rookie. Let me flag down this other bus to take you to the ER."

"But it's just a cut!" Crosby complained.

"It requires stitches, not a Band-Aid, hero. That needs a hospital. Suck it up."

"Ugh."

Gambini drew alongside Crosby as the medic strode away and grimaced at the slash on Crosby's arm. "He's not wrong," he said apologetically. "What happened?"

Crosby outlined the situation, and Barnes got there in time to hear the wrap-up. Gambini eyed him with exasperation.

"Where's your *live* perp?" he asked.

"You mean our victim?" Barnes asked facetiously. "She's in the back of their shop," he said, nodding toward the department-issue SUV with the cage in the back for perpetrators. They'd been on foot patrol in the area—the shop was a luxury, since it meant they didn't have to drag their perp back to the station, which was a good eight blocks away.

"Yeah, and where were you?" Gambini asked, voice hard. "Because I'm hearing what Young here *isn't* saying. He told you he was heading up the stairs. Where were you when he got jumped by a junkie with a meat cleaver?"

Barnes gave Crosby a "thanks for trying" look and sighed. "I was hauling my fat ass up as fast as I could, Cap. What can I say? Too much good living, not enough PT."

Gambini groaned and tilted his head back, appealing to the heavens. When he looked back at Barnes, he said, "Rufus, I would *love* to put you on a PT regimen and give you six weeks with your rookie to get back into shape. I really would. But we are short staffed, and you *know* how hard it is to find guys for this department. Division Commander Davies is absolutely hardline on—" He gave Crosby a surreptitious glance, and Crosby suddenly got it.

None of that Sons of the Blood crap. It was impacting her personnel recruitment in this division. Ah.

"I run in the morning," he said helpfully. He used to run on the treadmill at HQ, but in the last three weeks, he'd taken to running the streets at 5:00 a.m., when it was quiet, since he couldn't get any fucking sleep in his flop. "You close?"

"Could meet you at the precinct," Barnes said reluctantly. He looked at Crosby's wrist—the bleeding had gotten worse, not better—and sighed. "Fair?"

"I'll bring my gear. Tomorrow?"

"Next week," said the medic, coming up behind them. "And you, right now, in the bus. I can see your blood trail from here."

Crosby groaned, and as he got into the bus, he saw the one thing he'd been avoiding. The medical examiner and forensic crew clustering 'round the shattered brick façade and the dead gunman behind it.

It was his turn to close his eyes and gaze up at the sky.

"Cap?" he asked, as the medic lifted his arm and started injecting him with anesthetic.

"Yeah, son?" Gambini was not that much older than Crosby, but Crosby appreciated the attempt at comfort.

"Who'd I kill?"

Gambini's sigh was as old as he sounded. "Curtis Miller—ex-policeman and addict. You arrested his wife, Janine." He grimaced. "She used to run the department's Toys for Tots charity and made a hell of a chicken salad for department functions."

"Oh Jesus," Crosby muttered. He wanted to scrub his face with his hands, but—"Ouch!"

"Yeah, you were cut to the bone," the medic muttered. "Make your Captain go away so I can irrigate this and we can get you to the ER."

"Meet you there," Gambini told him.

Great.

CROSBY MANAGED to text Harding with an update while he was on the bus, and he'd barely pressed Send when Garcia popped up on his screen.

You got what?

Crosby smiled a little, wanting to hold the phone to his chest. They'd texted at night over the last six weeks, making updates on the case, exchanging observations.

Talking about dreams.

About how Garcia actually *wanted* a family, but he'd always assumed it was out of the realm of possibility because he'd known he was gay from the get-go.

About how Crosby had been very evenly bisexual but had hidden it because he'd wanted to be a cop more than he'd wanted to be out.

About how Garcia wanted a dog or something, but he was worried about his hours.

About how Crosby would totally be up for a golden retriever and maybe they could hire a walker?

And how Garcia used to love the dance clubs in Miami, where he'd go to jump up and down and primal scream after a bad run in the ATF or his stint as a county mountie.

And that Crosby thought he was clumsy on the dance floor, but he'd love to see Garcia dance.

And Garcia wanted to dance with him, so very bad, because he'd never danced with someone he cared about and he thought it might blow his mind.

They'd assembled a list of movies they wanted to watch together, television shows they needed to shotgun, places they wanted to visit where nobody knew them or would care.

That Garcia had texted him was not a surprise—but that he knew what he'd texted Harding was.

Are you in the field? Crosby asked unhappily, thinking they had to be close together for Garcia to jump his shit so fast. *Don't worry about me in the field!*

Back from the field. The op was successful. YOU'RE BLEEDING?

At the same time Harding texted him, and he sighed.

I'm fine. Gonna brief Harding—going to get stitched now. He paused. *Not that I don't wish you were here. This never would have happened if you'd had my back.*

If Garcia hadn't been able to make the climb, he would have said something. But then, Garcia would have learned to levitate to have his back.

Is that the only reason you'd want me there?

Without warning, Crosby felt the full weight of the last hour. The ripping fire and burning ache exploding in his left arm, the moment of horror of seeing the rookie shot, that fearful, breathless pause before checking to see if he was okay.

The dead man behind the shattered remnants of the brick façade.

That total second of terror when the woman had jumped on his back and he'd realized that he was alone, totally alone, and no backup was coming.

I want you here because I'm a pussy and this whole fucking day sucks. But that's not gonna happen—just know it would if I could.

He ignored Garcia then because he had to, updating Harding on the sitch. He finished with *The Forty Third needs people Davies can trust. If you've got some ideas, hit her up.*

There was a pause, and then, *Do you need us to pull you out?*

Crosby closed his eyes and fought the temptation to beg.

We still don't know the big fish, he replied, feeling like shit. He thought of Barnes and his willingness to come in and run to be the cop his division needed, and of the poor rookie who'd been so afraid to contradict Crosby he'd almost gotten killed.

Good people, dammit. Gambini, Davies—good people. *They* needed to trust their fellow officers. They needed help.

I can't abandon the division, he answered after gnawing on his lower lip. *They need us.*

Roger that. But we need you too, kid. Don't forget to holler for help if you need it.

Roger that.

And throw Garcia a bone. He looks like you kicked his puppy.

Oh God. Apparently this was his day to suck. He switched to Garcia's text string and saw, *I want to be there for you too.*

Unexpectedly his eyes burned, and his thumb started to cramp as he texted, he needed the words down so bad.

When this is over, we can go find a cat or something. We can go to Chartreuse's dance club. We can take a week and go to California and play on the beach. It's supposed to be fucking cold, but I don't care.

And then? Garcia, who usually sounded so together, was begging, and Crosby couldn't let that stand.

Then we go back to your place in Queens and play house until I tread on your last fuckin' nerve.

Won't happen, Cowboy.

Good. I like that house.

I like you in it.

I want it more than anything. And that was true. He wanted it more than making this bust—even more than working with the rest of the team, and he'd never thought that was possible.

Then we'll make it happen. Get stitched. Text me when you can. Love you.

Crosby caught his breath, and he saw the thought bubbles coming, and wondered if Garcia was going to try to backpedal, to take it back so Crosby didn't panic.

He wasn't panicking—he was so damned grateful Garcia had given that to him to cling to. Like a piece of flotsam in a torrent of chaos, Crosby had those words.

Love you too, he texted quickly, hitting Send before Garcia could overthink himself, take away those words that Crosby needed so badly. *Text later.*

The medic gave a particularly tough scrub on the wound she was cleaning, and Crosby grimaced as he slid his phone in his pocket with his free hand.

"Telling your girl you'll be okay?" the medic—a twentysomething woman with a hint of purple in her dark ponytail and a silver ring in her eyebrow, contrasting with her bronze skin—asked.

"Yeah," Crosby said, leaning against the back of the bus with relief. Texting in the car made him queasy even when he wasn't getting worked on.

THE DEBRIEF in the hospital was pretty much what Crosby expected.

The staff cut off his long-sleeved uniform shirt, leaving him in his T-shirt and slacks, both of which were bloodstained by the time they'd put twenty stitches in his wrist and forearm. The whole area was aching fiercely under the local anesthetic by the time they were through, and they'd given him a sling so he could keep it immobile for at least a day.

Iliana joined him, Gambini, and Barnes in discussing the bust, particularly since Iliana was the one who would have to face the press later that day.

"You had no idea who the guy was," Iliana reassured him, looking grim. "He'd been let go by the department months before you arrived *because* he had a drug problem, and it got a lot worse." She frowned, and she and Crosby made eye contact. "Shit," she muttered.

"Shit?" Gambini said. "Shit what? This whole day is shit—don't give us any more."

Crosby grunted, about ready to throw some bullshit on, when Iliana did him one better.

"When Rick was hired, his old captain called me. They were having some problems with meth flooding the streets, cut with fentanyl, really easy to get addicted to and available like candy on every street corner. He told me Rick knew what to look for, and that's what we were both thinking, right, Rick?"

Crosby nodded, grateful for the cover. "Yeah—that sort of thing where a habit becomes a dragon—that's the sort of drugs we're looking at. And it's flooding the two-four." He remembered the clusterfuck that happened when Toby had been rescued. "That thing where the precinct was surrounded, about a month ago? Right before I started up here? They lost two guys there that they thought had been using."

Gambini and Barnes looked suitably impressed, and Iliana gave the slightest tip of her chin to taking a lie and embroidering it with more truth.

"So have the drugs analyzed," Gambini said. "Done."

"And tell the detectives to look into who was dealing to the guy and his wife. I gotta be honest with you," Crosby added, "I didn't know the couple, but you know. That was a pretty good walk-up. They didn't start out doing meth and stabbing flatfoots. They had to work up to that shit."

Iliana nodded. "I'll brief the detectives. I've got a couple in mind." She swallowed and met Crosby's eyes in a "help me out" sort of expression. "Should I go to the press with that?"

Oh yes, Crosby thought, his anger very close to the surface. "Absolutely," he said with satisfaction. "Let the community know that the drugs are taking good men—good cops—down the tubes with them, and that's no way for a community to be healthy. We want accountability for everybody."

Iliana's eyes lit up, and he could see her processing that soundbite in her head, spinning it to make her department and her precinct look good and self-aware and on top of the shit going down on their turf.

"That's good," she admitted, and Gambini and Barnes both nodded. "You guys get lost for a sec," she said. "Me and Young here need to have a chat." They buggered off, and she gave Crosby a look. "Now for you."

Crosby grimaced, and she did too. He couldn't be taken out too long—she knew that.

"Desk duty for two weeks," she said. "Starting in three days. That's when you get the sling off and just have a bandage, right?"

"Roger that," he said, thinking wistfully about a little house in Queens.

"In the meantime, Ricky," she said, pleading in her voice, "would you get some fucking sleep?"

"Roger that," he mumbled, his head already aching with the lack of it. He thought momentarily about simply leaving from the hospital, but he was wearing a bloody T-shirt and his service weapon—he would need to go to the precinct and change and then take his clothes to get laundered for his return.

But he could do all that, he thought almost desperately. He could do all that if he had Garcia's house at the end of the pain rainbow. He could get that done.

Iliana nodded to Gambini and Barnes, her eyes sharp on his.

"Let me give you a ride to your flop and then to the train," she said softly. "I don't have to be in my dress blues for another two hours."

"I'm not sure that's safe," Crosby said, frowning. "McEnany pops up there every so often. He actually knows what you look like."

"I'll keep an eye out," she said, eyes still sharp. "I can do paperwork in my car for half an hour while you go get your shit in order, tell your guys you're going to visit your girlfriend, whatever. I just...." She grimaced. "You're in pain, you're exhausted—I just don't like you going in there without backup after this, you understand?"

Crosby nodded, appreciating it. "Yeah, but you're gonna blow my cover. I gotta get to the precinct and change, then get to the flop and pack—"

"Let me put a new uniform in your locker," she said. "It's the least I can do. That way you can come straight from Gar... your girl's place to work in three days."

Her face turned tomato red, and he suddenly realized what she'd almost said, and then *his* face went tomato red, and he wondered if he was going to die right there, in the hospital, from a cut on his arm and mortal embarrassment.

And then he realized how close she'd been to painting a big target on Garcia's back.

"You can't tell anyone my girl's name," he growled, and she swallowed and nodded.

"Sorry Cr… fuck, *Rick.* Goddammit. I've *been* where you are, and I know better." She let out a sigh. "I just… you know. Gail texted me and said, you know, your *girl* is missing you, and, uhm, I knew who she was talking about and…." She scrubbed at her face. "Shoot me now."

"I would, but they made me put my gun in a lockbox when I was admitted for stitches," he said dryly. "But you can stop talking now."

"Thanks, Rick," she whispered, obviously mortified. Then she looked him in the eyes. "I've had to tell my friend that her friend, who stayed with her for six weeks when her leg was broken and I was too broken to function like a rational adult, has been looking like hell every day for the last month. Please let me pick you up and drop you off at the train station, just to make myself feel better."

He smiled a little. "After your presser. Have Barnes drop me off. It'll look legit."

She nodded. "Fair. Let's get you out of here."

HE FIGURED that he had two hours after Barnes dropped him off, giving the building a look of profound distaste. "This place ain't on my beat, thank fuck, but gods, somebody's in hell watching this shithole."

"I haven't seen a lot of blue here," Crosby told him, which was only half true. The fact was, his building was on the beat of a Son's of the Blood precinct, which meant they ignored all the crime there and let their buddies take are of it.

God help anyone who wasn't male or white. Crosby's skin crawled more every day he walked up the fucking stairs.

"That's 'cause the precinct that serves this place is crooked and full of white powder," Barnes told him baldly. "You know that or you wouldn't be in our place, helping to keep those guys from the Twenty Fourth."

"Shh!" Crosby would have flailed if his arm didn't ache so fiercely. "Do you want me dead before I hit my front door?"

Barnes grimaced. "And *this* is why I've been a beat cop for twenty years. If I was doing your shit, I would have died a long time ago." He rolled his eyes and glared at Crosby like it was all his fault. "All I know is those goddamned Blood-fuckers haven't moved in on our precinct, and a lot of that is Davies and her commitment to not hire them. Suddenly you show up, and you're better than a good cop—you're like super-cop—and Davies and Gambini treat you like you're God's gift, which is fine, and you live *here*? Yeah. I'm old and I'm stupid, but I'm not *that* stupid."

Crosby's stomach churned—worse than usual because it was pretty much a twenty-four seven acid volcano these days.

"We need to find the guys higher up," he said after a moment. "My unit is working on that while I'm here pretending to be working for the bad guys." He didn't add that the bad guys had threatened his unit if he hadn't gone undercover in the first place—it was one level too far for poor Rufus Barnes, he figured.

Barnes grunted. "You still want to go running when you get back?"

Crosby gave a slight smile. "I'll be doing it anyway. Might as well drag you with me."

"Yeah. You're under enough stress, kid. It would be great if you could count on me to have your back when it's time."

"You're a solid cop," Crosby praised and then realized what he'd said. "I mean a *good* cop—"

Barnes burst into a raucous round of guffaws. "You need to go rest and find your girl, Young. Call it a fucking day, right?"

"What about you?"

"I'm gonna go sit with the rookie for a bit." Barnes let out a low whistle. "Poor kid. Helluva welcome to the force."

"Keep having his back," Crosby said seriously. "And being a decent human being. Believe me, it's better than I ever had."

Barnes looked embarrassed. "Get going before I take you home and make my wife feed you."

And with that Crosby absolutely had to leave.

THAT WAS the plan, right? Crosby made his way up to his room, eschewing the elevator per usual and wishing he felt safe enough here to take a pain pill. The impairment to his reflexes, to his cognition, was just too damned much to risk.

But pain alone can be distracting, and as Crosby rounded the landing for the floor with Creedy's flop on it, he heard the door to the stairwell open but was still not prepared for McEnany, barreling into him like a dragon made of white rage.

"You fucking *asshole!*"

Crosby caught three fists to the face, one, two, three—and by the time the fourth would have landed, he'd ripped his arm out of the sling so he could block with his bad arm and land a powerhouse to McEnany's jaw with his good.

McEnany howled and backed off, but he didn't go down. Instead he pulled back and circled Crosby, looking for an opening that Crosby refused to give him. Crosby's arm was a lightning fire, and one of his eyes was already swelling shut, but the idea of kicking McEnany down the stairs and hoping his neck broke was the fury point that kept him on his feet.

"What the *fuck!*" he snarled, parrying a feint without losing sight of McEnany's shoulders and core, where all fighters telegraphed their moves.

"You're supposed to be working for *me!*" McEnany growled. "And you had to go shoot up one of Creedy's top guys!"

Oh fuck. It fucking figured. "Creedy's top guy?" Crosby shouted, blocking a rabbit punch toward his throat—fucking nasty assed fighter, god*dammit!* "Creedy's top guy was a *meth addict.* He shot a rookie through a wall because he was a fucking *coward.* We got called in because he was holding a knife to his wife's throat. You wanted me to cover for that?"

"I want you to be some goddamned *use!*" McEnany shouted, and he went sideways for a chamber kick, but Crosby had inches and pounds on him. Blocked the kick with his arms, blocked a flurry of them and then used the wall so he could throw his body sideways, catching McEnany with both feet in his core.

McEnany flew backward, landing on the stairs behind him, and it must have hurt, because he took his time getting up.

"I *am* being goddamned use," Crosby hissed. "I'm being your fucking poster boy. You want to get your recruits in the unit? Do it now, because they're starting to think white boys might not all be racist shitbags. But don't blame me if your fucking candidates are too stupid or too crazy to pass the entrance qualifications. That's on *you* for not training them up, and that's on *them* for thinking they're God's gift."

He stood back for a minute and assessed what McEnany was going to do next, because the man's shoulders were forward and his fists were up, and this fight was not over.

"All I wanna do," McEnany snarled, "is get back in good with the Sons—do you get that? The brass. That's all you gotta do for me—"

"Well, whose ass am I kissing, tough guy? I don't got no pride. You're threatening my team, you're threatening my girl. Whose balls do I gotta suck to get you out of my hair? 'Cause I don't know what tales you had to tell the FBI to get me out on assignment this long, but I'm betting you're running out of time."

McEnany flinched, and Crosby realized he'd scored a direct hit. Someone must be riding McEnany's ass to either produce a bust through Crosby or to return him to Special Crimes Task Force, and McEnany was feeling the heat. And today....

Crosby's eyes narrowed, and he braced himself, ignored the fucking pain, and let loose with the final hit, the one that would turn McEnany into a berserker, more intent on carnage than on saving his own skin.

"And not just the brass," Crosby finished, dancing a little on his toes. All those hand-to-hand training sessions, all those times he'd been pitted against Garcia, who was little and wiry, like McEnany, and who fought dirty 'cause he'd have to on the streets. Crosby knew he had to be quicker, knew he had to use his strength but not as a crutch—knew what had to be done.

"Shut up," McEnany snapped. "You don't know what you're talking about—"

"Creedy's pissed, isn't he?" Crosby went on, feeling light on his feet and strong in his heart. A cut above his eye was pouring blood, but he wiped it off with the back of his bloody fist, the bandage taking most of it, even as his popped stitches seeped through the other side. "You promised him I'd get his boys hired, but Iliana Davies isn't the problem, is she? His boys are the problem. And you lost *men* on this gamble, and you can bet someone at the two-four is taking notice. So he's riding your back, and *you* should be captain, right? And you gotta take orders from *him*, gotta take orders from the *feds*, from whoever in the alphabets you're trying to impress, and this whole time, the guy you planned to fuck the most, *me*, I'm doin' okay, right? I'm a flatfoot, right where I started, and you're *screwed*, McEnany. You couldn't piss down your own leg if your shoe was on fire, could you?"

McEnany's roar reverberated up and down the stairwell, and he charged Crosby with all his might.

He got in a blow to Crosby's jaw, but Crosby was stepping wide, so it hit just hard enough to bruise but not break. At the same time, McEnany's momentum carried him past Crosby, across the landing, and he was overbalanced, expecting Crosby's bulk to stop him. When that didn't happen, his legs tried to take the stairs like a cartoon character's, but his chest and shoulders and head leaned forward, forward, until he pitched down the steps, rolling as he went, landing on his back, bruised and bleeding but still breathing.

Thank fuck.

Crosby took the stairs two at a time, getting there before McEnany even thought about getting up. McEnany glared from his position, prone, right up until Crosby's police issue boot came down to rest ever so gently on his throat.

"Crosby…."

McEnany swallowed, and Crosby saw real fear in his eyes.

"Who do you got watching my team?" he asked, flexing his foot.

"Creedy's guys—he's managing… gah!"

Crosby relaxed his flex because crushing McEnany's larynx would have been too damned easy.

"Whose ass are you trying to impress?" Crosby growled, and when McEnany whined in protest, Crosby flexed his foot again.

"Cavendish," McEnany whispered. "Courtland Cavendish. He's the one who got me this job."

Aces. Crosby flexed his foot again. "You fell down the stairs," he said brutally.

"Creedy won't—"

"You got drunk and fell down the stairs," Crosby reiterated. "I hear a whisper of anything else, we're gonna have this fight for real."

McEnany whined, wind whistling through his broken nose and spattering blood, and Crosby thought sourly that he wanted to arrest the guy, take the guy in, but Creedy had his goons watching the squad—and a room full of methed-out cowboys half a flight of stairs and a hallway away. If Crosby tried to get McEnany out of this building, his odds of seeing daylight were not great, but McEnany was a coward, and Crosby had the goods on him, the thing that would get Creedy gunning for him too.

Crosby needed to talk to his team, talk to Harding, see how they could use this situation to their advantage. But first he headed to his room to grab his stuff.

He unlocked all three locks in record time and strode in, peering around the room with a practiced eye to see if everything was as he left it.

It wasn't. There was a kid crashed on his couch.

"Goddammit, Junior," he muttered, and Junior—fully clothed and looking like someone had caught a good one in the eye himself—rolled off the couch and onto his knees.

"What? Sorry, Ricky, I—"

"How did you even get in here?" Crosby demanded, locking his door again and shoving the kitchen chair under it. "I have three goddamned locks there for a reason!"

Junior gave him an almost bashful glance. "Well, you know, I can pick a fuckin' lock—" And then he seemed to see Crosby for the first time. "What the hell happened?"

Crosby was rooting under his bathroom sink for a box of bandages and first aid supplies he'd bought on his first day, and he didn't answer.

As he stood up, Junior answered for him. "Did my old man give you what for 'cause you killed that guy?"

Crosby stared at him with his one good eye and wished there was some way he could staunch the blood dripping from his nose. "What're you talking about?"

"'Cause he went pretty bananas when he found out. I guess Curtis Miller and him used to be tight back in the day. So word came that you killed the guy—he lost his shit."

"Well, Miller shot my rookie through a wall and wasn't stopping. I had to do something or what kind of cop would I be?" Crosby asked bitterly.

"Was the rookie okay?"

Crosby sighed and leaned his head against the mirror. "He'll be in the hospital for a while, but his vest stopped the slugs. But that didn't stop Miller from shooting."

Junior nodded. "See, nobody told my dad that. Wait, if my dad didn't do that to you, who did?"

Crosby grunted. "Three guesses."

"McEnany?" To his credit, Junior sounded very, very disgusted. "Man, that guy. Comes in here and talks to my dad like he's dirt. My dad was born here. He's been with the Sons since he was a baby. He shoulda been a cop like his old man, but fuckin' Equal Opportunity wouldn't let him be a cop 'cause he's white—"

Crosby squinted at him through the blood on his face. "What are you even talking about? Three-quarters of my division is white, and that's definitely not what the people we patrol look like. If your dad didn't get in, there had to be another reason."

Junior gaped at him, because this was obviously something that had not occurred to him. "I just… he's said—"

Crosby sighed and splashed water on his face, wincing when it hit his cuts. He had to get out of there. He'd text Iliana later that he made it to the train.

"Junior, you're not a bad kid. You make enough at the warehouse—maybe save some money and get a flop with some guys who don't spend all day doing meth and playing video games and then pound you when you get back from work." Crosby had seen him sporting black eyes, fat lips, and limping in a suspicious, painful way that had nothing to do with his legs and everything to do with strained muscles in his glutes. God, poor kid. He stayed away from the meth most of the time, probably because he didn't want to get caught unawares, but there was no doubt about it. Sometimes he *did* get caught.

"They're my friends," Junior whispered, looking away.

"They're your father's friends. You deserve better."

Junior huffed out a breath. "Yeah, but they can get me the job working the night deliveries with the big bitch—that's where the money is. I've told you that."

He had, but Crosby hadn't put it together as important, and suddenly it seemed like something he should be telling Garcia and Harding.

"Man, you don't need the prime shift. Work the shifts you got and spend your money on rent," Crosby told him and punctuated that by wiping blood from his lip. Shit. Priorities.

With a grunt, Crosby began to dress the cuts on his face, taking off his T-shirt to use as a washcloth since it was pretty wrecked. Slowly and patiently he washed off each cut, applied antiseptic, and then, if needed, a tiny butterfly bandage before moving to the next one. When he was done with his face, he started on his knuckles, and somewhere in there, his nose stopped bleeding, and he finally got to—very gingerly—clean up the mess on his upper lip and chin.

Finally, *finally*, he looked less like a disaster survivor, and he turned toward the front room so he could find himself some clothes.

And caught Junior staring at him with naked hunger.

Oh. Well shit.

"Junior," he said quietly, "you can't look at guys that way within a mile of your father and his friends. You know that, right?"

Junior met his eyes and swallowed. "It doesn't matter. They use me and call me a fag anyway."

Crosby closed his eyes and breathed softly through his mouth. "Like I said," he told the boy, "you deserve better. But I can't be it."

"'Cause you've got a girl," Junior said glumly.

"'Cause I'm taken," Crosby agreed, wanting to say the truth, even if Junior didn't know the difference. "But more than that. 'Cause right now, with your dad and his friends, I'm dangerous. I'm toxic."

With a sigh he went to the mini fridge and pulled out a water, opened it, and swigged half of it before it even hit him that he hadn't heard the crack of the seal—and the fridge had been unlocked.

The bitter, medicinal aftertaste burned his nasal passages as the liquid hit his esophagus when he swallowed.

The drugs struck him like a mallet, starting with the surcease of pain, and he stared at Junior in outrage. "Man, I was nice to you!"

Junior looked surprised, and Crosby fought not to fall down. "What? My dad gave me water to bring up here!"

"And you bought it?" His vision was swimmy. Fuck. Narcan—did he have his Narcan?

"He said you were always bringing us beer like a friend. I should bring you some water since you were too good to get high with us." And if the kid could pick the locks on his door, the mini fridge had been no big deal. Even with swimmy vision, Crosby didn't miss the look on Junior's face when it hit him.

"God, kid," Crosby slurred. "You're so fuckin' dumb."

Frantically he rooted in his pants pocket while his heart thundered in his ears. He had no idea if he'd OD'd or not. He'd started sweating profusely, and it was hard to breathe. Was this what an OD felt like? Was this just being high?

His knees went out from under him right as he pulled the package with the ampoule in it. Junior knelt beside him, eyes rolling wildly. "What's wrong with you?" he asked. "Ricky, what's the—"

"Drugged," Crosby managed. "Open this. Shoot it up my nose. *Now!*"

He fumbled the ampoule into Junior's hand as his vision went from swimmy to wild, wonky, and dark, and his head bounced off the cheap tile floor before he knew he was going over backward. There was a debilitating freeze of all his nerve endings. His heart thundered hard enough to drive a freight train, but he couldn't move his limbs. His skin burned, his lungs burned, the darkness all around him burned....

Then cooled, so soft, so soothing, that's right, just fall into it... fall into the darkness and—

He sat up suddenly, the burn in his nose and nasal passages acidic and painful. The nastiness of it all tripled when he leaned over and vomited mostly water onto the floor.

For a few moments, all was silence as the roar in his ears subsided and his breathing—still fast—slowed down enough to think.

About the time he registered that every body part and joint ached like it was in an acid bath, he finally remembered Junior, who was crouched back against the bed, arms around his knees, still clutching the exhausted ampoule of Narcan and crying.

"Thanks, kid," he rasped. His brain was still fogged, the world swimming in front of his eyes, his muscles shaking with, well, everything from an adrenaline dump to... fuck. Meth? Fentanyl? Narcan?

It was all rushing through his bloodstream, and the only clear thing was that he had to get out of this flop, out of this building, *right the fuck now*.

"Kid," he rasped, "get me some clothes. I can't go out like this."

Junior seemed to gather himself then, and without a word he went through Crosby's drawers, coming back with the sweats Crosby himself had bought, and the underwear and socks, a new T-shirt, and a plain blue hoodie.

It took Crosby three tries to stand, and when he did, he couldn't get away from the vomit fast enough. He moved to the sink as if wading through poisoned gravy, but the cold water on his battered knuckles, his wrists, his face where it shocked his cuts and bruises, in the nasty pit of his mouth, all served to help him breathe easier. He wiped himself down with a paper towel and threw a bunch of them on top of the vomit puddle.

"I'll get that," Junior mumbled, and Crosby let him.

Clothes. Clothes were hard. Small holes for arms, for legs, and pulling the neck over his face was the worst. He was just looking at his hoodie in despair when he felt capable hands on him, helping him, stretching the neck of the thing out so it didn't rip open his bandages. The same hands sat him down and helped him with his sneakers and socks and then gently placed his phone in his hands while Crosby tried to formulate a plan.

To his immortal embarrassment, he had a terrible, aching erection and thought, *Aha—so I finally know why people might like meth,* but he also knew that faded after the first couple of uses, so he wasn't too impressed.

His brain was wandering.

Shit.

He looked at his phone again, and only the constant use, the double life, helped him remember to pull up group two.

Drugged. Out of it. Need to get clear of here.

He hit Send and stood with an effort. Get clear. That was the thing. The thought of the stairwell made him want to vomit again, but even worse, McEnany was probably still there. Hell, Creedy was probably waiting for him on the third platform—everybody knew he took the stairs and not the north elevator.

There was a south elevator.

He looked at Junior, who had sprayed the floor off and wiped it down and was now washing his hands.

"Take me to the elevator at the far side of the hallway," he said.

Junior grimaced, horrified. "The one that always smells like someone took a crap?"

"Nobody will expect me to come down in that one. We all avoid it." Crosby hoped. "I need to get clear until my head's straight. C'mon, kid, help me to the elevator. I'll disappear. Your dad will never know you were here."

"You'll get slaughtered if you go out like this!" Junior protested, sounding legitimately frightened.

Crosby's phone buzzed.

Hold on, Cowboy—we're coming.

Gonna be walking outta the south end of the building, he texted. *And heading west down the cross street.*

He stood and wove his way to the door, and Junior followed. Crosby had rescued his keys from the pocket of his uniform slacks, and he made Junior lock each lock down the line before they turned toward the far end of the building and started to walk.

Junior hadn't been exaggerating about the smell in the tiny graffiti-encrusted elevator—it was always a fresh dump too. Someone must have cleaned it up every morning, Crosby thought, because the floor was always oddly spotless. But still, a good place to avoid.

Going down fifteen floors was pretty fuckin' awful, and only the thought that he didn't want to spend the last five floors wallowing in that smell *plus* vomit kept Crosby from losing it again.

When he got to the bottom, he turned, his head still swimming, every muscle in his body aching and weak. He took a step out of the elevator and his knees went, and only Junior's shoulder under his arm kept him going.

"You're sposed to be getting clear of me," he mumbled.

"My dad tried to kill you," Junior almost sobbed. "He drugged your drink. Jesus, I'm so fuckin' dumb. How... how come I'm so dumb?"

"Not yer fault," Crosby slurred. "Keep goin', kid. But if ya stick with me, yer life's gonna fuckin' change. Ya gotta know tha'. You help me, ya gotta run far and fast."

"I don't know what to do," Junior whispered, and Crosby wanted to take it back about the kid being so fuckin' dumb. He wasn't dumb at all—just scared. Well, you get beaten and violated most days of your fuckin' life and that's how you end up, right?

"I'll think of somethin'," Crosby mumbled as they made it outside the building. The street running west was a two-lane, almost an alley with a sidewalk. Nobody came up this street because it had no access to the train, no access to uptown. All it had was access to another big cross street in four more blocks.

"Yeah?" Junior snapped, some spirit back in him, although he kept Crosby's arm slung about his shoulders. "What're you gonna do?"

"Help ya land," Crosby repeated. "'S wha' we do. Swear. But your dad fin's out—he'll kill ya, Junior. Don't wan' ya dead. Jus' a baby. Swee' swee' lil kid."

God, whatever was going on in his head it was getting worse. His heart was building up in his ears again, and he wondered if he needed another dose of Narcan. Fuck. Fuck—he hadn't brought one.

His phone buzzed in his pocket, and when he looked, he realized it had taken him nearly fifteen minutes to get this far.

I'm walking up behind you, Cowboy. Don't panic.

And then suddenly, oh God. Calix's arm around his waist, strong and capable, and his shoulder under Crosby's arm. A firm hand took Crosby's phone from him, and the next thing Crosby knew, a department issue was up on the curb, and Garcia and Junior were helping him into the back.

"Junior's gotta come with," Crosby managed before falling into comfort—and unconsciousness. "Compromised. Dad'll kill him. Needs protection."

"Gotcha."

Something was weird with Garcia's voice—something off. Choked and clogged and rough, and Crosby thought, *Don't cry, baby. I've got three days to spend at gnome,* before all communication between his brain and his body stopped completely, and he was out.

Landing Zone

GARCIA WAS asleep in the chair next to his bed when Crosby sat up yelling his name.

"Here!" he exclaimed, standing in his stockinged feet, clutching his fleece blanket around his shoulders. "Here! Crosby, I'm here!"

Crosby fell back against the sheets and started tugging at the needle taped to the back of his hand. "Wha's this?" he asked. "It stings!"

"Leave it in!" Garcia grabbed his fingers to stop him from pulling the IV out. "It's fluids and stuff to counteract the three different drugs rabbiting through your system. And painkillers and antibiotics for your stitches and your bruises and your ribs and your scrawny, underfed ass. Jesus God, Crosby, those guys tried to kill you!"

Crosby grunted and glanced around the bedroom, looking befuddled and almost dear. "Lots of fuckin' times," he said, a little bit of outrage tinging his voice. "I mean, stabbed and beaten and drugged—holy crap, what a fuckin' day!"

Garcia let out a cracked laugh and, disregarding all social boundaries, pulled Crosby's covers back so he could climb into his own bed next to him.

"Jesus, Cowboy, you scared me."

He'd stopped breathing just as Swan had gotten the SUV into the hospital ambulance bay. Gail had sat on his chest and slapped his bruised face, screaming at him, while Garcia…. Garcia had heard of people disassociating before, but never in his life had he thought it was something he'd do. Crosby had been dying, his head in Garcia's lap, eyes wide and vacant, and Garcia had been floating, far, far away, waiting for the knife that would come from nowhere and rip out his heart, leaving him in blissful darkness.

Crosby's first breath had brought him back to himself, and the knife was right where he'd known it would be, still in his heart, but he'd forced himself back into his body, back into the car, because the boy he loved was breathing now, and he could live through the pain of survival like he didn't think he could live through the pain of loss.

Crosby drew him closer, bringing him back to himself, and Garcia went. Crosby's arm—no longer weighty with muscle--tightened to the point of discomfort, but Garcia wasn't going to argue. "How'd I get here?" Crosby asked rustily. "With… doctor stuff in my arm?"

"That was all Harding." Which was good, because Garcia's and Gail's brains had not been functioning at the time. "He didn't want you in a hospital—didn't want a soul to know you were in such bad shape. He had us haul you to a medical bay where the paramedics and a doctor treated you. He met us there. Then we shoved you back in the SUV and brought you home."

Crosby frowned. "I'm not in the guest room."

Garcia gave a short, barking laugh. "I tried, Crosby. I swear. Harding and me were dragging your sorry ass through the house, and I was like, 'Guest room's here—' and he just grunted and rolled his eyes, and we kept going to here." Garcia's next laugh was saner, if broken. "We set you up, and the doctor showed up again. I think he was a friend of Harding's, 'cause they seemed tight. Anyway, he set up the bag and put all the medications in it and made sure your wounds and your bandages were okay." He let out a little sigh. "Lucky you. They just left. Chadwick and Carlyle spent an hour outfitting Nana and Pop-Pop's old house with lots of fun surveillance toys. I think we're safe here."

"Mm." Crosby let out a sigh, but Garcia could tell he was still exhausted. "Junior? Where'd the kid go?"

Garcia shook his head. "Harding wanted him in protective custody, and I guess Junior was pretty scared of his old man. I…." He grimaced and hoped he'd made the right call. "He was looking at you like it was love, man. I asked him if he'd mind rooming with… you remember Jesse and Kurt?"

Crosby tried to open his eyes, but the attempt obviously failed. "First case?" he asked, voice blurry.

"Yeah. Anyway, they're rooming together in the city now. Not boyfriends, just friends. And I thought… you know. Sort of redneck debriefing 101, being in the city with two guys who are *also* gay and who are not entirely white."

Crosby's lips tilted at the corners, although his eyes stayed closed. "God, you're good. Good thinking. But still—feds are watching them?"

"Yeah, we put Henderson and Doba, the two guys from the Twenty Fourth, on them. They've both been vetted and tested and shit in the last month. No security clearance per se, but we trust them on this. I think your guy Junior's going to land."

"How long'm I gonna be down?" Crosby asked next.

"I wanted a month," Garcia said bitterly. "But Harding wants you to go back in if you can—at least as Rick Young at the Forty Third. Carlyle and Chadwick are going through your apartment right now, checking for bugs, more drugged waters, getting your laptop—that sort of thing. We're having a debrief in two days, so you gotta get your sleep now."

Crosby nodded, and then, to Garcia's horror, two silvery slips of water slid down on either side of his nose.

"Oh, papi," he whispered. Oh, baby. What they'd done to him—oh hell.

"Just… just stay," Crosby whispered back. "For a while. Just stay."

"'Course, Judson." Garcia snuggled in tighter, mindful of the bruises and the fact that Crosby's body probably felt like a jigsaw puzzle in a box right now. "God, I missed you."

"Every minute of every day," Crosby confirmed, and while his arm relaxed around Garcia's shoulders, his words held him tight as he dozed off on Crosby's much thinner chest.

Garcia got up an hour later to put on pajama pants and use the bathroom. Crosby started to thrash around in his sleep before he got back.

Garcia slid next to him again, soothing, calming, making sure his IV was still in place. He paused for a moment to smooth Crosby's shaggy hair back from his forehead and wondered how soon he'd start demanding to get a haircut, because he usually wore it pretty closely cropped. Not shaved, just tight on the sides and a little longer on top.

Maybe he wouldn't, Garcia thought, a lump in his throat. It might be hard for that version of Crosby, with his broad chest and his quiet swagger, to emerge from this one, his face still battered from his run-in with McEnany, if Junior's story was to be believed. But it was more than the long bandage on his arm, the swollen eyes and jaw, the broken nose, the bruises blooming everywhere on his chest—it was that he'd lost maybe forty pounds in the last two months, and he held himself, even in sleep, like he was warding off a blow.

"How bad's the face?" Crosby asked, startling Garcia because he'd thought Crosby was still sleeping. It was hard to tell. One eye was completely swollen shut, and the other one was just swollen, as was his jaw.

"Remember the end of *Rocky*?" he joked weakly.

"Which one?"

"Two," Garcia said promptly, because that was the one where Stallone's face had looked the worst.

"Ugh, I'm a troll. How can you stand me?"

Garcia laughed softly. "Don't get all vain on me now, Cowboy. All this humble shit. You gonna tell me that was for show?"

Crosby's cut and swollen lips twisted. "You can be humble and still want to make a good impression," he said, and Garcia had to smile, albeit bitterly.

"Impression made," Garcia whispered. "Or did you think I told just anybody 'I love you.'"

Crosby made a sound almost like a sob. "God, I was hoping that was real. You wrote it, and I thought, 'He's gonna walk that back. I can't let him. I need that too much.'"

Garcia groaned in embarrassment. "I didn't want to saddle you with that shit, Crosby. Jesus, how embarrassing—"

"Naw." Crosby took a happy breath. "It kept me sane. It did. The whole day was a shitshow from first to last. Right up until I woke up here, and you were with me, and I was okay. But those words—if you hadn't given me those words, I might have given it up before Junior and I got to the street."

Garcia's eyes burned. "I love you, Judson Crosby," he whispered. "I love you when you're not scaring the hell out of me, but I still love you now."

"Love you too, Calix. Now would you stop looking at me like I'm dead?"

"Sure." Garcia took a breath and tried to remember how to treat his lover like he was whole and well. "You know, pretty soon everybody's going to want to come here to make sure you didn't die. Really pisses me off that we don't get no sex between now and then."

Crosby squeezed his eyes shut and made some rusty hip thrusts on the bed from his prone position. "Yeah. That was it. My sex drive. What a shame."

Garcia couldn't help it—he laughed. "You're shameless."

"Yeah, well, last time I was home, it was a lot more fun, you gotta admit that."

"But it was too long ago, baby. You need to be here more so you got the fun and the regular and sometimes even the shitty. I'm told that's how relationships work."

"You sound really wise here," Crosby told him. "Tell me more about relationships. It seems I'm in one." He grunted. "By the way, Iliana almost blew my cover today to tell me I should go home and get laid. That was great."

"Oh God. Tell Gail to stop talking to her roommate."

"You tell her," Crosby returned acerbically, and then he let out a long sigh. "I miss Elsa. God, I miss everybody. I only get so much out of you on text. You sure I'll see the unit tomorrow?"

"Yeah." Garcia took a breath. "We might even convince Toby to come."

Crosby's face crumpled a little, and Garcia, lying on his side, smoothed a gentle hand down his chest. Garcia had kept him apprised of Toby's recovery, but it was slow. Toby's fragile bones had needed surgery after surgery after being broken in jail, and he'd needed extensive dental work as well. He'd needed to sell the big apartment since he wasn't working, but Toby had always been smart with money. A smaller apartment—and only a few good friends—had gotten him through the last two months, as had his parents coming to stay with him while he recovered. Garcia had visited as often as he could—sometimes sitting in Toby's apartment on a new, more comfortable couch, and listening as Toby relived his and Crosby's college years had been the only way he'd managed not to drive his department issue down to Brooklyn so he could throw Crosby in the back and force him to be home.

It had also let Garcia see the earnest young college student he'd had no doubt Crosby had been, the sweet kid who would befriend and protect a young man with a bright talent and personality but who could be easily bullied physically. Crosby had believed in good then—had wanted badly to be a part of it.

It had hit Garcia forcibly how much the betrayal of Sons of the Blood must have hurt him. The all-business agent, who had proclaimed himself "not that fast and not that bright" hadn't just been trying to prove he was still good in his heart, he'd been protecting himself from any more betrayals.

"He doesn't blame you," Garcia told him softly. "He blames McEnany. He blames the dead cop who beat him. He doesn't blame you."

"He should," Crosby whispered. "I... I should have seen how vulnerable he was."

"Why?" Garcia asked harshly. "You had a day's warning, and you got out." He smiled a little. "I mean, I would have moved you out regardless, but still."

To his immense relief, a gentle smile fought for purchase on Crosby's battered face. "You were pretty insistent."

"I'm still insistent," Garcia told him, his heart aching. "We finish this case, you come home here, papi. We need your ass prints on my barstools, and I need to yell at you for stupid shit like dumping your beard trimmings in the sink."

"What kind of animal does that?" Crosby joked weakly.

"Good. Then I yell at you for absolutely nothing, and we… we get up on our day off and go get bagels and shit. And this thing…." His voice caught. "This thing that happened to you. It never happens again because *I*'ve got your back, and I'm not stupid enough for any of this bullshit to hurt you."

"You *are* the best partner I've ever had," Crosby said, and for a moment Garcia preened, and then it hit him.

"You are *not* comparing me to McEnany!" he gasped in outrage, and Crosby's laugh, a little cracked but still mostly whole, warmed him.

"Actually, I was comparing you to Gail—but don't tell her."

Garcia pressed his face against Crosby's bare chest—avoiding his taped ribs—and laughed until he sobbed. Crosby let him, soothing him with a hand on his back, and when Garcia pulled himself together, he realized that Crosby's hand had gone limp and he'd fallen back asleep.

Good. His boy needed his sleep if they were going to bring this thing home.

HARDING'S DOCTOR friend came by a couple hours later. Garcia answered the door in his sweats with a hoodie, beyond the niceties at this point. Harman Blodgett was perfectly average—average height, average build, with a widow's peak of average hair not too far receded and average brown eyes. But he had a lovely smile, a little shy but gentle and strong as well.

He'd been almost angry as he'd attended Crosby the first time— snapping out orders to the medics and focusing a lot of his ire on Harding himself. Garcia had a clear memory of this unassuming man snarling, "Look at him! He's been through hell and then, for all intents and purposes, poisoned. You couldn't have pulled him out of the meat grinder a little earlier, Clint?"

"All of us are in danger, *Bärchen*—and if they get to me, they get to you," Harding had replied. "He's staying under by choice."

Harman had cast Harding a flinty look before continuing to work on Crosby, for which Garcia had been grateful. And at the time he'd made the assumption—silly him—that they were friends or colleagues, but now, as Harman gave an apologetic look while wearing a much-laundered set of scrubs and asked if he could come check on Garcia's "young man," Garcia wondered if he hadn't missed something big in his worry over Crosby.

If nothing else, he should have looked up the word Harding had used—*Bärchen*—to see what, exactly, it meant.

"He's still asleep," Garcia murmured. "Down the hall. You remember, Dr. Blodgett?"

"I do," said his guest. "But please—call me Harm. Clint talks about all of you. I feel like I know you all."

Garcia cast a quick glance over his shoulder, almost panicked. "Uhm, I wish I could say the same—"

He got a compassionate look in return. "He keeps his family and friends very close to the vest," Harman told him. "But I remember him telling me that you and Crosby stayed with him all night over Christmas. It was such a kind thing to do."

Garcia searched his memory for that moment, remembered Harding asleep on the couch while using his suit coat for cover. "We didn't think he had anybody," he said.

"I was on assignment," Harman told him, and Garcia blinked. "With...?"

"FBI," Harman said, as though he hadn't just blown Garcia's mind. "Profiling division. I actually suggested Clint recruit Crosby. That work he did on Brandeis was some first-rate detecting, some excellent puzzle assembly. I've never seen someone so intuitive." A shrug. "I know it probably felt like the end of Crosby's world to get recruited to the SCTF and have to move to New York, but he was wasted as a patrol officer."

Garcia gave a rusty chuckle. "Roger that. And he's told me—more than once—that he really loves it here. I think he regards this as a second chance to do some good."

"So not only a good puzzler," Harman Blodgett said, "a good man. I know Clint's been *very* worried about him."

"We all have," Garcia said, his voice like dust.

"You more than most," Harman observed compassionately. "I'm going to get very personal with this examination. He may not want you here."

Garcia nodded. "I'll leave if he wants me to." He'd meant it, those months ago; he didn't care where Crosby put his pecker as long as he brought it home. But he also knew Crosby would have told him if something like that had been needed. He trusted.

"Fair enough," Harman murmured. Garcia opened the door, and his voice brightened. "Mr. Crosby, how nice to see you again!"

Crosby squinted through his swollen eyes. "I wish I could say I recognize you," he said, "but I seriously can't see that much. They weren't this swollen after the fight!"

"Methamphetamines," Harman said, his voice still compassionate as he opened his bag and took out a pair of examination gloves. "And I'm sure the fentanyl didn't help. There was something else in there—I think aspirin, just to make it cheaper—and that also makes your bruising worse. And the Narcan made your heart beat extra fast, pushing blood under your skin. All in all, not a great day to get poisoned." He grimaced. "The cut on your arm was a *drag* to stop bleeding, and your nose wasn't much better."

Crosby groaned. "God, I'm a train wreck. That was *not* how I planned to start my day."

Harman chuckled. "Nobody does. But yeah, you were in bad shape. It could have been worse. I talked to the boy who helped bring you in. The proximity of all the injuries with the poisoning—that wasn't good for you either. And Narcan helps you recover from an overdose, but it leaves its own marks, including a racing heart. You were lucky he helped you outside. Any delay in getting you to treatment might have made things much, much worse."

Crosby groaned. "Man, I gotta get back in there. The Forty Third is vulnerable, and so are my people."

"We've got some news on that," Garcia said softly. "I get that you might have to go in to protect the Forty Third, but we're making inroads on the higher-up. We're close, Crosby. I swear."

They had *so* much to say to each other about the op, but Garcia would keep the personal texts and hug them to himself for the rest of his life.

Crosby gave a brief smile. "I mean, not gonna argue. Not the worst thing, taking a few days off."

"Good," Harman said, probing delicately at the tissue around Crosby's nose. "You shouldn't go running until this is cleared up, anyway. It's hard to tell because of all the other things jostling around your bloodstream, but I think you may have suffered a mild concussion."

"I already wasn't too bright," Crosby said with half a laugh, but Garcia couldn't laugh.

"You got out alive," he muttered, half angrily. "You…. Dammit, Crosby."

Crosby's eyes darted toward Garcia. "'S no worries. M'fine."

Harman took a deep, exasperated breath. "Calix, would you mind leaving the room for a moment?"

"'S fine," Crosby said. "Knows everything."

"Does he know your sexual history for the past year?"

Crosby let out something like a distorted giggle. "Yes!" he laughed. "Believe it or not, he knows the whole shebang."

"Does he know the he-bang?" Harman asked, voice steady.

"He *is* the he-bang," Crosby told him seriously. "Had one she-bang and one he-bang in the last year. All the bangs were on the PrEP protocol."

Harman nodded. "Fair enough. We still sent your blood to the lab to have it tested for everything, but it helps to know. Was that the only medication you're taking?"

"Had some antibiotics this morning, after the stabbing, before the fight," Crosby said. "And whatever you put in my hand here." He grimaced. "That stings like a mother, by the way. I mean, it's dumb, right? My body got hit by a train and poisoned, but that burn on my hand is the thing driving me the most batshit."

"I have heard that before," Harman murmured. He stopped fiddling with Crosby's face and checking his stitches to take his gloves off so he could pull an iPad out of a case from his bag. He tapped some things in with a stylus and then flicked what was going into Crosby's IV. "Judson, when was the last time you ate before your no-good-very-bad day?"

Crosby grimaced—a grotesque expression on his battered face that probably hurt as well. "I dunno… probably the night before. Yeah, that's right. I had a broccoli-cheese baked potato from a vendor the night before."

"Solid choice. Healthy for a cop," Harman murmured. "Do you always eat so well?"

Crosby grunted, averting his eyes right out of Garcia's bedroom window. "I… I mean, yeah, if I can. But, you know. My stomach's been off. Like, way off. Like… like bran muffins and apples for breakfast aren't enough to take away the burn."

Harman sighed. "I'm going to get personal here. Are you still comfortable with Calix in the room?"

Garcia would have needed a gun to his head to get kicked out now. "Yeah. Sure. What's up?"

Harman pulled Crosby's T-shirt up, and the first thing Garcia noticed, besides the bruising, which made parts of his ribs almost black, was how thin he'd gotten. Garcia could count the ribs, and the muscle mass in his chest had diminished.

Gently, Harman probed around the bruises, finding something under Crosby's skin which he poked at deliberately. Crosby put his hand up to his chest and made a pained sound, and underneath that, Garcia heard his stomach grumbling.

"What's that?" Garcia asked.

"Well, for starters, he's hungry. But for finishers, his blood tests showed markers for a peptic ulcer. I'm going to prescribe something to counteract the stomach acid, but Crosby, you need to keep up the good eating habits. Except don't skip any meals, okay?"

Crosby grunted. "I never knew what I could eat in my flop," he muttered. "The one time I let my fuckin' guard down, and look what happened."

"I hear you," Harman said, looking at him worriedly. "Now, am I to understand you didn't have any of these symptoms before you went undercover?"

Crosby shook his head and smiled a little, catching Garcia's eye and winking. "Lots of chicken sandwiches to keep the weight down, but no. No acid in my stomach. You know—I *like* my job normally."

Harman nodded and then glanced at Garcia, then back at Crosby. "Your relationship," he said delicately. "I take it you're not out to your team?"

Crosby shook his head, but Garcia made a noise. Crosby pursed his lips and held the hand in the sling up just enough to tilt it back and forth.

"I get the feeling we're not as secret as we'd planned," he said. "We, uhm, became roommates two days before I went under. At least one person on the team figured it out, and I think she told her partner." Crosby grunted. "And her roommate."

"Ouch," Garcia said. "Awk-*ward*."

Harman glanced at him.

"Her roommate was the she-bang," Garcia told him, and Harman laughed.

"Gotcha."

"She almost blew my fuckin' cover in the ER to tell me to go home and get laid," Crosby muttered, and it was Garcia's turn to laugh.

"That woman should know better!" he said, because that really *had* been a close call.

"It was a weird morning," Crosby mumbled. "But Garcia thinks Harding knows."

"Oh, he knows," Harman said. "Because he's the one who told me." He regarded them both. "And he's the one who told me that the young man who helped bring you in had a terrible crush." He sighed and pinched the bridge of his nose like he'd like to say more but couldn't, and Garcia made an intuitive leap.

"And some raging STDs," he said sharply, glancing at Crosby. "And maybe an HIV infection."

Harman tapped his nose because Garcia had apparently scored a direct hit.

Crosby groaned. "Poor kid. Okay, I get why you were asking all that now. Look, I know the kid landed and shit, but you need to have a counselor visit him, because from what I understand, a lot of that was *not* consensual."

"Gah! That's unfortunate," Harman muttered. "Okay, good. Not good that it happened, but good to know. I'll have that done. So now you know why I was asking, but about this ulcer...."

"I can't come out of undercover yet," Crosby said. "I mean, give me the treatment, and I'll keep eating right, but you guys.... McEnany is the least of our worries. We need to pin this guy Cavendish because Iliana's division is under siege. She can't hire anyone because she's got Creedy pushing every racist asshole born in Brooklyn into her ranks, and she can't trust any of the people above her to help her hire from within the department. And who*ever* is funding Creedy, he's pushing the whole meth/fentanyl/aspirin thing, and it's causing people to spiral super fast. Yesterday, I killed a user who was a cop four months ago, and the guy's wife used to do charity work, and she's the one who stabbed me. This whole Sons of the Blood thing needs to be brought down."

Crosby took a hard breath, probably fighting the pain in his ribs, and then spoke again while Garcia was trying to formulate an argument.

"And they have trackers on the team, waiting for Rick Young to fuck up his assignment. So… you know. I'd rather not."

Harm huffed out a breath. "As much as I appreciate that, you need to maybe look at alternatives. We need to take some ultrasounds and some CT scans, but have you seen blood in your stool?"

Crosby groaned slightly. "Now see, you couldn't have sent him out of the room for *that*?"

"You guys insisted," Harm Blodgett muttered. "But maybe it's a good thing he *is* here for that. There has got to be a way to wrap up this case before your stomach blows wide open and three other people try to kill you!"

"I'm *sayin'*!" Garcia snapped. "You have literally been crapping blood?"

"I hate that you know that about me," Crosby muttered.

"I'd rather know about your first kiss and first communion," Garcia told him angrily. "But I'd settle for something that's trying to kill you in the here and now!"

Crosby blew out a breath and closed his eyes. "I'm still alive," he muttered. "You are overreacting."

Garcia was about to show him what *real* overreacting was all about when Dr. Blodgett did what even Garcia could admit he should have done from the beginning and kicked him out to go make Crosby something to eat.

Garcia was back in ten minutes with a bowl of chicken chowder that he'd gotten from the deli two days before, when he'd had the day off and he'd been missing Crosby something awful. He'd dressed it thick with crackers and walked it in tentatively after he knocked on the door.

Harman was packing up his bag, and he gestured for Garcia to put the soup on the bedstand so he could sit in the chair.

But first he gestured for Garcia to talk to him in the hallway after he set the soup down.

"Anything else I miss?" Garcia grumbled. "Knife wound in his back? Gunshot he forgot to tell us about?"

"A serious reluctance for you to see him incapacitated?" Harm asked acerbically.

Garcia grunted. "I hate that this is what bothers him."

"Well, it takes time to trust someone when you're vulnerable," Harm said, gentleness in his voice. "Trust me, Cl—uhm, my significant other resents that I get to see him so much as sleeping."

Garcia kept his expression neutral, but behind his mask, he was remembering Harman's impatience with Harding when he'd brought Crosby in and the way he seemed to know all of the people in the unit personally, like old friends.

Because Harding had told him.

Clint Harding.

Oh God, did Garcia feel stupid.

"You train yourself," Garcia murmured, "to keep all your emotions far, far away." That moment in the SUV, with Crosby's seizing body in his lap would never not haunt him. "You don't want anybody to know who you are, and then, when you find the one person you don't mind knowing, you are so… afraid. That they'll get…." His anger surfaced. "Shot, or stabbed, or poisoned, or beat to death or…." He flailed.

"Or develop a peptic ulcer and bleed out," Harman added softly. "Yes. All of that. But he's stronger than you think. And he's accomplished a *lot* for someone who isn't cut out for this. Your team will figure out a plan to finish this quickly." He gave a quick smile. "I have faith."

Garcia couldn't help himself. "You should, uhm, tell Harding he could tell us, you know. I mean, I get… most bosses don't want you to know anything personal about them. But… but Harding takes good care of us. And he picks us carefully. None of us are going to turn on him."

Harman grimaced. "Yeah, but you know. His choice. Always."

"Of course," Garcia had to concede. "Unless, of course, your ex-she-bang tells half the ER after you've been stabbed. Man, I haven't even *met* Iliana Davies, but I want to slap her. Dick. Move."

"Stress move," Harman said, and that perpetual gentleness undid all of Garcia's anger.

"When would *you* send him back in the field?" he asked.

"Two months, after at least two weeks on a beach with nothing to worry about but slathering on another coat of sunscreen."

"Fair." Garcia could live with that. "When are you going to recommend to Harding he goes back?"

"Five days," Harman told him soberly. "Use them well. Plan your ops. And give him a failsafe if you want him to get home. He can only protect himself so much when he's trying not to puke blood."

"I hear you," Garcia muttered. "Anything else?"

Harm grimaced. "The antibiotics and NSAID painkillers are going to mess up his stomach even further."

Garcia glared. "I hate this. I... I can't do this. I literally need to kill something." He would give his left nut for a heavy bag in the basement or some such bullshit, but he'd never had time to set up a home gym. It's why he always used the equipment at work. It could take more punishment than the small set of free weights in the spare room.

And also, Crosby would usually be there, and they could work out together.

"You're growling," Harm said softly. "Perhaps you should take a run or something?"

Garcia gave a tired smile. "Or I could always talk to him."

"Yeah, hey. You could always talk to him!"

They both laughed, and Harm let himself out after telling Garcia he'd be back in a few hours to take out the IV.

Well, it was just as good he had to leave it in; it meant Crosby was a captive audience for a little while longer.

Garcia paused at the doorway for a moment before he walked into the room. Crosby was leaning back, eyes still closed, only the restless flexing of his IV hand revealing that he was still awake.

"What?" he asked irritably, eyes still closed, and Garcia had to smile.

"I was letting some of the mad out, papi. You really made a mess of yourself for me."

"Wasn't *for* you, exactly," Crosby grumbled. "I'm just mad you have to clean up the mess."

"Not have to," Garcia said, moving to sit in the chair Harm had recently vacated. He picked up the soup, still warm, and said, "I want to be here for you. Don't freak out. I think it means it's serious."

"Only bang this year I care about," Crosby murmured. "That way," he corrected, grimacing. "Iliana's been a stand-up friend in the last two months."

Garcia grunted and said, "Open up, papi. Both your hands are out of commission for the moment. Gonna feed you some soup."

"Gah!" Crosby's open mouth was the perfect opportunity to pop in a spoonful. He swallowed and glared and then said, "You will never respect me again after this. I'll have to move out and change my name."

But Garcia wasn't having any of that. "As. If. With all the trouble we went to getting you here? For fuck's sake, you're lucky you're not cuffed to the bed. Now open up again."

Crosby did, scowling, but this time he took a moment to really taste the soup. "This's good," he said reluctantly. "Where'd you get it?"

"Deli around the corner. Just one more thing to look forward to when the op's over. Incentive enough?"

Crosby moved his IV hand, putting it on Garcia's knee. "*You* are incentive enough. I promise."

Garcia smiled a little. "Sweet talk gets you more soup."

Crosby opened his mouth and ate, and after he swallowed he said, "So Harding's boyfriend's something, isn't he?"

Garcia paused before scooping out another spoonful. "How'd you know?"

"I heard him cussing Harding out in the ambulance when I was being treated. I didn't remember until he came in and talked to me. Sounded like you when I've pissed you off."

"Like now, when you're hurt and your stomach's ripping itself apart and my heart hurts looking at you?" Garcia asked.

Crosby's expression was hard to read, but his hand on Garcia's knee squeezed gently. "Yeah."

"How're we gonna get you out of this?" Garcia asked, setting the soup down and covering that hand.

"I think we gotta trust the team," Crosby murmured. "I think… I think Harding recruited us all for different reasons. I know that Harman's a doctor, but he's also a profiler. He's the one who helped me nail Brandeis. I remember those conversations—he told me to trust Harding." A corner of his mouth pulled up. "Called him Clint. Told me to trust Clint. Repeatedly. I remember once when we were both really frustrated, he said—and I'll never forget this—that Harding had this vision of what law enforcement should be. And that if he had his way, it would never be just one guy trying to figure something like this out."

Garcia frowned. "Why didn't the feds get called into that, anyway?"

Crosby grunted. "'Cause I was the only one who saw the connection—the only one who didn't write those kids off 'cause they were from the wrong neighborhood. I think Harding had some words with the higher-ups to even send feds down after I made the collar."

"Baby," Garcia murmured, finally feeling the words instead of the fear and the worry. "My fear here—and I can see it so clearly—is that you were alone for so long. And not just when you were a flatfoot in Chicago, and not only when you got to New York and only knew Toby and nobody else. I think all of it—from liking boys to not following the crowd even in school—I think you have never felt... safe."

Crosby swallowed and squeezed his eyes shut tighter. "I have," he whispered. "For two days. Here."

Garcia took a deep breath. "Here. We gotta get you back here for a while."

Crosby nodded, and as worried as Garcia was about his stomach, he sat there, the soup on the nightstand, holding Crosby's hand until he fell asleep.

I Have a Plan!

THEY HAD to put off the team meeting because Crosby slept for almost twenty hours after Harm left. He woke up to use the bathroom—awkward, with Garcia following him with the IV—and to eat, because Garcia was nagging him to. And then, after a few more intense conversations with Calix and some gentle touching on both their parts, he fell asleep again.

He finally woke up enough to shower and get dressed, but he waited until after Harm came to take the IV out and to check his dressing on the slice on his arm. Harm agreed to take the sling and shoot it into the ocean, per Crosby's request, but he had lots of advice while he did that, including the admonition that running or heavy exercise of any form was still out of the question.

"Good," he'd said, able to see without squinting, thanks to the anti-inflammatories running through his system. "I'll just couch and eat starchy foods and plan world domination."

"So you *do* understand how this works," Harman had joked.

"Garcia's been giving me pointers," Crosby replied dryly. "Bad news is, I've only got three more days to master it."

"You need more practice," Harman said, sounding stern, but Crosby remembered how kind he'd been when they'd talked over the phone about the Brandeis case. Harman only got stern with people when they were ignoring medical advice.

"It's important," he said softly. "Harding knows it too."

"Clint pushes everybody on his team as hard as he pushes himself," Harman muttered darkly. "I'm not okay with this."

"Aren't you an ER doctor *and* an FBI profiler?" Crosby asked, proud that he had a secret weapon in this war.

"And I'd cut one of those jobs loose if my partner would back off the throttle for a damned minute," Harm groused, rubbing something soothing over the back of Crosby's hand to ease the burn from the IV needle.

Crosby raised his eyebrows. "Garcia tells me we might have two more recruits in the office. That should give him a little more downtime once I'm back."

"Well, kid, it's not often people like you or Garcia just drop into his lap."

"I thought Harding stole him from ATF."

Harman grunted. "But first he read the report in which Garcia went undercover for a month and then broke the case *after* getting the mother and children who were being held hostage in the drug house out and into WITSEC without the dealer knowing they were even connected to the bust. Harding saw that and said, 'He's got Crosby potential.'"

Crosby groaned. "You know, my college professors were always surprised I was passing their classes. I don't know where Harding got all this damned faith, yanno?" He paused. "But that's pretty badass about Garcia."

"Your college professors were stupid," Harm said, and gave him a perceptive, studied gaze. "And you use that. The assumption that because you're big and blond, it means you're not bright. But I will tell you something. Harding does an IQ assessment the two of us worked out together years ago when he was first starting this unit. He wanted something that would show him the kind of person he needed—someone who could work fast, think on their feet, retain information, and not leave a wreckage path in their wake. Your work on the Brandeis case showed that you were quite good at that, in addition to having a solid moral center that he depends upon."

The recitation was almost clinical, and Crosby squirmed. "Yeah, but I'm not a doctor by day and an FBI profiler by night," he said uncomfortably.

Harman Blodgett snorted. "Don't kid yourself, Crosby. The whole team is made up of superheroes. That includes you."

Crosby remembered the video Garcia had sent him. Garcia had kept his phone recording the entire time, including that moment when the team emerged from the fog, every one of them from maternal Natalia to tiny, fey Gail responsible for a kill.

They'd been angry. And proud. And determined to keep Toby, Garcia, and Chadwick alive.

He smiled a little. "They really are sort of badass."

"And so are you," Harman said. "Just remember—even badasses need some help. Batman was better off in the Justice League, right?"

"Yeah, but I still can't figure out what Green Lantern was doing there. I mean… that ring—that could do everything, right?"

"You're missing the point, Crosby, and you're not that dumb."

"Fine." He sighed. "I'll be Batman."

"Be Crosby," Harman muttered, throwing his supplies into his black bag. "But be a live Crosby. You won't just break Garcia's heart if you don't come back. You'll break *everybody's*, including Harding's and Natalia's. Just don't take all my hard work keeping you alive and throw it away, okay?"

"I'll do my best," Crosby said humbly. "Thank you."

"Whatever. I need some sleep. I'm cranky. I'll be here for your little confab tomorrow night. Get some rest between now and then."

Crosby rolled his eyes. "I have to. *Somebody* told me not to go running."

Harman's thin face took on a trace of arrogant pride. "Yes. Yes I did. Go me."

"Go get some sleep," Crosby said kindly. Harman really *did* look exhausted. ER doc, profiler, Harding's significant other. All those things added together probably made for a very tired boy.

Harman nodded and made his exit, and Crosby moved on to his shower. He came out in sweats, his shaggy hair drying, and smelled food.

"Ooh… chicken and rice again?" he said as he entered the kitchen. A song was playing over a house speaker, something smokey and syncopated about stealing a dance with a lover on the downlow.

Garcia gave him a sideways look as he flipped what was in the pan. "Lightly breaded fish," he said, and his voice was a little clogged. Crosby wondered what he and Harm had talked about and had a sudden need to comfort instead of being the one comforted.

He moved behind Garcia, cupping is hips and swaying a little to the music.

"Hey," he murmured, dropping his face into the hollow of Garcia's neck and shoulder. "You know what?"

"What?" Garcia seemed to melt back against him, and Crosby tightened his grip around his waist, ever so grateful Harm had taken the damned sling.

"We've got three days. That's longer than we had last time. And maybe this time we can plan the op so next time I stay. What do you think?"

"I think we're not having sex before I feed you," Garcia said, and while he tried to keep his voice tart, Crosby could hear the yearning.

"That's fine. Feed me. We can start on that list of movies we talked about. Then sex. At night, in the dark, like we've been married for years."

Garcia let out a choked laugh. "That's your fantasy, Cowboy? No orgies with the cast of *Yellowstone* or nights out with Johnny Depp?"

"Nope. Toldya. Straight ol' vanilla me. My fantasy is that this assignment is long past and you and me have worked a busy day with SCTF. And we come home, after some beers with our friends and colleagues maybe, and make ourselves some dinner. We clean up, watch some TV, and then slide into bed. One of us," and he thrust his groin very gently, to indicate it was Garcia, "may think we're all done, but the other one," and he hugged Garcia tighter to let him know that this was him, "reaches across the bed and starts touching. And then kissing." He kissed Garcia's neck. "And then touching." He slid his hand down under Garcia's waistband, teasing but not intruding. "And pretty soon we're doing our favorite thing. And when we're done, we just fall asleep, because the alarm's set, and we're gonna wake up in the morning and do it all again. And when we wake up, you say, 'Oh my God, we had sex!' and I'm all smirky and proud, and maybe the next day, *you're* the one reaching for *me*."

"Mm." Garcia sighed into his embrace. "Let me move the fish, Cowboy. It's done and I have to kiss you."

Crosby stepped back long enough to let him do his thing, which was good because it smelled delicious, and then stepped into his arms when he turned around. For a moment he was afraid. They were so close, Garcia's eyes enormous in his almost peaked face, and Crosby wondered if he could force the iron cage he'd held around his emotions, around his heart, down enough to touch him.

Then Garcia closed his eyes and held his face up for the kiss Crosby had promised, and Crosby knew he couldn't leave his partner hanging.

Garcia's lips were soft, and for a moment, Crosby just let the feel of them suffuse him, melt through his reserve, permeate his heart. Then his arms did that gathering thing in earnest, and he opened his mouth and swept his tongue in, wanting more taste.

Garcia reacted, putting his hand on Crosby's shoulders, clenching his fingers in his T-shirt. He had to stand on his toes, and Crosby bent down, pillaging Garcia's mouth like a kid with a sack of candy, and everything was sweet, and everything was better than the last thing he'd tasted.

A frenzied beeping penetrated his senses, and Garcia groaned and ripped himself away, turning back toward the stove. "Set the table, Cowboy," he ordered gruffly. "If you kiss me any more, my brain's going to leak out my ears, and then Harm's going to need to come back and fix *me*."

Crosby chuckled, feeling pretty good about himself, and set the table in short order. Garcia plated the food at the oven—always a good sign—and set the plates down with a rather pleased expression.

"What?" Crosby asked, as they sat down kitty corner to each other.

"There's leftovers," Garcia said, chuckling a little.

"That's a big deal?" Crosby had no idea.

"It means you'll be here tomorrow to eat them for lunch."

Crosby grinned at him—gently, because his face still hurt, but it was nice to be able to react to Garcia's optimism.

"See?" he said, giving a soft shoulder bump. "Small fantasies."

"Best kind."

IT REALLY was simple. They watched a romantic comedy that night—one of Garcia's favorites—on the understanding that they could watch a gritty crime drama the next night for Crosby. Crosby started nodding off midway, and he found himself asleep on Garcia's chest, Garcia's arm wrapped protectively around his shoulder. After the movie he woke up and stumbled to the bedroom, *his* bedroom, all dumb jokes about living in the spare room burned away after over a month of living in a flop that could have been his coffin.

He didn't need to reach for Garcia; Garcia rolled into his space, rubbing gentle hands on his skin while he fell asleep dreaming about sex. He woke up in the darkness, shivering in Garcia's arms, while a dream about being locked in the tenement stairwell rocked him, a viscous goo flooding the tiny room, flowing into his mouth, his nose, his lungs....

"Shh, papi," Garcia whispered, and Crosby woke up, shuddering out his reaction in Garcia's arms.

"There's no poisoned water," he mumbled.

"It's all gone."

"I can breathe here," he said, and he heard the earnestness in his own voice as he tried desperately to tell Garcia something important.

"Always, baby. Take a deep breath and go back to sleep."

So he did, and this time he slept until morning.

GARCIA WENT into the office that day, refusing all of Crosby's entreaties to go with him. As a consolation prize, Crosby got folders on Courtland Cavendish, Marshawn Devereaux, and Marcy Beauchamp, their three suspected Sons of the Blood members in higher-up positions, and he got his first good look at how his team hadn't been idle during his absence.

Kicked back on the made bed, clean, fed, wearing sweats and socks, oh gods, *comfortable* for the first time in nearly two months, he took a look at the research the team had done in between their regular nine-to-nine jobs of saving the world.

Open this one first, read Garcia's handwriting on a Post-it. Dutifully Crosby opened the file on Marshawn Devereaux and saw a candid picture of a handsome, stern-looking Black man with his family, including his daughter and her wife with their two small children and a note from Natalia, making Crosby remember what Garcia had told him about Devereaux from the beginning.

Sorry, guys—I asked my father-in-law to check on Crosby and help backstop his cover. I can assure you, nobody in this family has any connection to a white supremacist group.

Crosby laughed outright and spent a moment looking at a happy family, some of whom looked *very* familiar. In particular Natalia caught his eye, holding her son while playfully bussing his cheek while her wife balanced a toddler on her hip, and just their smiles made him smile in return. After a sweet moment, he set the folder aside. He wanted to go directly to Cavendish's folder, particularly after McEnany's revelation, but another Garcia Post-it stopped him.

Don't dismiss Beauchamp—smells like an outhouse.

Oh?

Hmm…. Marcy Beauchamp, originally Marcy Lamb, graduated from… CSU Stanislaus, California? The actual hell? What was someone from the sinking center of the West Coast doing in New York cop politics?

"Marcy Lamb, Marcy Lamb, where did you come from…?"

Marcy Lamb was the daughter of a cop who was the son of a cop who was the son of a cop in an area of California known for its sharp dividing lines between the Mexican immigrant community and the rich landowners who drove the area. She'd gotten her criminal justice degree—but just barely—having blown off, ignored, and probably pissed off the professor who taught a required course on hate crimes and the racism built into the criminal justice system. Crosby was reading between the lines here—but he saw the D-, the D+, and finally the C because Marcy had needed to take the class three times to get a grade that would let her graduate. He also noticed a surprising dearth of letters of recommendation in her file from her other educators. She'd had to, in fact, rely on her sponsor, a notoriously right-wing councilman, and his son to get her through the academy.

The councilman's last name was Beauchamp.

After marrying up, Marcy followed her husband to Texas, where he'd accepted a job in charge of border patrol. Crosby grimaced because the number of citations for human rights violations and brutality had been reduced to six pages of bullet points in small font, and it told him that the Texas Rangers—one of the country's peacekeeping forces with their roots deepest in the toxic well of racism—were alive in spirit.

Marcy had worked under him and had gotten a lot of commendations for things Crosby thought should have gotten her fired.

When Kent Beauchamp was killed on the job, Crosby imagined a lot of people breathed easier. Including his wife, who politicized her husband's death to further her own political ambitions.

Crosby studied these notes carefully, frowning.

She hadn't been well-liked, he thought. Either the well of misogyny ran deep—always a possibility—or she had rubbed people the wrong way. He saw a lot of good records, but a lot of denied promotions. He saw good scores on detective exams, but no recs for the job. When she ran for police commissioner in her hometown, she lost to a man who had only moved there a few years before.

Finally, she'd taken her commendations and her lack of likability and moved them to New York, where she was appointed as an expert on border patrol via the harbors smuggling in immigrants and proceeded to terrorize the harbor TSA.

Her picture showed a woman who could have been handsome, but a squint of dissatisfaction in her eyes and a pinch around her mouth put her into the category of someone Crosby would cross the street to avoid.

But none of that explained to Crosby how she'd ended up in the commissioner's office.

Narrowing his eyes, he pulled out the other file, the one on Courtland Cavendish, and started to read.

Ugh.

Courtland Cavendish was the kind of career politician both sides of the aisle claimed to detest.

Born to old money in Florida, he'd campaigned on all the usual suspects—family values that devalued families, small government that tried to legislate everything from who people married to what they did for a living to what they read, and law enforcement that only enforced laws in certain neighborhoods and were praised on their conviction rate of minorities. He'd been hired out of Harvard Law School directly into the commissioner's office, and Crosby would bet that if he looked *really* close he'd find that Cavendish's old man did some favors for the chief of police or something to make that happen. His was one of those careers that didn't do a lot—no legislation bore his name, and nobody owed him a debt of gratitude for finding money for training or opening up more drug rehabilitation centers or anything—but boy did he mouth off on social media *all* the fucking time.

And he did a lot of community photo ops in some of the poorer precincts in the city. Crosby could see how he'd be a big hit with the Sons of the Blood, in spite of the fact that Cavendish's family tree was hydroponic—none of those roots got anywhere close to getting dirty for the sake of the family wealth.

Okay, he thought, staring at the two folders. There was the local girl who married up and widowed into politics and the glad-hander who'd failed up, given his lackluster grades in Harvard, and who was now a small fish in a big pool and trying to make himself bigger.

What did they have in common?

Frustrated and intrigued, Crosby started flipping through the files, looking at the pictures, both the promotional ones and the candids taken by investigative forces.

Ten minutes in, he saw a familiar face. Standing at one of Cavendish's community photo ops, glaring from the background, was none other than Jimmy Creedy.

With a grunt, he texted Garcia.

Who's on overwatch? I need computer skills right now.

I am. What do you need?

I need facial recognition run for Jimmy Creedy with all the pix of Marcy Beauchamp. I think he might be the connection.

FINALLY, a lead I can research. I'll get back to you.

Thanks!

In the meantime, get some rest. People are coming after we wrap up the case, and you need to be awake.

Nag nag nag....

It's done with love, Cowboy, now let me work.

Fine. Love you too.

But how could he rest? There was weight equipment in the spare room—he should get up, stretch, and go in there to work out a little. He was too *pumped* to rest. With determination, he gathered the folders, making sure to replace the material in the same order in which he'd found it before stacking them once again. Then he stretched, his back against the headboard of the bed, and yawned, and for a moment his mind let go of all the possibilities of Marcy Beauchamp and Courtland Cavendish and how to nail them both for conspiracy.

And that's when he fell back asleep.

Wet Work

GARCIA WAS all for the cases that ended quickly and quietly, no gunfire, just a troubled person who could be tracked down and brought in to be dealt with by the legal system—particularly when the team had a bigger fish on the line that needed to be caught, skinned, and fried.

"Paperwork tomorrow," Harding said as everybody stalked onto the SCTF floor. There were curt nods, and Swan, Pearson, Denison, and Chadwick all headed for their locker rooms, where they'd shower if they needed it and lock away their armaments for the time being.

Harding frowned, though, as he saw Chadwick. "Where's your deadlier half?" he asked.

Gideon Chadwick grimaced and gave Garcia a grim look. "We stopped for food," he said. "Shake Shack, for Garcia, and we caught our tail."

Harding and Garcia stared at him.

"And you what?" Garcia asked. "Disappeared him?"

Chadwick gave a bloodthirsty grin. It had occurred to Garcia in the past month that Carlyle's skill set was that of an assassin, although he seemed a lot less sociopathic than Garcia imagined most assassins could be. But the stealth, the ways of killing silently, the murky "alphabet" training he'd had, it all told a story of covert ops. And the way he'd emerged from the fog the night of Precinct Twenty Four—he'd had a look on his face like a predatory cat with a whopper of a rat in its jaws.

"Tracked him?" Harding asked carefully.

Chadwick nodded. "Permission to take a covert vehicle and be his backup, sir?"

"Do you know where he is?" Garcia asked, not so carefully. He didn't care if they were partners, like him and Crosby, or partners like Harding and Denison—they were bonded with trust, love, and a dependency that defied analysis or description, and Garcia couldn't breathe when Crosby was away.

"He's been keeping in touch," Chadwick said with a twitch of his lean lips that told Garcia they probably had their own language, just like him and Crosby. "But I would like him to not have to be alone."

"Would you like backup?" Harding asked.

Chadwick shrugged. "Not so much." His look grew hooded and almost sinister. "What we would like is… permission."

Harding raised his eyebrows. "Permission?"

"Mm-hmm. Permission."

Harding's eyes grew flinty. "Nothing gratuitous. Nothing that can be traced back to us. And if you think you can avoid it, do."

Chadwick gave an absolutely chilling smile and placed his hand on his heart. "I solemnly swear we will avoid any wrongdoing if at all possible."

With that he wheeled about, tactical gear still on, and strode toward the elevator.

"I, uh, don't believe he and Carlyle are going to find it possible," Garcia muttered.

Harding turned those flinty eyes toward him. "They've tried to kill you once and Crosby three times. They were going to sacrifice an innocent man just to bait Crosby into a meat grinder. If Carlyle and Chadwick can get some information…." He let the sentence trail off, and Garcia nodded, understanding.

This was a silent, very deadly war. And Harding was ready to strike a killing blow to end it.

"Fine," he said, not sure where his conscience was, because it didn't seem to be speaking up, "but let me text Crosby and have him order pizza. If there's no Shake Shack at the end of the rainbow, I've gotta have something to eat."

THEY TRICKLED in from different routes—tradecraft, taking different paths through the city to get from their homes to the office, had become so ingrained in all of them in the last month, Garcia didn't think they'd ever get the stink out of their cell phones. He'd started stopping at different places for breakfast and coffee, changing the route up every day. He had three different grocery stores he ordered from, and he placed the orders at different times for different things. He knew that since that night with the Twenty Fourth, they'd all become nth level paranoid because the idea that they had tails on them—whether or not the tails were lost—was terrifying.

And tonight, of all nights, nobody could afford to be tracked.

But something seemed to have been cut loose in them, something savage and feral, now that Crosby had been attacked, because Chadwick and Carlyle may have been the last ones to arrive, but they were by no means the only ones who were... bloody.

"Rough ride in?" Crosby asked, sounding worried. They were both still wearing their vests under their long-sleeved shirts, and Carlyle had scrapes on his knuckles.

"Nope," Joey Carlyle said and glanced at Gideon as if in confirmation.

"Smooth as silk," he said.

"How smooth?" Harding asked, eyes sharp.

"You know that place on the Hudson where the bodies keep washing up?" Carlyle asked almost clinically. "That construction foreman keeps finding people in very nice suits without a mark on their faces?"

"Yes." Harding sounded wary, and Joey had everyone's attention by now.

The poor foreman—Garcia had needed to interview him once, and the guy had been legitimately confused as to which body they'd been talking about, because in five years of work, he'd recovered over twenty.

"I did an analysis of local tides and currents to see where the most likely dumping spot was for those bodies to end up there," Gideon said. "Turns out it's about three blocks behind one of those places that has the real good ice cream." He held up a bag with two half-gallon cartons packed inside a wash of ice packs, and Manny stepped forward and took it from him, getting nodded permission from Garcia to put the ice cream in the freezer.

Harding took a deep breath. "So, how many bodies does that take our poor engineer up to?"

"Twenty-three," Joey said promptly, before laughing low and deep from his belly.

"Wait," Natalia said. "Wasn't it only at twenty-one—"

"Turns out we were both tired of having tails," Gideon told her. "And since they both attacked first, I'm afraid we had no choice but to fight back. Until they were... wet."

"Very, very wet," Joey added darkly.

Garcia tried not to gape. "Are they just attacking us now out in the open?"

Joey shook his head. "No, I think we provoked them. Not on purpose," he added, looking virtuous. "We weren't doing a damned thing that was illegal—or even unseemly."

"All completely aboveboard." Gideon Chadwick's sober nod almost blew the entire façade.

Harding swallowed. "I don't even want to ask," he decided after a moment. "I...." He took a breath. "I am taking your word for it that you had no choice."

"We responded to an attack with proportional force, sir," Carlyle said.

Coming from the hall, dressed in Crosby's shirt and Garcia's sweats, Gail made a raspberry sound. "Weak shit," she muttered. "My guy rushed me with a knife, and Swan blew him away with his drop piece."

Chadwick and Carlyle stared at her. "But—"

"And then she threw a knife at the guy at my back," Manny said dryly. "Which she then had to retrieve, and—"

"Yuck," she muttered. "Fortunately we were in one of those alleys where bodies are sort of a regular occurrence. Our two guys might be found in the morning."

Harding gave a pained look. "I don't know if I have to say this or not, but—"

"Don't worry, Chief," Joey told him. "We'll do the paperwork on our air-gapped units at home so they can't be hacked. Then we'll print out a hard copy that you can keep in your desk or submit in triplicate or whatever you have to do when one of us makes a kill." He looked at Garcia and Crosby. "I know that our paperwork goes up the federal food chain, am I right?"

They all nodded.

"Then its fine. On a federal level, a supervisor you trust knows your agents were forced to defend themselves. On the state level...."

"The local po-po knows nothing," Crosby said. "I remember seeing kills like this—ones the old guys took in stride but us new guys were sure were hinky. Hello, now I'm on the other side of that mirror."

"I never wanted a hit squad," Harding told them soberly. "But that said, better them than us."

Gail laughed and misquoted "March of Cambreadth," "How many of them can we take out!" complete with accent. There was a scattering of laughter, and Natalia spoke up.

"But we can't do this forever, Clint. I've got my wife and kids living with my in-laws. We have got to put this thing to bed."

Harding gave a grim smile. "And Garcia thinks he has a way to do that. Garcia?"

They were standing in the kitchen, and Garcia made a pained sound. Crosby had the pizza waiting for them when he arrived, but Gail and Manny had gotten there first, and in the excitement over her run-in with her suddenly aggressive tail, nobody had eaten.

"Cap?" Crosby spoke up, and Garcia blessed him. "Food?"

Harding took a deep breath, as though *he* could barely contain himself from running out onto the street, guns blazing.

"Fine. Everybody get food and something to drink and gather around the coffee table. *Then* we talk about how to end this shit."

At that moment there was a knock on the door, and Harm showed up, looking tired in his sweats with a battered gray hoodie, and something in Harding's expression eased up and they were ready to roll.

A FEW MINUTES later, they were in position—Crosby in his "big and tall" chair with Garcia sitting on one side of him, not exactly clinging, but within casual touching distance. Gail was on the other side, and she *was* clinging. Garcia couldn't be mad or jealous or anything, though; they had been Olaf and Elsa long before he'd shown up, and they hadn't even texted in the past month. It had made sense to have Garcia be the one point of contact, but Crosby had obviously missed his team.

"Hey," Natalia said softly. "First, can I just say how glad I am to see Crosby not looking dead? Kid, you gave us a helluva scare."

Crosby shrugged in that way he had, the way that drove Garcia crazy in two completely opposite ways. "Thanks, Tal. I, uh, would rather not do that again." He made his eyes big and earnest. "Drugs are *bad*, kids. Don't do them!"

There was some strained laughter, and then Gail and Manny shook their heads, and Gail tightened her death grip on Crosby's leg.

"Man, don't even joke about it," Manny said with a shudder. "You didn't see you when Garcia shoved you in the car."

"Worse than the dog?" Crosby asked, obviously trying to pull up the sudden pall on the room.

"Worse than the dog," Gail whispered.

He stroked the tight braid down the back of her head. "Sorry, Elsa."

"Don't scare me like that," she murmured, resting her head against his thigh.

"Yeah, I'll do my best. It sort of sucked."

Garcia and Manny met eyes. They'd sworn a pact between them to never bring up Gail's screaming, half-hysterical moments, straddling Crosby and slapping his face, urging him to breathe. Swan had pulled the SUV into the ambulance bay by then, and they were waiting for Harding and the medics to show up, and Crosby had seized, the breath stopping in his chest. Garcia had gone to the faraway place in his head by then, someplace cool and isolated where nothing happening in the SUV had any relation to him or Crosby or the fact that the boy he loved was dying in his arms.

"We'd appreciate it," Manny said gruffly.

"Indeed," Harding murmured. "Okay, then. Crosby, good to have you back for the moment—"

"We are *not* sending him back in there," Natalia said, and it was so rare that she ever contradicted anything Harding said that the shocked silence was actually puzzled, because nobody could believe she'd done that.

"Let's get through the briefing, Tal," Harding murmured. "I don't want to make any promises in case we can't come up with a better plan."

She growled. Actually growled, but Crosby looked at her evenly.

"Your wife and kids, Natalia," he said. "They're exactly the people we're trying to protect here."

She growled again but subsided when Harding glared at her.

"Okay, so Crosby took his rest day seriously and spent it studying the data we've pulled up on Marcy Beauchamp and Courtland Cavendish, and he discovered something interesting."

All eyes turned to Crosby, who picked up the thread. "Cavendish has ties to Jimmy Creedy," Crosby told them. "The paper called him a union leader, but I know that's bullshit because I hear him badmouthing the real union leader of warehouse and dock workers as a pussy. His words. Don't get mad. So Jimmy apparently got enough *community* clout to not get anyone up in arms about that, and he's cozy with Cavendish, which is good. We know at least one member of McEnany's brass that he keeps trying to please." He paused for breath, and Garcia took his turn.

"And Crosby sent this to me to ask for facial rec, and I think we have another."

Crosby grinned at him through his still healing face, looking excited to have helped. Garcia wanted to lay on the praise thick because nobody else had seen Jimmy Creedy's nasty, ugly mug in that series of pictures they'd pulled on Cavendish, but then, Crosby had been to Creedy's apartment once every other day for the last six weeks. Crosby was maybe the only one of them who could.

"It wasn't Creedy," Garcia told them. "But Crosby's been pretty good at sending me pix of his known associates, as well as any info he's got. Most of them work in the same warehouse Creedy works at, so I did two things. The first is I took a look at who owns that warehouse. Crosby's been telling us that meth is what's for dinner in this sitch, and two things hit me today. One was that a warehouse would be really spiffy place to get shipments of drugs in from God-knows-where, and another is—"

"Holy shit," Harding said, and Garcia grinned at him and nodded.

"Yessir. We all missed it."

"What'd we miss?" Gail asked. "I did the deep dives on Beauchamp and Cavendish—what'd we miss?"

"What's Beauchamp do for a living?" Natalia asked, sounding frustrated, like she should have gotten it too.

"Oh my God," Gail said.

"Could we share with the class?" Manny asked desperately.

"She's in charge of immigration through the ports and harbors," Chadwick said, shaking his head. "So all that meth coming in through the harbor is...."

"Oh my God. Coming in through the warehouse where Creedy works!" Manny filled in. "Shit! That was bothering me. What did the meth have to do with anything? Where was it coming from?" He looked at Crosby apologetically. "I know that meth is usually really easy to cook up, and fentanyl is supposed to be everywhere, but what you got hit with was high-grade stuff. All those samples you gave us? They were super consistent. This wasn't backyard kitchen meth—this was cooked by a skilled chemist and cut with exact proportions of fentanyl. When it's not being dumped in your water and glugged down, it's optimum design for addicting people but not letting them overdose until their money is all gone and they don't have any teeth."

"Great," Crosby muttered. "At least it was good bad stuff."

"Not even funny," Harm said quietly to Harding. "Get this shit off the street. I saw three overdoses *today*."

They all shuddered, and then Joey Carlyle spoke up. "So Beauchamp is getting the stuff through the harbors, and let me guess. Does *Cavendish* own the warehouse?"

Garcia groaned. "That was going to be my second big reveal, but yes! Carlyle wins all the prizes for the giant intuitive leap, everybody. Somebody get our boy an extra slice of pizza."

Joey grinned at everybody, a feral smile that hinted at the blood he'd spilled just to be sitting there in Garcia's living room, and grabbed his own slice of pie.

"Okay, then," Natalia said, calming the whoops and cheers—a sign of stress relief, yes, but they weren't out of the woods yet. "So, you've got their function in the Sons of the Blood organization, but do you have the connection for how they met?"

Garcia failed to not look smug. "Oh yes. Like I said, we've got pictures and histories of *all* the assholes Crosby's been feeding us. Including this one."

He'd printed out a folder at work and then wiped his browser history off the work unit *and* the cloud. A competent forensic technician could figure out what he'd been researching, but unless somebody was specifically after what he'd been doing, it wouldn't jump up and bite anybody on the ass.

He opened the folder he'd kept balanced on his lap and pulled out a picture and a history and passed them both around.

"Meet Donny Mazursky. He works security at the warehouse, which means his best talent is being a thug and a bruiser, and he's got the minor-crimes rap sheet to prove it. Donny has a family of brothers, three of whom went out to Texas to work for... anyone? Anyone?"

"Border patrol," Crosby said, getting it.

"Winner, winner, pizza dinner!" Garcia proclaimed. "So I went back and cross-referenced Mazursky and Beauchamp, and I came up with...." He waggled his eyebrows in the pause.

"You're enjoying this," Crosby said, and Garcia grinned at him.

"Only 'cause you're here with us, papi, but yes I am."

"So...." Harding was making impatient motions with his hand, and Garcia brought himself back to the meeting.

"Mazursky and Marcy Beauchamp's husband, Kent, were both on the board of a legit political organization called Americans for America, which is... anyone?"

"A white supremist organization!" Carlyle guessed, his voice a brutal imitation of a gameshow host's.

"And another prize for the gentleman with blood on his knuckles," Garcia replied in kind.

"I thought I'd washed that off," Joey muttered, and Gideon passed him, of all things, a baby wipe.

"You never clean enough," Chadwick muttered back.

"Shit." Carlyle wiped off the back of his hand and nodded for Garcia to go on.

"So," Harding mused, "is it, like, another branch of Sons of the Blood, or—"

"It was short-lived," Garcia said. "Lasted three years before getting branded a hate group. But since Mazursky was from the East Coast, it's not hard to jump from that to Kent Beauchamp and his wife starting their own... uhm, *poker game* at their place with their fellow travelers."

"And then Kent gets killed," Natalia said, "and Marcy runs for city council, and it falls through, and Mazursky talks to Creedy."

Garcia nodded. "And Creedy talks to his friend, the lawyer at NYPD Cop Central, and Beauchamp gets a job there."

"And she's perfect," Harding said thoughtfully. "She knows law enforcement, she's pretty, she can make her way around a bureaucracy—"

"But only if the price is right," Crosby added. "I studied those files today, Chief. I think there's a lot of... of *unlikability* about this woman. Now normally I'd say being well-liked isn't a factor with a coworker, but...." He made a face, and Garcia knew he was searching for words.

"She's working with the public," Natalia said. "She was supposedly working with the community. Likability is part of her job. So to have someone who seems to have alienated *everybody*, including her hometown, rising so high so fast over there, it does seem as though she's working for a price."

"And Cavendish can pay the price," Swan said. Suddenly he frowned. "Garcia, he's a lawyer working for the commissioner's office, right?"

Garcia nodded. "Yeah, why?"

"Is there any way we could get a look at what cases he's tried? Because I'd bet my ass he ran across criminals during a criminal interaction. I've been studying up on white-collar crime. You'd be surprised how many white-collar criminals meet their street connections in court."

Harding frowned and stood up, pacing for a moment. "He mostly dealt with civil suits, am I right?"

Everybody in the room nodded because Garcia knew everybody in the room had read the files he'd given Crosby, including Natalia's sweet little joke file at the beginning.

Crosby turned to Garcia. "Give Elsa your computer. I know it's not associated with SCTF, so maybe she could take a lookie-loo and see if there's some names we could check out."

Garcia nodded and opened his laptop, making all the necessary modifications to keep any searches from being traced back to his IP address. Then he handed the laptop to Gail, and she grinned at him.

"Don't worry. I've got a couple of tricks you might not know. It'll still be clean as God's fingers when you get it back."

The problem with Gail being *such* a good field agent was that she was so much better at overwatch than he was, Garcia thought with a sigh.

"I have faith," he said with a wink. Then he turned to Harding. "Okay, so we'll find the connection. I'm surprised Gail couldn't access it on the back of her eyelids already. But what do we do with it then? I mean, we'll have a case. We'll have the connections between Cavendish and Beauchamp and between both of them and the Sons of the Blood. What else do we need?"

"We're building a case," Harding muttered. "But we also need a trap. So let's look at the case first. To begin with, we're only assuming about the warehouse—"

"Gid and I will take care of that tonight," Carlyle said, so casually Garcia stared.

"Uhm, how?" Swan asked.

They exchanged bloodthirsty glances. "Well," Chadwick said slowly, "turns out we were just there earlier this evening."

Harding glared at them. "I'm sorry, what?"

"We told you where we, uhm, shook our tail!" Carlyle protested. "Look at the address for that warehouse—where all the, uhm, bodies keep coming from. I didn't even put it together until right now!"

There was a stunned silence in the room.

All those bodies, turning up in that one place in the river, originating from that one warehouse where all the drugs were coming in and all the crooked would-be cops were working.

The case—the entire case—just fell into place.

"So, uhm, tomorrow, if we don't catch anything we can't pawn off on the FBI," Harding muttered, "Swan, Pearson—"

"We will be looking up all the dead people," Manny said, speaking for Gail, who was apparently in the zone on Garcia's laptop. "And cross-referencing them with all the names I have written right here!" He held up his copy of the file folder, with all the new information and questions written on a legal pad he'd secured to the back.

"Oh my God, Swan," Crosby said, sounding proud. "You are like magic. I don't think any of the rest of us were keeping up."

"I am a champion notetaker," Manny said primly. "So what else is on the list?"

Harding and Natalia met eyes, and Natalia was the one who said it. "Me and Harding are going to One Police Plaza tomorrow to introduce ourselves to Cavendish and Beauchamp," she said softly. "I for one want to get a look at how they talk to us, what they have to say. If they're Sons of the Blood, you can bet they're going to be *really* unhappy that I'm even in the building."

"And if they're just sociopaths," Harding said, "there should be tells."

Harm, who had been sitting quietly on the floor, practically behind Harding's chair, spoke up. "Body cams."

Harding looked at him in surprise. "You think?"

Harm nodded. "If you've got something more discreet you can rig, do it. I want to see the interviews."

Harding nodded in return. "Can do." He sighed and looked around the room, and Garcia didn't have to double-check to see what he was seeing. They were tired. Gail was clicking away, and Swan was writing ferociously, his pencil making scratching sounds in the sudden silence. The two teams who'd had run-ins were coming down from the adrenaline rush. Harding and Natalia looked frazzled and angry—and exhausted. Even Harman was resting, his head against the overstuffed chair Harding was sitting in, his eyes closed.

Suddenly Harding's lips twitched up as he glanced in Garcia's direction, and Garcia turned his head and looked up.

Crosby had slumped into the chair, eyes closed, breath coming regularly, and Garcia wondered how long he'd been like that.

"Ten minutes," Harm said without opening his eyes. "He nodded off ten minutes ago. He didn't eat much. Has he been taking his meds?"

Garcia grunted. "I would have no idea about that. I just got home." He looked around. "But we've got a spare bed if anyone needs it."

Harding nodded. "Nobody goes home alone tonight," he said soberly. "Swan, can you sleep on Gail's couch? With her roommate, that'll put three of you under that roof."

Manny nodded curtly, without looking up from the notes he was taking as he did some surfing of his own with his encrypted phone.

"Natalia, we... I've got a guest room you can sleep in," Harding said.

She snorted, and that, of all things, seemed to lighten up the room.

"Give it up, Clint," she said softly. "It's like Garcia and Crosby—everybody knows."

Harding's cheeks turned a gentle pink. "Very well," he intoned, obviously trying to keep his dignity. "Would you like our guest room?"

She nodded. "Thanks, guys. It would suck, going into an empty house."

"Carlyle?" Harding said. "You and Chadwick?"

"He listens to pirate metal," Carlyle said soberly. "Do I get some sort of compensation for having to listen to pirate metal in the morning?"

"Yeah, asshole," Chadwick retorted. "You get me as your awesome partner, and fuck you with an anchor!"

Carlyle gave a lazy, almost satiated smile. "Looks like I'm in," he said, and Garcia's gut gave a little dance then about Carlyle and Chadwick, but unlike the whole rest of the world in *his* business, he wasn't going to pry.

But as everybody yawned and stood, and Harding made plans to meet at his and Harm's house in Staten Island the next evening, where "I'll cook pork adobo," Harm volunteered quietly, "since we're out now, and it's my day off," Garcia was struck by a sudden worry.

"We're all... we're all going to make it home, right?" he asked, hating himself for sounding weak and quavery.

"Hold up," Chadwick muttered, going to the new laptop set up on the end of the counter. With quick twitches of the keys, he rewound the picture to three hours earlier and then sped through the feed from all six cameras, past everyone's arrival two hours before, and on until they were viewing it in real time.

"Still safe," Chadwick said, glancing around. "But Garcia, be sure you check the feed every so often."

"Will do," Garcia murmured, and then he sent a troubled glance over to Crosby, who hadn't moved. "Two more days?" he said, looking at Harding and almost begging for more time.

"Let's see what we find tomorrow," Harding murmured, and the rest of the room glanced at Crosby too and then nodded soberly.

They departed after that, in groups. Natalia left her department issue in front of Garcia's house and the keys on the counter before leaving in the back of Harman's little Audi.

"I wonder how they met," Crosby mumbled from the chair, surprising Garcia.

"Harman and Harding?" Ooh... yet another reason not to come out, because wasn't that precious?

"Harding and Denison," Crosby said, standing up and wobbling to grab the counter, obviously still disoriented and in need of more sleep. "They're such good partners. Do ya think there was a group or somethin', fer people like us, like them, in the service or the alphabets? I mean, you 'n' me, Tal 'n' Harding, Chadwick 'n' Carlyle—what're the fuckin *odds*?"

Garcia gave a short laugh as he made his way to Crosby's side. His boy needed help to bed. "How long've you known about Chadwick and Carlyle?"

Crosby grunted. "Mm... dunno. Right after you got here, I think. They... they look and move so different, but they're still so in sync. It's spooky."

"We've never been to Carlyle's apartment," Garcia wondered as Crosby fell in step with him. "Do they live together?"

"Dunno," Crosby said. "Cops have picnics, go to each other's weddings, have bowling night—often live in the same suburb. This job is different. I think... I think fewer of us get married. Most of us are too focused on the job to start families. I think... I think it's hard to keep a balance." He paused and slouched against the doorway, pulling Garcia against his body, and Garcia complied, indulging in the chance to lean on someone. "I clung to you, Calix. Our texts. They were a lifeline. But if I'd let go—*become* Rick Young—it would have been like becoming another person. One who didn't feel the pain. But the minute I became me again...."

Garcia swallowed, his heart suddenly beating so hard he wasn't sure he could fathom the rest of that sentence.

"I'd be lost," Garcia said, his voice echoing inside Crosby's as he said the same thing.

They both took a deep breath.

"Bed, Cowboy," Garcia murmured. "Sleep while you're here."

"Seriously," he muttered. "Sex. It was a thing, right? We *had* sex. I did not imagine that."

And Garcia was able to pull a smile out of his boots. "You did not imagine it. And tomorrow we may have it again."

"But not tonight. This blows." And with that Crosby pushed off from the wall to the bedroom, and Garcia helped him get undressed, because he was that exhausted. But as he ran his hands tenderly over Crosby's back, smoothing his T-shirt over his shoulders before wrapping his arms around his waist, just to breathe him in one more time before letting him lie down, he had to agree with Crosby.

The no-sex thing totally blew.

AT THREE in the morning, Crosby sat bolt upright in bed.

"There's someone outside," he whispered fiercely, and Garcia, who had fallen into a fitful sleep next to him after watching some TV on his computer, did the same thing.

"Wha—"

But then he heard it too. Looking in the corner of the room, he spotted one of the alarm beacons Chadwick had installed. It was blinking madly, and he hissed in a breath. With a flip of his computer screen, he called up the security program and scoped out the six quadrants of the video feed.

"Ooh... there."

Crosby looked over his shoulder and saw it.

"Oh my God," he breathed. "That cat is fucking *huge*."

Garcia scowled and noticed the cat, three feet long from tail to nose, washing his paw in front of the door. "Right?" he muttered. "But he's not the asshole dressed like a ninja who's on the side of the house!" He pointed to another camera angle, and Crosby grunted.

"Wait—is he headed toward the front? *He's headed toward the cat!*"

And with that, Crosby grabbed the knife he'd kept under the mattress and went hauling down the hallway in a sort of shamble, whispering, "Go out the side and get him while I go get the cat—wait until you hear me at the door."

And before Garcia could say, "That is the dumbest fucking thing I've ever heard," Crosby was rummaging through the cupboard for tuna while Garcia had no choice but to crouch by the window that overlooked the area over the garbage cans on the side of the house. Carefully he peered outside, toward the front, where their intruder seemed to be heading, and for a moment, he had misgivings. What if it was the cat's owner or their next-door neighbor who'd heard the cat too? What if there was a perfectly innocent explanation for the cat, the ninja guy, and the automatic weapon sticking out of the guy's pants—

Yeah, no.

Very carefully, Garcia unclipped the old-fashioned windowsill and raised the sash, knowing that he'd spent all last summer making sure the operation would be smooth and soundless for those days when he could catch a breeze.

He watched their intruder edge near the front porch, back to the house itself, working to a place he could turn and look, probably scoping out his chance for an entrance.

To Garcia, what happened next sounded like Crosby was shouting, booming across the whole neighborhood to scare children and small wildlife for a mile around, but it must not have been that loud because their intruder simply gasped and pressed back harder against the outside of the house, as though trying to make himself smaller.

"Sampson," Crosby crooned, and Garcia could hear the screen door open. He used that opportunity to shimmy down the side of the house and land silently in his bare feet on the short strip of grass and pebbles that made up the walkway between the house and the fence next door.

"Kitty," Crosby continued. "C'mon, man, we missed you. Brought your favorite. Yeah, that's it, you big squishy asshole. Come get tuna. Definitely tuna. You can eat that shit for days. C'mon in, big guy, you and me got some bonding to do."

Bonding? What, they owned that enormous fucking cat now?

Garcia shook his head and continued to advance on their intruder, who was so engrossed in what Crosby was doing that he didn't hear Garcia coming until Garcia was close enough to grab the gun hanging out the back of his pants and hold his own gun to his temple.

"Don't move," he said very softly, "and I won't have to kill you."

Garcia was expecting the elbow to the face, so he ducked it, rolling, both guns in hand. He bounced to his feet, ready to crash into the guy and take him out, but Crosby was leaning over the rail, knife to the guy's throat, a hand holding his head back.

"Pidgeon," Crosby said pleasantly. "How you doin'? Where's Kinsey tonight? I thought you two would be joined at the groin." He punctuated that last with a little jerk of the knife, and Garcia noticed a trickle of blood down Pidgeon Smalls's neck. Now that his eyes had adjusted and he wasn't fighting the guy, Garcia could recognize one of the faces on the "known associates" board in the office.

"Not sayin' nothin', faggot," Pidgeon snarled. He was a crookedly built, ugly little man with hunched shoulders and a face that looked like it had been built from scowls and mean laughter. Crosby jerked the hand with the knife again, and Pidgeon let out a whimper.

Garcia remembered the conversation with Harman about how Junior might have gotten infected, and he had a sudden sick sensation in his gut.

Crosby *would* kill this man if Garcia didn't stop him. Crosby had been forced to watch this guy and his buddies violate that poor kid who'd saved his life. Crosby wouldn't hesitate to saw the hunting knife in his hand right through Pidgeon Smalls's neck.

"You better say something," Crosby purred, "or pretty soon you won't be able to."

"All right! All right!" Pidgeon whined, and to Garcia's relief, he saw Crosby's grip on his head loosen just a tad. "Kinsey was at the docks tonight. There were four of us. Two of 'em disappeared. Kinsey was pissed." His eyes darted right. "We had a line on a car, right? McEnany gave us some trackers, and one of 'em was here. We thought, you know— find that car, find the guys who fucked our guys up."

Crosby met Garcia's eyes and frowned, and Garcia had a sudden insight.

"Department issue," he said, and Crosby nodded, both of them refraining from glancing at the department-issue vehicle Denison had left in the driveway. Garcia's heart started beating in retroactive panic for Natalia and her family. God, talk about instincts that were right on point!

"So much to unpack there," Crosby muttered. "We're gonna need to cuff this guy and call it in."

"Bullshit," Pidgeon muttered. "You're a corrupt piece of shit, Ricky, you know that? You sit in Jimmy's front room and play video games with all that meth lying around and you're gonna call *me* in?"

The laugh that shook Crosby's shoulders wasn't entirely sane, and Garcia really didn't like how close that knife was.

"Easy, *Ricky*," he said. With a few deft movements, he situated the guns, slinging the automatic over his head by the strap and aiming his personal piece, a Berretta 9mm, under Pidgeon's chin. "Go get the cuffs and call it in. If you hear a shot, come out with some cleaner and a scrub brush for the brains."

He watched the struggle, watched Crosby's shoulders rise and fall with a few controlled breaths, watched his death grip on the knife ease up enough to pull the weapon slowly out of the cave made by Garcia's gun and Pidgeon's neck and chin.

"Yeah," Crosby said gruffly, his body shuddering as he let go of his rage. "We probably shouldn't kill him. We've got some information to get."

He moved quickly then, while Garcia frog-marched Pidgeon forward, gun to his back, across the porch and into the front room. Crosby met him with cuffs, and while Garcia took care of frisking and restraining, Crosby set up one of the kitchen stools in the center of the entryway, leaving Pidgeon sitting in the middle of a cleared space. With a furious glare at Pidgeon, Crosby handed Garcia ankle cuffs.

"Wow," Garcia said, because Pidgeon was short enough that his legs dangled. Nevertheless, he cuffed Pidgeon's ankles around the stool legs, leaving him helpless to so much as run.

"We can't kill him," Crosby ground out. "We need his information. So he can't try to escape."

Garcia nodded, getting it. He looked at Pidgeon and said, "It's a good thing our boy here is dedicated to his job, 'cause he *really* hates you."

Crosby took a measured breath. "And for the record? I never did your fuckin' drugs, asshole. If I had, Creedy wouldn't have tried to poison me with it."

Pidgeon blinked. "He what?"

"You heard me. Sent Junior to my room with some water to pay back for all the beer. One of the bottles was drugged. So there's your hero, poisoning my fuckin' water. Chew on that and wonder which fuckin' supermax we're gonna send you to, 'cause, buddy, I'm too pissed for you to have a family reunion at Rikers Island."

Garcia took a breath and nodded to Crosby. "Go get your piece and make the call. Me and Pidgeon are gonna have ourselves a party."

Maybe some sweats over his boxer-clad bottom would ease that sizzle of rage Garcia felt thrumming under Crosby's skin. Or maybe Garcia could just let Crosby waste the guy. That might do it, but he'd rather not have it happen in his house.

Garcia took another breath. No, that might do for *Garcia*—Garcia understood revenge and hot-blooded fury—but not Crosby. Not his cowboy, who would talk family annihilators down and be the cool finger on the trigger when he was trying to save a child—and Garcia—with one shot. The guy who would calmly put himself between a scared kid and a slightly unhinged predator. That guy would never forgive himself for shooting this asshole in the back.

But that guy was still weak and recovering and angry and hurt, and this moron in the cuffs had quite literally raped his puppy. Crosby's protectiveness over Junior had been understandable; Garcia had known the kid for barely an hour, but he'd seen the innate decency in Junior Creedy, and apparently Crosby had too because there was no doubt Junior had saved his life. It wasn't that Crosby wasn't justified in wanting Pidgeon dead—it was that he wouldn't forgive himself if it wasn't a righteous kill. Carlyle and Chadwick had the souls of assassins. Gail and Natalia were streetfighters. Harding and Swan were soldiers. Garcia and Crosby were, at their hearts, policemen—not the Sons of the Blood bullshit, but the kind of cops that *should* have been. The kind who saw communities and protected them.

It would kill something vital inside Crosby to take this guy's life without extreme cause, and Garcia loved that about him. But it also made Crosby really fucking fragile right now, and he needed Garcia to save him.

He stood there, in his T-shirt and briefs, arms crossed, gun in one hand, and glared at Pidgeon.

"So," he said calmly. "You gonna tell us about this warehouse you work at? 'Cause I get the feeling that's really integral to how this story ends."

At that moment, Garcia heard an unlikely sound. Carefully assuring himself that Pidgeon was too secure to run, he stood on his tiptoes and peered over the back of his couch.

The giant fucking cat—a gray-and-white monstrosity with enough fur to make a whole other cat—was stretched out across the center of the couch, making biscuits against one of the throw pillows. In the kitchen, up against the baseboards, Garcia could spot the now-empty can of tuna. In spite of himself, Garcia had to smile. Well, maybe Crosby wasn't *that* fragile.

After all, he'd managed to save the cat.

Minor Thugs and Major Scumbags

CROSBY HAD calmed down by the time he was dressed, and called Harding.

"You've got him *where*?" Harding demanded, sounding grumpy and out of sorts. Well, Crosby had needed *his* sleep too.

"In the living room, cuffed to a chair. Hey, I didn't plan on going scumbag hunting in my underwear, but there you are."

Harding grunted. "How do you think he found you?"

This part hurt. "He was tracking Talia's department issue. I think we need to have the others swept, and we need to call them *now*."

Harding grunted, and a beeping sound emanated from what was clearly his phone. "Yeah, well, Chadwick and Carlyle just passed their contact deadline, so I agree." He sighed. "Look, you need to interrogate him. If I can't get Chadwick and Carlyle on the horn, we *all* need to go to that fucking warehouse by Red Hook and bail their asses out of the fire."

Crosby nodded. "Should we call for a unit?" he asked.

"I'll tag the FBI for your scumbag. They should be there in fifteen minutes this time of night, so you don't have much longer. Get all the info you can and leave something for them to throw in the slammer."

Crosby grimaced. He could feel the rage and the weakness coursing through his body in equal pulses. He wasn't physically ready to do this, but dammit… Garcia needed him. *The team* needed him.

He couldn't let them down, and he couldn't lose himself in the anger and the fear.

He could be hurt—he knew that. He got hurt on the regular. He couldn't deal with the disappointment in Garcia's eyes if he wasn't the man Calix Garcia had fallen in love with.

The strength was in there. He had to remember where to reach.

When he walked out to the living room, he was decked out in full tactical, down to his Kevlar, boots, the hunting knife now strapped to his thigh, and the weapons he'd pulled from the safe.

"Feds are on the way," he told Garcia as he strode into the living room. "Get set and get decked. There's more going down tonight than this."

Garcia nodded tersely and glanced from the knife on his thigh back•
to Crosby's eyes. An evil little smile twitched at his full mouth, and he
said, "You can make him bleed a *little*, right, Cowboy?"

From nowhere, Crosby found a grin. Oh yeah, that's where his
strength was.

"I'll try not to stain the floor."

Garcia laughed and started out. He paused at the hallway and said,
"Oh, nice cat, by the way. Is he staying?"

Crosby's grin softened a smidge. "That big ol' bruiser? Smelled the
tuna and just jumped into my arms. I think he likes me!"

Garcia's laughter echoed through the hallway, and Crosby turned
to the glaring excuse for a human being perched on the kitchen stool with
renewed purpose.

Pidgeon sneered. "This your real home, Ricky? You go slumming
with us real men and come here and live in your little fairy paradise?"

Crosby let an evil smile twist his lips.

"You think Queens is a paradise? You really been doing too much
product, Birtle."

Pidgeon flinched, and Crosby's black heart grew at least a half a size.

"You think I didn't know that was your real name? Cute, right? Birtle
to Birdie, Birdie to Pidgeon? And that was as good as you got, wasn't it?
Nobody's calling you Eagle or Falcon or Raven, are they. You're the street rat
of birds, Pidgeon. So don't worry. Nobody expects you not to fuckin' sing."

"You think I'm gonna sing to a *fag*—"

Crosby's hand flew out, flat and hard, and he cracked the guy across
the face. Pidgeon howled through a broken nose, and Crosby took a step
back, leaving his hands ready at his sides, and remembered that strength.

"You gonna call me that?" he asked, his voice low and pleasant.
"Given that I know you and Kinsey be swapping the same fuckin' STDs?"

Pidgeon's face washed so white it was almost green, leaving
every blemish, every broken blood vessel, every bad nutrition decision
standing out in stark relief. His mouth worked, but Crosby could tell it
had just hit him, maybe, where the itchy green gunk dripping out of his
cock had come from.

"That's different," he muttered weakly. "That's 'cause Kinsey's
stronger. He's the fuckin' alpha of our little tribe, right?"

"I got news for you, buddy," Crosby said cruelly. "If someone's
fuckin' you 'cause they're stronger, that's rape. That's not even sex—

that's power. If you're doin' that to someone for the same reason, that makes you a rapist. So there you go. Another crime on your jacket. More to look forward to in prison. It'll be great."

Pidgeon swallowed again, and if Crosby hadn't known—*known*—that Junior had been suffering under him and Kinsey on a daily basis, he might have felt bad for the guy. But he'd taken his pain and shared, spread it around, added salt to it, and Crosby was not impressed.

"What do you want from me, Ricky?" Pidgeon asked, mean little eyes rolling wildly, looking for an escape.

"Why're you here tonight?" Crosby asked, deciding to start there. "You were after someone on the team. You thought you had someone else, but you ended up here. Why were you making a move tonight?"

Pidgeon grunted. "'Cause two of our guys disappeared near the warehouse in Red Hook tonight, and two of the workers who were supposed to report in from the Bronx dropped off the map. We figured there was a war on. There's a big delivery on tonight. The big bitch is there to supervise and everything. We couldn't risk your people showing up when we're getting a shipment, you know?"

"Drugs?" Crosby said, although he knew.

Pidgeon gave a bitter snort through yellowed teeth. "You ever remember your life before something bad?" he asked. "Kinsey and me, we grew up together. We was friends. And then Jimmy starts working with the big bitch, starts saying we're gonna pump the Sons of the Blood up, says, 'Here, boys, have a treat—we're gonna party,' right?"

Crosby nodded. He did, in fact, remember life before something bad happened, but his bad thing had been an awakening. Pidgeon's had been a hammer to the skull.

"So was that it?" Crosby prodded. "There was a party tonight and your guys started disappearing? Creedy ordered you to go on the hunt?"

Pidgeon shook his head. "It was more than that, man. You fuckin' disappeared. Creedy said you were dead of an overdose, and Kinsey and me, we said no way, 'cause everyone knows you're clean. But he sends us up to your room to get your shit, and your room is clean, cleared out, empty." Pidgeon swallowed hard. "So, you know, you tell me Jimmy poisoned you with meth, I see maybe that could be true. And it's not like we've never been at war before. We were at war when the Puerto Ricans moved into the warehouse next door. We drove those little bastards out, and there was some fuckin' blood. But this time we were supposed to be at war with *cops*, man.

And…." Pidgeon gave a fractured laugh. "You were supposed to be our secret weapon. You were gonna go in, you were gonna feed us intel on the cops, you were gonna keep the cops off our back. But all we could see, really, was you went in and did your job—and not even in a bad way. You actually fuckin did what…." His laugh this time sounded like a sob. "I was supposed to be a cop. So I could help people. But you go in to help Curtis, and he's so trashed he ends up dead. And Creedy's so pissed he fuckin' *poisons* you. And we're at war with the feds, and our guys start disappearing, and…."

Pidgeon was shaking by now, sobbing, whimpering, and Crosby's reluctant pity stretched and made itself known. "And I don't even know who's the good guys anymore," Pidgeon moaned. "'Cause it damned sure ain't us."

Crosby kept his weapon at the ready as he backed to the refrigerator.

"Whatcha doin', Ricky?" Pidgeon asked, sounding afraid. Could he be faking? Maybe. But Pidgeon and Kinsey weren't imaginative men. They weren't crafty. They weren't smart. Faking was for a smarter breed of criminal.

"Been a while," Crosby asked. "Since you fixed, right? Been a while?" He could tell; the signs were there. The shaking hands, the uncontrollable emotions. Garcia had frisked him before he'd been cuffed to the stool, and there'd been several dime bags in his pockets. In anyone else, Crosby would have figured there was intent to sell, but he'd seen the guys use, and he was pretty sure that was a night's good run.

"Yeah," Pidgeon whispered. "Am I a junkie? Is this what bein' a junkie's like?"

"Yup," Crosby said, moving up from the refrigerator. He cracked the soda and held it up to Pidgeon, standing off to the side, keeping his gun aimed. Pidgeon opened his mouth and drank greedily, moaning slightly with the sugar and caffeine suffusing his bloodstream.

"You're good to me, Ricky," Pidgeon mumbled when he was done. Crosby set the soda can on the table, having collected DNA in case Pidgeon was wanted on any other crimes.

"Pidgeon," Crosby said, keeping his voice low. "Tell me about the delivery tonight. It's a big one. You said the big bitch is gonna be there. This bitch got a name?"

"Beechum," Pidgeon said promptly. "It looks like something ritzy, but even she says Beechum."

"Gotcha. You say she's the big bitch. Does she got a boss?"

Pidgeon frowned, and Crosby could swear he smelled burning rubber. "She does," he said. "Guy who owns the warehouse. I heard her talking to Jimmy tonight. She was like, 'He told me there was a shipment tonight, and I don't give a shit what your assclowns are doing about that other thing, have them here tonight to do their fucking jobs!'"

Crosby let out a small laugh. "Sounds like a ballbuster," he said, and he could see that Marcy's track record of not making friends had followed her.

"She's someone… I dunno. Big. McEnany sucks up to her all the time. Asking her for money, making sure Creedy can take samples of the blow. If she had a knob, he'd wax it, you know?"

Crosby nodded. "What about McEnany. How's he doing?"

Pidgeon shook his head. "Dunno. Someone broke his face three days ago. He's been shitting kittens ever since." Pidgeon lowered his head conspiratorially. "I'll be honest," he whispered. "He and Creedy been pulling each other apart. He was pissed 'cause Creedy said you OD'd, Creedy was pissed 'cause he said McEnany got you Narcan. All that 'this is my brother' bullshit, that's been flushed down the fuckin' tubes. Now it's both of them trying to push each other in front of the truck that's Big Bitch Beechum."

There was a solid knock at the door. "FBI. Is this the home of—"

"Don't say his fuckin' name," Crosby snapped through the door. "Were you or were you not told it's silent running tonight?"

There was a silence. "Apologies" came a more subdued voice. "FBI arriving for a joint mission with the SCTF?"

"I got it," Garcia said from the hallway. "You opened him up like clam with a screwdriver, Cowboy. Good job."

Pidgeon gave a weak, wet little snort. "And now you're jus' gonna throw me away," he said.

Crosby turned toward him, not sure there was redemption in his future—not sure there could be. "You're gonna get clean in prison," he said. "You're gonna get clean, and prison's gonna fuckin' suck. But you know what you said about remembering how stuff was after something bad?"

Pidgeon nodded glumly.

"Remember this moment. You smell, Pidgeon. You ain't changed your clothes in a week. Your teeth are fuckin' falling out. And you're running around doing bad shit and you don't even know why. You ask yourself if prison's worse than this, yeah? And if it's not? Maybe you can change shit when you get out."

Two guys with FBI windbreakers walked in, handcuffs and manacles in their hands. Garcia handed them the keys and pointed them to everything on the end table that they'd cleared out of Pidgeon's pockets.

"Make sure you get all the fuckin' dime bags," Garcia groused. "I don't want that shit in my house." Which was fine. Crosby didn't want it either.

"Understood," said the Special Agent in Charge, a slender, no-bullshit woman named Downey who took in Garcia's house at a glance. "Was this a home invasion?"

"Attempted," Garcia said. "I'll forward you the video of him casing the house and looking to get in."

"What alerted you to the prowler?"

Garcia laughed and looked over the couch back again. Crosby risked a glance and saw that their friend the enormous cat was still there.

"My roommate heard our guy there disturb the cat," Garcia said, still chuckling. "Woke me up and the alarm beacon was flashing."

The agent looked over the couch and gave a ghost of a smile. "Your cat?"

"Is now," Crosby said mildly. He gave himself a mental pat down to make sure he had all the gear he needed. "We gotta go," he said. "Did our chief give you the lowdown?"

"We understand there's shit going on tonight," Downey said shortly. "Your SAC told us to give you a unit so we could sweep the one here." She pitched the keys to Garcia, who pitched them to Crosby in one smooth move. Downey laughed. "So we know who drives?"

Crosby could see the smartass retort in Garcia's eyes, so he answered quickly. "I, uh… go fast."

"He makes the other cars pregnant by riding up their tailpipe." Garcia snickered, and that at least was safe to laugh it.

"Ready?" he said to Garcia.

"On it."

He glanced at Downey and said, "Could you… I dunno, make sure the cat's still inside when you're done with Pidgeon? He's got water and tuna and shit, but I don't want him out on the streets alone. He's got no collar, and he's a little skinny under all that fur."

Downey's dark eyebrows hit the line of her dark blond hair. "Sure, Agent. We'll take care of your cat."

Garcia cackled. "Oh my God. Wait till I tell the chief you said that. You're getting a whole new coffee mug!"

Crosby grunted and gave Pidgeon one more nod, indicating their business was done, before following Garcia out into the night.

THEY BOTH grunted after they'd climbed into the department issue and Crosby steered it away from the curb.

"Same make, same model, same windows, same chassis," Garcia muttered.

"It's like our mechanic got his degree at wizardry school or something," Crosby agreed. "This thing steers like ass."

Garcia's next words were tentative. "So, uhm, you sure it's the steering?"

Crosby grimaced, because he could hear where Garcia was going with that and didn't want to admit he might be right. But if they were going out on an op tonight, he owed it to *everybody* to be honest about his physical condition.

"I am stupid tired after not doing much at all," he admitted. "I mean, put me in if I'm needed, but I may serve you all best by hanging back with the long gun and keeping you safe that way."

Garcia let out a breath. "I cannot tell you how happy I am to hear that you're only stupid tired and not full-out stupid. Keep us briefed on how you're doing."

Crosby let out a raspberry. "I *am* stupid. I hung out with them. I listened to them talk. They talked about video games, they talked about getting polluted and trashing places, and they bitched about their foreman. They may have mentioned 'the big bitch' two or three times, but I swear to God, I always thought they were talking about a piece of equipment!"

Garcia's rather manic chuckle warmed him. "I mean, that's fair, right? Guys I worked with in ATF used to call our grenade and missile launchers 'the big bitches.' It took us a long time to assemble that file on Beauchamp—I mean Beechum. We were spending all our time on Cavendish."

"Yeah, well, if we can link him to this warehouse and to Marcy Beauchamp or Beechum or whatever, it'll be worth it," Crosby agreed grimly.

"But first we gotta see what's what." Garcia pulled out his phone and hit Harding's preset, making sure the whole thing was on speaker.

"Harding," came the growl over the phone. "I'm on my way to Red Hook and the warehouse with Natalia—"

"And me!" Harman snapped from what sounded like the back of Harding's personal vehicle.

"You're not supposed to be here!" Harding retorted, before getting back on the line and trying to sound professional. "What can you tell us?"

"Carlyle and Chadwick picked the wrong goddamned night to make a stand, sir," Crosby said. "They're getting a big fucking shipment tonight, and Beechum's going to be there. Pidgeon told us that she does look to somebody. We figure Cavendish, but—"

"I finally found the shell company that owns the warehouse," Natalia said. "And we have the link."

"Way to go, Tal!" Garcia crowed. "Because if we all survive tonight, we can walk right up into Police Plaza and arrest that sonovabitch."

"That's who you want to arrest?" Crosby asked, curious. "Because I'm more excited about McEnany and Creedy."

"We all have our goals," Garcia declared magnanimously. His face hardened. "Those boys, I wouldn't mind killing."

"Anyway," Harding ground out, obviously too focused to want to ride herd on them like he usually did. "Carlyle and Chadwick have *not* reported in yet, but I got hold of Swan and Pearson. They'll meet us on-site with Davies. There's an empty vehicle depot about a block away from the warehouse, so we can meet there and stick to the shadows."

Garcia cleared his throat, and Crosby took a shaky breath, realizing his back, neck, and arms were shaking just from steering the shittily maintained department-issued vehicle around.

"Sir," Crosby said, hating to admit this but afraid of what would happen if he didn't.

"You sound like shit," Harding said. "Are you good to go?"

"Sixty percent," Crosby assessed coldly, his stomach knotted. "Unless things get bad, you may want to keep me in overwatch." If his team was in trouble, he was damned if he sat on the high ground and watched them get hurt—or worse.

"Good call," Harding said, his voice gentle.

"My team needs someone they can count on," he said miserably, and then Garcia spoke up.

"He says that, but you shoulda heard him interrogate Pidgeon Smalls. It was a thing of beauty. He pegged Marcy Beechum and even calmed the guy down." Garcia gave a grim chuckle. "And as soon as this is over, I'll tell you how he saved the cat."

"Oh…. Calix, no," Crosby muttered, embarrassed all over again.

"In the morning, over breakfast," Harding promised. "Chadwick and Carlyle are buying."

Crosby and Garcia recognized that for what it was: a prayer that their friends were safe.

"Amen," they both said together. "Meet you at the auto depot," Crosby finished.

"I'll text coordinates," Natalia said, and they were out.

Assassins Freed

HARDING AND Denison apparently had the gate codes for the federal parking lot because the gates were open and they were waiting, along with Gail, Iliana, and Swan, in the shadows between what looked like an office building and an auto bay. Harman was there too, dressed in tactical gear like the rest of them, except his had FBI emblazoned across the back instead of SCTF. It occurred to Garcia to wonder if maybe the two of them hadn't met and partnered on the job, because for all his slender grace, Harman Blodgett looked *very* comfortable in Kevlar with a helmet, strapped with a semiauto and ordinance.

"The warehouse is two lots over," Harding said, pulling them all more deeply into the shadows. He pointed to the silhouettes of what looked like another warehouse building adjacent to the lot they were on. "I've got gate codes to that lot too, and a promise that the alarms are going to be off. I need overwatch parked on top of that building. Crosby, take the night vision and tell me if you see any place that could be useful. Garcia, Harm, you take south, between the cargo bay doors and the waterfront. Swan, Pearson, you take east, between the bay doors and the parking lot. Tal, you and Davies secure the parking lot, and you need to hide your stripes. We don't want anybody escaping, but if shit goes south, you're our calvary."

"Where you going to be, Clint?" Denison asked, stripping off her windbreaker and turning it to use the Velcro flaps to hide the reflective ID tag.

Harding held out the tablet he'd been studying and showed them the plans he'd been given for the lot and the warehouse itself.

"See this?" he murmured. "This is a back stairway. It leads right up to a loft over the main warehouse. It's where setups like this usually keep their office. If Carlyle and Chadwick have been captured but not disposed of, I'm going to bet they're up here. If we've got Crosby doing overwatch from across the way, he can keep hostiles off my back and hopefully take out anybody who threatens the rest of us. If Crosby's source was right and there's a shipment tonight, there's going to be a lot of shady warehouse workers off book—that usually spells muscle that doesn't mind violence. We'd prefer incapacitated to dead, but them dead to you dead, you hear me?"

Gail said it again, and this time it seemed to resonate. "How many of them can we take out?"

Harding didn't contradict her this time. "Our approach needs to be quiet until we've verified Carlyle and Chadwick, do you understand? Until then keep your blades out but your guns handy, you all read me?"

"Roger, Chief," or something similar came from the quiet assembly.

"First things first," Harding said grimly. He opened a box and pulled out comm links, then passed the unit to Crosby. "Mother hen, make sure us chickies are safe, would you?"

Garcia watched Crosby hook the comm link onto his belt and put in his own earwig. He looked grim and determined and up for the task, no matter what he said about physical fitness. That rage, that fragile, butt-hurt anger, seemed to have passed, leaving the calm, thoughtful partner Garcia treasured.

"We need to make sure Crosby can make it to overwatch," Harding was saying. "Garcia, Harm, help him out, and the rest of us will get into position. We rely on Crosby to execute, but Crosby, you wait on *my* signal to find Chadwick and Carlyle. We don't want this to be a hostage situation—they need to be found and out of there before this goes down."

Nobody said the words "What if?" Nobody had to. If Chadwick and Carlyle were found dead, the team would burn this place to the ground.

"We ready to go?" he asked, meeting their eyes in turn.

There was an assortment of grim nods and grunts, and then Pearson, with a bloodthirsty smile. "You know what I say, Chief," she dared.

Harding nodded. "How many of them can we take out," he growled, low in his throat.

The whole team, Harman included, echoed him, and they were off.

GETTING TO the top of the warehouse meant jumping to grab the outside ladder, which hung seven feet off the ground. Crosby went first because he could actually reach it with his hands over his head, and then he hung upside down, hauling first Garcia and then Harman up.

For a minute, Garcia was going to give him shit about "Sixty percent my *ass*," but when it came time to do the upside-down crunchy that would have gotten his hands into position to pull up, for a terrible moment, Garcia didn't think he was going to make it.

It was a maneuver Garcia had seen him do a thousand times in the work-out room—something big and macho that seemed particularly grandiose and stupidly unneeded, and he'd do two sets of ten and call it a day. But tonight he hung suspended, body cocked at pike position while he reached with his hands for the bars between his feet. Garcia was about to hand Harman his gear—he was holding the sniper rifle—when Crosby ripped out a groan and made the final two feet, grabbing the bar and letting his feet dangle while he pulled himself up by main arm strength until he could put his feet in the rungs.

When he was safe, he paused for a moment and panted, almost retching before he grunted and gestured with his chin for Garcia and Harman to keep going.

They did, but when they got to the roof, there was a six-foot gap between the last rung of the ladder and the handles at the top.

Harman reached up and grabbed the handles, hauling himself up to check out the roof. He whispered, "All clear," before completing the chin-up, the comm box and tablet strapped to his back. Garcia went next, and when he got to the top, he and Harm crouched to give Crosby the assist when he had to pull himself up.

Crosby took the aid, but when he was on the roof, he held up a finger and doubled over, throwing up water before glaring at Harm.

"I've seen junkies," he panted, "get up with one shot of Narcan and toddle off to their next fucking fix. The fuck is this?"

Harm sighed and cracked a water from his bag, handing it over. "Well, you piss on the slush by the side of the road, nobody notices," he said testily. "You, my friend, were like the fresh, virginal, newfound snow in the middle of the woods. And first a dinosaur stomped on it, and then someone pissed meth and fentanyl all over it. Your body can fucking tell."

"*Nnnggh!*"

Garcia let him express his frustration for a minute before they all stood and hunched over, heading for the spot on the roof with the ultimate view.

"Here, let me," Crosby murmured, reaching for the tools to bolt the frame of the long gun to the roof. It took him less than thirty seconds, and then he set his Maglite on the ground and took the gun out of the case. Carefully, scowling in concentration, he cleaned and assembled the gun, going at warp speed. Garcia and Harman looked on, and Garcia knew his own eyebrows were raised because he didn't think he'd ever seen Crosby so efficient.

"I had to," Crosby murmured when he was done. "It's the gun from the FBI unit—I don't know it. You gotta get acquainted or they tend to buck and bite, you know?"

"Are you trying to make me jealous of a gun?" Garcia asked.

"Is it working?" Crosby's grin and wink in the beam from the Maglite reassured him somehow.

"Yes. Now roll over so we can set a tarp under and over you. We've got dark gray—"

"Bottom," Crosby muttered, rocking back on his heels and letting Garcia work.

"And light gray for the top," Harm murmured. "Fair. You'll blend right into the roof. Here's some water, some trail mix, and your tablet and charger." He set everything out so Crosby didn't have to stand up completely and organize before he and Garcia army-crawled back to the ladder. "Clint says he wouldn't trust anyone else to back him up this way. I trust you too."

Crosby grunted and grabbed his night-vision goggles, the better to scope out the proceedings. "I probably won't need you all to show your IDs—none of the workers are wearing black, so we can be invisible." He tapped a button on the tablet. "Comms set," he said. "Earbuds on. Thing One and Thing Two are getting into position."

The others counted off, using the Thing designation, and Harm turned to go.

Garcia paused, just long enough to squeeze Crosby's shoulder. Crosby turned his head and winked. "Got your back," he mouthed.

"You'd better," Garcia told him softly, before following Harman Blodgett into the night.

"HE'S OKAY, right?" Garcia asked Harm after they'd worked their way to their position near the front of the warehouse—in the shadows of course. There was enough clatter and clamor coming from the guys unloading pallets inside the door to drown out death-metal karaoke, but Garcia still whispered in Harm's ear.

"You gotta remember," Harm muttered, making himself damned invisible back against the warehouse behind a stack of pallets. "Most people couldn't do that, *period*. He's tired. A few days, lots of electrolytes, he'll be fine."

Garcia grunted, and they both concentrated on what was going on with the others.

"Ricky," Iliana murmured, pissing Garcia right off because that wasn't his name. "Denison's got a license plate with a government tag she's sending you. I got pictures. Can you ID that?"

"Roger that, Thing Six. Give me a minute and…. Thing Four's internet upgrades for the win."

"Thank you, Olaf," Pearson murmured softly.

"Good job, Elsa. That is a government-issue vehicle leased out to… any guesses?"

"Marcy Beauchamp," Natalia said. "Very cool. Sending you photos. Start assembling a file so Clint can wake up a judge when all this is through."

"Can do," Crosby murmured. "Adding pictures of the warehouse, including those giant pallets containing plastic-wrapped bricks of white powder you can see being stacked in the doorway."

"Everybody hush," Harding ordered, and the sudden silence on the line was louder than the noise coming in from the warehouse.

There was quiet for a moment, and Garcia was pretty sure Harman was trying to grow eyes in the back of his head—detachable ones he could roll around to trace Harding's movements. They *could* hear him moving, his breath coming in harsh pants, and what sounded like a window opening.

"Shit," Harding hissed. "Shit shit shit shit shit, there's an alarm. I think it's time delayed. I see them, they're breathing, but we've got about thirty seconds—"

"Garcia, Blodgett," Crosby called, "Pearson, Swan, go in, make a fuss, start arresting people, give him cover in three, two, one—"

It was an audible—and later Garcia would be in awe, because it was a good one, and it worked—and Crosby made it from sniper distance away.

Crosby hit one, and Garcia and Harman rushed in from the waterfront while Pearson and Swan rushed in from the other side of the great bay door. Everybody had their guns out and their targets sighted as Garcia and Pearson called, "SCTF! Everybody on the floor, hands up, laced behind your head!"

There was sudden shock, and the bulk of the people in the warehouse did just what they were told.

In the back of the warehouse, near the inside stairs leading up to the office, a severe-looking woman dressed in a flannel shirt, hoodie, and jeans, stood up, pulling out her own pistol in one hand and badge in the other.

"Marcy Beauchamp," she said, and Pidgeon was right—she *did* pronounce it "Beech-um." "Harbor Patrol. What are you doing here?"

"Marcy Beauchamp," Denison said, scampering in from the parking lot with Davies on what felt like greased wheels. "You are under arrest, by order of the SCTF—"

Beauchamp's expression grew ugly as she registered Denison's presence and her own badge, and she raised her pistol, ready to fire.

The alarm went off, and a shot came out of nowhere, taking Beauchamp down, dead center mass, and chaos erupted in the warehouse.

CROSBY HAD been using night vision through the tablet. Given Beauchamp's lack of signature, he knew she had Kevlar, and given the way she was holding that pistol, he was pretty sure she was aiming at Denison's face and not her vest.

One shot and she was flat on her back, hopefully still alive, but down for the moment as the warehouse workers all decided to make a run for it.

"That wasn't thirty seconds," he said, exclusively for Harding's ear.

"So it was sixty. Sue me," Harding muttered.

"How are they?"

"Fucking drugged," Harding muttered. "Carlyle's barely breathing."

Crosby pinged Harman's earbud. "Harding needs you topside," he said, scanning the entrance to the warehouse. Marcy Beauchamp had the bad luck of standing front and center, and the stairs she'd been sitting on weren't too far recessed, so he'd been able to make that shot. Pearson and Swan were back-to-back, Pearson aiming inside the warehouse at the restless workers and Swan aiming toward the loading dock and the workers by the truck. Harman and Garcia were in the same position—moving Harman up to help with Carlyle and Chadwick would leave Garcia naked, and Harman would be walking up the wooden stairs to the second-level office alone as well. Crosby double-checked the environs again, sweeping both visually and with the infrared scope. When he was satisfied, he said, "I've got your back."

"Roger that." From his vantage point, Crosby watched Harman squeeze Garcia's shoulder. "Moving," he called. "Crosby's got cover."

Garcia repositioned himself. "Move," he called back to the warehouse door, gun facing outside while Swan pivoted, joining Pearson, Davies, and Denison to take care of the guys they could trap *in* the warehouse.

Harding made it up the stairway, and Crosby called to Harding. "Blodgett's coming in." Then he saw something that made his blood run cold.

He hit All Comms and called, "Four assholes coming in from the waterfront, automatic guns out. Find cover!"

"Sure they're hostile?" Garcia asked, although he was throwing himself back against the wall of the downstairs office, making sure he could still see out the warehouse door. While Crosby watched, a dock worker with a pistol tried to get a bead on the four other agents, and Crosby took him out so Garcia could keep lookout.

When the guy had dropped, probably dead without Kevlar, Crosby used the night vision to assess the landing party.

"No tactical gear," he said. "Just guns. I've got 'em, but I need a light on 'em for one hundred percent clearance."

Garcia edged around the warehouse door and shone his Maglite toward the dock. The first figure creeping off the skiff caught the beam in his eyes, and even Crosby could hear him swearing. Garcia shouted, "SCTF, drop your weapons!" and suddenly all four guys were pointing their weapons at Garcia. Garcia dodged back behind the door and Crosby picked them off, four sharp reports, one after the other, and four bodies dropped to the ground before they could get off a shot.

"Nice work," Garcia muttered and turned his attention back to the firefight/knife melee going on inside the warehouse. With an aim and a shot, he took out a guy lunging at Pearson, and she turned in time to watch him drop, giving a salute with her knife before squatting to secure the two men kneeling at her feet.

The fighting, though bloody, was also quick and contained. Crosby had to trust his people to take care of themselves. While he could see—and get a shot in—part of the bay, when there was that much movement and violence, his people were better off fighting close quarters.

"Garcia, report," he said crisply into the comms while scanning the surrounding area for more men.

"Getting secure," Garcia's voice was breathless, and Crosby could see him running to the others to assist in takedowns and securing hands, feet, and weapons. "Hey, there's a lot of fuckin' people here. Has anybody thought of calling for reinforcements?"

Crosby let out a harsh breath. "Gimme a sec. Details." Then he tagged Harding. "Chief, should we, I dunno, tag the DEA and the FBI to maybe jail all the scumbags and house the drugs?"

"There's a thought," Harding said, making it sound like he hadn't had perfectly legitimate reasons for not going through other resources. But they had a warehouse full of illegal drugs and hired muscle, as well as one of the ringleaders in custody, and all of it together made this more than an independent-department investigation. Along with the recordings they'd made from Crosby's bugs, as well as Crosby's own testimony and reports, the warehouse, Carlyle and Chadwick's imprisonment, Pidgeon Smalls in custody, and Marcy Beauchamp's very presence all worked to support their case that the Sons of the Blood not only existed but had been funded from within upper levels of the police department.

If nothing else, it was a drug bust of massive proportions, and SCTF was not equipped to handle it.

"Any, uh, ideas on that matter, Chief?" Crosby prodded.

"Wait a sec," Harding ordered, but not to Crosby. "We need to see if it's clear outside."

Crosby did his job, both peering at the night-vision screen and through his scope. Since Denison and Davies had needed to come in from the parking lot there'd been some losses of warehouse workers and henchman that way, but Crosby was pretty sure they'd had a chance to get license plates before shit had gone down. In the emerging gray of predawn, the river entrance looked clear—not a boat to be seen—and from Crosby's vantage point, anyway, all their bad guys were either cuffed and restrained or, well, dead.

Except…. "Shit!" he snapped, making sure he was talking to everybody. "Beauchamp! The fuck did she go?"

The entire team almost burst the comms with the exclamation of "Mother*fucker*!" until Denison said, "I bugged her vehicle. She's not going far."

"Fair," Crosby muttered, mad that she'd managed to slip away. "Harding and Blodgett exiting with packages in tow. Someone give them backup."

Garcia returned to his corner with his back to the office wall, and Swan disappeared, only the muzzle of his pistol visible against the warehouse opening as he aimed toward the stairs in case someone came in like Harding had, through the roof.

The upstairs door opened and Harding appeared, a barely conscious—and very bloody—Gideon Chadwick hanging on his shoulder. Blodgett was behind him with Joey Carlyle.

Crosby let out a breath and some tension from his shoulders before saying, "Chief?"

"Tag the DEA and FBI," Harding said into comms. "And get us a fucking bus. They need treatment."

Through Harding's comms he heard Chadwick, sounding weak but furious. "I need a fucking *gun*. Why don't *I* get to kill somebody?"

"You got caught," Harding retorted. "Play stupid games, win stupid prizes. Now move."

Through Harman's comms, Carlyle gave a raspy chortle. "He told *you*, Gid—I *said* stay in the fuckin' car!"

"And let you get all the flowers in the hospital? Not on your life."

"Jesus," Denison said clearly. "Harding, shut them up before we gag them and dunk them in the river."

Harding's disgusted and pained answer made them all a little more indulgent of their banter. "Looks and smells like that already happened after they were beaten, Tal. They're wet and freezing."

"We *were*," Chadwick said loopily, "but then whatever they shot us up with warmed us right up."

Harman's grunt of absolute fury rumbled in everybody's ear. "Screw Chadwick—why didn't *I* get to fire a single shot? Goddammit!"

"Yeah, Harm, everyone's getting hurt to piss you off," Harding told him. From Crosby's vantage point, he could see Harding and Blodgett hauling Chadwick and Carlyle down the final flight of stairs, and he glanced at his tablet, seeing confirmation of his emergency call for federal officers on-site immediately.

"Chief, ETA five minutes on those reinforcements you requested."

"Awesome," Harding murmured, setting an exhausted Chadwick down on the foot of the stairs. Blodgett set Carlyle next to him, and they both huddled together, Chadwick's arm around Carlyle's shoulders, under emergency foil blankets. "What's our ETA on the buses?"

"Two minutes," Crosby murmured. "You want I should stay in place until they're cleared?"

"Roger that, Overwatch," Harding replied. Then, loud enough to carry to the team in the warehouse. "Can somebody *please* get their hands on Marcy fucking Beauchamp?"

"Pearson and I will," Swan volunteered, and Gail nodded fiercely, grumbling something sotto voce about slippery bitches.

The emerging light helped Crosby track them as they ran toward the parking lot, taking directions from Denison for where the state-issue vehicle had been. In the meantime, Crosby entered the plates into the database for the tracking information, but Gail's disgusted, "Don't get too comfy, guys, she's still here," made that unnecessary.

Crosby took a moment to study the map of the compound, trying to figure out where she would be—

And was distracted by the clank of someone on the ladder.

He knew the location of every member of his team, and none of them were back there.

"Don't panic, guys," he said, carefully disassembling his gun and tucking every piece but the firing pin into the case. "She's coming up the ladder behind me."

He heard another rattle, this one higher than the last, and continued with every piece, making sure the ammo was tucked in his pockets and the gun was clean and ready to reassemble. Then he threw the night-vision camera and the tablet into the padded interior, knowing it would be safe for what came next. Quickly, he scrambled to his feet, his body stiff from the long time on the hard surface, and did a few stretches before double-checking the locks on the case and pitching it off the roof. He didn't watch its arc against the pink sky or wait for it to hit—the gun case was stainless steel, practically indestructible, and the gun was a danger to nobody as long as he had the firing pin on his person. The record of their night, of what they'd done and why—as long as two quickly fired-off requests for warrants sent off to judges Harding had specified in his contacts had been signed—were all safe in the tablet, and it was time for Crosby to deal with his own op.

By the time Marcy Beauchamp made a leap of faith and hauled herself onto the flat of the warehouse roof, Crosby had taken the only cover available, one of three HVAC units clustered near the river end of the warehouse. Crosby had a momentary fantasy of running off the building into the river, but although the perspective said otherwise, reality was that the concrete apron extended twenty feet over the harbor, and he'd hit the ground with a painful splat.

Nothing to do but keep his tactical gear on, get out his 9mm, and make a stand.

Over his comms, he heard Garcia speaking out over the babble that had erupted when he'd told them he'd found Beauchamp.

"Don't worry, Cowboy. Help is on its way."

GARCIA STARED at the ladder up the side of the warehouse in disgust. She'd sabotaged it with the simple expedient of lard—the first three feet or so—and his first attempt to jump up and grab a rung had landed him painfully on his ass.

"I will rip her spleen out through her nose," he growled, and in his ear he heard Crosby chuckle.

"I'd pay to see that. You gonna have a show?"

"You just keep breathing, son," he promised direly. "Give me a second here—" His voice cracked on the "here," and he found himself ignominiously hefted up between Harding and Swan, both of them unfairly tall and unfairly broad as they put his feet on their shoulders and walked, in unison, toward the ladder.

"Feel the rungs around your head," Harding told him. "Are they still slippery?"

He took off his gloves, fouled from their contact the first time, and reached above his head. The usual rough, untreated metal met his grip, and he said, "Hoist me a few inches higher so I can grab that far, Chief."

"Roger... that...."

Garcia knew he weighed, at the outside, 160–180 with full tactical kit and weapons. It could not have been easy for either of them to grab his ankles and lift him, and he did his best to assist by locking his core, his thighs, and his knee muscles. His entire body was shaking as he latched on to the clean ladder rung and chinned himself up. Without even trying with his feet, he reached up to the next rung, and then the next, doing a painful walk-up with his hands that would have looked great if he was showing off in the gym, but right now, after watching Crosby pitch the sniper gun off the roof so Beauchamp couldn't use it, the whole situation was both deadly and terrifying.

And the next rung. And the next. And the next. Figuring he'd gone up far enough to avoid the slippery ladder rungs, he began using his feet, grateful beyond words when they stayed stable. The harsh crack of an automatic weapon coming from the roof made his muscles clench, and he moved faster now that his feet were underneath him.

Until he heard a breathless little squeak below him.

"Fuck!" He looked down and saw Gail, blood dripping down her right arm, hanging on determinedly with her left. She must have come up after him, he thought numbly, still running on adrenaline, and what looked like a knife wound in her shoulder hadn't meant a damned thing until she got halfway up.

"Dammit, Elsa," Garcia muttered, torn between Crosby on the roof and Gail right here. There were two sharp reports, from a Beretta, not an Uzi, and Beauchamp's round swearing from above, while Crosby remained silent.

Garcia's cowboy was holding his own, and Crosby would never forgive Garcia if he let their little sister down.

Muttering to himself, Garcia put his feet on the outside of the ladder. "Hang on, Elsa," he told her, before allowing himself to slide, feet straddling, hands lowering him down. He got even with Gail and grabbed her weak hand, putting it on the next rung, where she slid it through the rungs to her elbow and locked herself in.

"You good?" he asked as she clung to the ladder, scowling in disgust.

"I'm fine. Go help him!"

Garcia grinned and saw that Swan and Davies were directing a newly arrived firefighting team to inflate a bag against the side of the warehouse. Good idea, but it wasn't time for him to use it just yet.

With a burst of resolve, he hauled himself up above Gail again, and when his feet hit the rungs, he scampered as fast as he possibly could.

As he cleared the top, pulling himself onto the edge of the roof, he heard Crosby's grunt of surprise and pain, both through his comms and in real time.

"Cowboy!" he called out, and Crosby shouted, "Hit but mobile!"

"Who else is here!" Beauchamp called out, the first time Garcia remembered her talking after Crosby had put her flat on her ass.

"None of your business," Crosby called back, giving Garcia the distraction he needed to scope out what was going on. Beauchamp had her back to the roof access, probably because she figured nobody would make it up past her child's trick of the lard on the rungs. "I'm the only one you really want, right, Marcy?"

"I don't even know who you are!" she shouted.

"Well for starters, I'm the guy who knocked you on your ass," Crosby said with a bit of mean humor, and Garcia was there for it. Scrambling, he scuttled sideways in the opposite direction Beauchamp was facing, hoping to make it to the other side of a ventilation fan, which was the only other cover besides the HVAC units.

"Yeah, I owe you for that, motherfucker," she snarled. Aiming her weapon, she fired toward the sound of Crosby's voice, and Garcia's heart jumped into his mouth until he heard the return fire. With a scramble, he slid behind the fan unit, pulling out his weapon and situating the shot.

"I've got her," he said into the comms.

"We need her info," Harding and Crosby said at once.

Out loud, Crosby said, "You can't kill me, Marcy. You take me out and my associate behind you takes off your head."

"You're bluffing," she said, and in response, Garcia stood, pistol in hand, and shot her in the back.

She fell forward, her weapon clattering from her hand while she fought for breath.

Crosby stood, gun still out, a bloody red patch on his shoulder testifying to a duck he hadn't made fast enough. After he skirted the HVAC units, he and Garcia converged on her, until they were standing, one on either side, holding their guns to her head.

"Can't breathe," she gasped, twisting as she slid down the smooth surface of the units. Garcia half expected Crosby to help her down, because he was just that gallant, but his boy was breathing hard, his face pale and sweaty, and Garcia figured he'd had enough. Instead he took her weapon, put the safety on, and slung it over his shoulder while Garcia frisked her and cuffed her and she gasped for breath.

"Did the vest hold?" Crosby asked.

Garcia ran his hand impersonally along her back and then down her front, making sure it didn't come back bloody.

"Looks like it. Can't vouch for her lungs, though."

"Lots of shit can happen through a vest," Crosby agreed. "Especially when you get hit twice in the same day. How you feelin', Marcy? You feeling like being a Son of the Blood is a prime deal right now?"

She grunted, "I'm true to my people," and Garcia wanted to sigh. It was just so fucking pointless.

"No you're not," Crosby contradicted, squatting to look her in the eye. "You think paying your people in drugs is being true to 'em? 'Cause I've seen the junkies on your payroll. They coulda had lives, Marcy. You took them. How's that feel? You think you're being true to the police force? 'Cause how many cops have you killed with drugs or in this stupid war with cops who do their job? You being true to white people? I gotta tell you, most of us think you're giving us a bad name. We *hate* you. So far, you're a murdering, drug-pushing attention whore, so don't ask me to respect your integrity, okay?"

She fought for breath, but Garcia could tell it was getting a little easier. "What do you want?" she asked.

"Who do you report to?" Crosby asked. "We've got a warrant looking into your communications, your financials, your living space, vehicle space, and colorectal health, but give us the name anyway and we won't make messing with you our mission for life."

"She shot you?" Garcia asked, not sure he was okay with that deal.

"Twice," Crosby said on a deep breath. "Kevlar. Wonderful stuff. Naming our first kid Kevlar."

It was on the tip of Garcia's tongue to say they were naming their first kid Gabriel because they'd need all the strength they could get when Harding's voice came over comms.

"If you two have a kid, we're naming it Joliet Jake Blues. Now hurry the debrief because we've got to land a helicopter on that roof and it's not that sound, so you two have to jump off first."

"I'm sorry," Crosby said, sounding numb. "Did you say jump off?"

"Fucking genius here greased the bottom rungs," Garcia muttered, flicking *at* Marcy Beauchamp's forehead.

"Don't... touch... me... you—"

The racial slur she uttered was no surprise, but the fear and venom were a bit of a shock.

"Look, lady," Crosby muttered. "We'll get out of your hair, but we want names, numbers, and where to look in the financials. You would not believe how many people in prison do not believe your white supremist bullshit. Not even the white supremacists. You're going to want all the help you can get."

At the mention of prison, Marcy's expression went from pained to stricken, and Garcia knew they had her.

"Drug trafficking, Marcy," Garcia all but sang. "Drug trafficking, corruption, attempted murder, obstruction of justice—"

"And a partridge in a pear tree," Crosby hissed. "And remember you'll be tried here in New York with us liberals. Nobody's going to give you a fucking break for being a Son of the Blood."

Garcia squinted. "How does that work, anyway? I mean, those people don't like women. We've been listening to their tapes. As far as they're concerned, you are—and I'm quoting here—'a hole, a gash, or a whore.' I mean, the *best* you got is 'the big bitch.' What's the appeal?"

She was still breathing, but he had to check that when she swung her cold, lifeless eyes to meet his. "At least I'm better than somebody," she said, and Garcia sucked air through his teeth.

"Sad, lady. Who's your boss?"

"Courtland Cavendish," she murmured, and she sounded broken, like that little bit of truth was the last little bit of fight she had in her.

"Will we see that in your phone records?" Crosby asked.

"I've got a second laptop," she said. "In the gun safe." She did something funny with her eyes then, something that said she wasn't being entirely truthful.

"She's got a gun safe with a booby trap in her apartment, Chief," Crosby said. "I'd bring the explosives team."

"Fuck... you...," she breathed, and Garcia realized the color had washed out of her face.

"Look, Marcy," he said, "we're going to have to leave you so the medevac can get you on a stretcher and take you away." In the background he could hear the choppers closing in. "You've got exactly one minute to give us something we didn't fucking know or you get no deal from us."

"Second phone," she said. "In my locked office drawer. Cavendish was my boss, and some prick named McEnany, a fed who works in the IA office, kept promising us a new mole. Some guy named Rick Young was gonna infiltrate the Twenty Fourth for us. We needed it. All our workers lived there—the cops kept getting close. The fuckers killed off our main distributor a few days ago."

"*Rick Young* killed off your main distributor," Crosby rasped, growing almost as pale as she was. "But it's good to know we should search that guy's phone and computer. We just thought he was another junkie. See what poisoning your work force does for you? Anything else?"

"Two guys in the DOJ—don't know their names. Cavendish creamed himself whenever they called. They gave him cases, he gave them fuckin' money. Their numbers are in there."

Garcia grunted and looked up to see the guys in the medevac lowering a stretcher, two of their medics taking a ride down.

"Thanks, Marcy. You've been a peach," Garcia said. "And I don't mean that in the gross way any of your people do. Good luck with that pneumothorax. I understand those are super fun."

"So fun," Crosby muttered. "So. Much. Fun."

And with that they moved away and let the medics have her, after Garcia called a warning not to take her cuffs off even if she was anesthetized and seemed out of it.

They nodded—they understood criminal patients, apparently—and the next stop was the edge of the warehouse. Garcia took a good look at Crosby as they stared down at the big rescue air cushion at the foot of the building. It had been set up about six feet to the side of the ladder, probably because the ladder could be problematic for a jump. Or for deflating the thing.

"How's your lungs, partner?" Garcia asked. He was never taking that for granted again after Crosby's last encounter with a bullet and Kevlar.

"Fine. Shot hit me in the back shoulder." Crosby took a breath. "The next hit grazed my arm. Fuck. Me."

"Not with comms on," Garcia muttered, and he knew there would probably be hell to pay, but he was not expecting Elsa's snort.

"Yeah, right. We all know Olaf tops," she muttered, and he and Crosby met eyes and managed a tired smile.

"So much for being undercover," Garcia said, and Crosby gave a one-armed shrug.

"I was never any damned good at it anyway," he said, and then he looked over the ledge again. "So we ready to get down from the fuckin' roof?"

Garcia grabbed his hand. "On three."

They had to let go of each other's hands as they fell, and the landing was a confusion of rubber-coated canvas and tactical gear, but Crosby struggled to his feet just like Garcia, and together they set off to find their team.

Bad Guys in Suits

IT WAS sweet of Harding to get him, Chadwick, and Carlyle in the same room, but Crosby didn't *speak* Chadwick and Carlyle, just like *they* didn't speak Crosby and Garcia. By the time they'd all been checked out and given fluids and—in his case—antibiotics and stitches and pain relievers, and—in their case—CT scans regarding their organs and heart rates and so forth, he was as convinced as Garcia that they'd been sleeping together for the last year.

A thing he planned to discuss in earnest with Gail, because *she'd* already been treated and released, *dammit,* and sent off by Harding with the others to do who knew what. Which meant she'd missed the show.

"Seriously, you guys," he said at one point, "how much musical theater can two people watch?"

For that transgression he was treated to a full-throated duo rendition of "It's Hard to be the Bard" that dissolved into the two of them giggling loopily, but hey, that's what happened when you were given a pure dose of opioids and left to marinate for two hours.

"How you doing, Crosby?" Harding asked, giving Rogers and Hammerstein a disgusted look as he strode in.

"Seriously, Chief, how long are they gonna be that stoned?"

Harding grimaced. "Well, for one thing, they're lucky they're not dead. The doctor said they were given borderline overdoses of heroin. The only thing that kept it from being lethal was that apparently they'd been fighting like hell, and they *kept* fighting even as the drugs took over. Add that to the fact that it was a pure opioid and not a highball like you got, it basically sedated them until they finally slept."

"I don't care," Crosby said earnestly. "Drugs are bad, kids. None of us will ever do drugs again. When can we get out of here and go arrest the fuckers who shipped the drugs?"

Harding laughed a little. "Don't you want to know why they got *different* drugs?"

Crosby squinted at him. "I'm going to assume it's because Cavendish was expanding the operation and tonight's little delivery was not just meth and fentanyl?"

"Winner, winner, chicken dinner," he said, and Chadwick picked up on it and started singing "Funiculi, Funiculà"—some sort of version involving food—and Carlyle joined in.

"Dear God," Harding muttered. "Somebody find them some Led Zeppelin on Spotify. I'm begging you."

"You're just lucky you missed the second act of *Hamilton*," Crosby snapped. "Now go on about different drug deliveries and whether or not we should care."

"We should care," Harding said, manfully tuning out a not-bad version of "The Immigrant Song," sung by Carlyle with Chadwick on air guitar. "Because those four guys in the boat you took out weren't the Florida dealers Beauchamp was using for the fentanyl and meth. They were *Turkish* dealers, and we used their identities to pinpoint the guys in the DOJ on Beachamp's phone who had just abandoned cases against the dealers for—as they claimed—lack of evidence."

"Was there a lack of evidence?" Crosby asked, feeling a little bloodthirsty.

"No, young Judson, there was not," Harding said, relish in every syllable. He looked up at Rogers and Hammerstein and snapped, "If you two don't sober up, you're going to miss all the fun, and haven't you missed enough?"

Immediately, he had Chadwick and Carlyle's complete attention.

"I don't know, Chief," Chadwick said. "Seems like we already missed quite a bit of fun."

"Will we get to kill someone with this fun?" Carlyle all but begged.

"No killing, I don't think," Harding said consideringly, "but if we bring you clothes and let you shower and change, would you like to go arresting? 'Cause I've got five warrants, and Natalia, Swan, Pearson, and Harm are on their way to Washington with two of them, but I thought the lot of us plus Garcia could go arrest our hometown scumbags. What do you say?"

Crosby grinned at him, feeling an entire surge of adrenaline. "Would I *know* one or two of those scumbags, sir?"

Harding's grin was all teeth. "You just might."

TWO HOURS later, Harding pulled his department-issue SUV right in front of the steps of One Police Plaza, and Garcia followed suit.

When they got out of the vehicles, four uniforms met them, trying to insist they couldn't park there, and they had to go around to the parking complex down the block.

Harding held up a warrant on his tablet and said, "This is signed by three different judges, and this case is big and ugly enough that if we don't walk these two perps down the front steps, the entire city is going to get *very* upset. Do you understand?"

The ranking officer paused to read the warrant and then blinked. "We'll guard your vehicles, sir," he said, leaving the five of them, in tactical gear and fresh uniforms, to make their way up the stairs. Carlyle and Chadwick had been worked over before they'd been drugged, and their faces were flush with new bruises, split lips, and cuts over their eyes, but Crosby knew his face was still worse, and the fresh bandages over his stitched stab wound and the gunshot graze gave emphasis.

Garcia just looked tired, and as they were walking up the stairs, Crosby said, "Hey, did anybody feed you?"

The other three men looked at them, and Garcia smacked his uninjured arm. "Are you fucking kidding me?"

Crosby grunted and pulled out a protein bar he'd bought at the vending machine in the hospital while waiting for Chadwick and Carlyle to be discharged.

"I'll take that as a no," he muttered. "When we're done here, I could fuckin' eat. Anybody else?"

It was weird—it was like they all realized it was suddenly ten o'clock in the morning.

"Yeah," Chadwick muttered. "I could eat. Pizza for breakfast, anyone?"

"Steak and eggs," Carlyle said dreamily. "And bacon."

"Egg-white omelet," Harding said as they neared the pillared entrance. "Goat cheese."

"Eggs Benedict," Garcia said promptly. "Extra ham. Crosby?"

Crosby thought about what they were about to do. "Steak and potatoes," he said, feeling his smile get bloody. "Extra rare."

Harding had called ahead and learned, fortuitously enough, that their two subjects had a meeting together that morning—along with some other gentlemen. "Community leaders" is what the receptionist called them. The receptionist had been asked not to relay any information about Harding's team incoming, not even to the other officers and detectives at the plaza.

He flashed his credentials at the desk and was directed to an elevator several floors up. Every step, every floor, every breath in the small car was a buildup of anticipation, and none of them spoke a word.

When they got to the double doors of the conference room, Harding took one door, Crosby the other, and they entered the room like they'd enter any other hostile space, busting open the doors and identifying themselves as Garcia, Chadwick, and Carlyle went in low and in formation before them.

"SCTF!" Harding boomed. "Hands in the air, weapons down. I *will* shoot the cell phone out of your hand!"

Crosby got there in time to see Jimmy Creedy and Kinsey Sizemore flanking Colin McEnany, all of them dazed as hell, and—he could revel in it—very, very afraid.

So was the lawyer with prematurely silver hair and a gray pinstriped suit, also flanked, but by two gentlemen in suits of their own. One looked Latino and the other Slavic, and here, Crosby thought, were the Turkish and Cuban delegates to the drug trade.

"What the fuck!" McEnany snarled. "Crosby! What do you think you're doing here!"

Crosby smiled. "Arresting the fuck out of you, McEnany. Yeah, I took your assignment. Did you think I wasn't keeping my team briefed on your every fucking move?"

Creedy's gun came out before anybody could even predict it. "You fuckin' traitor!" he screamed, aiming at Crosby. "Where the hell is my son?"

Crosby pointed his weapon at Creedy while Garcia said, "Watch McAsshole. He's moving his hand."

"You watch him. I've got Creedy," Crosby murmured, keeping his weapon up. "Creedy, drop the weapon. And your son is somewhere you and your boys will never fuckin' touch him again. D'you hear that,

Sizemore? Nobody will touch him—he's fuckin' free of you assholes. Only good thing to ever happen to the kid."

Creedy gaped at him, uncomprehending, his gun lowering, no longer aimed. "I'm the boy's father—"

"The hell you are!" Crosby shouted, aware that his team was looking at him. "A real father doesn't… doesn't teach his kid to hate. A real father doesn't fill a kid's head with poison or let his buddies beat on the kid because he thinks it's funny or will turn him into a real man or whatever. You're a shitty fucking father, and don't ask me where your kid is, because I got him away from you to save his fuckin' life. *You* may think he'd be better off as a meth-addicted gorilla, but the guy next to you is no way to live."

Crosby's entire team was staring at him, but Crosby couldn't seem to stop his mouth from running. McEnany stepped behind Creedy— the better to use him as a human shield—and Crosby just couldn't stop talking.

"Don't fuckin' do it, McAsshole," he snarled. "You got five guys in tactical who want to blow your head open like a watermelon—you feeling helpless yet? Feel like a victim? I bet you do. You had this coming, McEnany—like Damir Calvin did *not*."

"And you know what, kid?" McEnany called from behind Creedy. "I told you before—I don't care how many bodies I gotta walk on to get where I'm going."

With that, McEnany pulled his gun out and aimed it under Creedy's arm.

"*Gun!*" Chadwick called, and Crosby was dimly aware that the two thugs flanking Cavendish had gone for their weapons too, but he'd called Creedy, and Creedy had a weapon, and he knew his team would back him.

Creedy jerked his weapon back into place as Sizemore pulled his own out, and the SCTF was no longer interested in talking.

"Fire!" Harding called. The eruption of gunfire was sudden and brutal.

And short.

One shot from each of them—Harding took Sizemore—and each target went down. Cavendish had been the only one without a weapon, and he stood in the middle, blood spray across his suit, looking like he was about to scream.

The team crossed the room quickly, each one of them kneeling down to secure the weapons and check the pulses. Sizemore's big body had gone over backward, and he sprawled in a cheap suit without dignity, Harding's bullet through his chest. Creedy had two bullets—one from Garcia's piece and one from Crosby's piece busting his chest open, leaving him looking surprised in death as he'd never had the smarts to be surprised in life. Checking their pulses was a mere formality.

McEnany had been shot through Creedy's body, and he was wounded but not dead.

"Chief," Crosby said crisply, kicking McEnany's weapon away before kneeling down to cuff him in spite of the two big, sloppy bullet wounds from Creedy's through-and-throughs. "We're going to need a bus."

McEnany scowled at him from his back, bleeding profusely from the gut. "You couldn't even kill me right, you fucking screwup."

But Crosby was surprisingly okay with that. "Are you kidding? You being alive to serve your entire life in Leavenworth is seriously the best fucking news I've had all day." There was legitimate fear in McEnany's eyes, and Crosby felt a slow evil smile twist his own mouth.

McEnany saw that smile and paled.

"Kill me now, you sorry piece of shit," he moaned. "Don't be a fuckin' coward—"

"I think you're mistaken, McAsshole," Harding said, keeping both eyes on Cavendish. "That's a stomach wound, and you pulled your weapon from cover. The real cowards shoot a kid in the back."

McEnany opened his mouth and then groaned in pain, blood spattering from his lips, and since he was cuffed now, and probably going to live, Crosby took a sec to see what Harding was doing about the guy in the suit who had instigated all this bloodshed.

"I'm sorry," Cavendish said, speaking for the first time and trying to contain his expression of horror at the bodies that had piled up on either side. "I have no idea what this is about, but—"

Harding rounded on him, grabbing the cuffs at his side. "You don't know what this is about?" he asked, some of his fury coming to the fore. "Why, Mr. Cavendish, this is about drugs, and about redneck racists trying to infiltrate the police department, and about unscrupulous suits like you who don't really care one way or another, capitalizing on ignorance, greed, and addiction. This is about how you are going to spend the rest of your natural life in prison and not learn another fucking thing."

Cavendish gaped at him, and Harding swung him to the boardroom table where he bent him over to cuff him before he kicked his feet out and read him his rights.

Crosby called the ambulance for McEnany, enjoying every bitter word of recrimination the man made, and Garcia glanced from the dead to the wounded and back up to Crosby.

"You, uh, still hungry after this?"

Crosby grinned at him. "God yeah. You?"

Garcia started laughing then, and Crosby followed, and the rest of the guys picked it up. By the time the bus got there, and the FBI to take their statements and deal with the bodies, SCTF was unofficially done. Just fucking done with the entire affair.

Officially there were statements and reports and fuck all the all, but nobody still standing in that room was going to do another productive thing for at least a week.

Harding told them all so even before the feds arrived.

And then there was breakfast.

And the Walls

Two Months Later

GARCIA LIKED to brag extensively about how many improvements he'd made to his Nana and Pop-Pop's house in Queens, but one of the best things he'd done, Crosby could freely admit it, was completely renovate the HVAC system.

This was important because in July, when the heat and the humidity had everybody in the office surly and angry and pissed off, Garcia and Crosby's house was a gorgeous, serene oasis of cold air, cold beer, and one very large, very cool cat, who had enjoyed his can of tuna that one night and decided never to leave.

That air conditioning was particularly blissful when the sun was high and light was flooding the windows from the skylight Garcia had just installed in the living room, and their heavily shaded bedroom window was cool and breezy, and they were naked, sweaty, and unashamedly fucking each other's brains out.

Garcia straddled Crosby, his ass milking Crosby's cock slowly, so slowly, every movement, every gasp and moan, triggering a response in the other person, until they were caught in an exquisite loop of almost painful arousal, their pleasure building and building and building, until Garcia cried out, his head tilted back, his fine muscular body arching even as his ass muscles rippled, squeezing Crosby until he absolutely had to close his eyes.

Climax washed over them both, blasting through their bodies in slow, sensual waves until Garcia gave another little cry and fell forward onto Crosby's chest, sweat dripping from the little lock of hair that had swung over his squirrel-bright eyes.

Crosby gave a luxurious sigh and embraced him, although they were both wringing wet, and Garcia met his mouth in a long, sloppy kiss that would have ignited another bout of lovemaking if that had been round one, or even round two. But this was their day off, and they'd awakened and showered, and then Judson Crosby had seen Calix Garcia frying bacon in his boxer shorts and a tank top and had been absolutely, positively required to take him back to bed.

Garcia hadn't objected—just took the bacon off the burner. They'd eaten most of it with toast after round one and had then gone for a quick smoothie after round two. Feeding Crosby had quickly become as important as feeding Garcia—the ulcer was under control and healing slowly, but going without food was still a no-no, even considering all the wonderful endorphins he was releasing with the sex! After the smoothies, Crosby had stood up to wash their dishes in his briefs and nothing else. Garcia stood behind him, kissing his way down Crosby's spine, pausing to tease the cleft of his ass with absolute intent.

They barely made it to the bedroom, and rounds three and four kind of blurred together until it was now three in the afternoon and Garcia insisted on food.

"Are we done?" Calix asked, his breathing still a little elevated.

"For now," Crosby said. "I mean, you know, we're gonna have to do this again after we break another big case."

Garcia chuckled. This had, indeed, been a celebration.

The day before, after two months of depositions, of lawyers, of filing paperwork, of more lawyers, and of testifying in court, they'd finally wrapped up the last of the Cavendish/McEnany/Beauchamp trial. The Grand Jury had indicted, the lawyers had copped pleas, and the three ringleaders of what was now known as the Sons of the Blood drug ring really *were* in prison for the rest of their lives.

It was a hard win. The body count at the warehouse that night had been pitifully high—an entire neighborhood in Brooklyn had been wiped out, and drug users or not, they'd been sons and husbands and fathers. The drugs that had flooded the streets of that neighborhood suddenly dried up, but the addictions hadn't, and the resulting crime wave would have overwhelmed Iliana's precinct if the SCTF hadn't stepped in to help with screening, recruiting, and emergency hiring over the last two months. The SCTF had been bolstered by their two honest cops from the Twenty Fourth, Doba and Henderson, who had attended FLETC and been full-on instated in Crosby's absence. Henderson was still better used in research and tracking, but Doba and Henderson had been on some calls together, and Garcia said they were doing okay.

Crosby had gone back to the Forty Third for a month as a flatfoot, to help with training and simple manpower, and while he'd missed working with Garcia and the SCTF for that month, he'd gotten to come home to the house in Queens every night and share his day with Garcia, and that had gotten him through. He started to understand how Harman Blodgett could have learned to care for all the members of Harding's team just listening to Clint Harding talk as they shared their lives together, although Crosby's hunger to hear about his team was even greater because he knew them, had fought beside them, had shed blood.

They had a weeklong vacation planned for the beginning of September. Garcia wanted to go to California to try surfing and Disneyland, and Crosby was down with that. But that was in September. Now, in July, they were celebrating the fact that Crosby was walking into the SCTF on Monday morning and they'd get to be partners again.

Crosby had missed it—had missed *Garcia*—in ways he didn't think he could miss another person when he'd thought of sharing his life.

But lives turned out differently than planned, and his final conversation with his father had proved that. On his last day of sick leave, two weeks after the showdown at the warehouse, he'd been sitting in his chair, wrapped in a blanket, reading a Tom Clancy novel with the cat on his lap. Garcia had been at work, and he was getting ever so slowly used to the idea that he was no longer under assignment—he could *do* this, with nobody looking over his shoulder, nobody to account to, nobody asking him how he spent his time.

There was no more Creedy. McEnany was in the hospital. The team—well, what they did was dangerous, but nobody was stalking them to actually *kill* them, and they were relatively safe, and he could... he could *breathe* on his own. He'd fielded a call from Toby that morning, and they'd been planning to get together later in the week to compare battle scars, and he'd been looking forward to telling Calix (as he thought of him more and more when they were at home) about the promise to go to Toby's apartment for dinner.

And just then, in that moment of contentment, his phone rang. It had been his father.

"So, uh, Judson," his father said, his once powerful voice uncertain. "I've heard some... some troubling things from the guys back in the precinct. Have you heard about your old partner? That he's in the hospital?"

"Yup, Dad. In fact, I sort of put him there."

"Judson?" He sounded appalled. "Judson—McEnany's a good cop—"

"No, Dad. He was never a good cop. He was sort of a racist shitbag. I told you that two years ago—it didn't change when he got here and tried to have me and my team killed."

His father gasped. "You… you must have it wrong," he said weakly. "Collie McEnany—he's from the neighborhood—"

"And the neighborhood was fine with him murdering a kid in cold blood," Crosby said, remembering his words to Creedy. A real father didn't raise his kid on hatred. "And he may not go to prison for *that*, but believe me, my unit found lots of other stuff that's going to put him there to rot."

Crosby felt particularly liberated saying the words out loud. His father, the guy he'd joined the force to be like, could either be proud of him, or he could not. Crosby had a home, and he had his book, and he had a cat.

And he had his integrity, a job he could be proud of, and a lover who would partner with him and have his back, literally through thick and through thin and better and worse, and probably through richer or poorer, although Garcia wasn't letting him pay rent.

"But…." His father's voice faltered. "Son, your mother and I—we can never go home again. Not after this. *You* can never go home again."

The Chicago FBI field office had been dealing with death threats aimed at Crosby from this exact thing. Three cops—or their spouses— had already ended up on the wrong side of the law because those threats had been easily traced. Garcia wasn't taking down the security system anytime soon.

"Dad," he said, and decided to go for the whole enchilada. "I'm living with a guy. I'm in love with him. Do you think I could go home again anyway?"

His father's caught breath had chilled him to the bone. "Is this why… is this why you didn't come visit over Christmas?"

Crosby had choked back a broken laugh. "No. The 'my father is a racist' thing is why I haven't come home during Christmas. The 'I can't believe the old man built his career on this bunch of douchebags' is why I haven't visited. The 'I'm bisexual and in love and actually happy' is a me thing, not a you thing. But I know what it means. It means the old man who thought I should just okay the shooting of a Black teenager because going along means getting along is not ever going to let me darken his door again."

"Son...." His father's voice had diminished somehow. "You'd do that? Cut your mother and me out of your life?"

Crosby had sighed. "I don't want to," he said, memories of what had seemed to be a decent childhood playing behind his eyes. "But Dad, I made my choice. I made my choice the day I testified against McEnany in Chicago. In fact I made my choice the day I told him I didn't want to come to poker night. My choice is, I'd rather die a good man than live as a bad one. I spent six weeks undercover seeing how the bad ones lived because McEnany was using me as a pawn, and it hasn't changed my opinion any. You need to either love me as a good man—one who lives with another good man—or despise me because I'm not who you think I should be. But that's all you. You know this number. Call me when you get it figured out."

He hung up then and leaned his head against the back of the chair, his phone—and the book he was reading on it—falling to his lap. The cat, who had stayed Sampson after Crosby had pulled him in the house that night, continued to drool and was not unhappy in the least when he buried a hand in that glorious white-and-gray fur.

Garcia found him there an hour later, still staring into space, his face wet with tears.

"Hey, Cowboy," he'd said into the lowering twilight. "What's up?"

"My father called," Crosby replied, his voice toneless.

"What'd you say?"

And Crosby's own words had echoed back in his head, making that moment clearer and, while painful, also more beautiful, etched in his heart forever.

"I said I would rather die a good man than live a bigot," he said, and it was as true now as it had been, over two years before. "And I was living with a good man, and I was in love."

Garcia's slow smile crinkled the corners of his eyes. "What a coincidence," he said softly. "So am I."

Crosby had grinned up at him from the chair, and Garcia had—gently but firmly—moved the cat to the floor and then kissed him, a gentle kiss because they'd both been healing over those weeks, resting, getting ready for the massive amounts of cleanup in the future.

But Crosby hadn't wanted gentle. He'd wanted firm and real and *alive*. They'd ended up having sex in the chair, Calix kneeling on the cushion, face mashed against the back, Crosby holding his hips and fucking him from behind while Calix spurred him on. They'd come together, and Crosby had collapsed against Calix's back as the chair had collapsed beneath their combined weight, leaving them on the floor in a heap of fabric stuffing and broken wood.

Calix hadn't stopped laughing, not through cleanup, not through lugging the chair out to the front curb for trash pickup, and not through picking out another sturdy "big and tall" chair online and arranging for delivery.

They'd eaten dinner in a daze of fractured conversation and random laughter and had fallen asleep, Crosby's back to Garcia's front, Garcia still giggling into the nape of Crosby's neck.

And while the next two months had been tough—working apart *sucked*—that beginning glimmer of happy, of *them*, hadn't faded yet.

Crosby was starting to suspect it might not fade ever. This moment here, Calix collapsed in his arms, still panting, the air scented with sex and sweat and a little of air freshener and a little like cat, seemed to be the best moment of their lives, made even better with the promise that it would happen again and again and again.

"When we get up," Calix said, sounding content as the damned cat, who was asleep in his cat bed *under* the human bed because he weighed a bloody ton, "we need to eat and then shower before we go out to dinner and eat some more. I mean, it's totally worth it, Cowboy, but sometimes you need food to *fuel* the sex."

"Yeah, well, we need to move if we're going to be ready for tonight. We've got people to meet, right?"

Garcia hid his face in Crosby's shoulder. "Are you sure you want to do this?" he asked.

Crosby used a finger to tilt his chin up. "Remember that whole idea of us hiding? Us being undercover as a couple while we worked with really good people who wouldn't judge us?"

Garcia grimaced. "Yeah, I remember."

"That was a fucking dumb idea."

Garcia laughed outright. "I had no idea how dumb it was going to be. I swear."

Crosby laughed with him, his stomach muscles jiggling Garcia up and down on his cock, which was still wedged inside him. Contrary to all laws of physics and human biology, that thing started to wake up, and Garcia gave him an almost indignant look.

"We have to *eat!*" he complained.

"Yeah, we do," Crosby told him, shifting him to the side. Crosby's cock slid out, and a rush of come sealed the fate of the soon-to-be-laundered sheets. Crosby rolled to the side and danced his fingertips along Garcia's sharp cheekbones. "You and me, we have to go meet our friends and be a couple and let them be together however they want to. We need to have dinner and a good time, and we need to dance and laugh and let Rogers and Hammerstein—"

"Carlyle and Chadwick," Garcia intoned dryly, "who have *still* not admitted they're banging."

"Well, that's their prerogative," Crosby said, smiling a little. "When they finally do, we'll tell them they've fooled nobody. But in the meantime, we've got to go be happy. Because you don't go through what we went through and not get some of the happy."

Garcia's grin was practically luminous. "You *are* happy, right, Cowboy?"

Unexpectedly Crosby's eyes burned. "Oh my God, yes. I mean, I thought SCTF was as good as my life was gonna get, but seriously—*you* make me *so* happy."

Garcia's grin never faltered, but he did squeeze his eyes shut with wry humor. "Yay! I rank right up there with work!"

Crosby grimaced, realizing how weak that had been. He kissed Calix on the mouth, and the moment turned unexpectedly tender. "More than work," he said soberly. "I love you. I love you enough for forever. You've got to know that, right?"

Garcia looked up at him soberly. "I love you too, Cowboy. That same way. We're gonna do great things. I believe it."

His stomach gurgled, and they both groaned.

"Yeah, yeah—as soon as we get out of bed and eat!" Crosby conceded, and they finally got moving to start their day.

THAT NIGHT, the team met for dinner at a place that served steak and had a banquet room so they'd all fit. Everybody was dressed nice. Natalia had brought her wife, and the two of them looked thrilled to be out on a date in elegant dresses and heels that no SCTF agent could run in. Gail Pearson was wearing a Little Black Dress, and her thick blond hair, always so tightly braided when they were on duty, rippled down her back in a wave. She looked enchanting and beautiful, and Manny Swan—wearing the regulation male uniform of a sport coat and slacks—kept looking at her like he'd never seen her before.

Clint Harding brought his *husband*—a thing nobody in the team had known but Natalia until the fallout from the Sons of the Blood trial had made it a thing the press had gone after. Harman Blodgett got all the props for putting on tactical gear and coming to be a badass when he had no reason other than following his husband into battle.

Crosby thought he loved Harman a little more for that, because that moment on the rooftop, when Marcy had been gunning for him and he'd heard Garcia swearing over comms that he was there, had been one of the sweetest in his life.

He and Garcia, they would be okay, as long as they could do their thing together.

Carlyle and Chadwick arrived looking surprisingly good together. Carlyle wore one of those super-tight suits with a little bit of sheen, which told Crosby he was *really* looking forward to going dancing after dinner, and Chadwick wore the kind of coat and slacks that made him look like a visiting professor.

Dinner itself was delicious, and the conversation had been quick and fun and sarcastic. In fact a whole lot like their conference table talk but with the added personal moments that made this a dinner and not work. Crosby got to see Natalia's wife, Emily, kiss Natalia on the cheek with nothing short of adoration, and he remembered that file Natalia had put together on why her family was *not* suspected of being the bad guys, and how it had been a bright spot, a soft moment in a really dark hour.

People needed those bright spots, those soft moments, even people who walked into battle and came out bloody. And hard. And mad.

The dinner place was close to the dance place—Chartreuse's place—and Garcia had cleared it with Chartreuse when they'd been planning. Having a big group of po-po—no matter what branch—was not always a good thing for business, and while some of the folks in the group fit in with Chartreuse's club clientele, not all of them did, and it was important to ask.

Chartreuse had been thrilled. Since Christmas, she'd hired both Dani, the young trans woman whose father had been so very lost, and Junior, because his roommates, Kurt and Jesse, vouched for him. She'd said Garcia's people were *always* welcome in her club, because they didn't just make the world safe for the straight, the white, and the rich. They made it safe for everybody.

Toby would already be there—he was DJing for the first time since his night at the Twenty Fourth precinct. Crosby had visited him as much as he could in the intervening two months, helping him with physical therapy, keeping his spirits up. Toby had been so bullied in high school and college, and Crosby was determined to help him keep the best, the bravest parts of himself as he returned to life after almost being bullied to death.

Garcia walked with the rest of the party because Doba and Henderson might need some vouching for, while Crosby stayed and quietly picked up the bill.

Or rather quibbled with Harding about picking up the bill.

In the end, Harding had won, simply by putting the whole thing on the federal government's tab. "I'm calling it a team-building exercise," he'd said shortly. "Given how much grief they've given me over the years for *building* this team, I think they owe me some steak dinners."

"And a bunch of salads," Crosby said in disgust. "I can't believe Pearson ate salad."

"She got steak on it," Harding defended, but he too sounded baffled. "But Harman had the vegan meal, so, you know, we have to love them for who they are."

Crosby had laughed then, liking the little peeks of human being that they'd been allowed to see in their boss. He would never *stop* being their boss, but God, he was such a good human being.

Finally they made their way to the club, where the bouncers—Junior included—let them cut the line.

"How you doin'?" Crosby asked, taking a moment to talk to Junior.

Junior looked better. Dressed in a suit, he'd taken his natural warehouse muscles and—with Kurt and Jesse's help—had bulked up a little, tightening his body. His complexion—which had been spotty after an endless diet of pizza and soda—had cleared up, and his teeth were clean and white. His hair was cut short—Crosby wasn't sure he'd ever seen it without his gray stocking cap to cover—and it was dark, like his father's, but a nice foil for his blue eyes.

"Doing good," Junior said, and his voice, which had been crisp and professional as he'd greeted dancers at the bar, dropped now, became vulnerable. "I… I miss my dad. Is that wrong?"

Crosby grimaced. He hadn't told Junior yet that he'd been the one to fire the bullets that had killed Creedy and wounded McEnany, but it didn't matter. Creedy was dead because he'd pulled a gun on a cop instead of surrendering, and he was pretty sure Junior knew that. He didn't think it was what Junior was talking about anyway.

"Hey," he said gently. "My dad—he's not talking to me right now. I lost him two years ago when I said I couldn't be the kind of cop he wanted me to be. The kind who'd gun a kid down in cold blood 'cause of the color of his skin. I started missing him then. I'll keep missing him, even if he outlives me. The dad we had as a kid—he's kind of a… a god, you know?" Crosby remembered seeing his father in uniform, having that pride. "And I guess, if you've got a good dad, once he's a person again, it can be a good thing. 'Cause we can't grow into gods, but we *can* grow into good people."

"But if they're not a good person…," Junior pondered thoughtfully.

"Then we gotta make our own good people."

Junior gave him a smile then, and it may have been a little battered and a little bruised, but it had the makings of a whole and healthy heart. "I'll tell Kurt and Jesse that. They'll like the sound of it." He glanced into the club and gave Crosby a sly look. "So, that girl you were always texting—she in there? Is she the tiny blond one, 'cause she's cute."

Crosby grinned and leaned over to speak softly in Junior's ear. "Got news for you," he said, winking. "It wasn't a girl."

Junior gaped at him, looking pleased, and Crosby gave him a little salute before joining the others in the bar.

Toby had the place rocking, and Crosby gave him a wave as he walked in. Toby's perpetual professional smile went shy and personal, because they were friends and Crosby would protect him like a brother till the end.

The team was on the floor, dancing, but not like couples would. Harman and Natalia were doing a graceful swing to the bouncy, almost ska beat, and Emily and Carlyle were trying to keep up. Chadwick, Doba, and Henderson stood by the bar, waiting for drinks, and Gail and Swan were doing the basic dance floor bop, grinning as they cut loose a little.

Garcia was standing by the bar, talking to Chartreuse, who couldn't seem to stop smiling. Crosby moved up behind him, standing intimately close, and moved his lips along the curve of Garcia's ear.

He didn't have to see Garcia's face to know he smiled.

"And I can see our conversation's over," Chartreuse said with a wink. "But you boys need to come back and talk to me some more, when it's not your song, okay?"

"How do you know it's our song?" Garcia asked, but his voice had dropped, gone throaty, the same tones that had driven Crosby wild in bed all day throbbing beneath the surface.

"'Cause look at his face, cute boy," Chartreuse said. "It's definitely your song."

Garcia turned in his arms then and, hips moving, backed Crosby to the dance floor. Together they danced their way to the center, close enough to talk to Gail and Swan if they'd been so inclined.

Harding arrived and took over dancing with Natalia, while Harman joined them in the middle, as did Carlyle and Natalia's wife. With a colossal jump, Joey Carlyle popped over the heads of the dancers and whistled loudly, getting Chadwick's attention, and Gideon moved Doba and Henderson to the center too.

Because this wasn't just Crosby and Garcia's dance, this was their team's dance. Their family's dance. And they could live a lot longer and do a lot more good with their family to watch their backs.

Crosby gave Garcia a spin, and he smiled, ducked, and gave Crosby Gail's hand so she could spin back. With another turn, he was dancing with Carlyle, who stuck out his tongue and gave him Natalia. The dance spun them all into each other's space, and because they trusted, they kept dancing.

Later tonight, it would be just the two of them again, Garcia's tight body tucked into Crosby's arms as they drifted off to sleep, still humming their song, ready to dance—and fight—their way into tomorrow, with their team on their six.

Keep Reading for an Excerpt from
The Tech,
Book #5 in the Long Con series by Amy Lane.

The Beauty of Paper

"Now there, Etienne—do you see?"

"Yes, Papa."

Etienne's father was a slight man with unkempt hair that fell to his collar, a pointed chin, and wrinkles in the corners of fine brown eyes. Tienne's mother had died when Tienne was very small, before the tiny family had moved to the coast using stolen passports.

"The light from the sun bounces off the clouds and hits the water so."

"Yes, Papa."

"And what do we use that looks like light?"

"White! White in the blue and white in the gray and light in the gold!" Tienne continued to sing to himself, painting the ocean view from the window of the seaside cottage looking off the coast of St. Tropez. While he did so, his father continued to labor painstakingly over an etching machine with a laminator and various colors of ink on beautiful rainbow paper. Tienne longed to paint pictures on that rainbow paper, but his father told him—repeatedly—that the paper cost very much money and the people who hired Papa to work on the paper would be *very* displeased if he ruined any of it before it had a chance to be used. Many other little boys might have tested their father on this, but Tienne's papa was so very gentle and so very kind, and he worked hard every day. Tienne only wanted to please his father. He knew, even as a child of six or seven, that his father worked to feed them and that he wanted so much more for his son than he had for himself.

So Tienne sang softly to himself while his father muttered to the machine and the laminator and the instruments he used to etch letters and pictures into that glorious paper.

The slamming of the cottage door startled them both. Tienne's brush went sideways, and he made a gasp of dismay, but his father grabbed his arm and tugged him away from the painting before he could complain. "Hide behind the couch," he muttered. "Don't say a word."

"Papa—"

"Not a word!"

Tienne wriggled behind the couch and held his breath, unsure of what was happening, knowing only that his father had never spoken to him in such a tone, not once in all of his seven years.

"Couvier! Couvier! We know you're in there!"

Tienne's father's voice was furious as he stomped across the floor. "You are never to bother me here in my home. *Never*."

The next sound Tienne heard was the sound of fist on flesh—and then a returning sound. Had his father been hit? Had he hit back?

"All right! All right! All right! I hear you. Never come to your house. I get it. But Mr. Kadjic wants his stuff, you hear me?"

"The order is due tomorrow," Antoine Couvier said coldly. "It will be complete tomorrow. I have been good on every order. I will be good on this one. But not if you come to my home, do you understand?"

"Yeah, sure, we understand." There was the sound of patting down and straightening. "Remember—we don't need to come to your house to make sure you pony up… or to see your pretty little son."

Tienne held his breath in the silence that followed.

"You are threatening my son?"

"I'm sayin', Couvier. Accidents happen. To everybody."

"If they happen to my son, I will be sure every member of your organization spends every day of their lives in prison. You need me. You need my skills. I am the only forger for a thousand miles who understands the new electronic implants in official documents. You can have your papers today, if you like, but they will trip every alarm in the EU, and Interpol will be down your pants so fast you'll wish you'd packed lubricant."

Tienne had to shove his fist in his mouth in fear. His father—*his* father—could talk to people like this, all in defense of Tienne.

"That is if we don't kill you first," the man snarled, but Tienne heard heavy footfalls and then the door slam. Tienne stayed hidden, keeping his breathing under control, until his father's face appeared at the other end of the couch.

"You are okay?" he asked gently.

"Oui."

"Good, then come quickly. You need to pack three changes of clothes, you understand? And a few possessions you cannot bear to be without. It all must fit in your school pack, and it cannot be too heavy."

"My paints and pencils?" Tienne asked, feeling pitiful and trying manfully not to cry as he scooted out from behind the couch.

His father's hands in his hair comforted him, and he worked hard not to tremble. "I will carry your paints and pencils," his father said gently. "We artists cannot be expected to exist without them, no?"

"No." Tienne offered his papa a timid smile and got a kiss on top of his head in return.

"Now go. Pack your treasures and your clothes." He heard a bit of tortured parent in his father's voice then. "Leave your schoolbooks. I suppose we shall obtain others, wherever we land."

Tienne nodded, also sad. Other boys hated school, but Tienne loved it. He could read and write fluently in English and French beyond his grade level, but other things too—math, science—it was all beautiful.

"It is okay, boy," Tienne's father said to his retreating back. "We shall land on our feet, if only we will jump now!"

Nine years ago—Marrakech

"So," ANTOINE said, holding tight to Tienne's hand as they made their way through the crowded streets of the bazaar. "What did you do today in school?"

"I kissed a boy!" he said excitedly. At twelve, he was well ahead of his peers, even in the Arabic language he'd needed to learn relatively quickly in the three years since they'd left Europe altogether and come to Morocco. Given that he was so far ahead of his peers in studies, Tienne had developed other goals.

He was not prepared for his father's sudden tightness on his hand.

"That is fine if you like to kiss boys, Tienne," his father said, pulling him to a quiet place in the bazaar right before their tiny apartment. "But here there are many devout Muslims who would kill you for doing so. Wait until you're in a place where kissing a person won't lose you your head."

Oh. How disappointing. Tienne had liked the boy immensely— Kamel had such amazing dark eyes. "Where would that be?"

Antoine laughed softly. "France, my boy. It would be in France. Two more years, I think. Give us two more years here. I have our passports made and ready for us. We need to be ghosts for a little while yet." His father was always so good at planning ahead.

"Being ghosts is not as much fun when there are no boys to kiss," Tienne said glumly, and his father laughed.

"Quieter, my son, or we will be ghosts for real." The rebuke was gentle, but Tienne took the hint. They'd been on the run for five years, since his father had betrayed Andres Kadjic. Yes, his father had finished the passports, but he'd purposefully included a flaw, a red flag, and some of Kadjic's men had been jailed.

It had been, as Antoine had confessed one particularly miserable night during which they'd been camped on a street corner, hiding under the eaves to avoid the rain, a stupid thing for him to do.

But Kadjic had threatened his son, and Antoine had reacted out of panic.

"Understood, Papa," Tienne said now, silently bidding the sloe-eyed Kamel adieu. "But someday…?"

Antoine smiled. "Someday you shall kiss anyone you—" He didn't trail off so much as stop abruptly, his eyes widening at someone behind Tienne, his tanned face leeching of all color, as though he'd seen a ghost.

"My boy," he said, voice unnaturally loud, "it's time to pack for Casablanca."

For a moment, Tienne was going to argue. But they'd *moved* from Casablanca, not a year ago! But then he remembered his father's code. When they were going to run, always talk about the place they'd run *from*, not the place they'd be running *to*.

"Immediately," he said, and without another word, he turned on his heel and went running up the tiny set of steps between adobe buildings to their one-bedroom apartment above the bazaar.

They were packed in ten minutes but spent the next five hours eating, drinking, and *waiting* for the cover of darkness. This time, as Tienne was bigger, he got to carry some of his father's equipment and some of their art supplies as well as the requisite three changes of clothes. Tienne thought wistfully of the next time they could paint. After they found a place, there was always a frantic bit of activity as they forged passports and plane tickets and papers of provenance and whatever other criminals needed from them before they could finally settle down to what they both loved: art!

It would be a long time before they could paint together, he mourned, but still, he and his father turned their eyes to the horizon and the coming veil of night. When it finally came, they did not leave by way of the stairs, but out the window and up and across the roof, jumping two more roofs before they finally slid down a drainpipe.

And landed right in a group of men—slick touristy men wearing leather jackets and leather coats—and one brothel boy in loose harem pants and a velveteen vest.

"Hello," said the inebriated brothel boy, who sounded much older than those men usually got. "What have we…? Andres, put the knives down. It's a man and his son. Why would you—"

"Go, Daniel," said the shorter, more muscular of the men in the leather jackets. He was clearly their leader, judging by the way the others kept seeking his approval as they shouldered Tienne's father against the adobe wall of the building at their backs. He was squat, this one, dark-haired, with a brutally planed face, and he spoke with a thick Slavic accent. "You like pretty things. You don't need to know the ugliness here."

The brothel boy—but wait. He was older than most brothel boys. Perhaps he was simply a kept man—shook his head hard, as though trying to dispel some of the alcohol or whatever had impaired his senses. "Andres, you are not going to harm these people," he said, pulling authority into his voice. "You cannot. It's a father and his son—"

"A father who has put two of my men in jail by betraying me, thinking he was protecting his son. They will not live another day!"

"Then you and I won't see another night," Daniel said, pulling himself up to his full height and moving, almost imperceptibly, in front of Tienne. "I won't sleep with a man who could do this—particularly not to a child, but not to anyone. So they saw jail time. It's the logical end for our sort. You know it, I know it. If you threatened his son, he had every right!"

"*Nobody* does that to me and mine!" roared Andres Kadjic—for this was clearly the man who had sent Tienne and his father running for the last five years. "And no lover of mine stands against me. Not in public, not in private."

"I'm not your lover, then," Daniel said. "I don't want a thing to do with you. If I hadn't been drunk off my ass, I would have seen you for the brute you are—"

Kadjic's hand came out, brutally fast, a backhanded fist that drove the slender Daniel to his knees. "You think I am a brute now?" Kadjic said with a sneer. "Before this night is over, you will know me for what I am. But first—"

He turned to his men and nodded at Antoine Couvier, and his man yanked a knife across Tienne's father's throat.

"*No!*" Tienne screamed, and he saw the whole world as in slow motion.

The man who'd killed his father dropped Antoine's body as it still spurted blood and turned toward him. At the same time, Daniel, Kadjic's lover, who would probably share Antoine's fate before the night was out, leaped at the man with the knife and looked Tienne dead in the eye, screaming, "*Run!*"

Tienne took off, running faster then he'd ever imagined he could, thinking he felt the hot breath of the man with the knife on his neck. He ran until he could run no more, finally taking shelter in an alleyway, where he sat with his back against the wall and sobbed.

The next morning, he awoke hungry, thirsty, and terrified. He knew this city, but he did not know where to go for help. He knew his father's friends, but he did not know if any had betrayed him. He knew who the authorities were, but so many were not to be trusted.

He had his pack, though. He and his father split their cash now, so with his cash and his passport and ID, he could at least get out of Marrakech and go to….

Where? Back to France, perhaps? He and Antoine had been happy in France. But Kadjic had been there too. Prague? Kyiv? Amsterdam? There were cities they hadn't been to—perhaps Kadjic wouldn't be in Amsterdam?

It was then, as he was rummaging through his pack, that he made a terrible discovery.

As he'd fled, the man with the knife had probably taken a swipe at him. There was a slice down the pocket of his backpack, and the bulk of his cash was gone, as was a tube of green paint that had apparently been slashed as well.

He was broke.

He was *found*.

And Kadjic's people were probably waiting at the mouth of the alley, intending to gut him like a fish.

He stood, frozen for a moment, until a young man appeared, right where Tienne had thought to see a mobster with a knife and an Uzi.

Instead, the man held a sizable wad of cash in many denominations, every paper covered with galway green paint.

"Looking for this?"

The man spoke English with a clear lower-class accent, and Tienne searched his face for any trace of a sneer or mockery. What he saw was a handsome young man, maybe ten years older than himself, with short brown/red hair and brilliant blue eyes, looking at him levelly as though assessing Tienne for damage. He held his robe back so Tienne could see his badge. It said something about Interpol, but Tienne didn't care.

He spat. "I know nothing about that," he said, not meeting the young man's eyes. Crooked authorities—he'd seen his father pay off his share of people with badges.

"Do you know something about the man who almost died to save your hide last night?" the young man asked softly. "Danny Lightfingers?"

Daniel. Tienne bit his lip, and his voice caught. "He is alive?"

"Aye," said the young officer. "Barely. I wanted to stay by his side to make sure Kadjic's boys didn't go after him again, but he told me to come find you. Turns out he has his own damned money to travel with, and he gave me permission to use it to get you to safety. You going to let me do that?"

Tienne met his eyes, knowing his own were overflowing. "Where is safe?" he asked gruffly. "They killed my father. Where is safe?"

"Would you believe Chicago's safe?"

Tienne squinted at him. "America?"

"Aye."

Two days later, with a neat haircut and dressed nicely, his luggage chosen to match, Tienne still didn't believe it. After flying for what felt like days, he was greeted at the gate by a woman—ah, such a beautiful woman. She wore her hair in a chignon and dressed like the women of France, in a summer dress with an elegant clutch bag.

"Etienne Couvier?" she asked softly, and he looked around, over both shoulders.

"Oui. But my papers, they say—"

"Bertrand Lautrec," she murmured. "I am aware. But I know that sometimes it's nice when somebody says your name. Come with me. I'm Julia Dormer-Salinger, and you may call me Julia."

"Am I to live with you?" he asked, confused. All he'd been told was that he would be safe. After five years on the run with his father, his twelve-year-old self couldn't imagine this woman could keep him safe.

She smiled at him gently. "I have a son, and his friend practically lives in our house. I wouldn't mind a third. Would you like that?"

He frowned, understanding from her tone that this was a surprise idea for her.

"What did Daniel plan?" he asked, remembering the brave man who had still been recovering from the injuries Andres Kadjic had given him even as Tienne had flown away.

"Art school," she said with a little shrug. "I've secured a place for you at a rather prestigious boarding school, if you like."

And part of Tienne wanted badly to go with this lovely, kind woman to her home, where there were other boys his age. But everything was so strange—down to his hair and his clothes and the clipped sounds of English in seven different accents gunning by his ears.

Art he knew. Art was his last link to his parents.

"Art school, sil vous plaît," he said politely.

She smiled sadly. "You can visit us during breaks if you like," she said and then frowned. "But let's not tell Felix where you're from, yes?"

"Who is Felix?" he asked.

She grimaced. "My soon to be ex-husband. But don't worry. We adore each other."

Tienne frowned at her, turning as she did to walk through the airport. "Then why are you...?"

"Getting a divorce?" she asked, laughing. "Because women are really not his type. Is this the only luggage you have?" She indicated his roller board and matching satchel.

"Oui," he said, remembering sadly that after his backpack had been slashed, he'd only had the clothes on his back. The young police officer had needed to buy *many* clothes in Marrakech's modern department stores to fill the small case. "Who is his type?" Tienne asked, thinking about his one kiss, and how he badly needed to know if he could die here if he mentioned who he wanted to kiss.

"Men," she said simply. "In particular, one man, whom he's pretending he's not in love with anymore."

Tienne frowned. This sounded terribly tragic. "Who is this man?"

She tilted her head. "You should know, my boy. He's the one who sent you to America and told us to make sure you had a home." She bit her lip, uncharacteristically diffident. "Did you… did he happen to say anything to you? About us, I mean?"

Tienne laughed humorlessly, remembering that one moment in the alley when a man he'd never seen, never met, had jumped on top of a man armed with a knife and defied his very dangerous lover to save Tienne's life.

"We had no time to talk," he whispered. "He… he saved me. From dangerous men. But then his friend helped me get far, far away." He saw her obvious disappointment, though, and thought of something to say. "He must have trusted you very much," he added. "Because if you were dangerous to him too, you could easily hurt him."

Her expression grew, if anything, even sadder. "And Felix and I have," she said softly. "But again, that is not your story. Come. The only interview I could get you for the school I have in mind is this afternoon. I know it's quite the whirlwind, and you won't have a chance to come home and meet the family, but if it's art school you want, it's art school you shall have."

And that was that.

Years later, after he'd met Josh and Grace and their friends, and had spent summer and winter holidays with Julia and Felix, enjoying their company very much, he would wonder at his choice.

They'd offered him family as often as they could. They found out his birthday and sent gifts or took him out to celebrate. He spent part of his holidays with them and received presents. He even painted them pictures. A part of him yearned more than anything to make himself comfortable in their home, to lie about on the couches with Josh and Grace and their friends Stirling and Molly and play games and chatter and live in their pockets as they lived in each other's.

But he'd seen his father die, and that wound, that terrible wound in his chest, it was still open, and he was still desperately afraid.

He made it through boarding school instead, and then into the School of the Art Institute of Chicago, with an emphasis on oil-on-canvas paintings. It was there that his original calling, the one his father taught him, came into play.

It helped that one machine, one stamp, one printer, one jar of ink at a time, he'd begun to build up his collection of forging equipment again. Everything from estate sales to government clearing houses and Army/Navy stores gave him items he needed, and without thinking of the reason, he spent much of his allowance on the tools of the trade he'd employed with pride as his father's journeyman.

And then he hit college at seventeen, and that foresight and patient collecting paid off.

It seemed that many teenagers were desperate to have beer.

"Tienne?"

Tienne looked up from the desk in his dorm room, where he sat with his forging equipment, and wondered if he could will the ground to simply swallow him up.

"Josh?" There, large as life—and *sixteen*—stood the son of his benefactors, along with Josh's best friend, Dylan "Grace" Li.

Tienne had seen Danny since that night in Marrakech—many times in fact. He'd shown up the day *before* Tienne's birthday dinner with the rest of the family, or the week *before* Christmas. Once a year he showed up a few days after Josh's birthday, and Tienne had understood that this was part of Danny and Felix's doomed love affair. Felix and Julia lived in a mansion, raising Josh and Josh's friend, Grace, while Danny snuck into their home like a thief and spent time with the boy he loved like his own son.

And also with Tienne, whom he treated with kindness and affection and unfailing thoughtfulness.

Tienne would look at him and see his father—not perfect, but kind. Fierce when he was needed to protect his child. Pining for a lover he could never have, although Tienne's father had lost his mother in death.

He would have gone with Danny, no matter how imperfect his life may have been, but Danny was hoping Tienne could have the family Danny left behind.

Tienne was not good enough for that family. He thought Julia and Felix and Josh lived a fairy tale life—right up until Josh Salinger made his way into Tienne's dorm room/workshop when Tienne had all his forging equipment laid out on his floor.

"Hey, Tienne," Grace said, peeking from behind Josh's shoulder and blinking at him in delight. "Good to see you. You're a criminal too?"

Josh elbowed him, and as compact and graceful as Julia and Felix's dark-eyed, dark-haired son may have been, the elbow was no joke. "The only criminal thing I'm going to do today is drop you off a building if you don't shut up," he said.

Grace—ethereally beautiful and a constant pain in the ass—smiled with all his teeth. "You promise that and promise that, and not once have I been dropped off a building." He blinked his tawny eyes at Tienne, and his smile relaxed. "And dropping me off a building doesn't change the fact that Tienne is here, making fake IDs, when your mother swears he's an angel who can do no wrong."

Josh laughed, but the look he turned toward Tienne was kind.

"You couldn't be that bad if Danny sent you," he said, and Tienne felt his face turn red.

"How do you know—"

"Danny and I write," Josh said, surprising Tienne very much. Josh put his finger to his lips. "Shh. It's supposed to be a secret, but everybody knows. One of those weird family things. Anyway, he asks me how you're doing and worries because you're alone. He really *does* wish you'd take my mother's invitation to heart, you know. She wouldn't offer if she didn't mean it."

Tienne flushed more and looked away. "I…." He didn't know how to say that he didn't know what to do with that much kindness. Instead, he scowled and peered back at Josh through the hair that had grown long again. "But what are you doing here? I…. You… why do you need my services?" he asked finally, resorting to the language of thieves because he had nothing else to explain this.

Josh looked exasperated—but not with Tienne. "Thank God, I got a tip from a guy at our school that 'some guy at the AI is the best.' Genius here"—he nodded at Grace—"left our last set of IDs in the club. I had to cancel all the cards I used with them too!"

Tienne blinked, stunned at this level of thievery from someone his age. "Who made you fake cards!" he cried.

"Oh, they were real cards," Josh said, affronted. "They were made out to fake names. Are you kidding? Felix showed me how to hide my money when I was ten." He sighed. "I was going to go after Danny, and he was trying to show me how hard it would be to trace him. I learned a *lot* the summer Danny left."

Tienne frowned, putting the timeline together. If Josh was sixteen now, and Danny had left when he'd been ten, then he must have been gone the better part of a year before the encounter in the alleyway.

Uneasily, he wondered if Felix and Josh knew how close Danny had come to death that night, on Tienne's account, and decided he wouldn't ever tell them.

And then what Josh said *really* caught up with him.

"Your father knows how to… to *lie*. To scam? To steal?"

Josh laughed kindly. "Well, *yeah*. Uncle Danny taught him and my mother all they know. But what you're doing here…." He trailed off delicately and made motions with his hands.

And Tienne couldn't help it—this was the first honest thing he'd been allowed to say about his father since he'd arrived in America by plane. "My father did this," he said. "It kept us fed and gave us money to paint." Some of his joy faded. "In the end, I think it got him killed." He shook that off. "But I never knew your family… they would understand."

Josh crouched down and regarded Tienne closely. "Was that why you never moved in like my mother wanted?"

Tienne shook his head, unable to explain, and Josh let out a sigh. "Never mind," he said, giving Tienne the uncomfortable feeling that Josh knew much more that he wasn't telling. "Forgive me for prying. Now, if you could get Grace and me our IDs, and some for Stirling and Molly too—hey, do you do fake credit cards as well?"

Tienne glanced up happily. It was a newly acquired skill. "Indeed!"

"Excellent." He gave a rather quiet smile then. "And I hope you don't mind, but I'm going to tell my father about your little enterprise. No, no, don't worry. He won't ask you to do anything you don't want to do. But that way he'll be ready with lawyers should you get busted, you know, that sort of thing."

Tienne sniffed. "Of all the things my father and I worried about, police were not among them."

"Professional pride," Josh said, and he and Grace nodded with such understanding, Tienne wondered what sort of "profession" they'd been active in. "We get it. But there can be dangerous people in these gigs, and if Dad knows now, he can help get you out of a mess. And if you keep wanting to do it, he can get you business. All sorts of things. He has friends who need green cards, passports for people who would like to see their families. He really doesn't like the guy he uses now—says he's way too seedy, and my dad doesn't trust him. So if your work is any good…."

"We were the best," Tienne said without conceit. "It has taken me some time here. Your papers, your electronics, they're different. But my father was the best, and I worked with him until…." He swallowed. "Until I came here."

Josh laughed. "Well, excellent. You know, it would figure. I didn't think Uncle Danny would take someone boring under his wing."

Tienne had laughed then, taking it as the compliment it was. But as the years progressed, and Felix brought him more and more business, all of it protected under a layer of anonymity, none of it as edgy and dangerous as his father's business with Kadjic, he came to realize that it had been yet another sally of the Salinger family, trying to let him know he was not alone.

It was not until Danny's return—and his and Felix's rather spectacular reunion—that Tienne truly began to take that idea to heart.

Award winning author AMY LANE lives in a crumbling crapmansion with a couple of teenagers, a passel of furbabies, and a bemused spouse. She has too damned much yarn, a penchant for action-adventure movies, and a need to know that somewhere in all the pain is a story of Wuv, Twu Wuv, which she continues to believe in to this day! She writes contemporary romance, paranormal romance, urban fantasy, and romantic suspense, teaches the occasional writing class, and likes to pretend her very simple life is as exciting as the lives of the people who live in her head. She'll also tell you that sacrifices, large and small, are worth the urge to write.

Website: www.greenshill.com
Blog:www.writerslane.blogspot.com
Email: amylane@greenshill.com
Facebook:www.facebook.com/amy.lane.167
Twitter: @amymaclane

Follow me on BookBub

A LONG CON ADVENTURE

The Mastermind

AMY LANE

"Delicious fun." – *Booklist*

A Long Con Adventure

Once upon a time in Rome, Felix Salinger got caught picking his first pocket and Danny Mitchell saved his bacon. The two of them were inseparable… until they weren't.

Twenty years after that first meeting, Danny returns to Chicago, the city he shared with Felix and their perfect, secret family, to save him again. Felix's news network—the business that broke them apart—is under fire from an unscrupulous employee pointing the finger at Felix. An official investigation could topple their house of cards. The only way to prove Felix is innocent is to pull off their biggest con yet.

But though Felix still has the gift of grift, his reunion with Danny is bittersweet. Their ten-year separation left holes in their hearts that no amount of stolen property can fill. A green crew of young thieves looks to them for guidance as they negotiate old jewels and new threats to pull off the perfect heist—but the hardest job is proving that love is the only thing of value they've ever had.

www.dreamspinnerpress.com

The Muscle

AMY LANE

A Long Con Adventure

A true protector will guard your heart before his own.

Hunter Rutledge saw one too many people die in his life as mercenary muscle to go back to the job, so he was conveniently at loose ends when Josh Salinger offered him a place in his altruistic den of thieves.

Hunter is almost content having found a home with a group of people who want justice badly enough to steal it. If only one of them didn't keep stealing his attention from the task at hand….

Superlative dancer and transcendent thief Dylan "Grace" Li lives in the moment. But when mobsters blackmail the people who gave him dance—and the means to save his own soul—Grace turns to Josh for help.

Unfortunately, working with Josh's crew means working with Hunter Rutledge, and for Grace, that's more dangerous than any heist.

Grace's childhood left him thinking he was too difficult to love—so he's better off not risking his love on anyone else. Avoiding commitment keeps him safe. But somehow Hunter's solid, grounding presence makes him feel safer. Can Grace trust that letting down his guard to a former mercenary doesn't mean he'll get shot in the heart?

www.dreamspinnerpress.com

A LONG CON ADVENTURE

The Driver

AMY LANE

A Long Con Adventure

Hell-raiser, getaway driver, and occasional knight in tarnished armor Chuck Calder has never had any illusions about being a serious boyfriend. He may not be a good guy, but at least as part of Josh Salinger's crew of upscale thieves and cons, he can feel good about his job.

Right now, his job is Lucius Broadstone.

Lucius is a blueblood with a brutal past. He uses his fortune and contacts to help people trying to escape abuse, but someone is doing everything they can to stop him. He needs the kind of help only the Salingers can provide. Besides, he hasn't forgotten the last time he and Chuck Calder collided. The team's good ol' boy and good luck charm is a blue-collar handful, but he is genuinely kind. He takes Lucius's mission seriously, and Lucius has never had that before. In spite of Chuck's reluctance to admit he's a nice guy, Lucius wants to know him better.

Chuck's a guaranteed good time, and Lucius is a forever guy. Can Chuck come to terms with his past and embrace the future Lucius is offering? Or is Good Luck Chuck destined to be driving off into the sunset alone forever?

www.dreamspinnerpress.com

The Suit

AMY LANE

A Long Con Adventure

Two and a half years ago, Michael Carmody made the biggest mistake of his life. Thanks to the Salinger crew, he has a second chance. Now he's working as their mechanic and nursing a starry-eyed crush on the crew's stoic suit, insurance investigator and spin doctor Carl Cox.

Carl has always been an almost-ran, so Michael's crush baffles him. When it comes to the Salingers, he's the designated wet blanket. But watching Michael forge the life he wants instead of the one he fell into inspires him. In Michael's eyes, he isn't an almost-ran—he just hasn't found the right person to run with. And while the mechanic and the suit shouldn't have much to talk about, suddenly they're seeking out each other's company.

Then the Salingers take a case from their past, and it's all hands on deck. For once, behind-the-scenes guys Michael and Carl find themselves front and center. Between monster trucks, missing women, and murder birds, the case is a jigsaw puzzle with a lot of missing pieces—but confronting the unknown is a hell of a lot easier when they're side by side.

www.dreamspinnerpress.com

A LONG CON ADVENTURE

The Tech

AMY LANE

A Long Con Adventure

Can two quiet con men who lost their childhoods find their places as a part of a family—and with each other?

Ever since he watched his father die, Etienne Couvier has kept to himself. Under the tutelage of his sponsor family, the Salingers, Tienne grows into a gifted forger and artist. But no matter how hard they try to draw him into their midst—and despite the singular pull their friend Stirling Christopher has on his emotions—he resists.

When computer tech Stirling lost his adoptive parents, he found shelter and love with the Salingers. Stirling knows firsthand what Tienne has been through, so when an attacker shatters Tienne's self-imposed isolation, Stirling urges him into the Salinger crew. Maybe they can finally explore the quiet attraction between them.

Then the Salingers announce their next project: an inquest into the mysterious deaths of Stirling's adoptive parents. They descend on the Caribbean for answers, with Stirling and Tienne the quiet centers of the human justice-seeking hurricane. As they stretch out of their comfort zones, they learn that being family means someone always has your back. Hand in hand, they'll solve the mystery. They might even be able to live with the consequences—as long as they do it together.

www.dreamspinnerpress.com